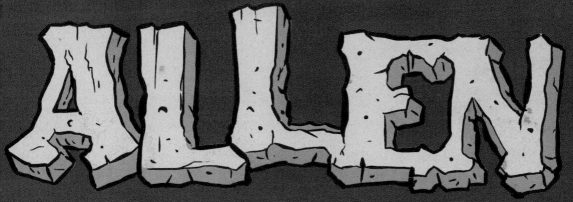

ALLEN
SON OF HELLCOCK

Written by
Gabe Koplowitz & Will Tracy

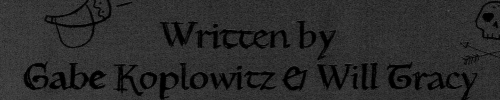

Illustrated and lettered by
Miguel Porto

Colors by
Kendra Wells

Supplemental Art by
~~Benjamin Marra~~
Natacha Bustos
and Ken Niimura

Printed in Canada 2017 Published by Z2 Comics Publishers Josh Frankel and Sridhar Reddy

Many thanks to our families, friends, Beau Bridges, Beau's Bridges, Dr. Razzle's Miraculous Write-Good Elixir, and the copyright lawyers of America, without whom this copyright page wouldn't be possible.

INFRINGE UPON THESE COPYRIGHTED CHARACTERS AND YE SHALL BE DICED INTO A MIREPOIX TO BE USED FOR MY AFTERNOON BOAR STEW

-HELLCOCK

Publisher's Cataloging-In-Publication Data

(Prepared by The Donohue Group, Inc.)

Names: Koplowitz, Gabe. | Tracy, Will, 1983- | Porto, Miguel, 1980- illustrator.
Title: Allen, son of Hellcock / [written by Gabe Koplowitz and Will Tracy] ; [art by Miguel Porto].
Description: New York, NY : Z2 Comics, 2017.
Identifiers: ISBN 978-1-940878-08-9 (hardcover)
Subjects: LCSH: Fathers and sons--Comic books, strips, etc. | Good and evil--Comic books, strips, etc. | Unworthiness of heirs--Comic books, strips, etc. | Cowardice--Comic books, strips, etc. | Swordsmen--Comic books, strips, etc. | LCGFT: Graphic novels. | Humorous fiction. | Fantasy fiction.
Classification: LCC PN6727.K66 A55 2017 | DDC 741.5973--dc23

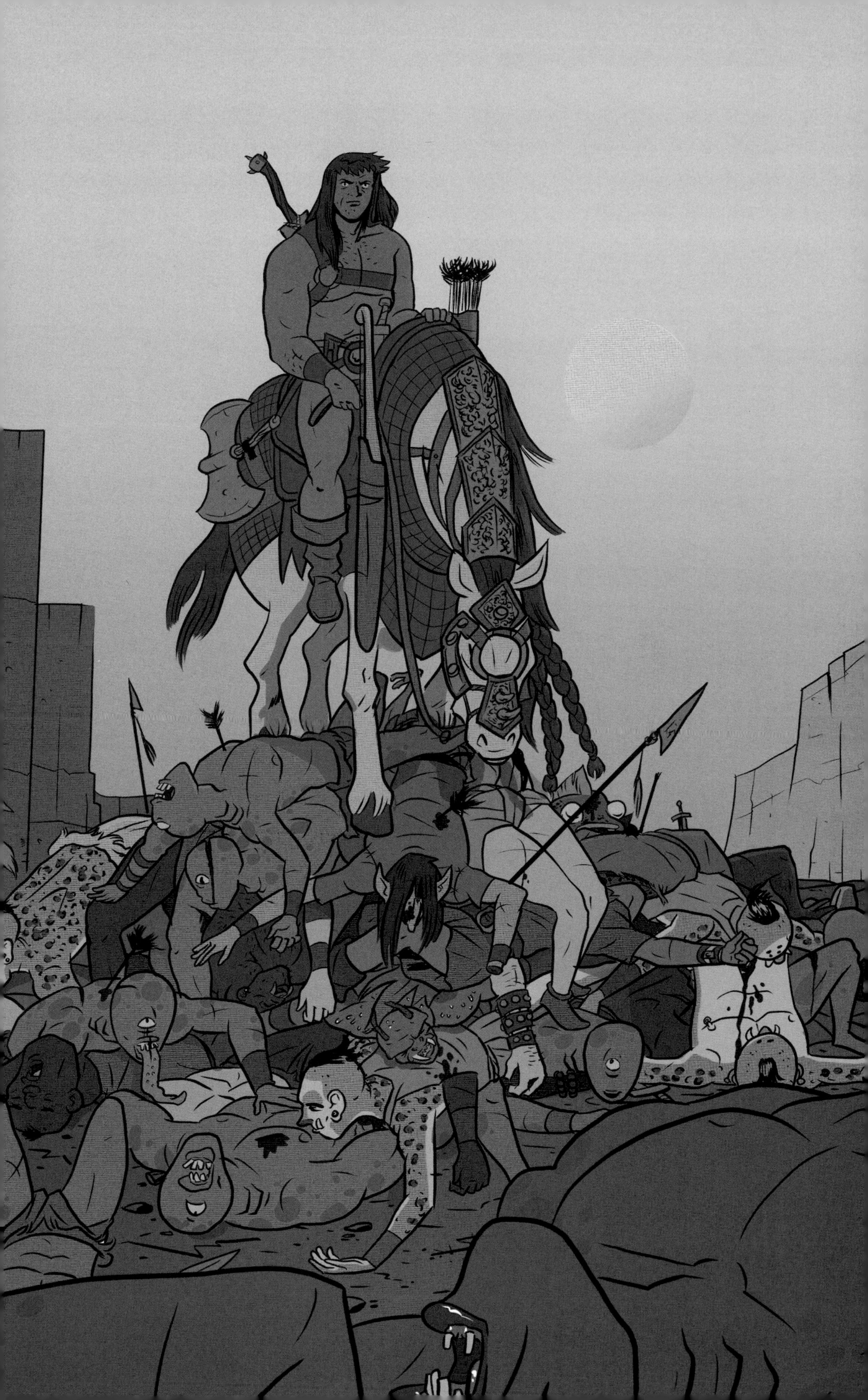

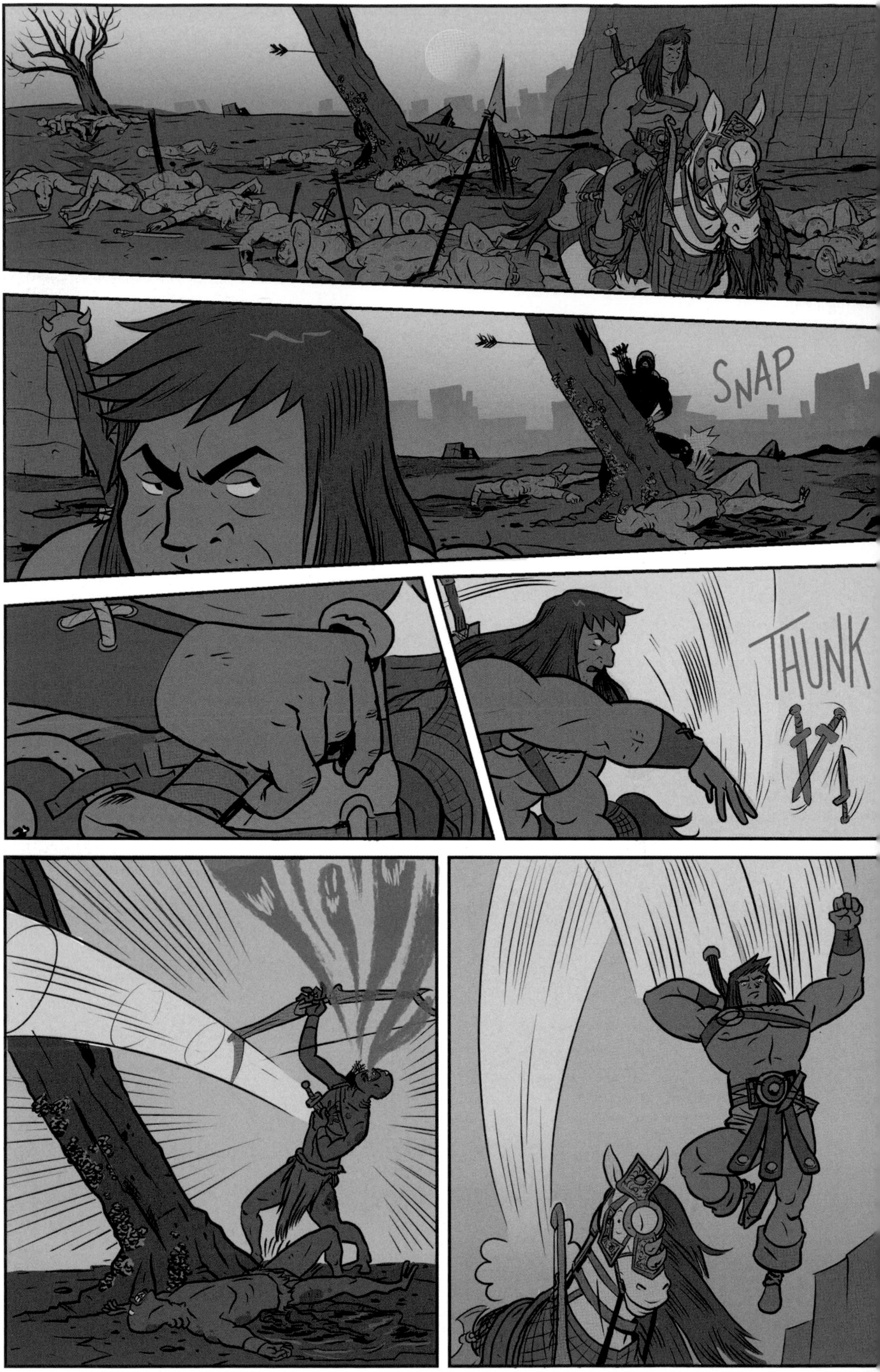
SNAP
THUNK

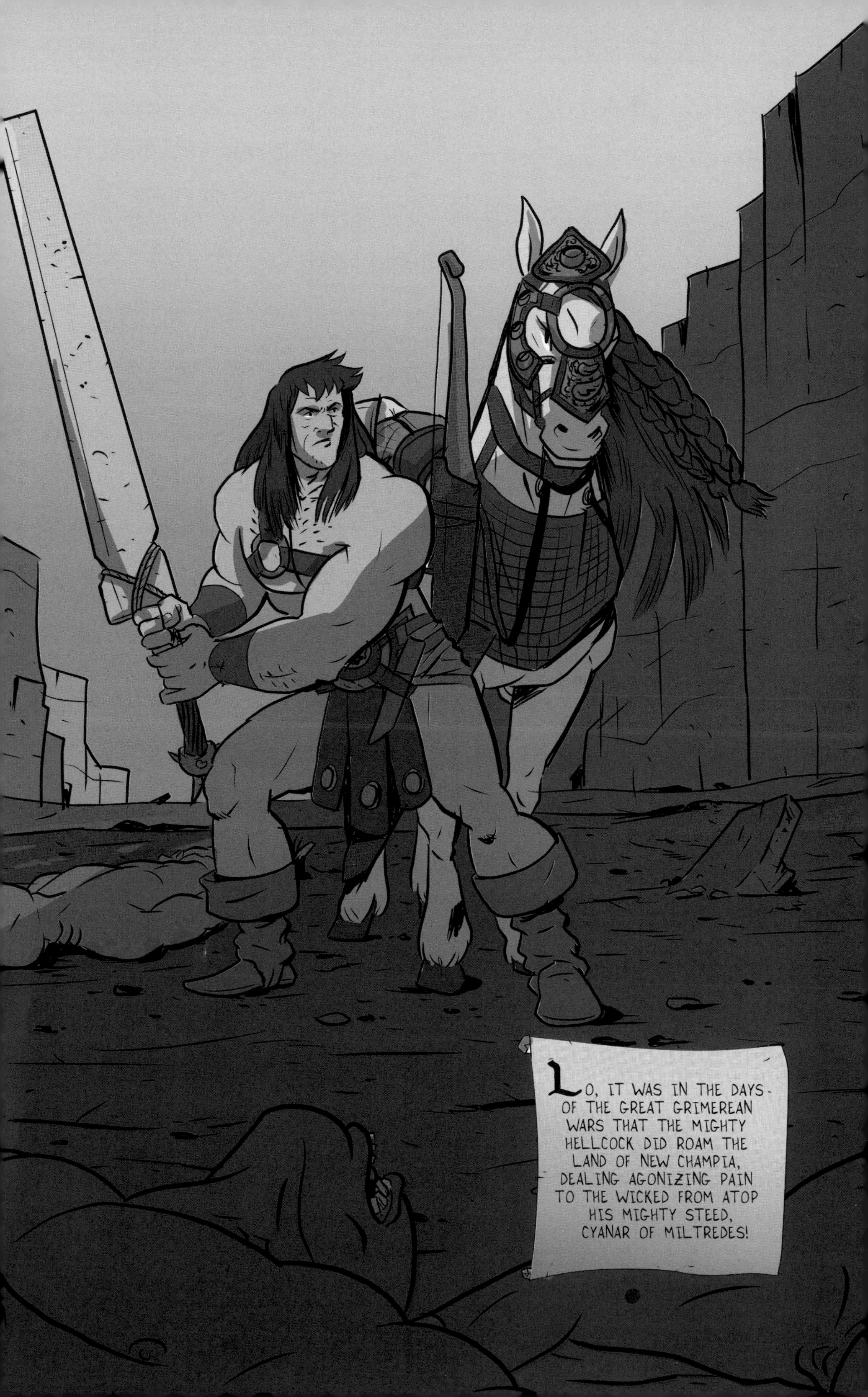
LO, IT WAS IN THE DAYS OF THE GREAT GRIMEREAN WARS THAT THE MIGHTY HELLCOCK DID ROAM THE LAND OF NEW CHAMPIA, DEALING AGONIZING PAIN TO THE WICKED FROM ATOP HIS MIGHTY STEED, CYANAR OF MILTREDES!

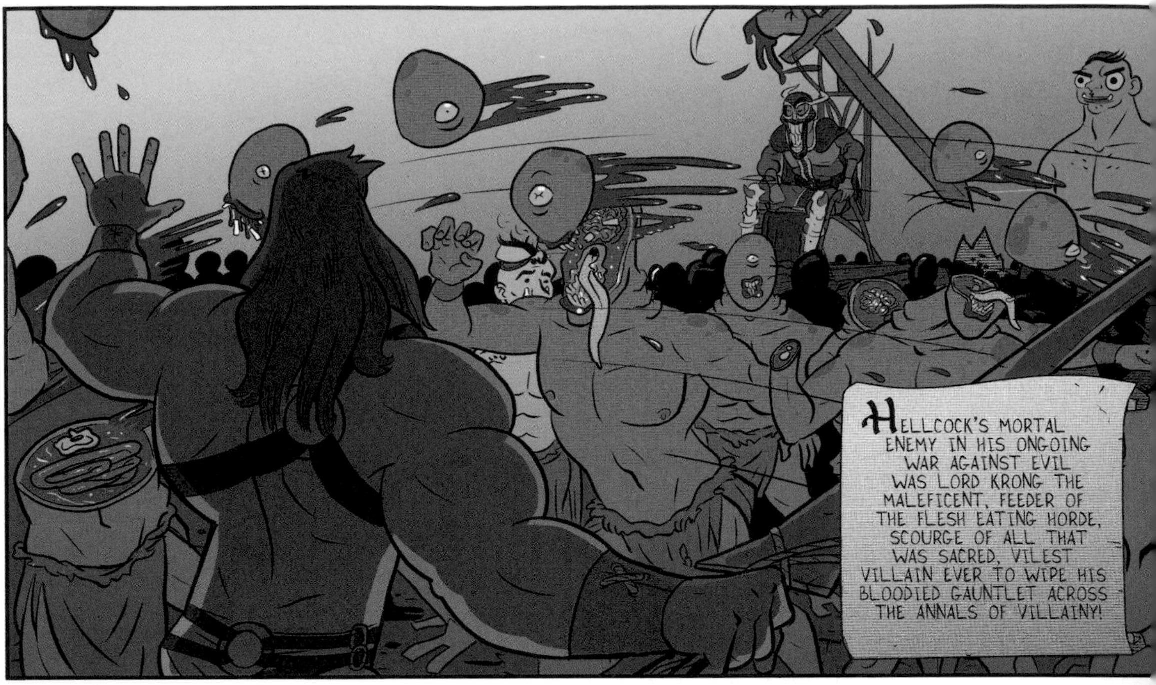
HELLCOCK'S MORTAL ENEMY IN HIS ONGOING WAR AGAINST EVIL WAS LORD KRONG THE MALEFICENT, FEEDER OF THE FLESH EATING HORDE, SCOURGE OF ALL THAT WAS SACRED, VILEST VILLAIN EVER TO WIPE HIS BLOODIED GAUNTLET ACROSS THE ANNALS OF VILLAINY!

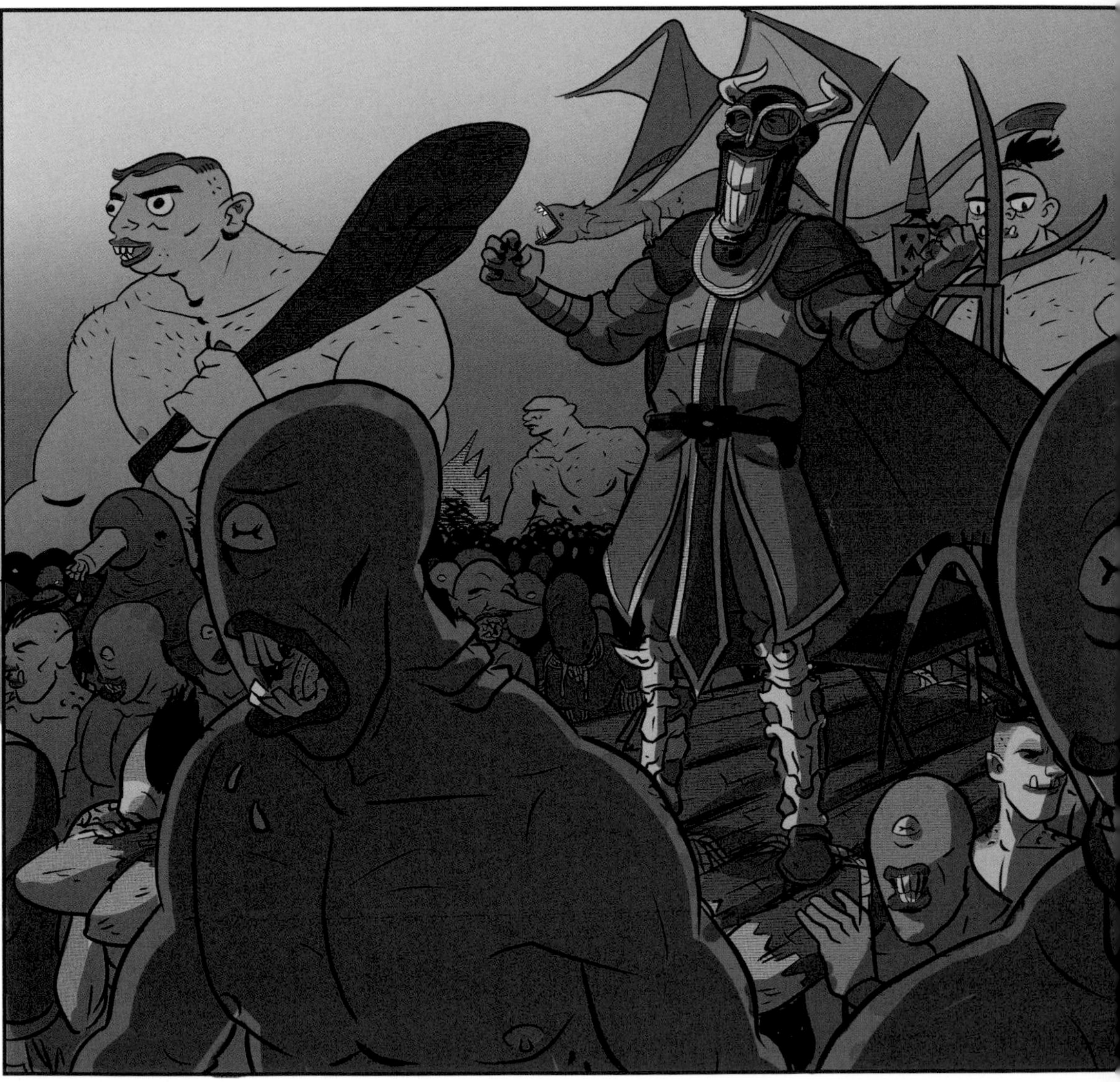

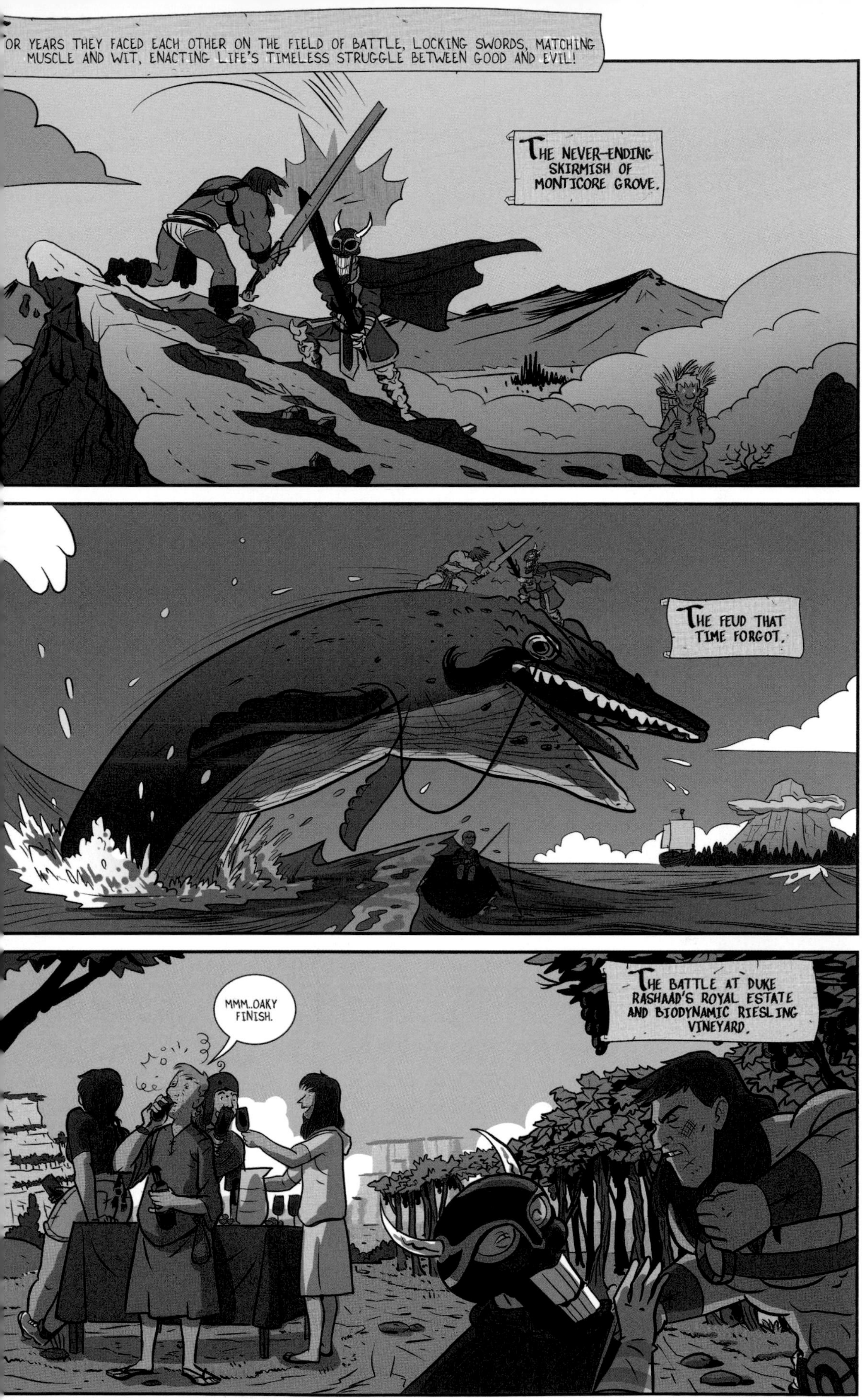

OR YEARS THEY FACED EACH OTHER ON THE FIELD OF BATTLE, LOCKING SWORDS, MATCHING MUSCLE AND WIT, ENACTING LIFE'S TIMELESS STRUGGLE BETWEEN GOOD AND EVIL!
THE NEVER-ENDING SKIRMISH OF MONTICORE GROVE.
THE FEUD THAT TIME FORGOT.
THE BATTLE AT DUKE RASHAAD'S ROYAL ESTATE AND BIODYNAMIC RIESLING VINEYARD.
MMM..OAKY FINISH.

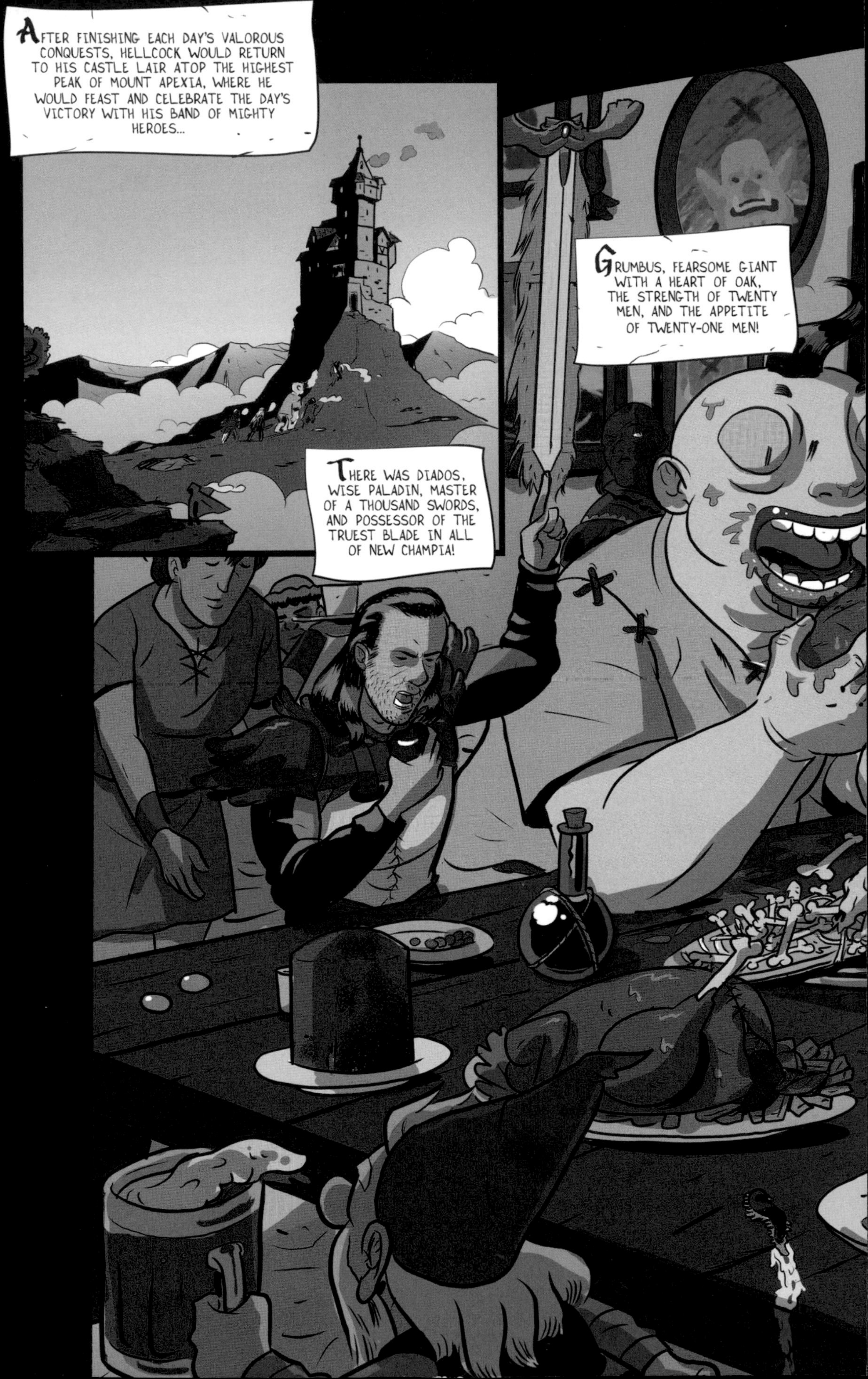
AFTER FINISHING EACH DAY'S VALOROUS CONQUESTS, HELLCOCK WOULD RETURN TO HIS CASTLE LAIR ATOP THE HIGHEST PEAK OF MOUNT APEXIA, WHERE HE WOULD FEAST AND CELEBRATE THE DAY'S VICTORY WITH HIS BAND OF MIGHTY HEROES...
THERE WAS DIADOS, WISE PALADIN, MASTER OF A THOUSAND SWORDS, AND POSSESSOR OF THE TRUEST BLADE IN ALL OF NEW CHAMPIA!
GRUMBUS, FEARSOME GIANT WITH A HEART OF OAK, THE STRENGTH OF TWENTY MEN, AND THE APPETITE OF TWENTY-ONE MEN!

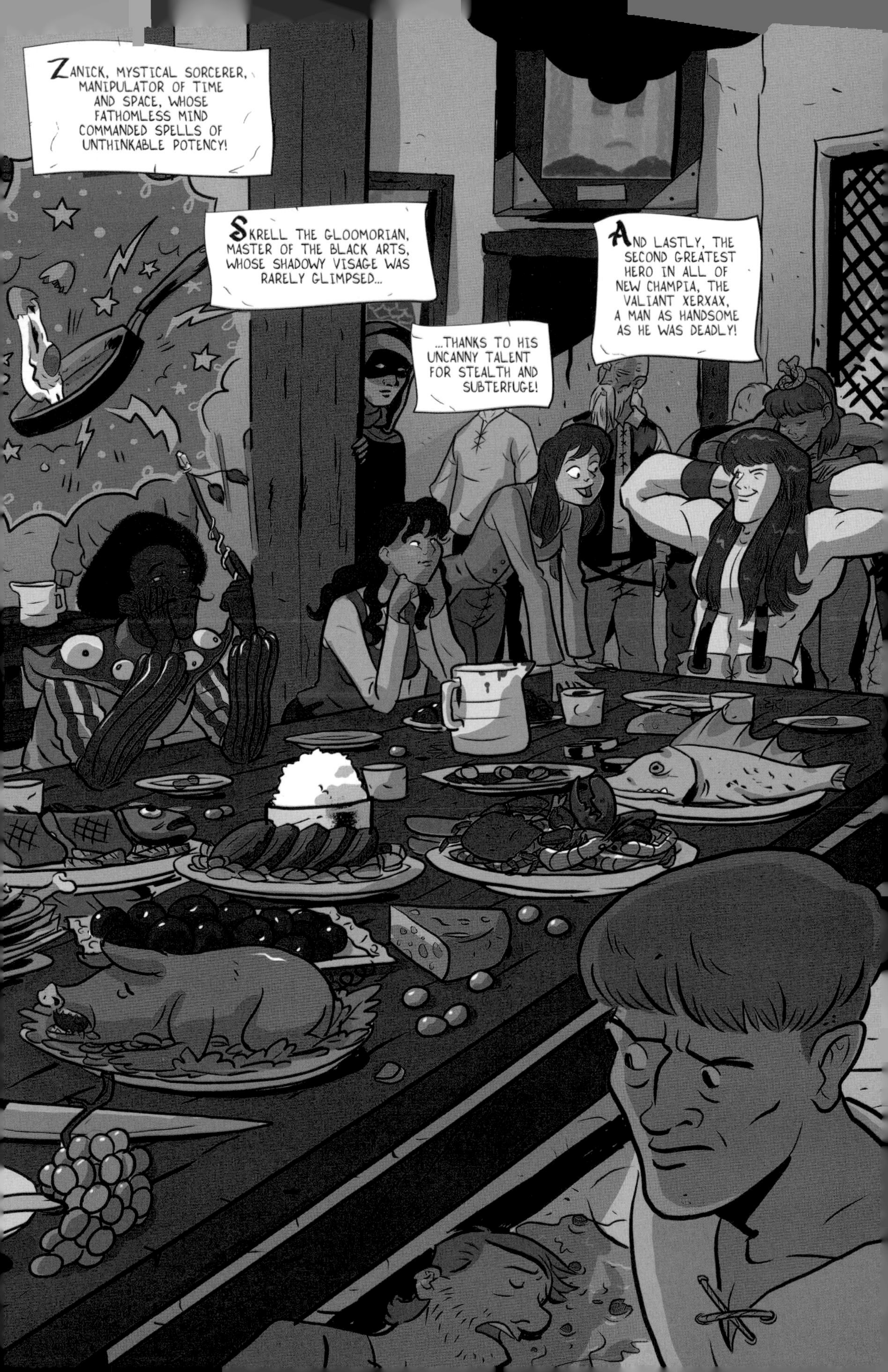
ZANICK, MYSTICAL SORCERER, MANIPULATOR OF TIME AND SPACE, WHOSE FATHOMLESS MIND COMMANDED SPELLS OF UNTHINKABLE POTENCY!
SKRELL THE GLOOMORIAN, MASTER OF THE BLACK ARTS, WHOSE SHADOWY VISAGE WAS RARELY GLIMPSED...
...THANKS TO HIS UNCANNY TALENT FOR STEALTH AND SUBTERFUGE!
AND LASTLY, THE SECOND GREATEST HERO IN ALL OF NEW CHAMPIA, THE VALIANT XERXAX, A MAN AS HANDSOME AS HE WAS DEADLY!

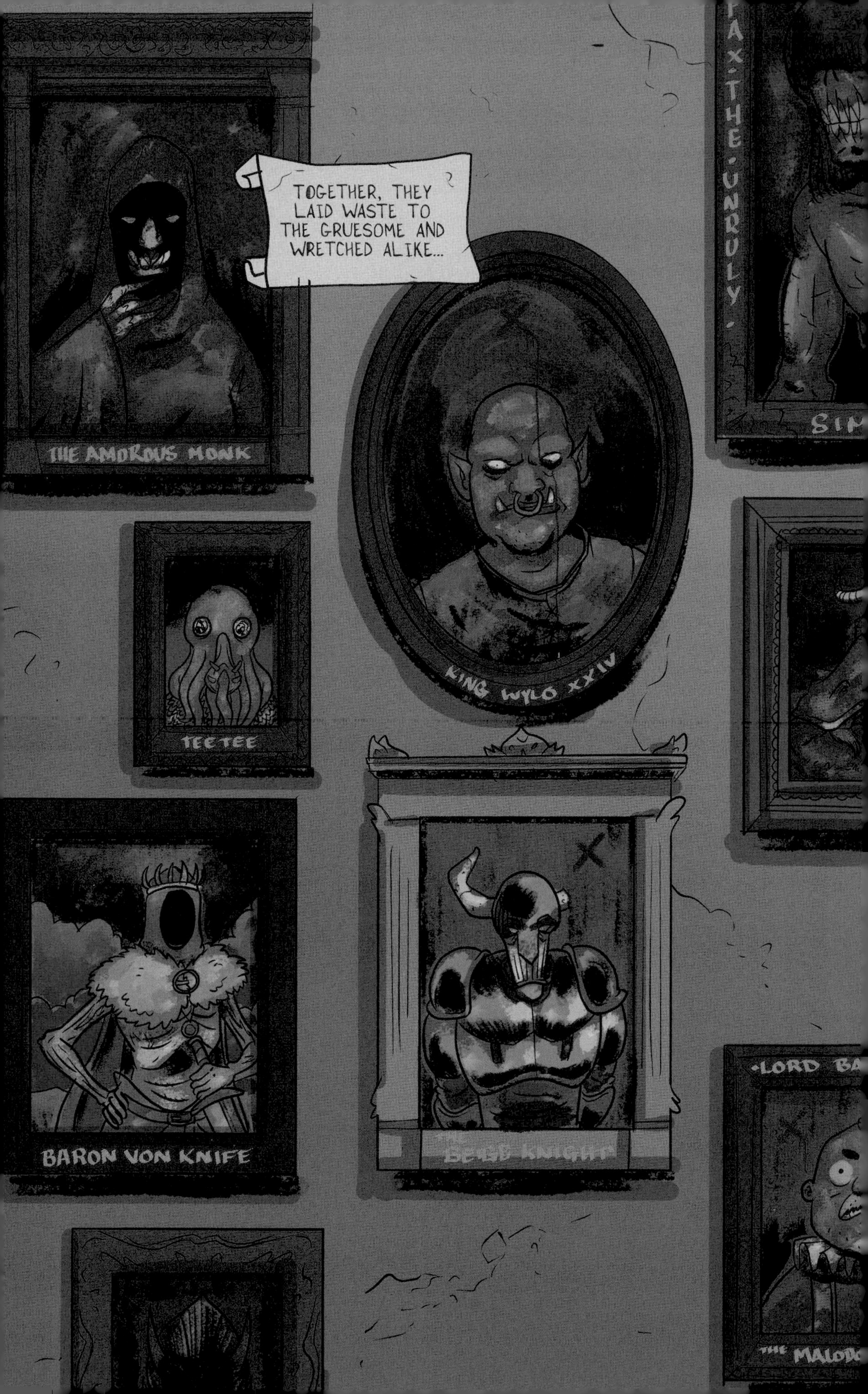
TOGETHER, THEY LAID WASTE TO THE GRUESOME AND WRETCHED ALIKE...
THE AMOROUS MONK
KING WYLO XXIV
TEETEE
BARON VON KNIFE
AX·THE·UNRULY·
LORD BA
THE MALOD

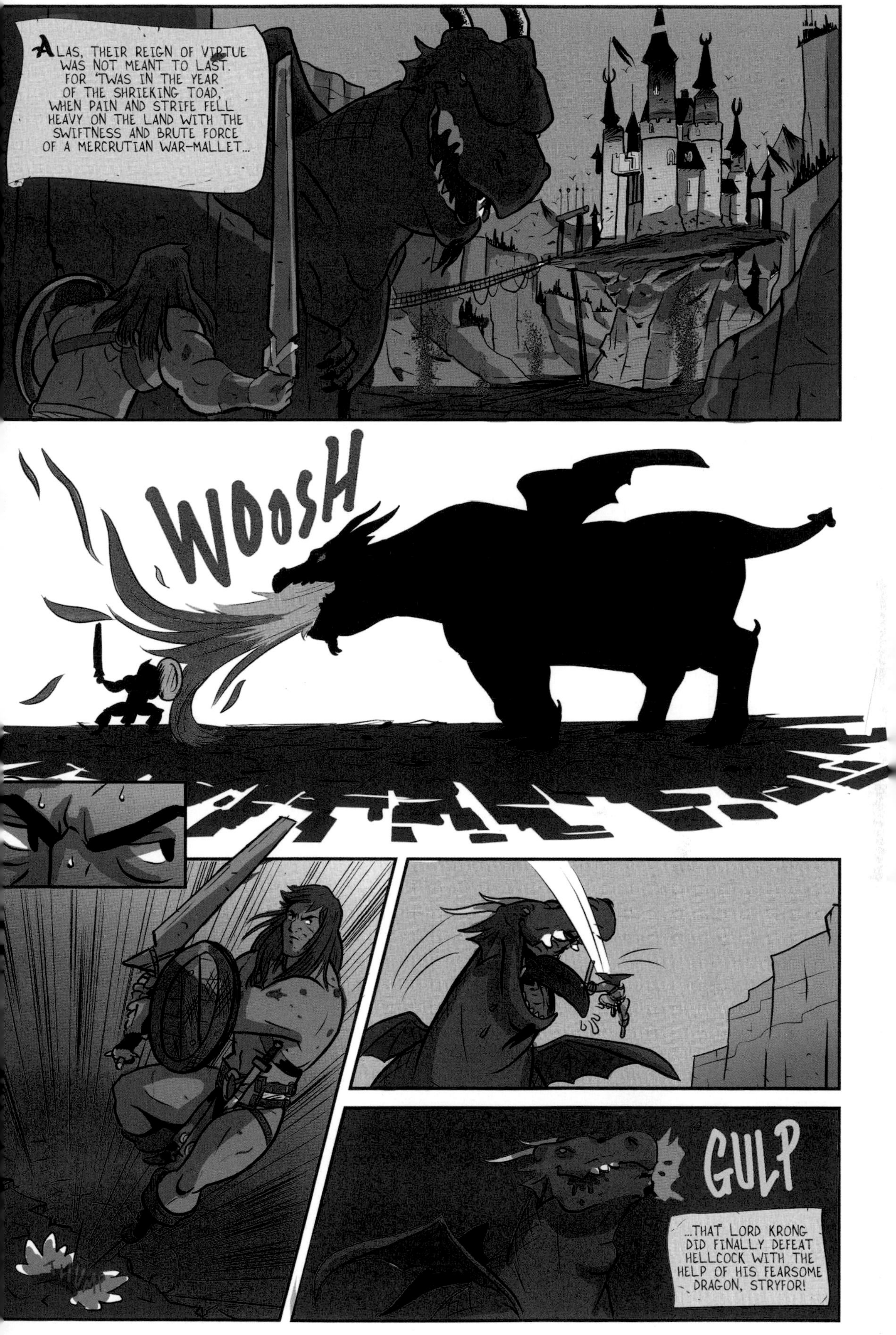
ALAS, THEIR REIGN OF VIRTUE WAS NOT MEANT TO LAST. FOR 'TWAS IN THE YEAR OF THE SHRIEKING TOAD, WHEN PAIN AND STRIFE FELL HEAVY ON THE LAND WITH THE SWIFTNESS AND BRUTE FORCE OF A MERCRUTIAN WAR-MALLET...
WOOSH
GULP
...THAT LORD KRONG DID FINALLY DEFEAT HELLCOCK WITH THE HELP OF HIS FEARSOME DRAGON, STRYFOR!

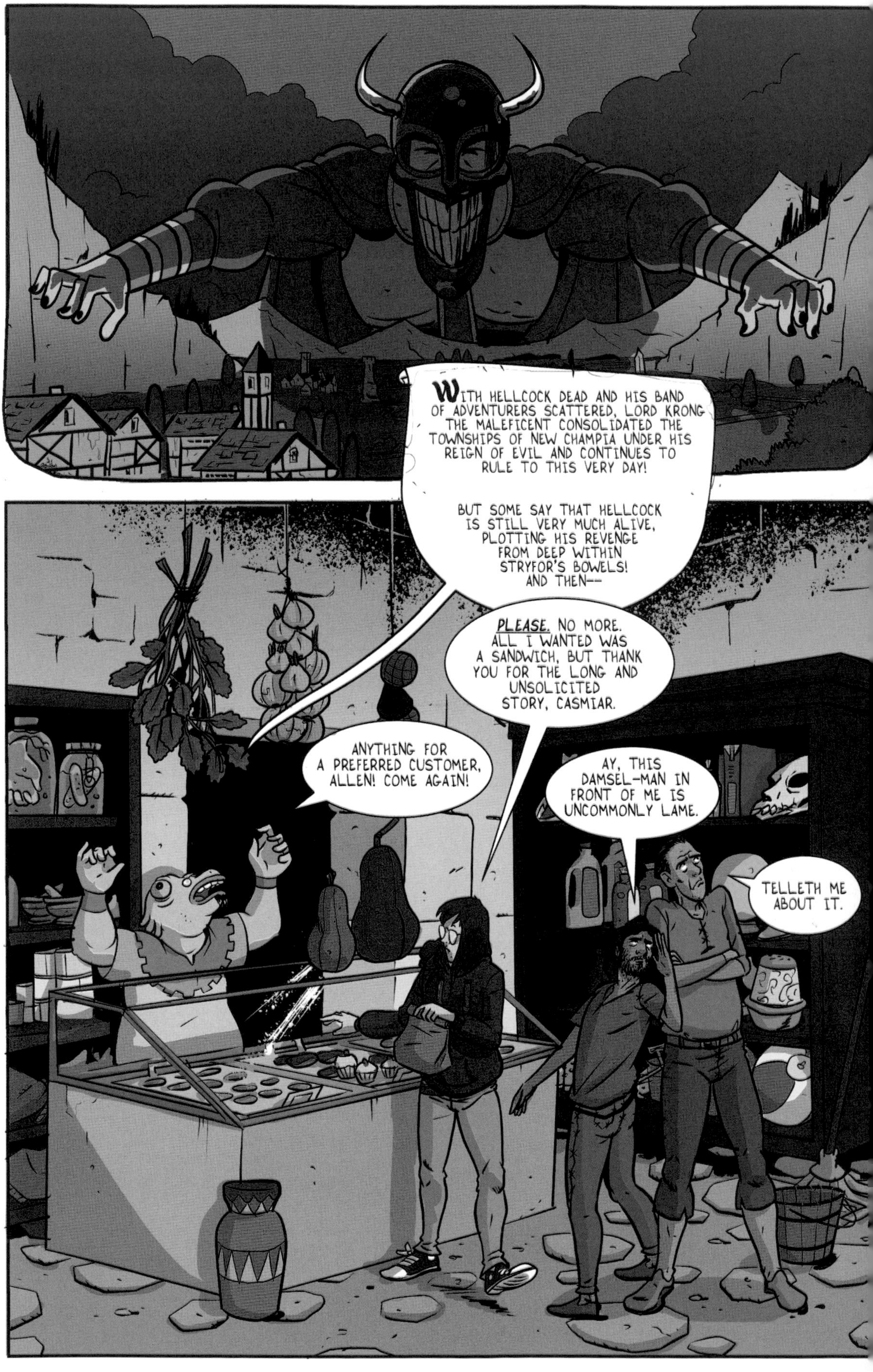
WITH HELLCOCK DEAD AND HIS BAND OF ADVENTURERS SCATTERED, LORD KRONG THE MALEFICENT CONSOLIDATED THE TOWNSHIPS OF NEW CHAMPIA UNDER HIS REIGN OF EVIL AND CONTINUES TO RULE TO THIS VERY DAY!
BUT SOME SAY THAT HELLCOCK IS STILL VERY MUCH ALIVE, PLOTTING HIS REVENGE FROM DEEP WITHIN STRYFOR'S BOWELS! AND THEN--
PLEASE. NO MORE. ALL I WANTED WAS A SANDWICH, BUT THANK YOU FOR THE LONG AND UNSOLICITED STORY, CASMIAR.
ANYTHING FOR A PREFERRED CUSTOMER, ALLEN! COME AGAIN!
AY, THIS DAMSEL-MAN IN FRONT OF ME IS UNCOMMONLY LAME.
TELLETH ME ABOUT IT.

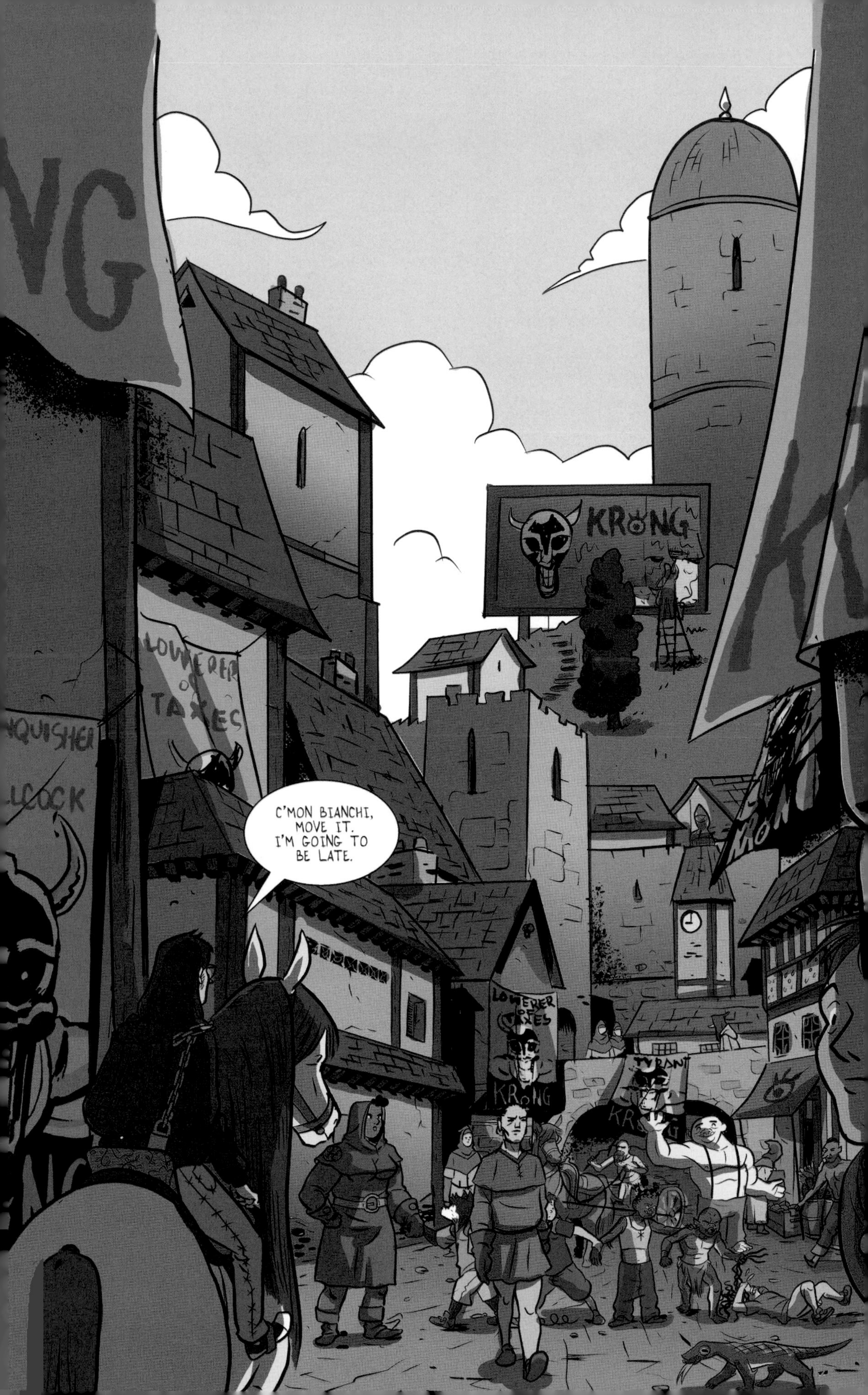
KRONG
LOWERER OF TAXES
C'MON BIANCHI, MOVE IT. I'M GOING TO BE LATE.
LOWERER OF TAXES
KRONG
TYRANT
KRONG

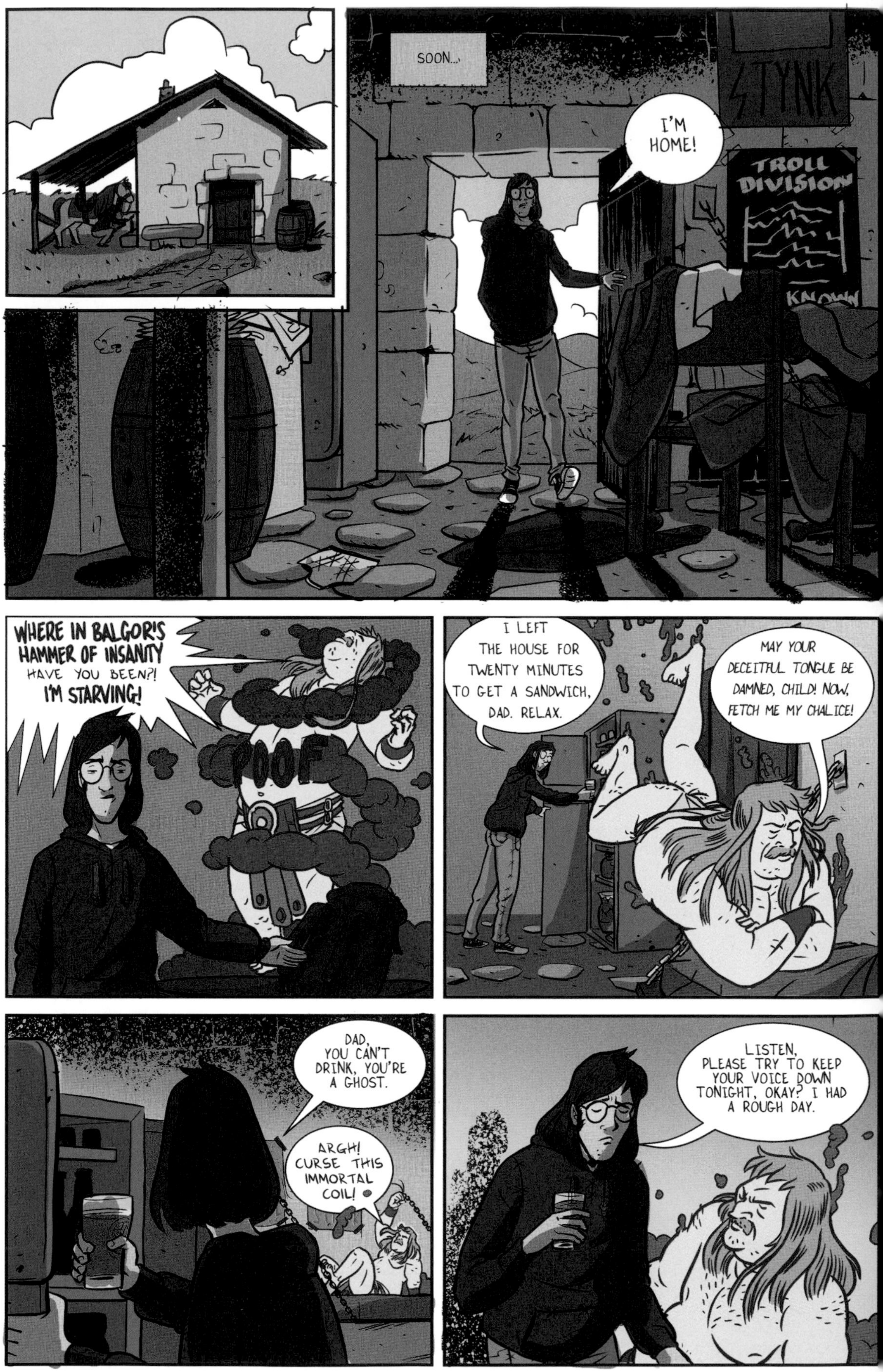
SOON...
I'M HOME!
STYNK
TROLL DIVISION
WHERE IN BALGOR'S HAMMER OF INSANITY HAVE YOU BEEN?! I'M STARVING!
POOF
I LEFT THE HOUSE FOR TWENTY MINUTES TO GET A SANDWICH, DAD. RELAX.
MAY YOUR DECEITFUL TONGUE BE DAMNED, CHILD! NOW, FETCH ME MY CHALICE!
DAD, YOU CAN'T DRINK, YOU'RE A GHOST.
ARGH! CURSE THIS IMMORTAL COIL!
LISTEN, PLEASE TRY TO KEEP YOUR VOICE DOWN TONIGHT, OKAY? I HAD A ROUGH DAY.

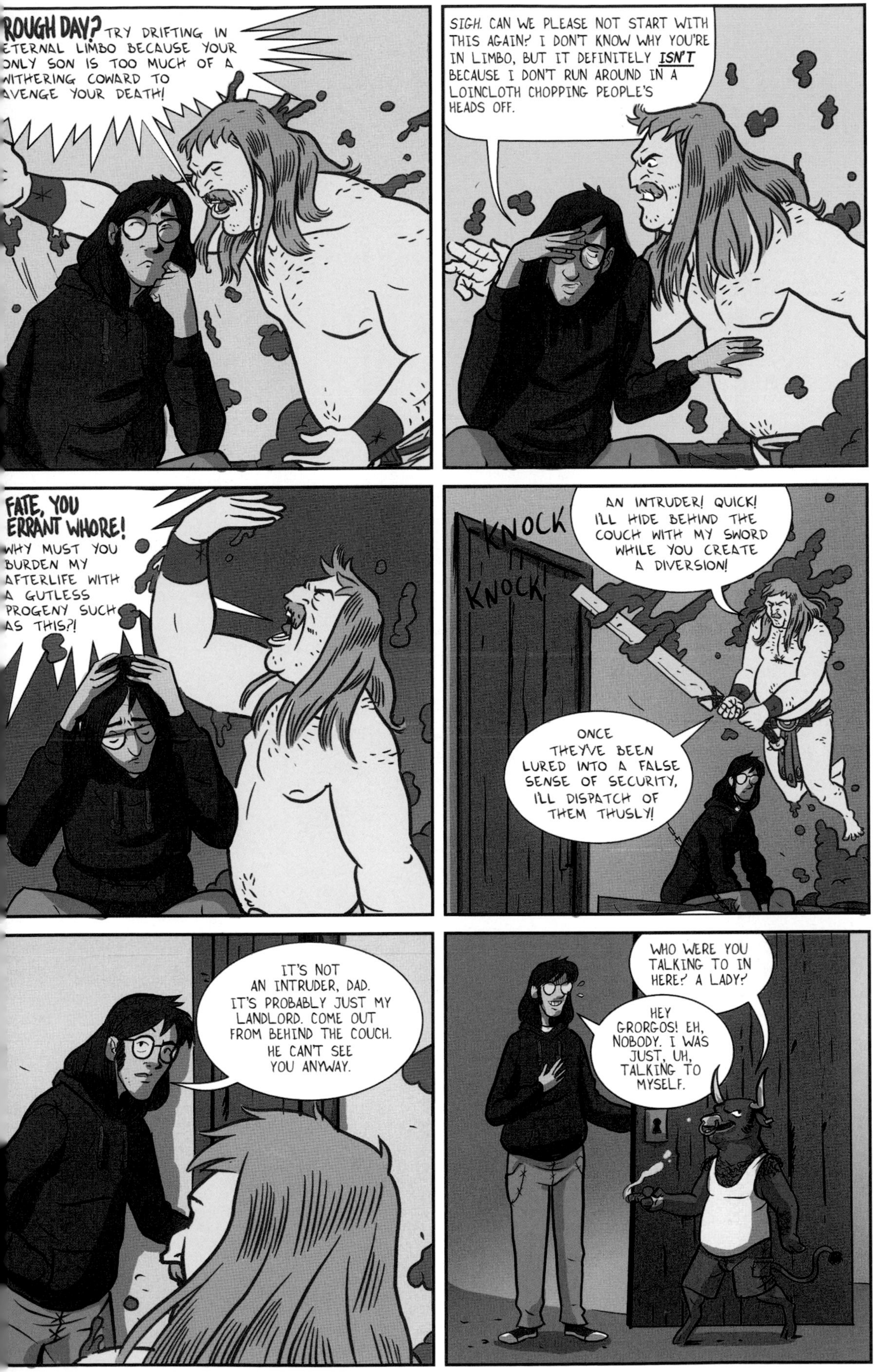

ROUGH DAY? TRY DRIFTING IN ETERNAL LIMBO BECAUSE YOUR ONLY SON IS TOO MUCH OF A WITHERING COWARD TO AVENGE YOUR DEATH!
SIGH. CAN WE PLEASE NOT START WITH THIS AGAIN? I DON'T KNOW WHY YOU'RE IN LIMBO, BUT IT DEFINITELY ISN'T BECAUSE I DON'T RUN AROUND IN A LOINCLOTH CHOPPING PEOPLE'S HEADS OFF.
FATE, YOU ERRANT WHORE! WHY MUST YOU BURDEN MY AFTERLIFE WITH A GUTLESS PROGENY SUCH AS THIS?!
KNOCK
KNOCK
AN INTRUDER! QUICK! I'LL HIDE BEHIND THE COUCH WITH MY SWORD WHILE YOU CREATE A DIVERSION!
ONCE THEY'VE BEEN LURED INTO A FALSE SENSE OF SECURITY, I'LL DISPATCH OF THEM THUSLY!
IT'S NOT AN INTRUDER, DAD. IT'S PROBABLY JUST MY LANDLORD. COME OUT FROM BEHIND THE COUCH. HE CAN'T SEE YOU ANYWAY.
WHO WERE YOU TALKING TO IN HERE? A LADY?
HEY GRORGOS! EH, NOBODY. I WAS JUST, UH, TALKING TO MYSELF.

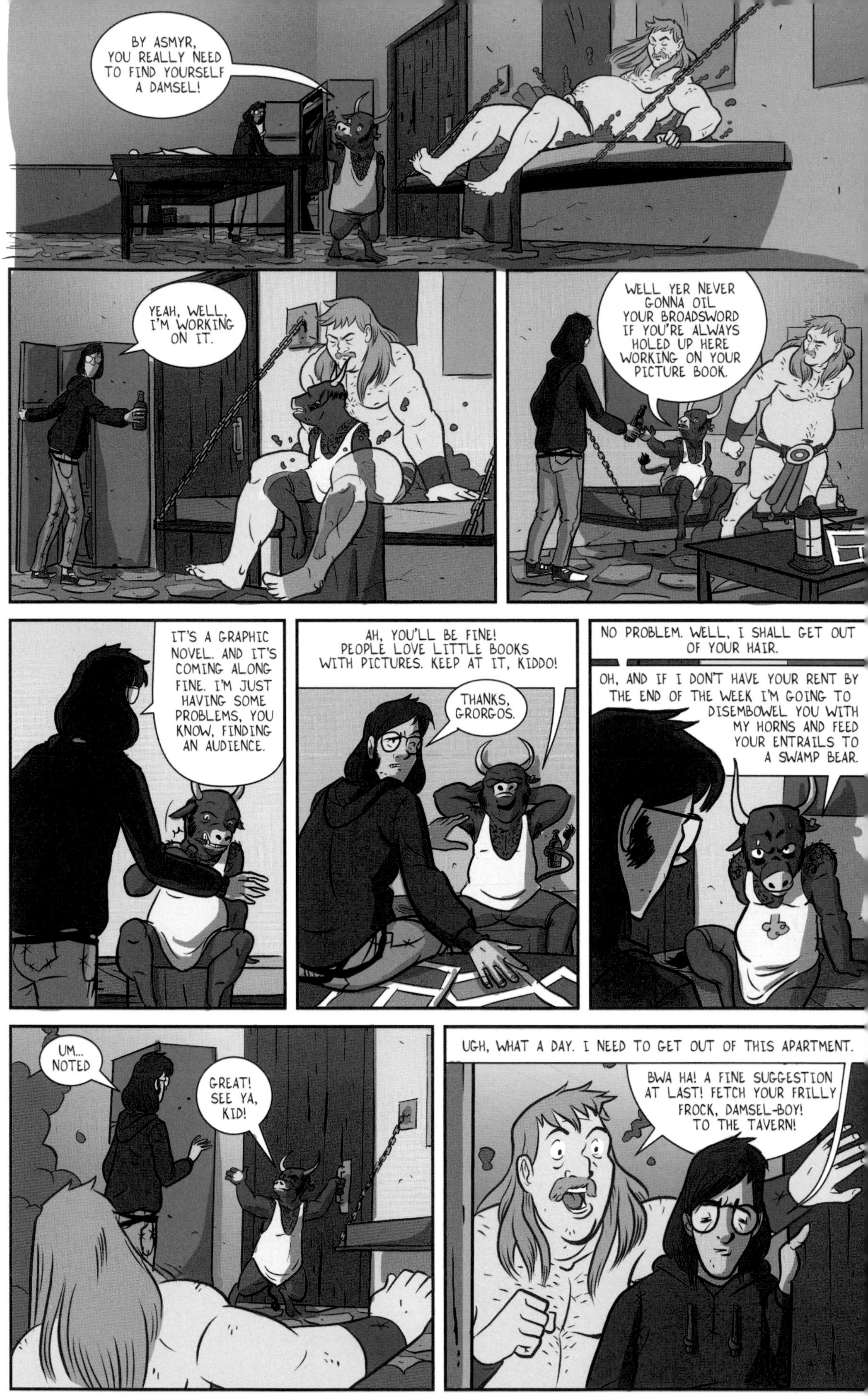
BY ASMYR, YOU REALLY NEED TO FIND YOURSELF A DAMSEL!
YEAH, WELL, I'M WORKING ON IT.
WELL YER NEVER GONNA OIL YOUR BROADSWORD IF YOU'RE ALWAYS HOLED UP HERE WORKING ON YOUR PICTURE BOOK.
IT'S A GRAPHIC NOVEL. AND IT'S COMING ALONG FINE. I'M JUST HAVING SOME PROBLEMS, YOU KNOW, FINDING AN AUDIENCE.
AH, YOU'LL BE FINE! PEOPLE LOVE LITTLE BOOKS WITH PICTURES. KEEP AT IT, KIDDO!
THANKS, GRORGOS.
NO PROBLEM. WELL, I SHALL GET OUT OF YOUR HAIR.
OH, AND IF I DON'T HAVE YOUR RENT BY THE END OF THE WEEK I'M GOING TO DISEMBOWEL YOU WITH MY HORNS AND FEED YOUR ENTRAILS TO A SWAMP BEAR.
UM... NOTED
GREAT! SEE YA, KID!
UGH, WHAT A DAY. I NEED TO GET OUT OF THIS APARTMENT.
BWA HA! A FINE SUGGESTION AT LAST! FETCH YOUR FRILLY FROCK, DAMSEL-BOY! TO THE TAVERN!

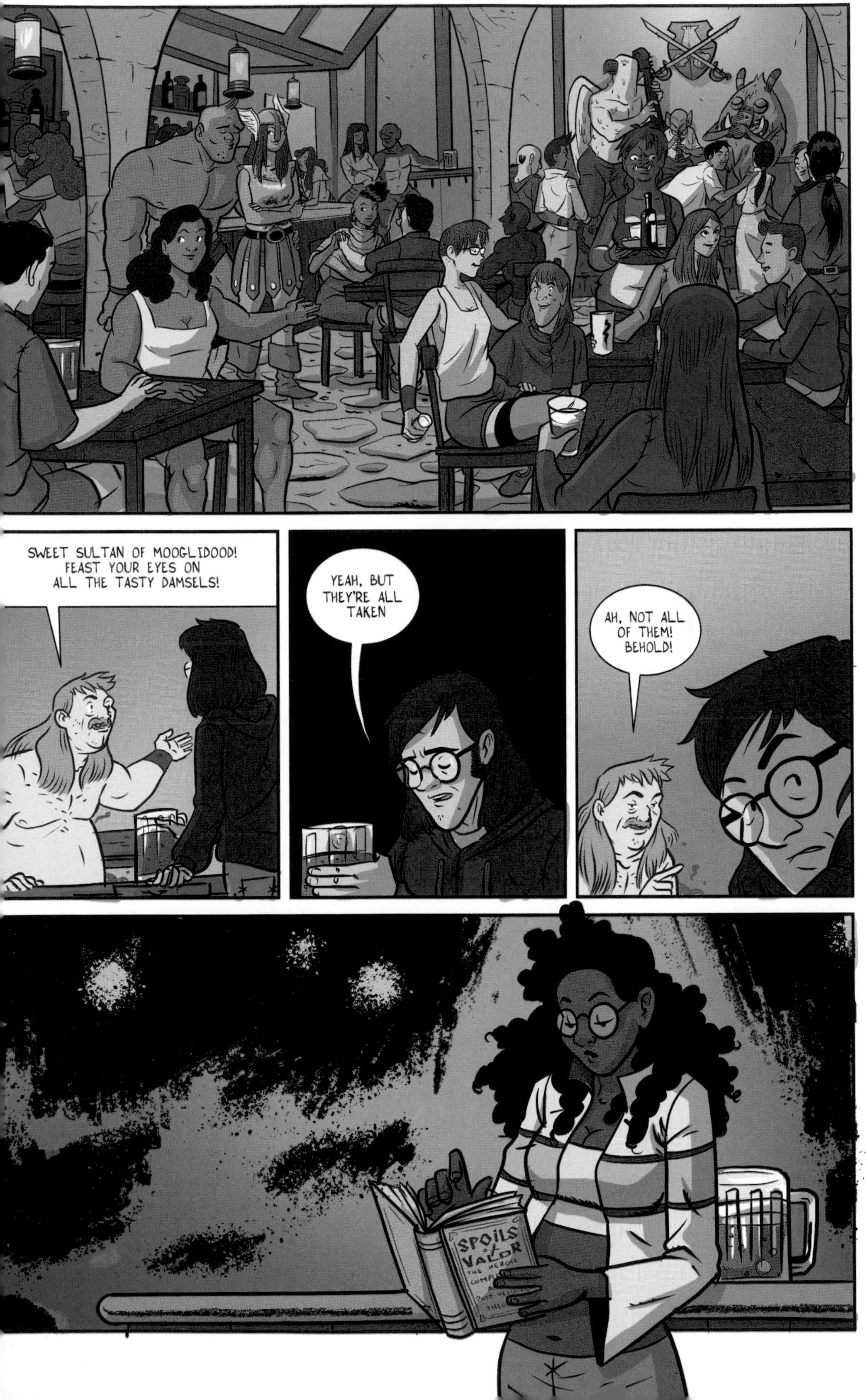
SWEET SULTAN OF MOOGLIDOOD! FEAST YOUR EYES ON ALL THE TASTY DAMSELS!
YEAH, BUT THEY'RE ALL TAKEN
AH, NOT ALL OF THEM! BEHOLD!
SPOILS of VALOR
THE HEROIC

GO, MY BOY! SPEAK TO HER!

YOUR LEAGUE?! YOU ARE THE SON OF THE GREATEST HERO WHO EVER BRAVED THE TARKAN SWAMPS! SHE WILL BE POWERLESS TO RESIST YOU!

SCREW THAT. I'M STAYING RIGHT HERE.

WHAT, ARE YOU CRAZY? SHE'S COMPLETELY OUT OF MY LEAGUE, DAD.

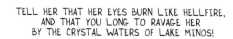

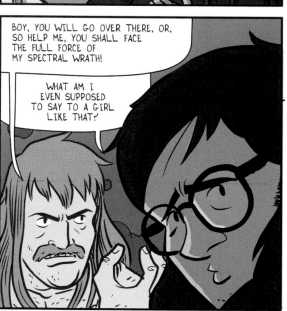

BOY, YOU WILL GO OVER THERE, OR, SO HELP ME, YOU SHALL FACE THE FULL FORCE OF MY SPECTRAL WRATH!

WHAT AM I EVEN SUPPOSED TO SAY TO A GIRL LIKE THAT?

TELL HER THAT HER EYES BURN LIKE HELLFIRE, AND THAT YOU LONG TO RAVAGE HER BY THE CRYSTAL WATERS OF LAKE MINOS!

WHAT? NO. ABSOLUTELY NOT.

TRUST ME, IT WILL WORK.

FINE, I'LL TALK TO HER...

BWA HA!

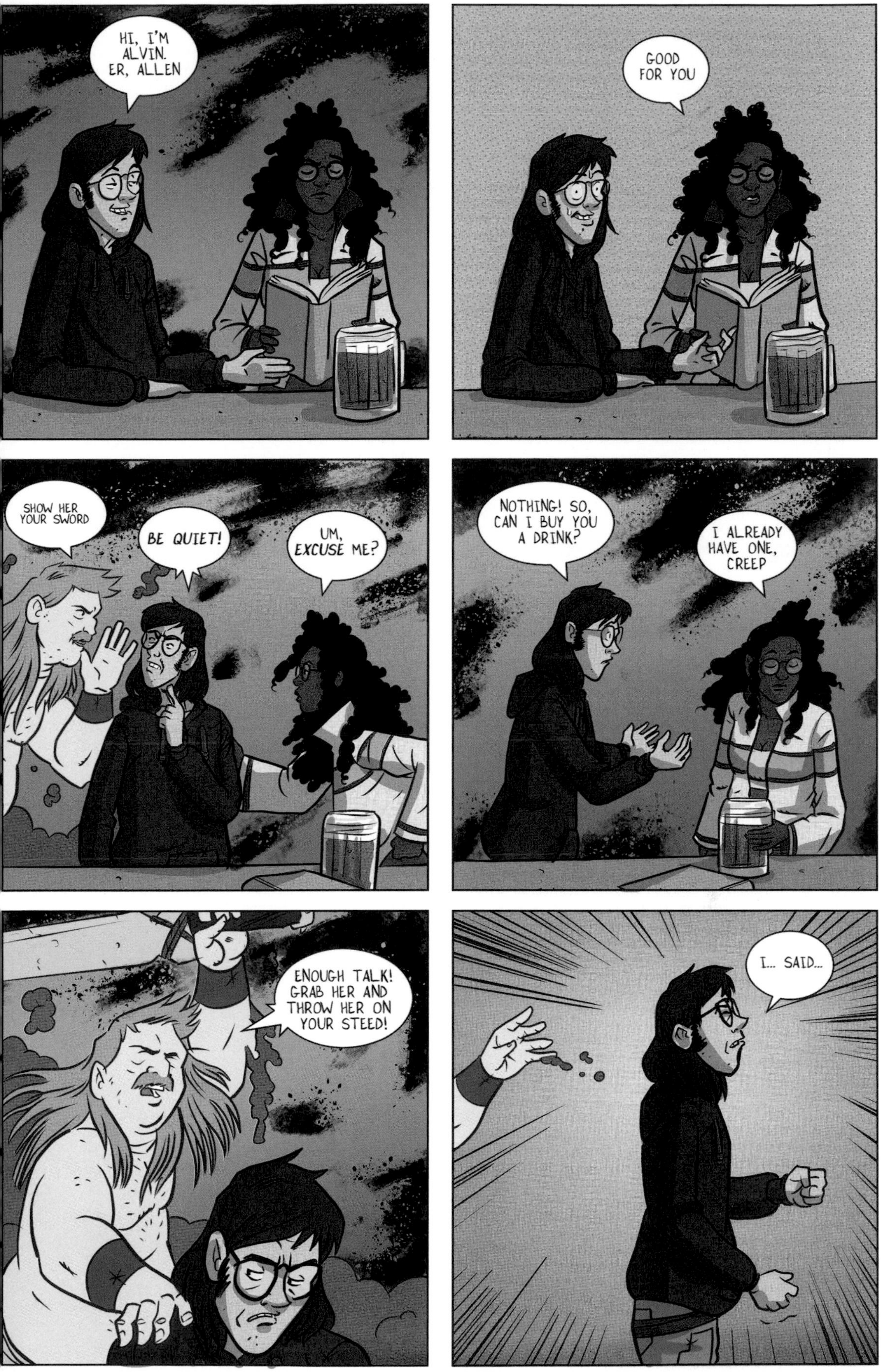
HI, I'M ALVIN. ER, ALLEN
GOOD FOR YOU
SHOW HER YOUR SWORD
BE QUIET!
UM, EXCUSE ME?
NOTHING! SO, CAN I BUY YOU A DRINK?
I ALREADY HAVE ONE, CREEP
ENOUGH TALK! GRAB HER AND THROW HER ON YOUR STEED!
I... SAID...

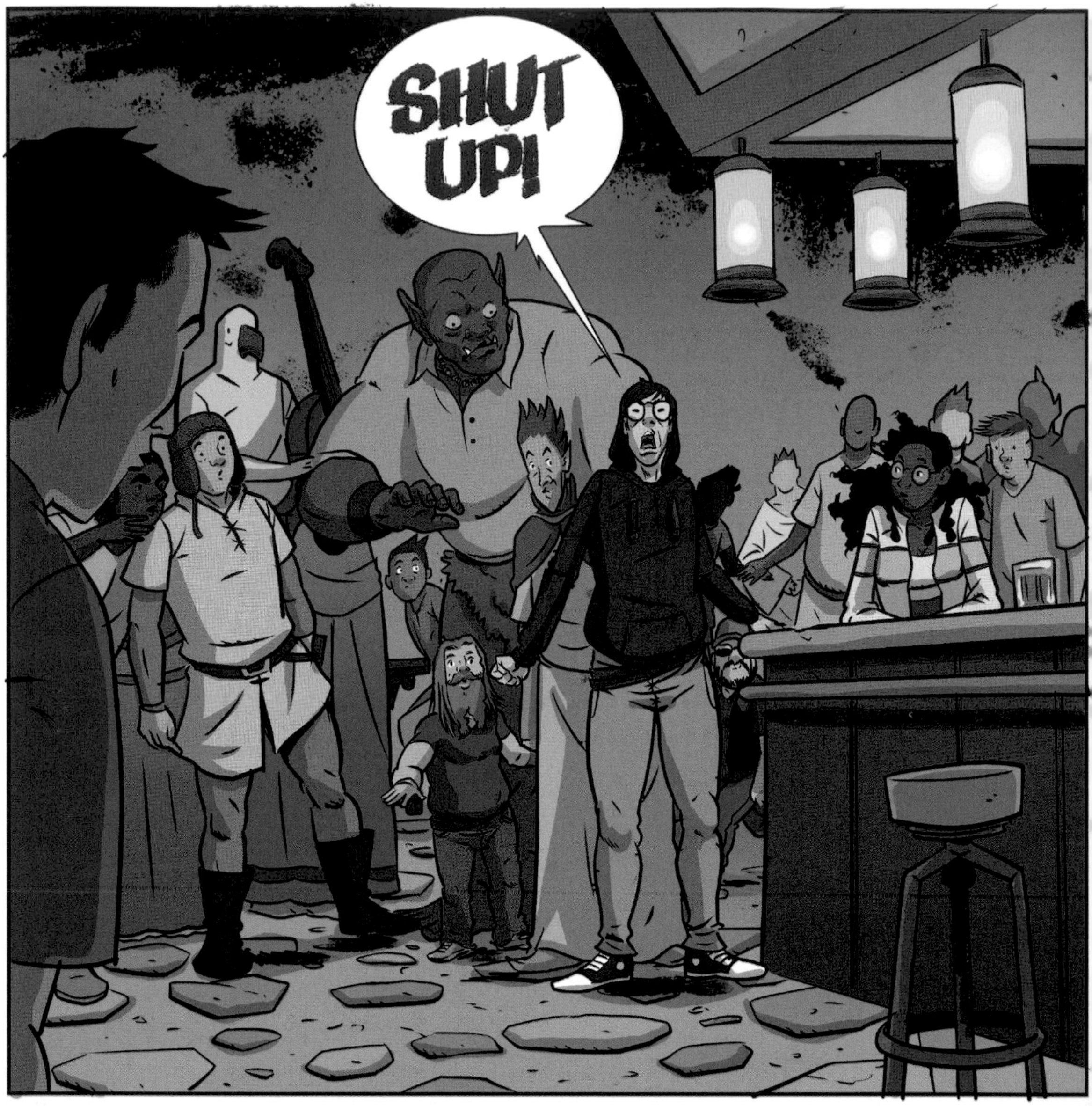
SHUT UP!

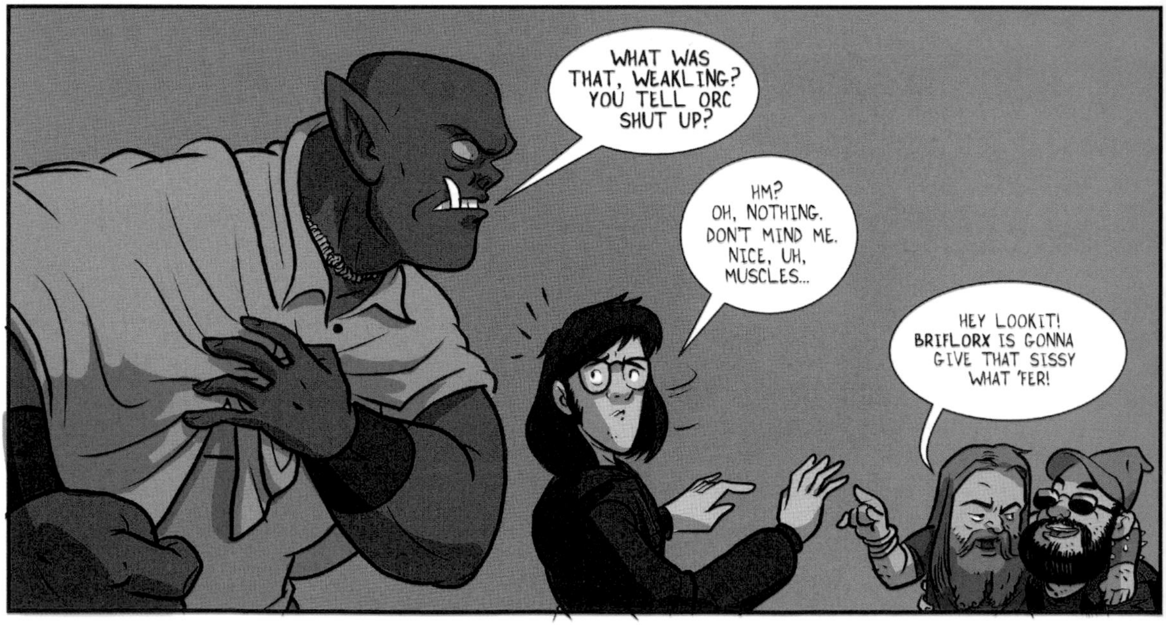
WHAT WAS THAT, WEAKLING? YOU TELL ORC SHUT UP?
HM? OH, NOTHING. DON'T MIND ME. NICE, UH, MUSCLES...
HEY LOOKIT! BRIFLORX IS GONNA GIVE THAT SISSY WHAT 'FER!

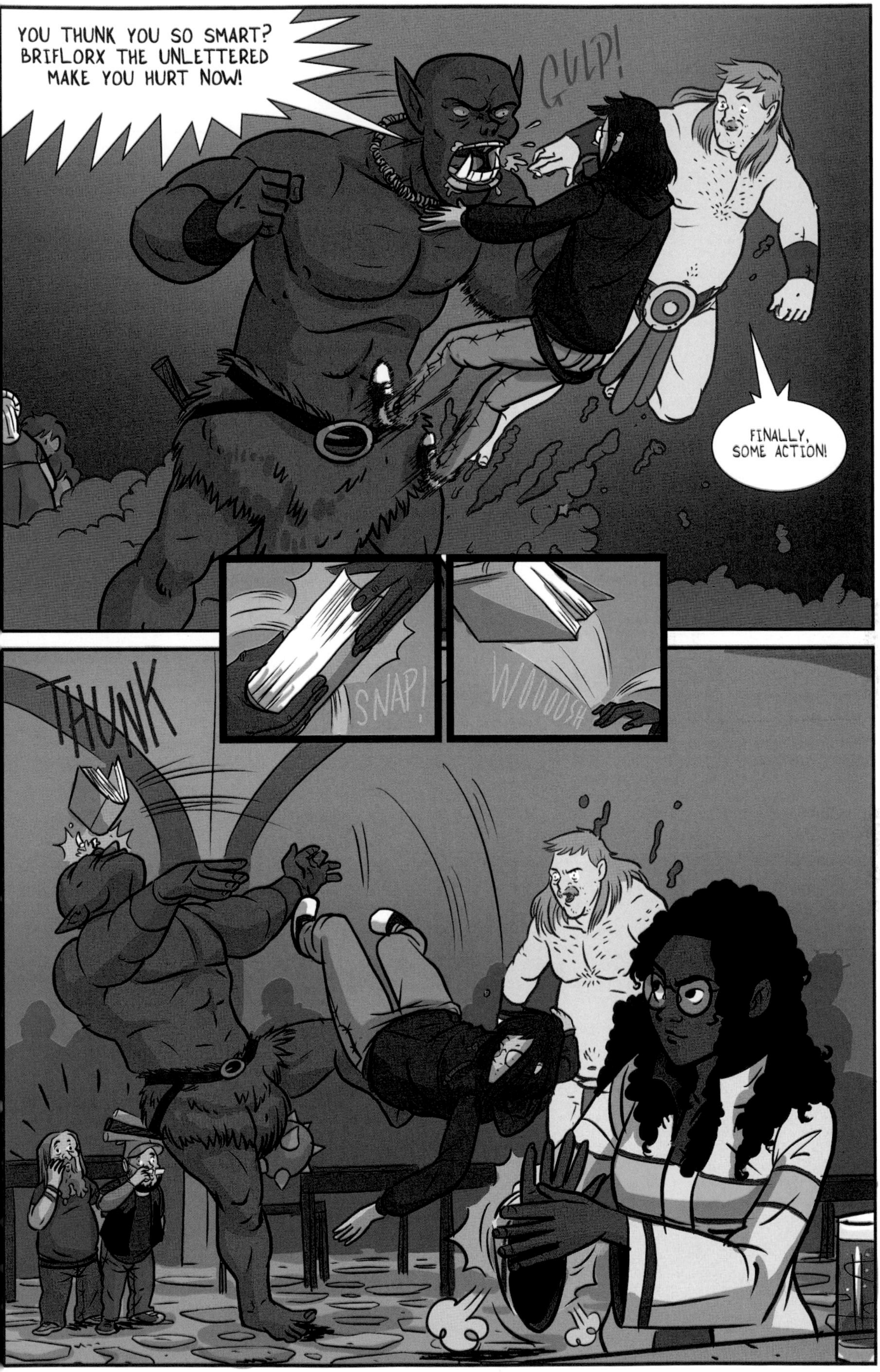
YOU THUNK YOU SO SMART? BRIFLORX THE UNLETTERED MAKE YOU HURT NOW!
GULP!
FINALLY, SOME ACTION!
SNAP!
WOOOOSH
THUNK

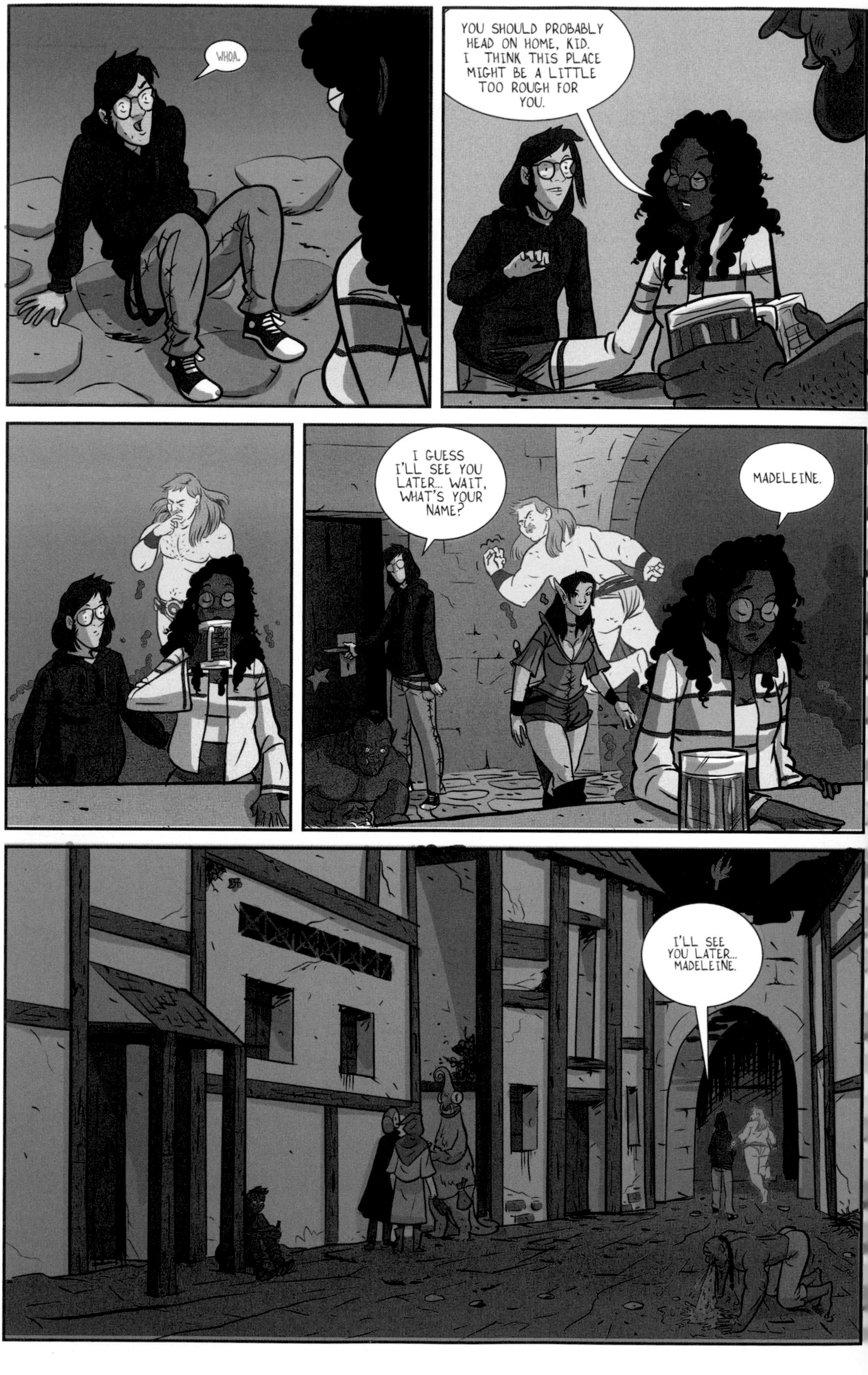
WHOA.
YOU SHOULD PROBABLY HEAD ON HOME, KID. I THINK THIS PLACE MIGHT BE A LITTLE TOO ROUGH FOR YOU.
I GUESS I'LL SEE YOU LATER... WAIT, WHAT'S YOUR NAME?
MADELEINE.
I'LL SEE YOU LATER... MADELEINE.

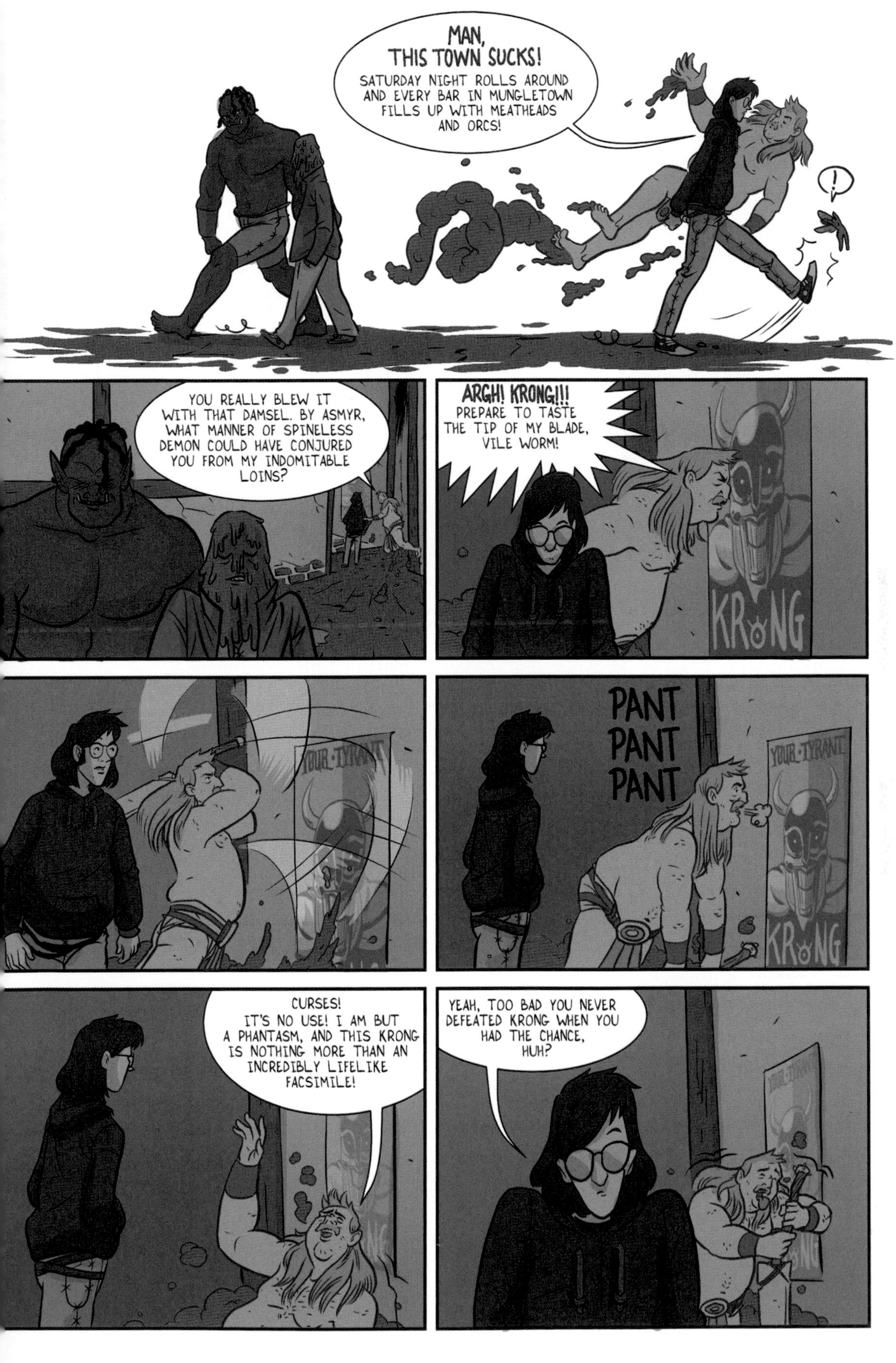
MAN, THIS TOWN SUCKS! SATURDAY NIGHT ROLLS AROUND AND EVERY BAR IN MUNGLETOWN FILLS UP WITH MEATHEADS AND ORCS!
!
YOU REALLY BLEW IT WITH THAT DAMSEL. BY ASMYR, WHAT MANNER OF SPINELESS DEMON COULD HAVE CONJURED YOU FROM MY INDOMITABLE LOINS?
ARGH! KRONG!!! PREPARE TO TASTE THE TIP OF MY BLADE, VILE WORM!
KRONG
YOUR TYRANT
PANT PANT PANT
YOUR TYRANT
KRONG
CURSES! IT'S NO USE! I AM BUT A PHANTASM, AND THIS KRONG IS NOTHING MORE THAN AN INCREDIBLY LIFELIKE FACSIMILE!
YEAH, TOO BAD YOU NEVER DEFEATED KRONG WHEN YOU HAD THE CHANCE, HUH?

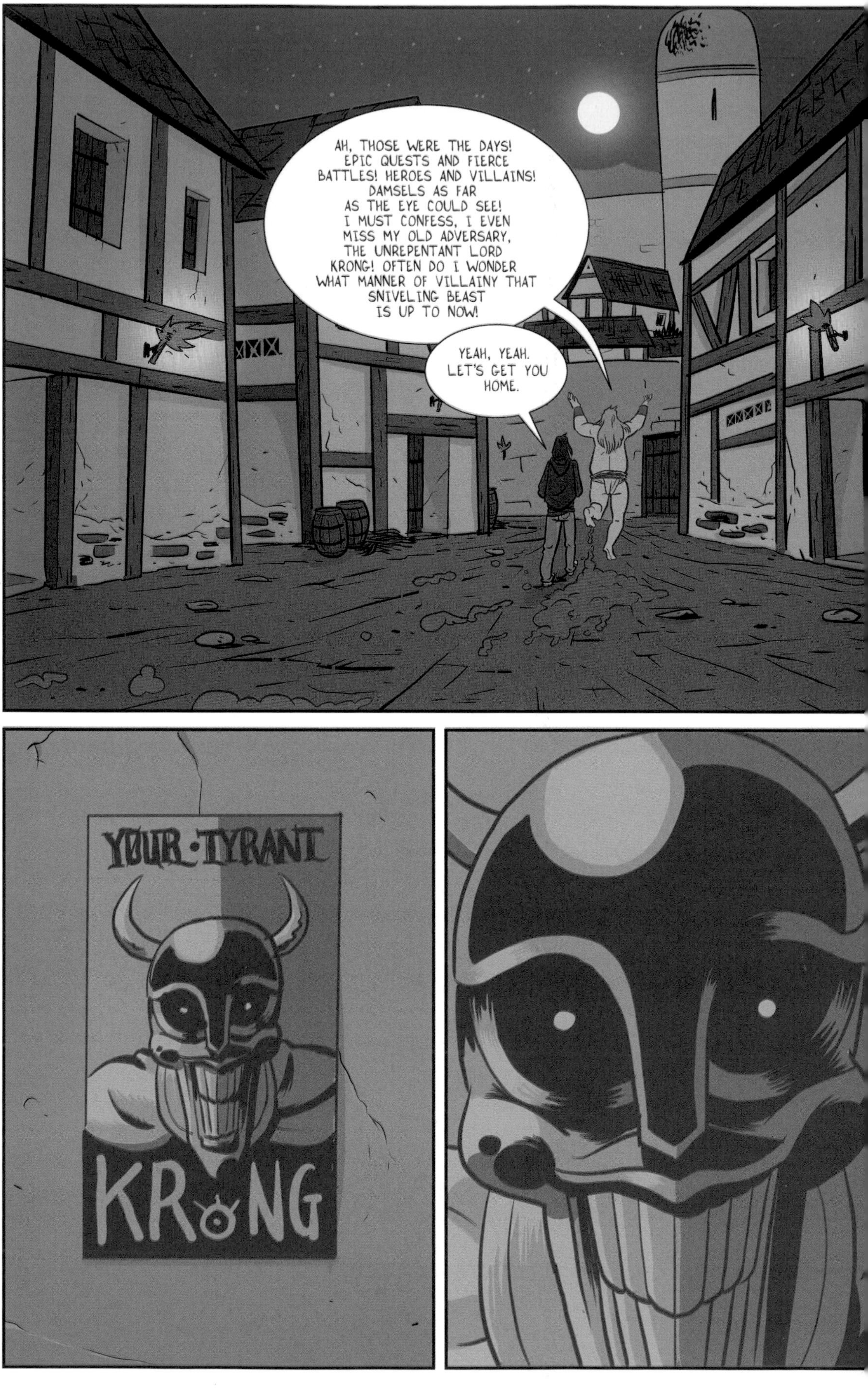
AH, THOSE WERE THE DAYS! EPIC QUESTS AND FIERCE BATTLES! HEROES AND VILLAINS! DAMSELS AS FAR AS THE EYE COULD SEE! I MUST CONFESS, I EVEN MISS MY OLD ADVERSARY, THE UNREPENTANT LORD KRONG! OFTEN DO I WONDER WHAT MANNER OF VILLAINY THAT SNIVELING BEAST IS UP TO NOW!
YEAH, YEAH. LET'S GET YOU HOME.
YOUR TYRANT
KRONG

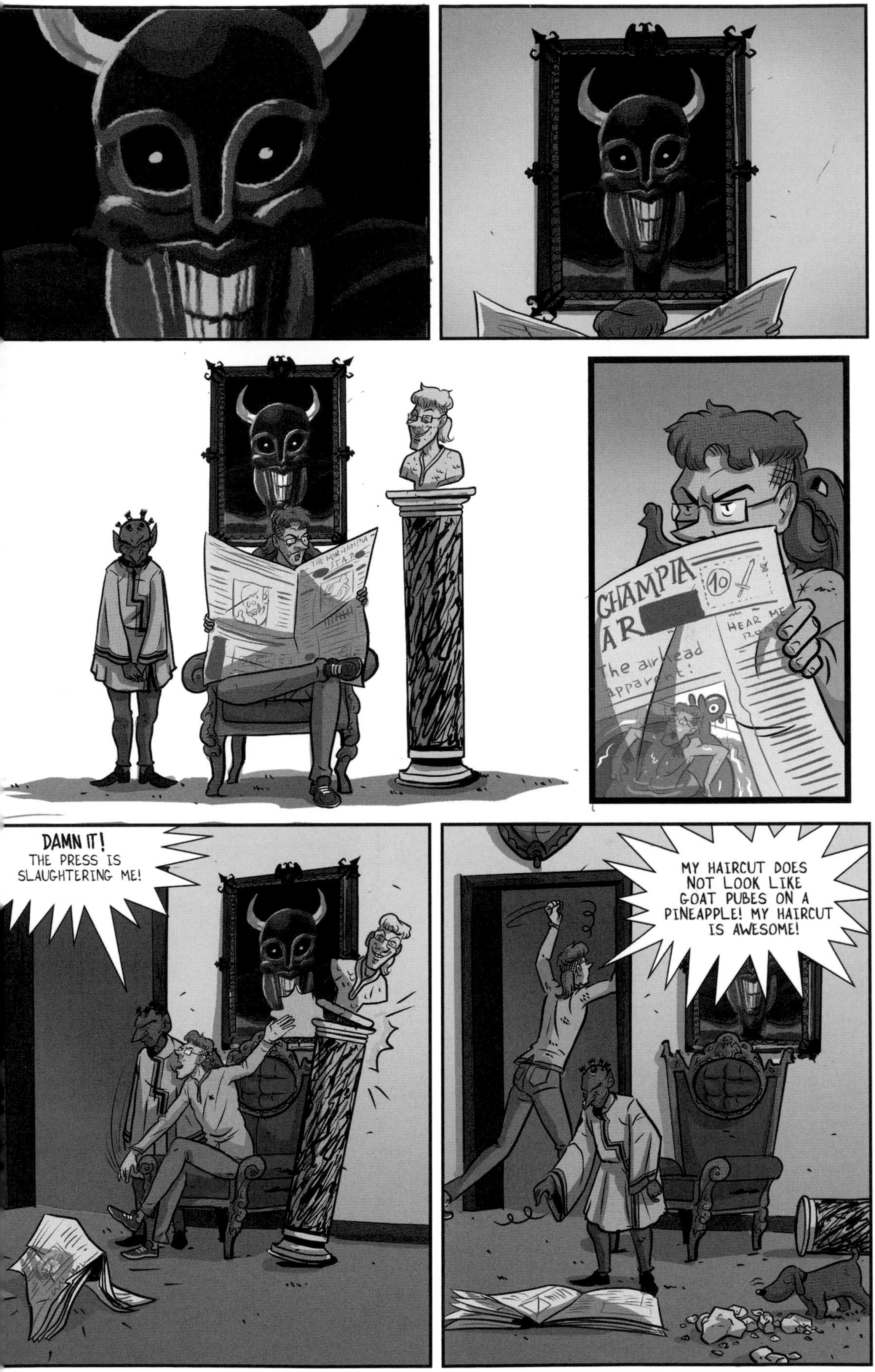
CHAMPIA
AR [redacted]
The airhead apparent!
HEAR ME
DAMN IT! THE PRESS IS SLAUGHTERING ME!
MY HAIRCUT DOES NOT LOOK LIKE GOAT PUBES ON A PINEAPPLE! MY HAIRCUT IS AWESOME!

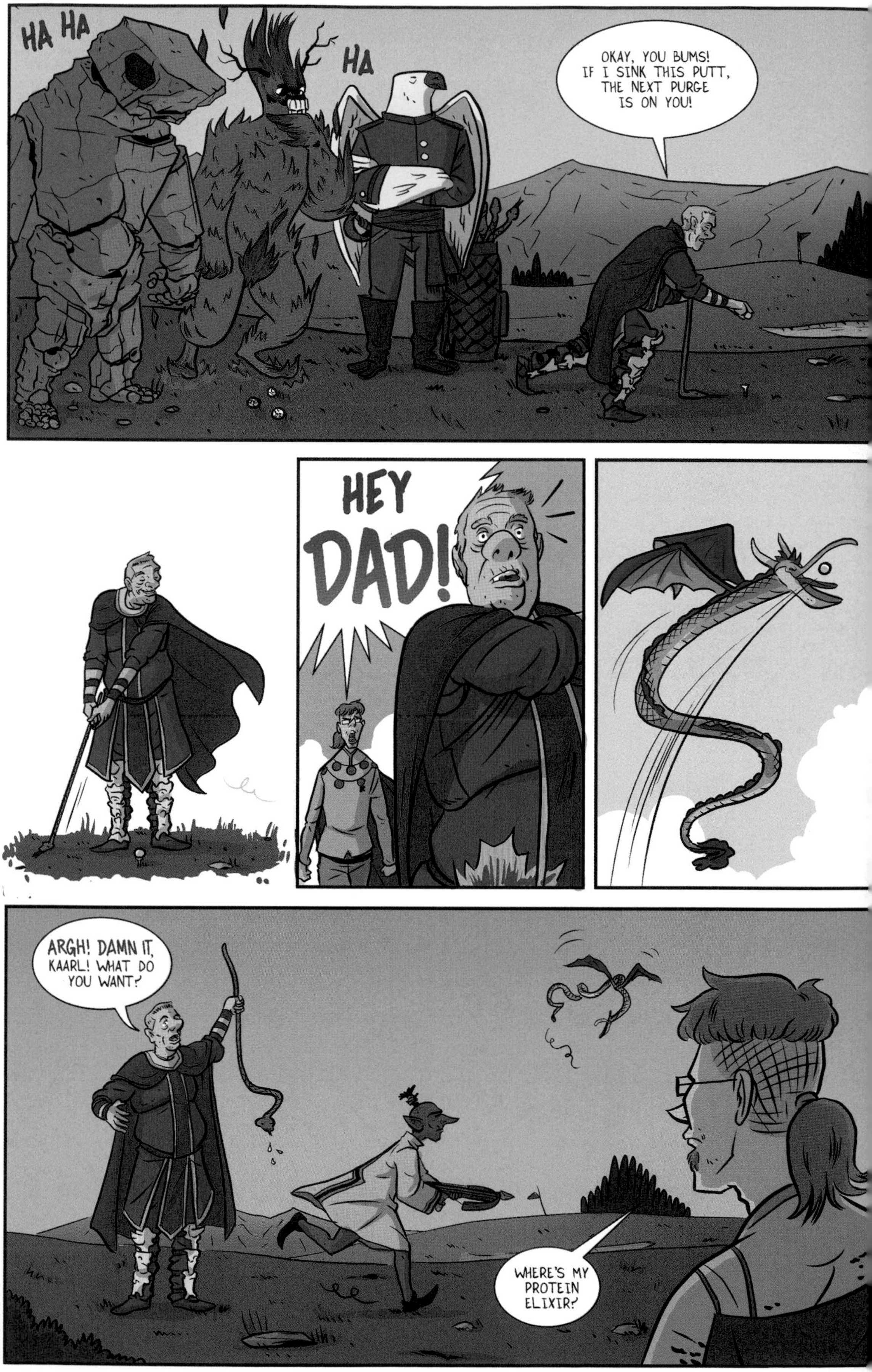
HA HA
HA
OKAY, YOU BUMS! IF I SINK THIS PUTT, THE NEXT PURGE IS ON YOU!
HEY DAD!
ARGH! DAMN IT, KAARL! WHAT DO YOU WANT?
WHERE'S MY PROTEIN ELIXIR?

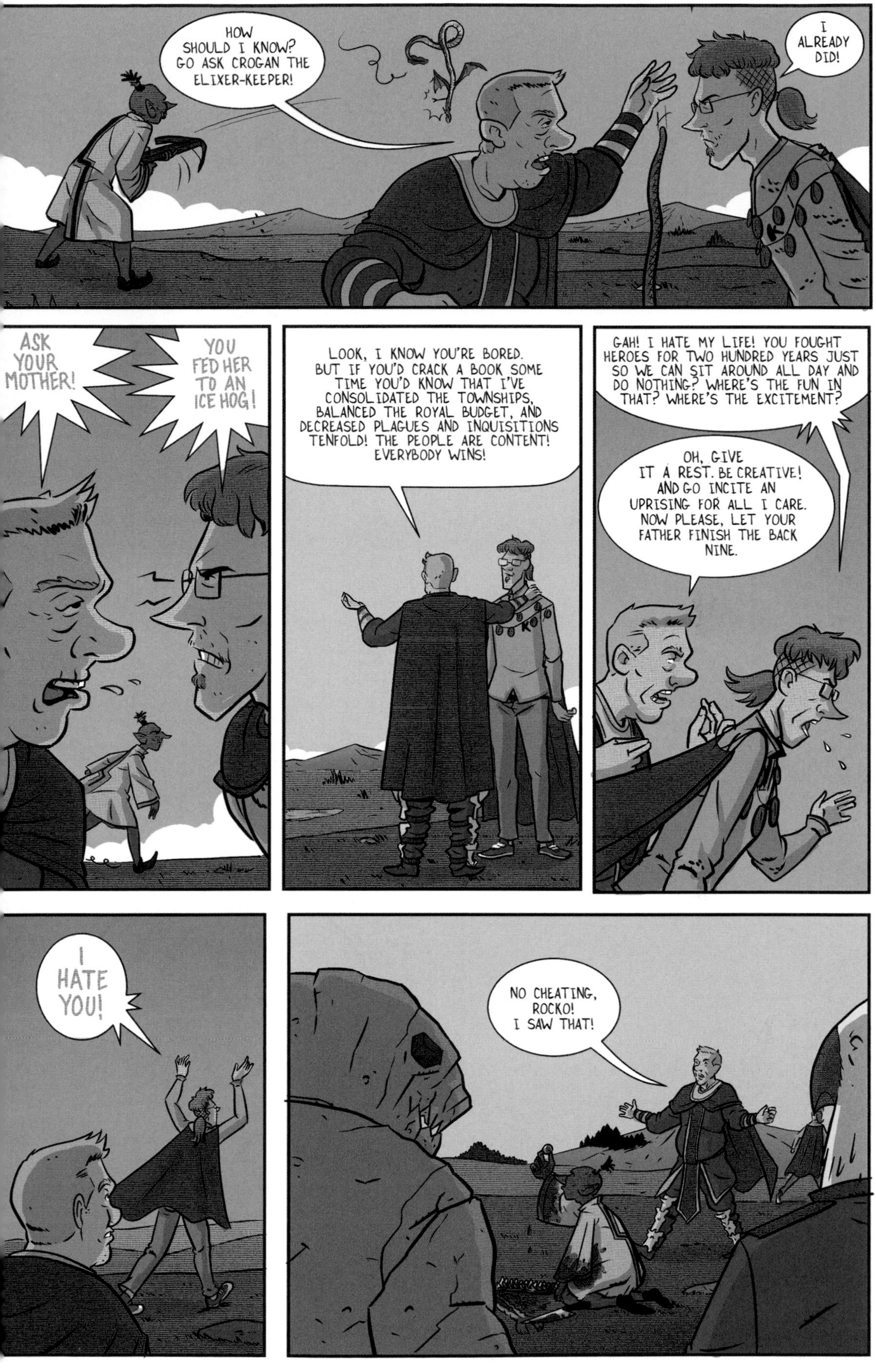
HOW SHOULD I KNOW? GO ASK CROGAN THE ELIXER-KEEPER!
I ALREADY DID!
ASK YOUR MOTHER!
YOU FED HER TO AN ICE HOG!
LOOK, I KNOW YOU'RE BORED. BUT IF YOU'D CRACK A BOOK SOME TIME YOU'D KNOW THAT I'VE CONSOLIDATED THE TOWNSHIPS, BALANCED THE ROYAL BUDGET, AND DECREASED PLAGUES AND INQUISITIONS TENFOLD! THE PEOPLE ARE CONTENT! EVERYBODY WINS!
GAH! I HATE MY LIFE! YOU FOUGHT HEROES FOR TWO HUNDRED YEARS JUST SO WE CAN SIT AROUND ALL DAY AND DO NOTHING? WHERE'S THE FUN IN THAT? WHERE'S THE EXCITEMENT?
OH, GIVE IT A REST. BE CREATIVE! AND GO INCITE AN UPRISING FOR ALL I CARE. NOW PLEASE, LET YOUR FATHER FINISH THE BACK NINE.
I HATE YOU!
NO CHEATING, ROCKO! I SAW THAT!

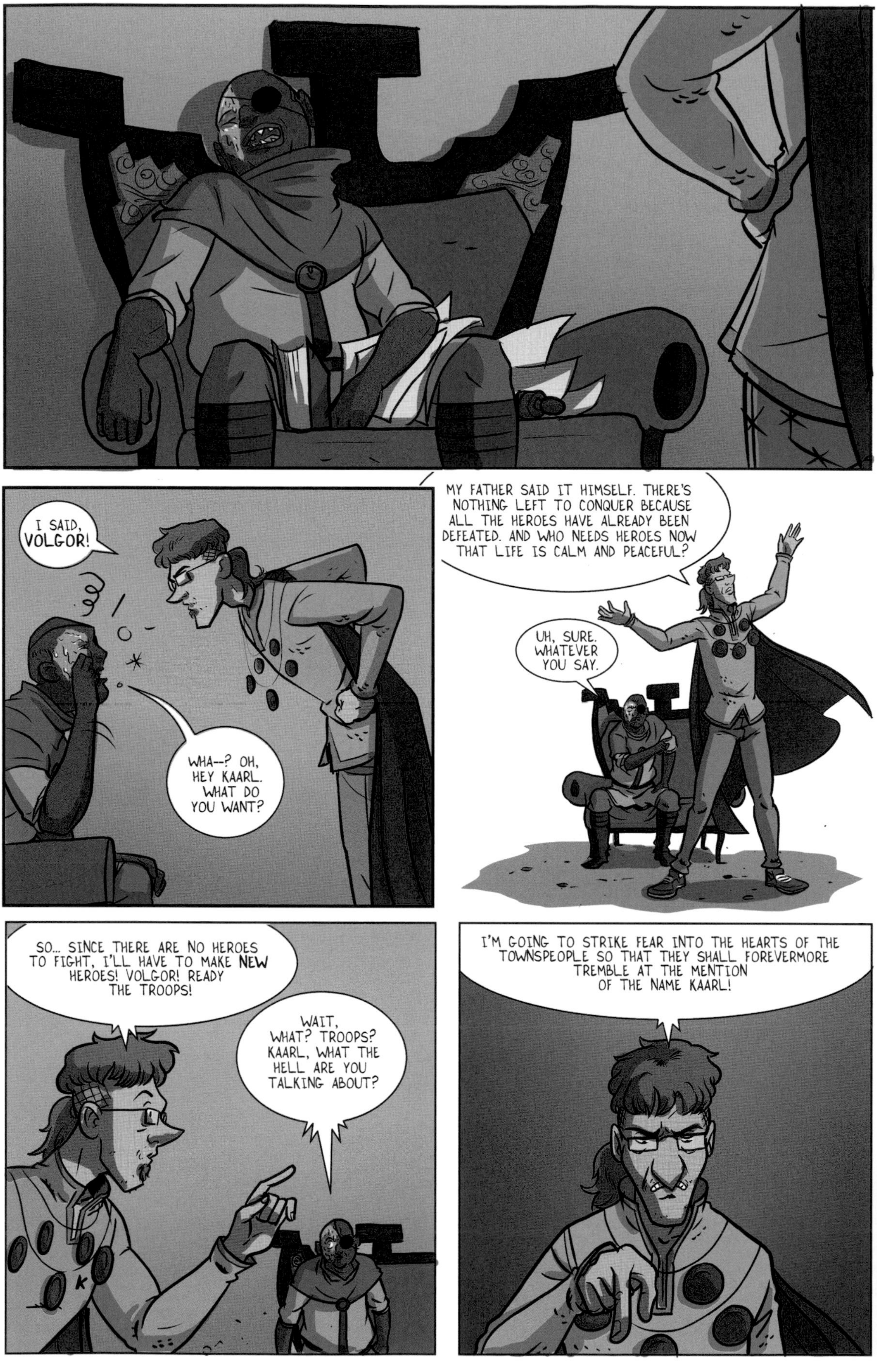
I SAID, VOLGOR!
WHA--? OH, HEY KAARL. WHAT DO YOU WANT?
MY FATHER SAID IT HIMSELF. THERE'S NOTHING LEFT TO CONQUER BECAUSE ALL THE HEROES HAVE ALREADY BEEN DEFEATED. AND WHO NEEDS HEROES NOW THAT LIFE IS CALM AND PEACEFUL?
UH, SURE. WHATEVER YOU SAY.
SO... SINCE THERE ARE NO HEROES TO FIGHT, I'LL HAVE TO MAKE NEW HEROES! VOLGOR! READY THE TROOPS!
WAIT, WHAT? TROOPS? KAARL, WHAT THE HELL ARE YOU TALKING ABOUT?
I'M GOING TO STRIKE FEAR INTO THE HEARTS OF THE TOWNSPEOPLE SO THAT THEY SHALL FOREVERMORE TREMBLE AT THE MENTION OF THE NAME KAARL!

AND ONLY THEN, ONCE THEY CAN NO LONGER STAND LIVING UNDER A FEARSOME AND RUTHLESS DESPOT, WILL NEW HEROES RISE UP WHO I CAN BOLDLY CRUSH! SO TODAY...
WE ATTACK!
OH, BROTHER.
HOO BOY, THIS IS GETTIN' GOOD! WONDER WHAT'S GONNA HAPPEN NEXT, EH ZORMOP?
I'M HUNGRY.

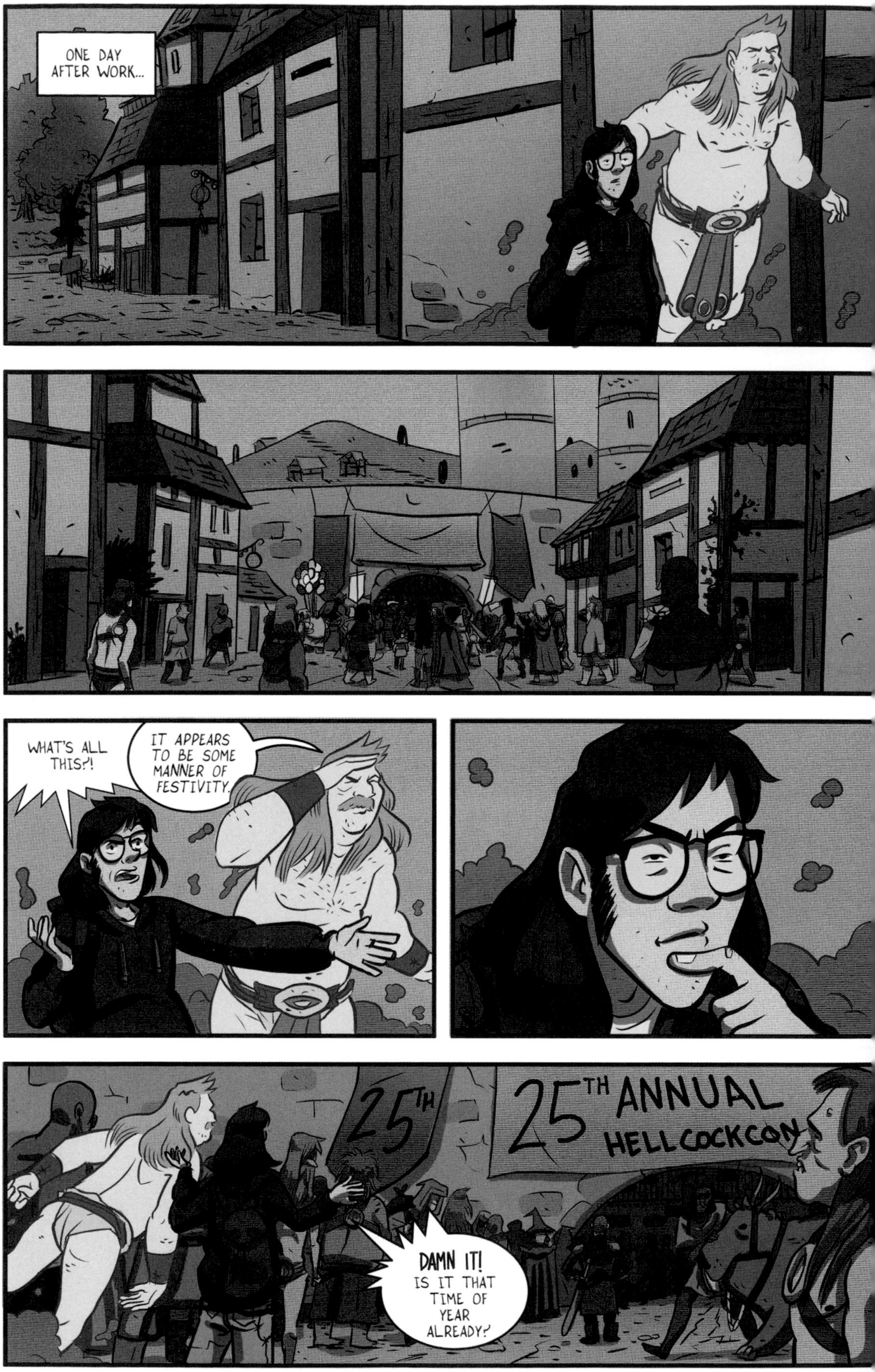
ONE DAY AFTER WORK...
WHAT'S ALL THIS?!
IT APPEARS TO BE SOME MANNER OF FESTIVITY.
25TH
25TH ANNUAL HELLCOCKCON
DAMN IT! IS IT THAT TIME OF YEAR ALREADY?

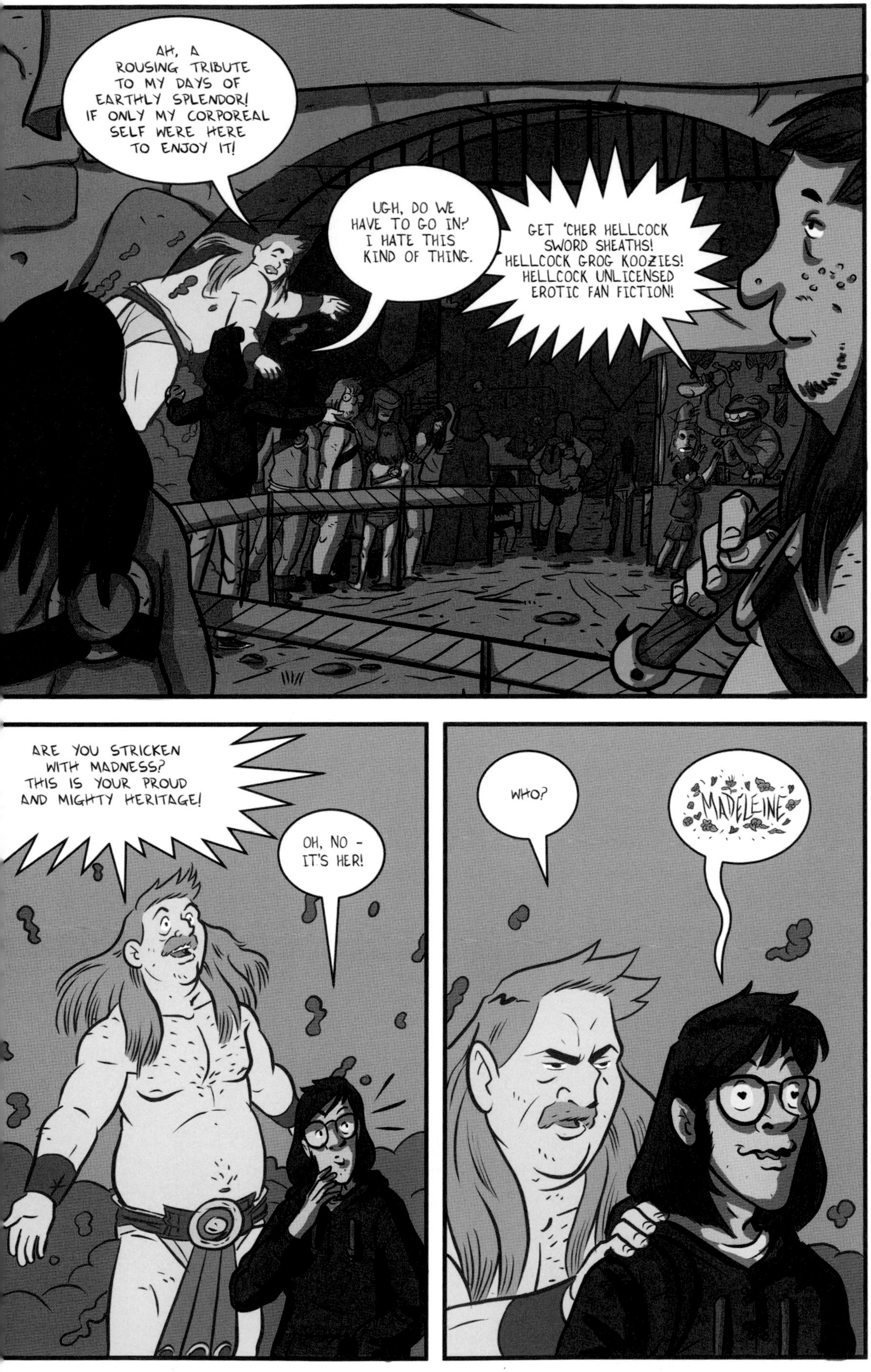
AH, A ROUSING TRIBUTE TO MY DAYS OF EARTHLY SPLENDOR! IF ONLY MY CORPOREAL SELF WERE HERE TO ENJOY IT!
UGH, DO WE HAVE TO GO IN? I HATE THIS KIND OF THING.
GET 'CHER HELLCOCK SWORD SHEATHS! HELLCOCK GROG KOOZIES! HELLCOCK UNLICENSED EROTIC FAN FICTION!
ARE YOU STRICKEN WITH MADNESS? THIS IS YOUR PROUD AND MIGHTY HERITAGE!
OH, NO - IT'S HER!
WHO?
MADELEINE

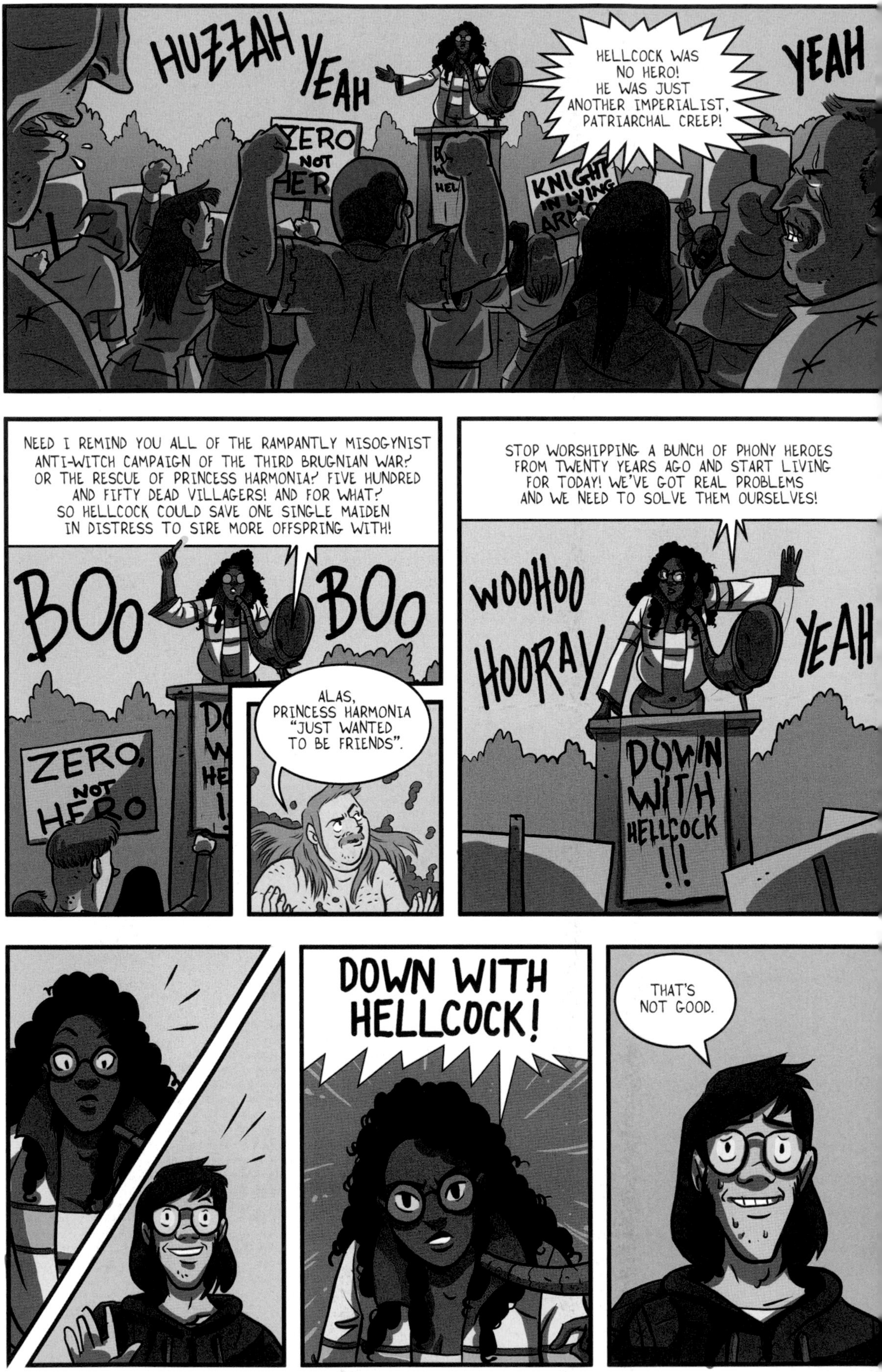
HUZZAH
YEAH
HELLCOCK WAS NO HERO! HE WAS JUST ANOTHER IMPERIALIST, PATRIARCHAL CREEP!
YEAH
ZERO NOT HERO
KNIGHT IN LYING ARMOR
NEED I REMIND YOU ALL OF THE RAMPANTLY MISOGYNIST ANTI-WITCH CAMPAIGN OF THE THIRD BRUGNIAN WAR? OR THE RESCUE OF PRINCESS HARMONIA? FIVE HUNDRED AND FIFTY DEAD VILLAGERS! AND FOR WHAT? SO HELLCOCK COULD SAVE ONE SINGLE MAIDEN IN DISTRESS TO SIRE MORE OFFSPRING WITH!
BOO
BOO
ZERO, NOT HERO
ALAS, PRINCESS HARMONIA "JUST WANTED TO BE FRIENDS".
STOP WORSHIPPING A BUNCH OF PHONY HEROES FROM TWENTY YEARS AGO AND START LIVING FOR TODAY! WE'VE GOT REAL PROBLEMS AND WE NEED TO SOLVE THEM OURSELVES!
WOOHOO
HOORAY
YEAH
DOWN WITH HELLCOCK !!!
DOWN WITH HELLCOCK!
THAT'S NOT GOOD.

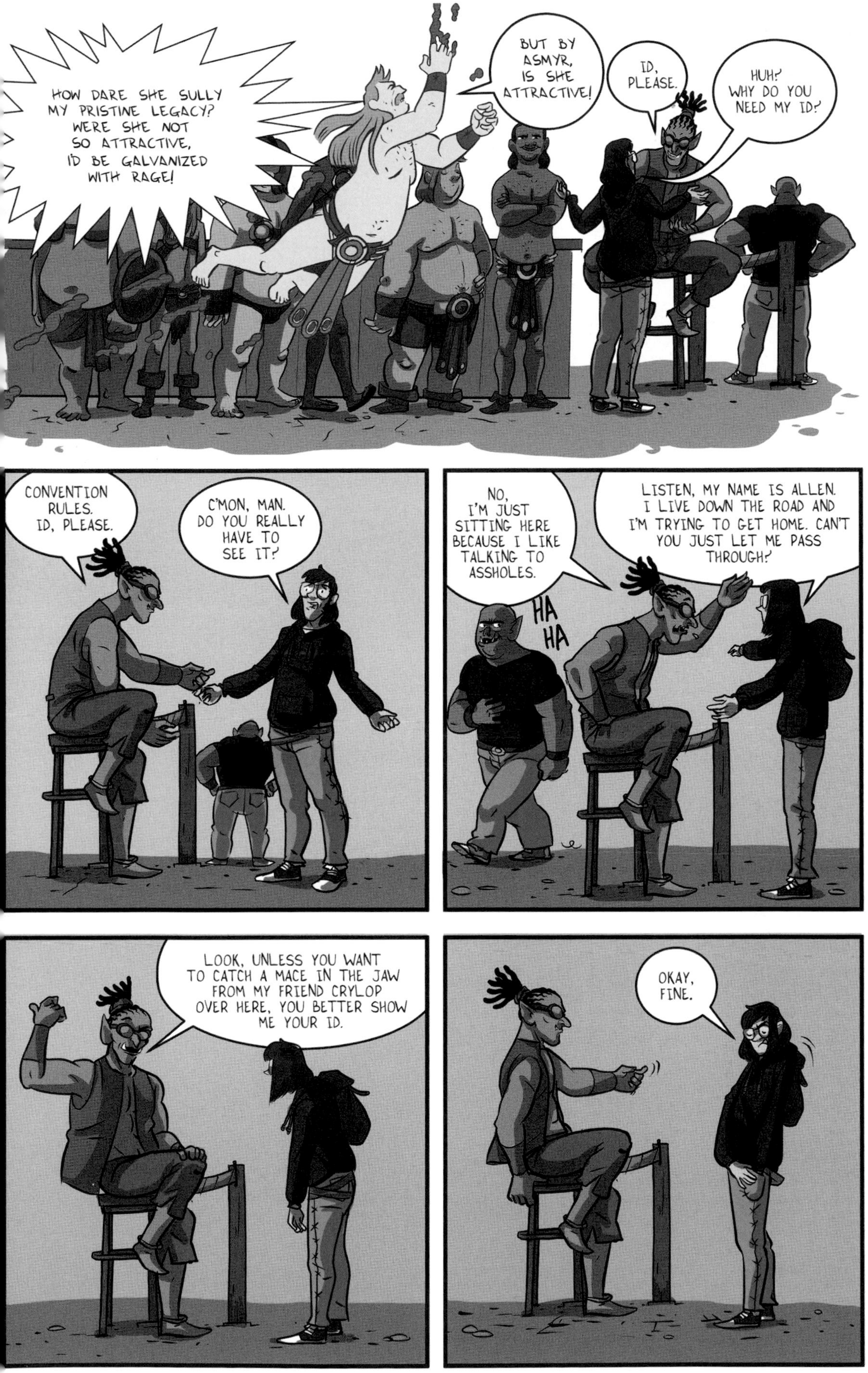
HOW DARE SHE SULLY MY PRISTINE LEGACY? WERE SHE NOT SO ATTRACTIVE, I'D BE GALVANIZED WITH RAGE!
BUT BY ASMYR, IS SHE ATTRACTIVE!
ID, PLEASE.
HUH? WHY DO YOU NEED MY ID?
CONVENTION RULES. ID, PLEASE.
C'MON, MAN. DO YOU REALLY HAVE TO SEE IT?
NO, I'M JUST SITTING HERE BECAUSE I LIKE TALKING TO ASSHOLES.
LISTEN, MY NAME IS ALLEN. I LIVE DOWN THE ROAD AND I'M TRYING TO GET HOME. CAN'T YOU JUST LET ME PASS THROUGH?
HA HA
LOOK, UNLESS YOU WANT TO CATCH A MACE IN THE JAW FROM MY FRIEND CRYLOP OVER HERE, YOU BETTER SHOW ME YOUR ID.
OKAY, FINE.

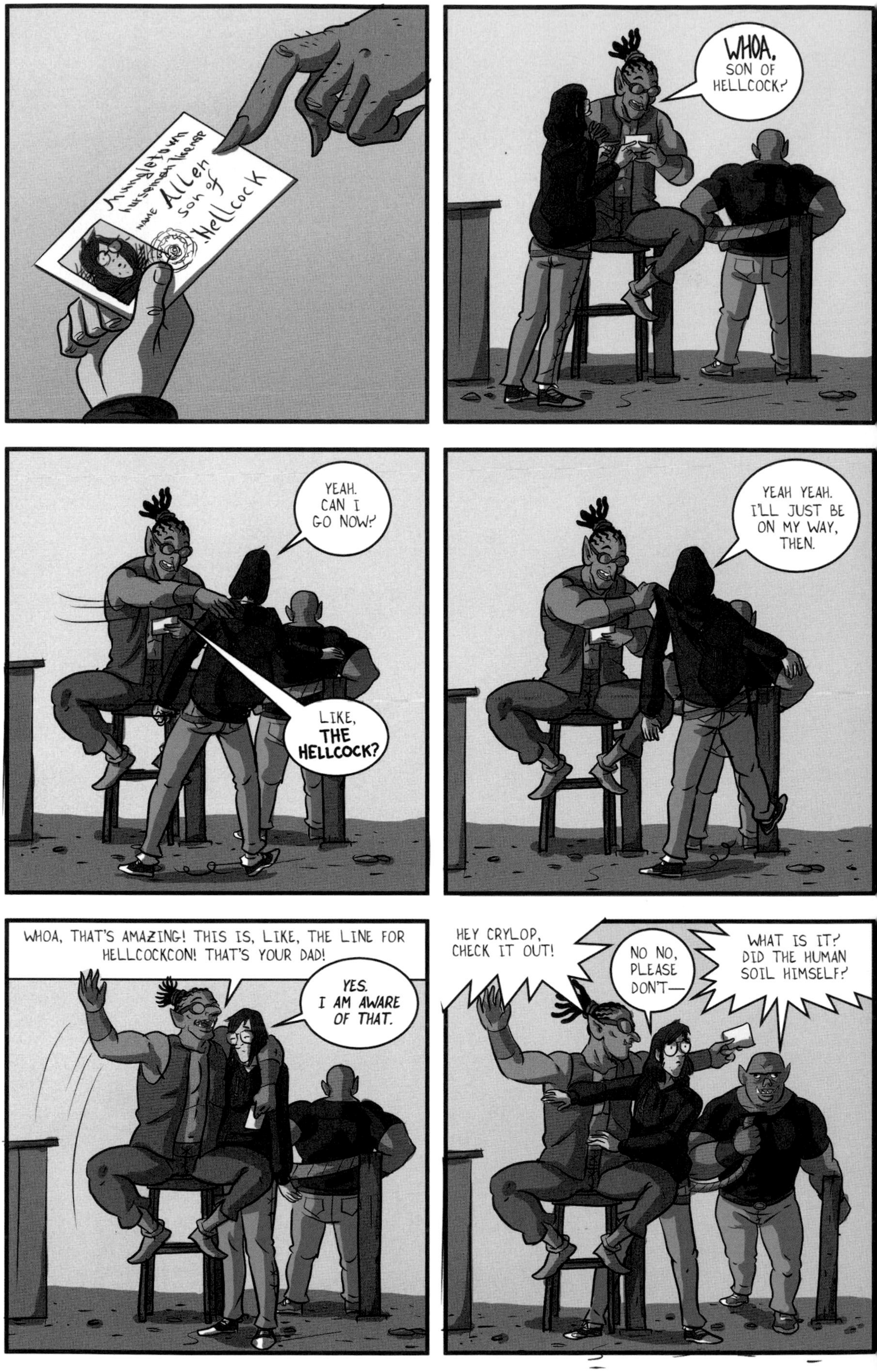

Munngletown hursemen license
NAME Allen son of Hellcock
WHOA. SON OF HELLCOCK?
YEAH. CAN I GO NOW?
LIKE, THE HELLCOCK?
YEAH YEAH. I'LL JUST BE ON MY WAY, THEN.
WHOA, THAT'S AMAZING! THIS IS, LIKE, THE LINE FOR HELLCOCKCON! THAT'S YOUR DAD!
YES. I AM AWARE OF THAT.
HEY CRYLOP, CHECK IT OUT!
NO NO, PLEASE DON'T—
WHAT IS IT? DID THE HUMAN SOIL HIMSELF?

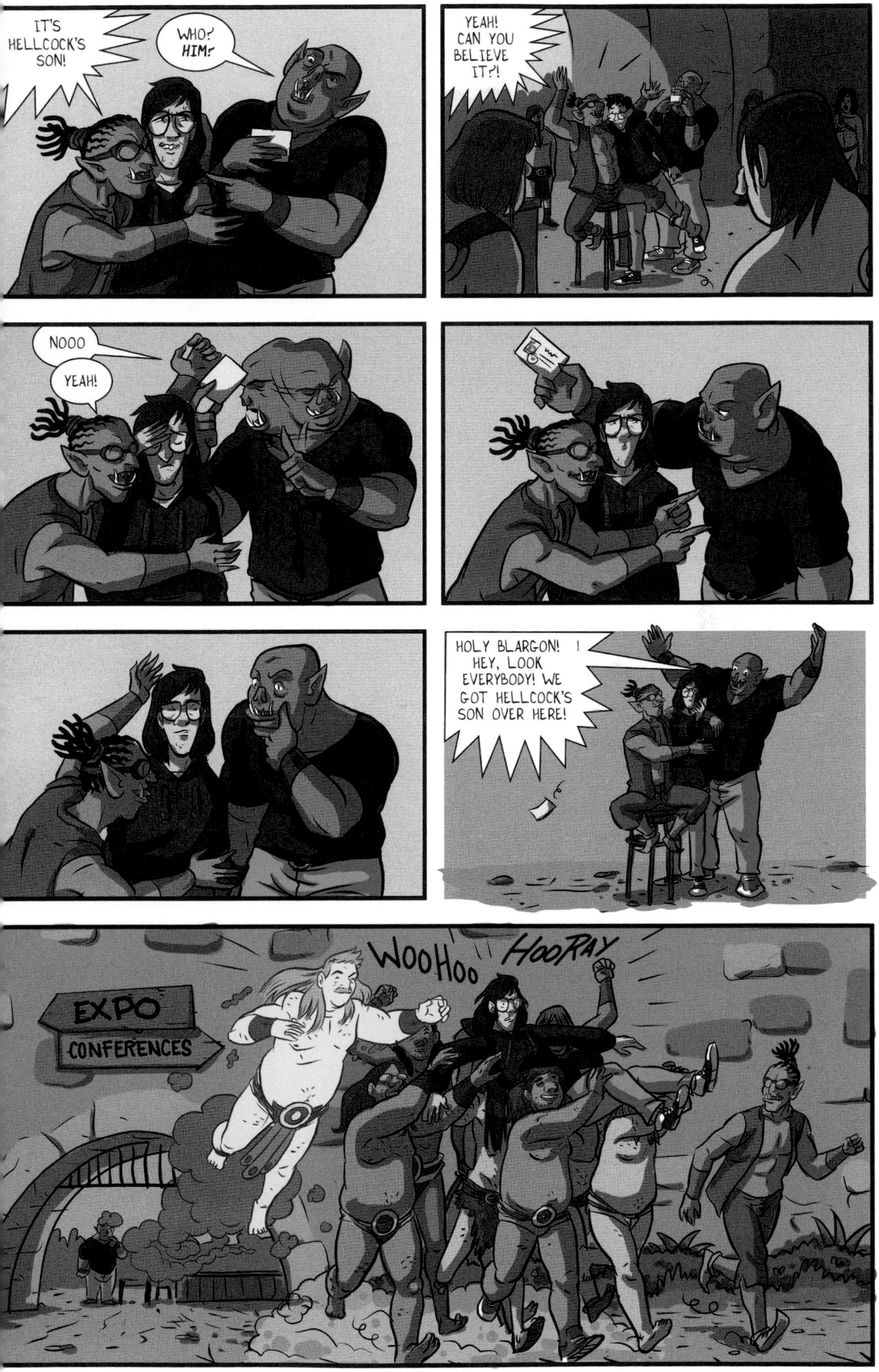
IT'S HELLCOCK'S SON!
WHO? HIM?
YEAH! CAN YOU BELIEVE IT?!
NOOO
YEAH!
HOLY BLARGON! HEY, LOOK EVERYBODY! WE GOT HELLCOCK'S SON OVER HERE!
WOOHOO
HOORAY
EXPO
CONFERENCES

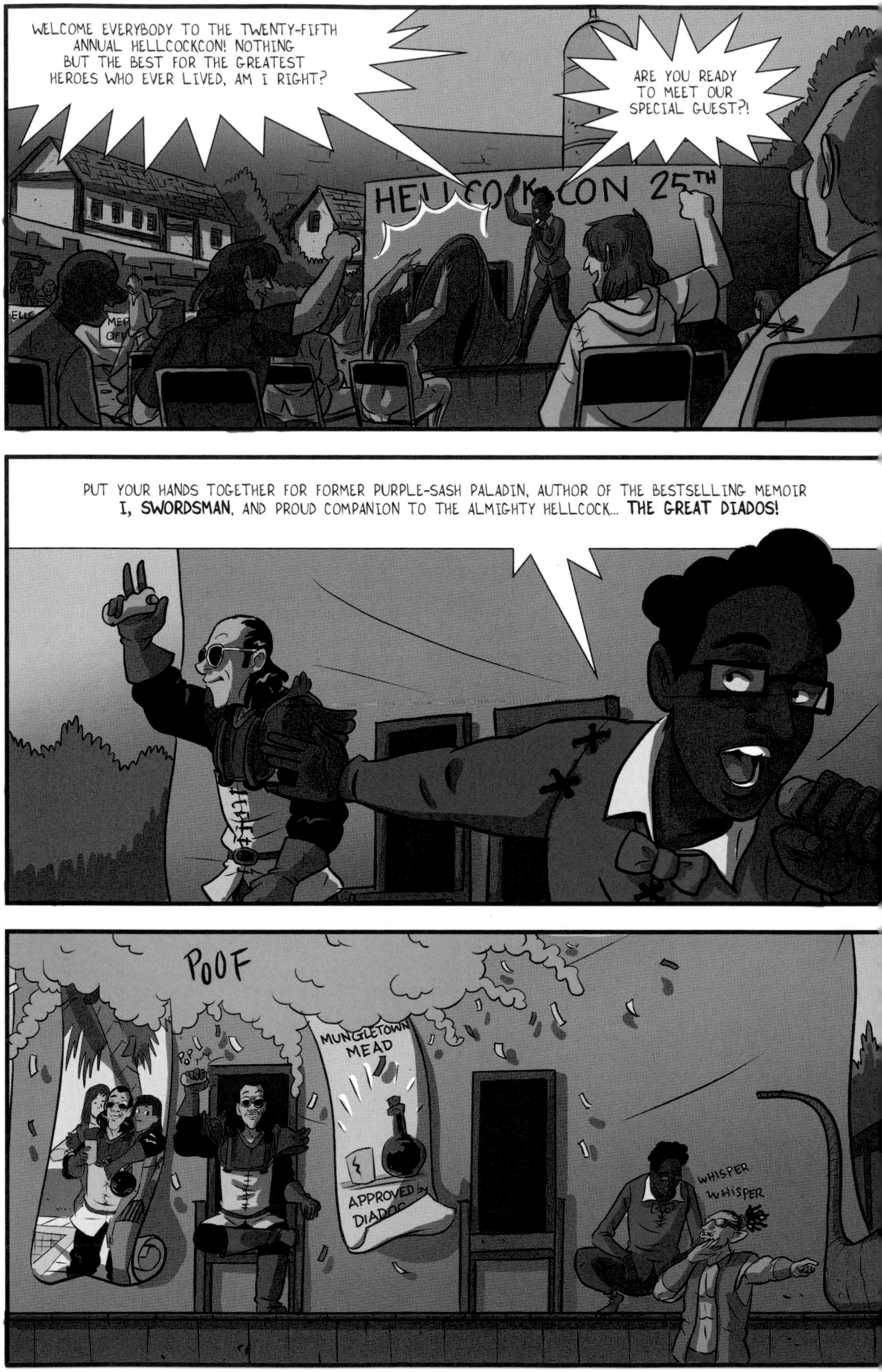
WELCOME EVERYBODY TO THE TWENTY-FIFTH ANNUAL HELLCOCKCON! NOTHING BUT THE BEST FOR THE GREATEST HEROES WHO EVER LIVED, AM I RIGHT?
ARE YOU READY TO MEET OUR SPECIAL GUEST?!
PUT YOUR HANDS TOGETHER FOR FORMER PURPLE-SASH PALADIN, AUTHOR OF THE BESTSELLING MEMOIR **I, SWORDSMAN**, AND PROUD COMPANION TO THE ALMIGHTY HELLCOCK... **THE GREAT DIADOS!**
POOF
MUNGLETOWN MEAD
APPROVED by
WHISPER
WHISPER

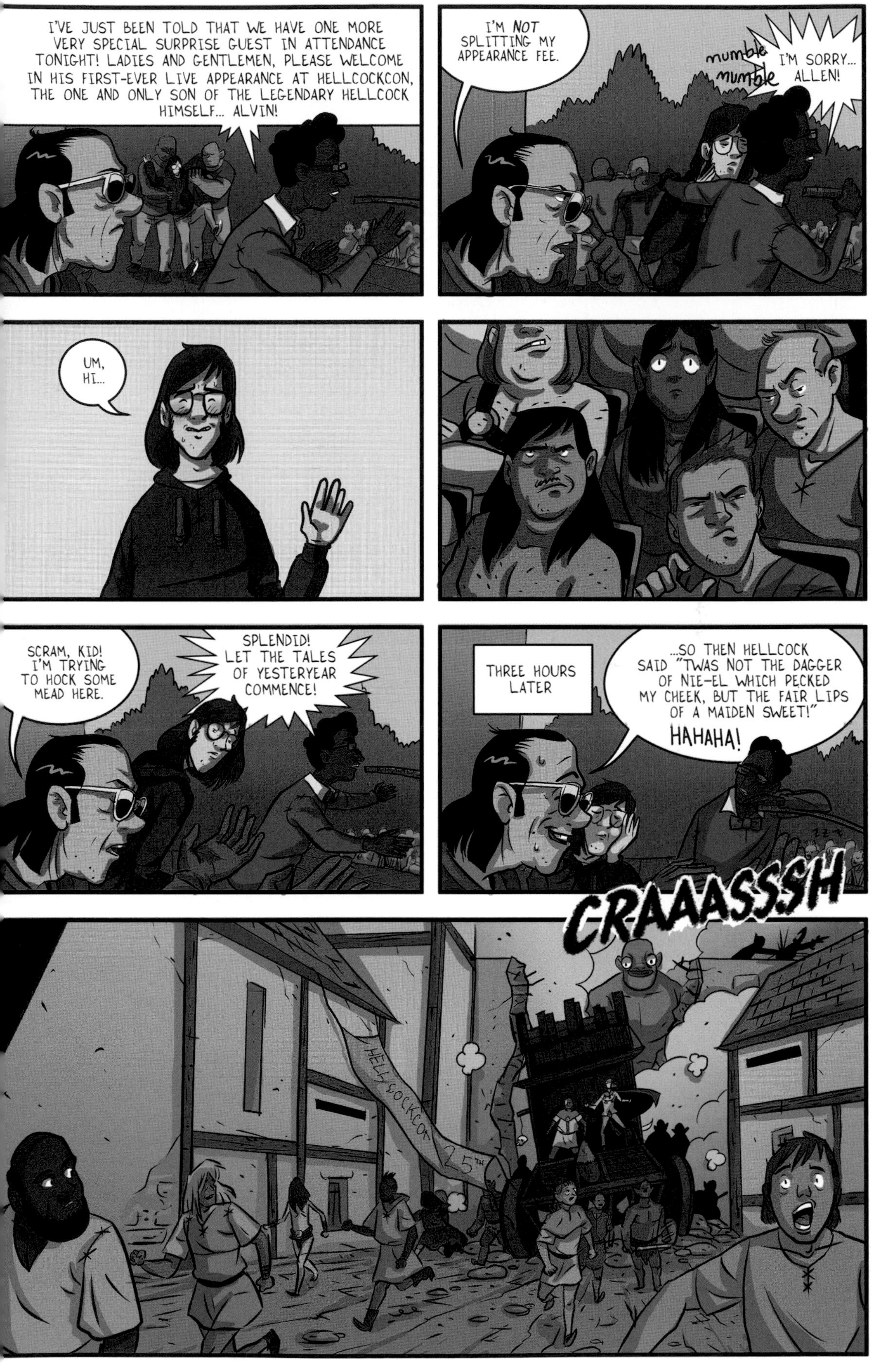
I'VE JUST BEEN TOLD THAT WE HAVE ONE MORE VERY SPECIAL SURPRISE GUEST IN ATTENDANCE TONIGHT! LADIES AND GENTLEMEN, PLEASE WELCOME IN HIS FIRST-EVER LIVE APPEARANCE AT HELLCOCKCON, THE ONE AND ONLY SON OF THE LEGENDARY HELLCOCK HIMSELF... ALVIN!
I'M NOT SPLITTING MY APPEARANCE FEE.
mumble mumble
I'M SORRY... ALLEN!
UM, HI...
SCRAM, KID! I'M TRYING TO HOCK SOME MEAD HERE.
SPLENDID! LET THE TALES OF YESTERYEAR COMMENCE!
THREE HOURS LATER
...SO THEN HELLCOCK SAID "TWAS NOT THE DAGGER OF NIE-EL WHICH PECKED MY CHEEK, BUT THE FAIR LIPS OF A MAIDEN SWEET!"
HAHAHA!
CRAAASSSH
HELLCOCKCON 25TH

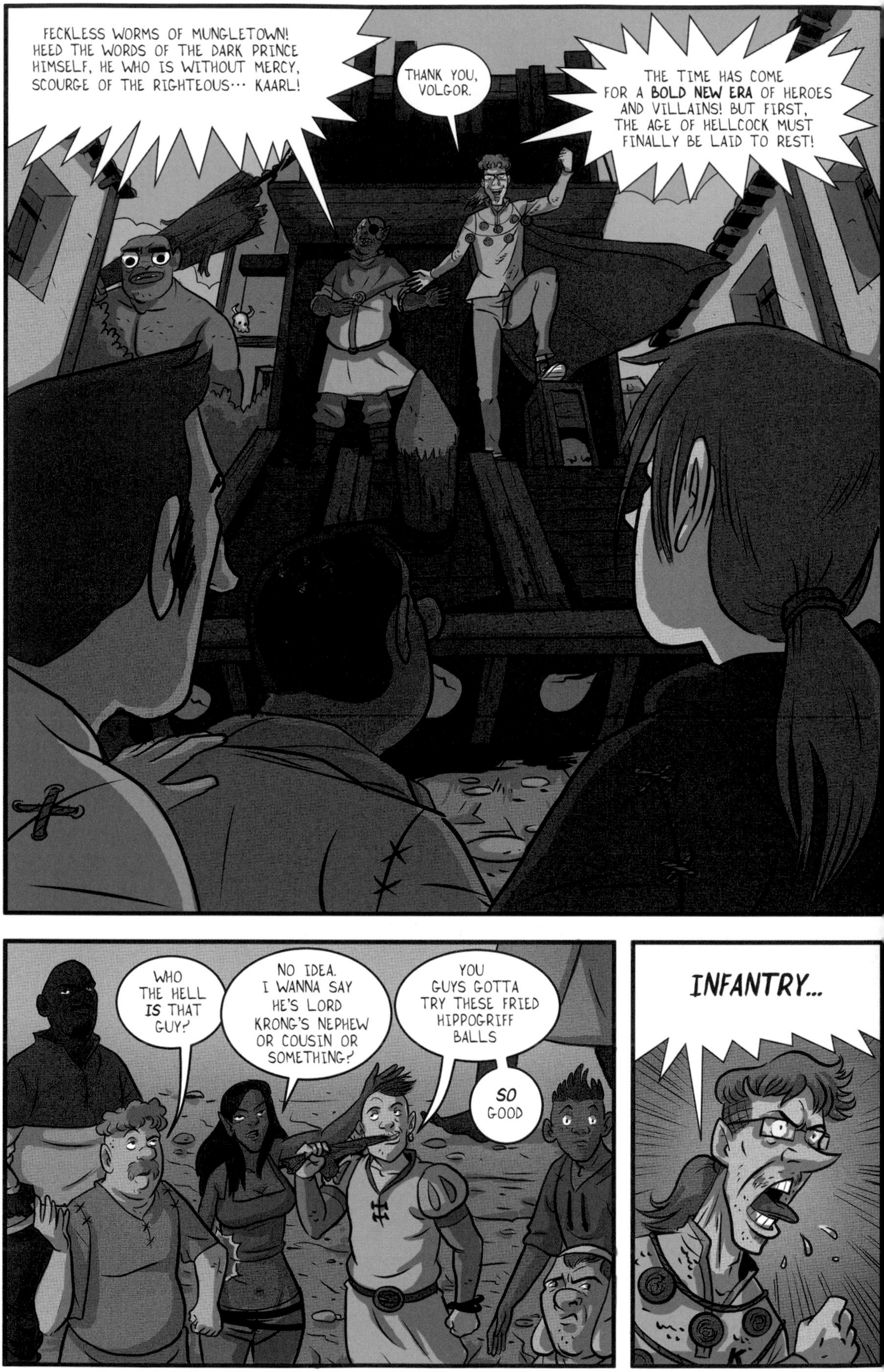
FECKLESS WORMS OF MUNGLETOWN! HEED THE WORDS OF THE DARK PRINCE HIMSELF, HE WHO IS WITHOUT MERCY, SCOURGE OF THE RIGHTEOUS··· KAARL!
THANK YOU, VOLGOR.
THE TIME HAS COME FOR A **BOLD NEW ERA** OF HEROES AND VILLAINS! BUT FIRST, THE AGE OF HELLCOCK MUST FINALLY BE LAID TO REST!
WHO THE HELL **IS** THAT GUY?
NO IDEA. I WANNA SAY HE'S LORD KRONG'S NEPHEW OR COUSIN OR SOMETHING?
YOU GUYS GOTTA TRY THESE FRIED HIPPOGRIFF BALLS
SO GOOD
INFANTRY...

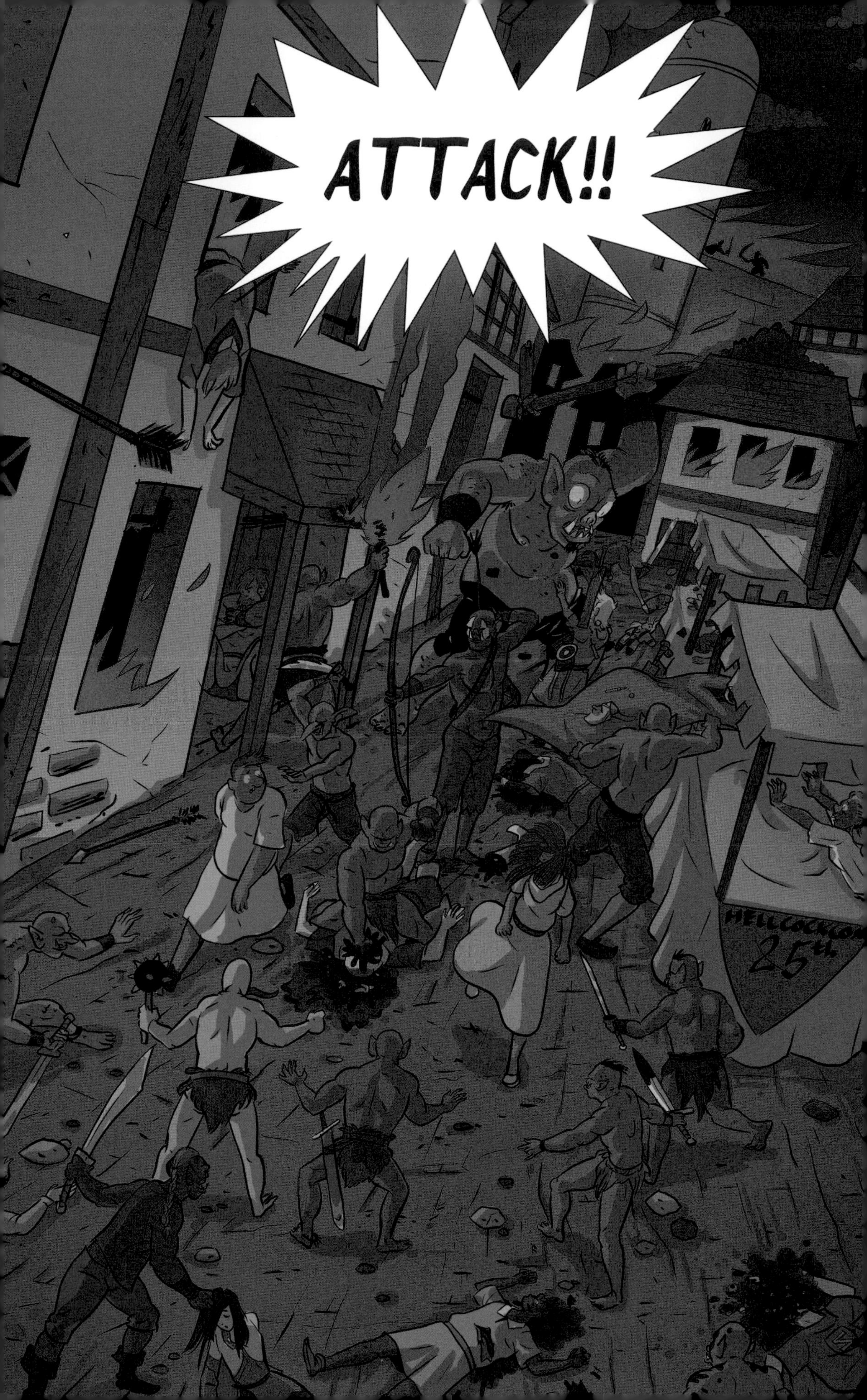
ATTACK!!
HELLCOCKCO
25th

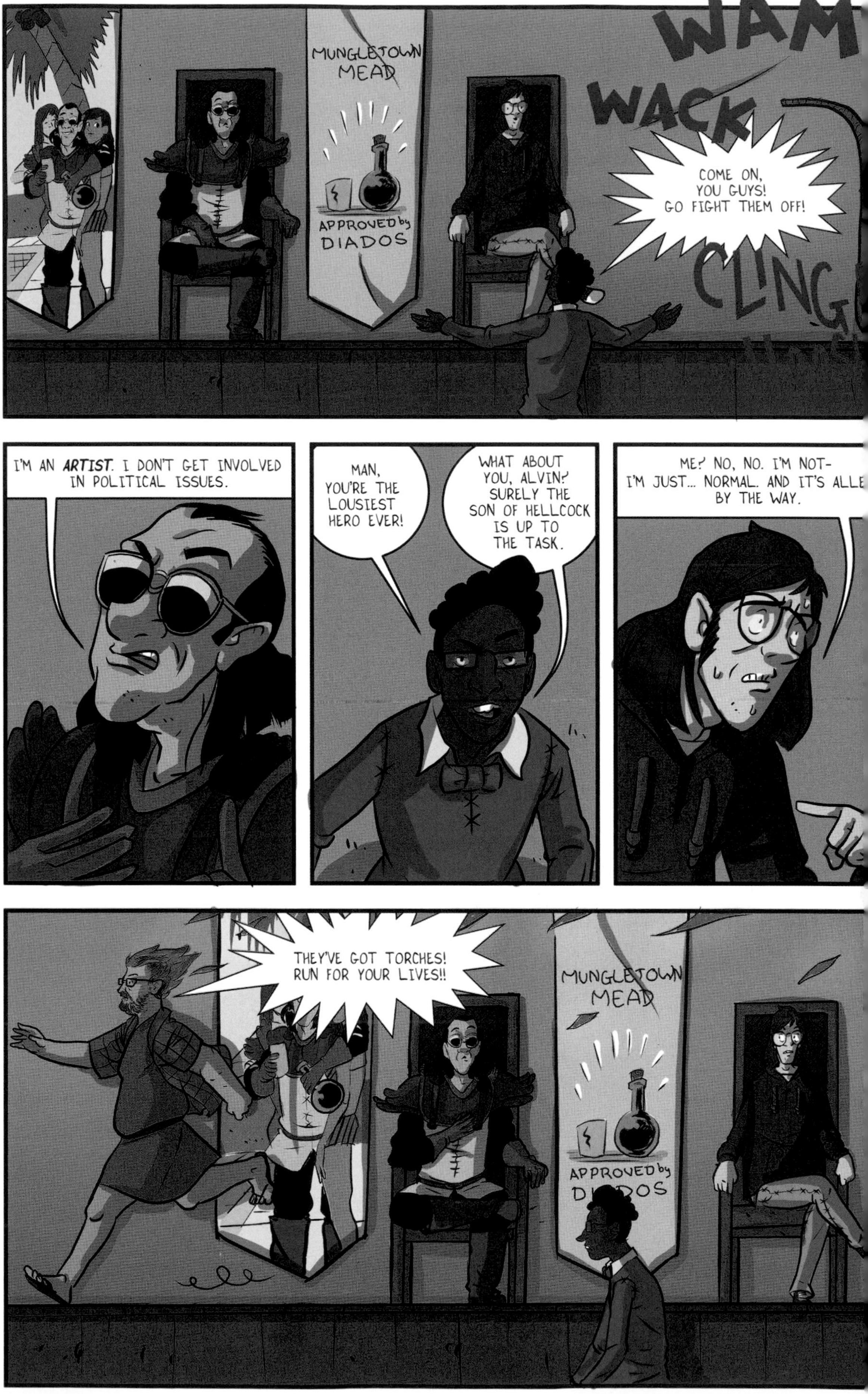

WAM
WACK
MUNGLETOWN MEAD
APPROVED by DIADOS
COME ON, YOU GUYS! GO FIGHT THEM OFF!
CLING
I'M AN **ARTIST**. I DON'T GET INVOLVED IN POLITICAL ISSUES.
MAN, YOU'RE THE LOUSIEST HERO EVER!
WHAT ABOUT YOU, ALVIN? SURELY THE SON OF HELLCOCK IS UP TO THE TASK.
ME? NO, NO. I'M NOT- I'M JUST... NORMAL. AND IT'S ALLE BY THE WAY.
THEY'VE GOT TORCHES! RUN FOR YOUR LIVES!!
MUNGLETOWN MEAD
APPROVED by DIADOS

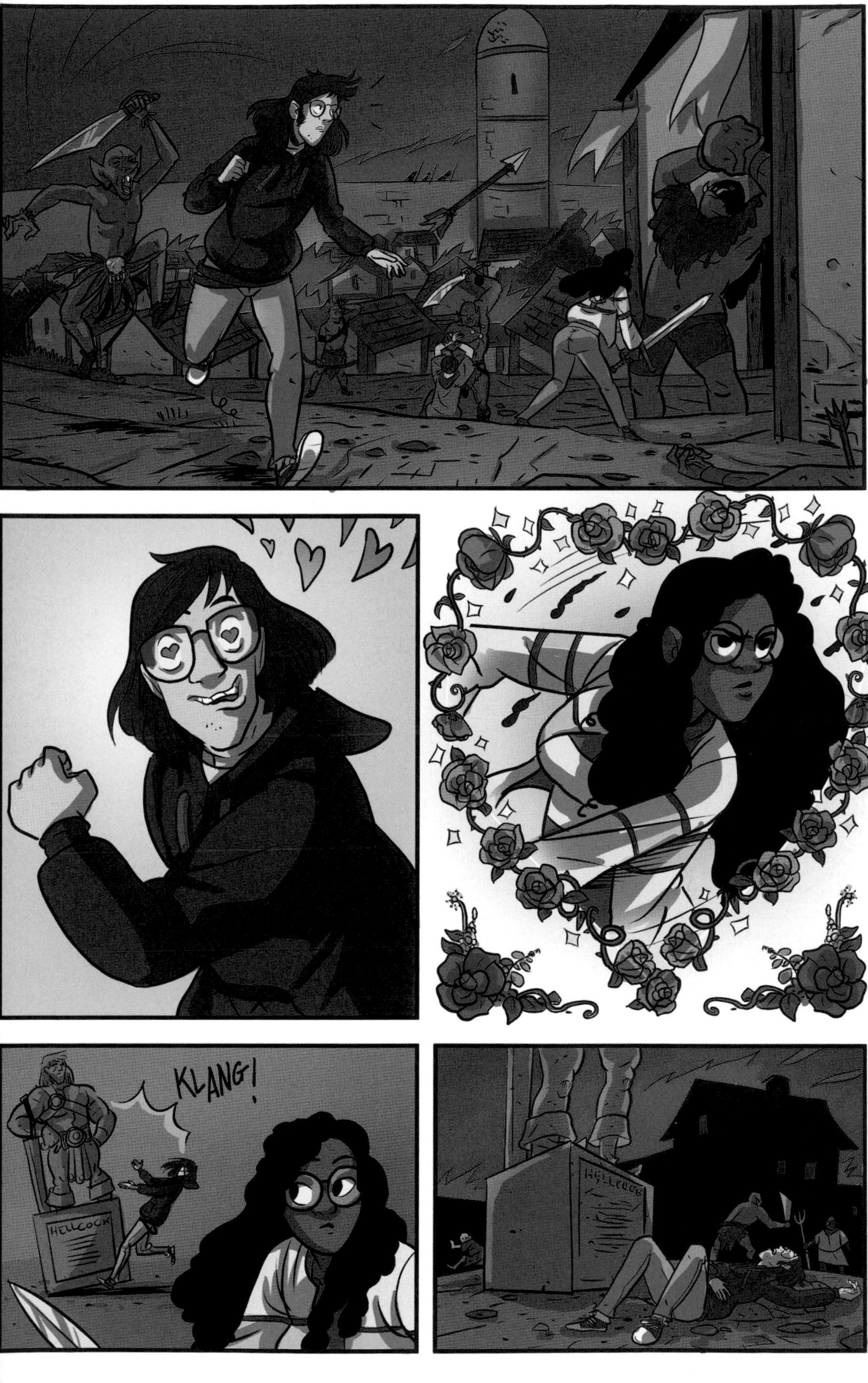
KLANG!
HELLCOCK

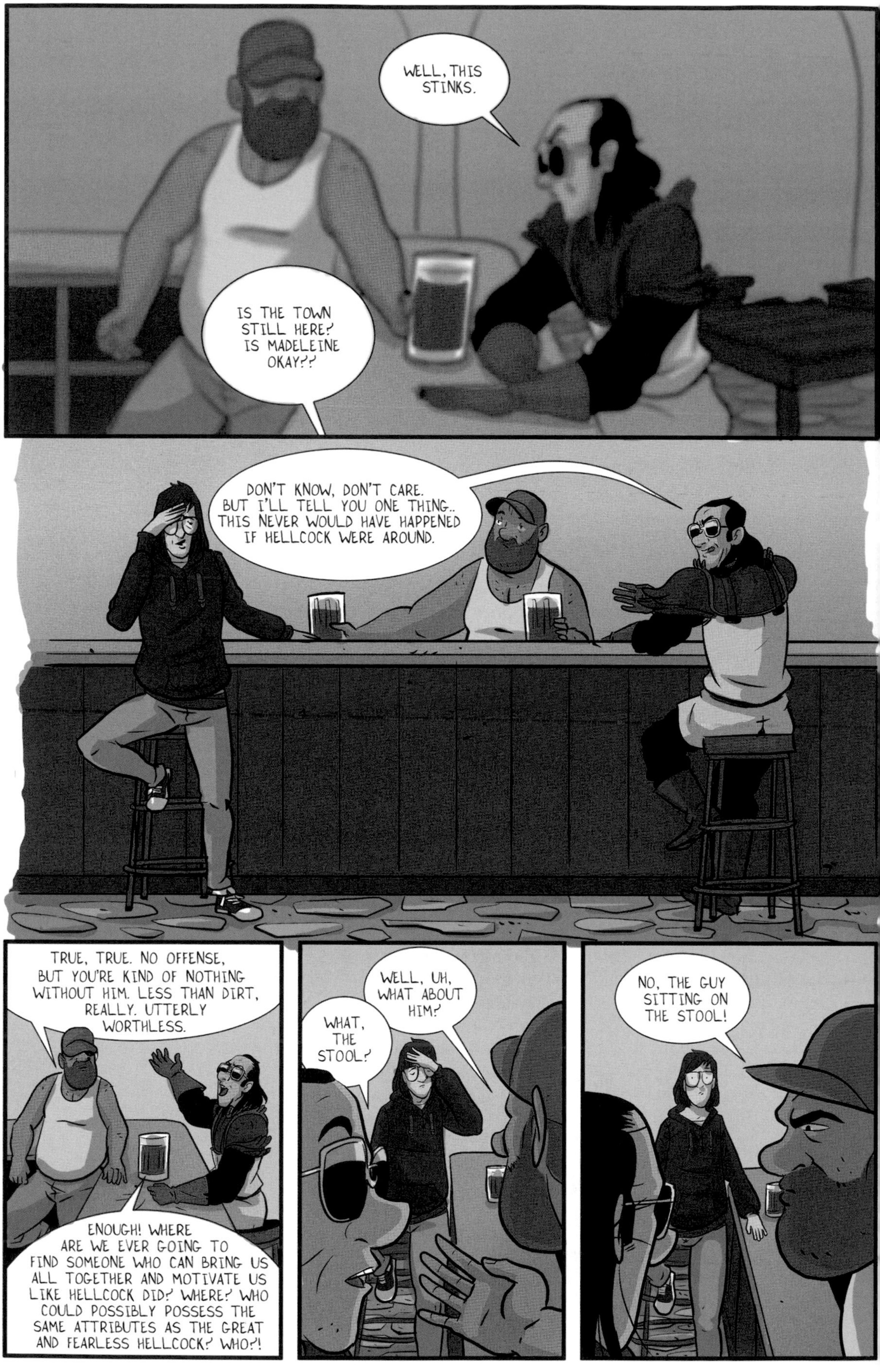
WELL, THIS STINKS.
IS THE TOWN STILL HERE? IS MADELEINE OKAY?!?
DON'T KNOW, DON'T CARE. BUT I'LL TELL YOU ONE THING.. THIS NEVER WOULD HAVE HAPPENED IF HELLCOCK WERE AROUND.
TRUE, TRUE. NO OFFENSE, BUT YOU'RE KIND OF NOTHING WITHOUT HIM. LESS THAN DIRT, REALLY. UTTERLY WORTHLESS.
ENOUGH! WHERE ARE WE EVER GOING TO FIND SOMEONE WHO CAN BRING US ALL TOGETHER AND MOTIVATE US LIKE HELLCOCK DID? WHERE? WHO COULD POSSIBLY POSSESS THE SAME ATTRIBUTES AS THE GREAT AND FEARLESS HELLCOCK? WHO?!
WELL, UH, WHAT ABOUT HIM?
WHAT, THE STOOL?
NO, THE GUY SITTING ON THE STOOL!

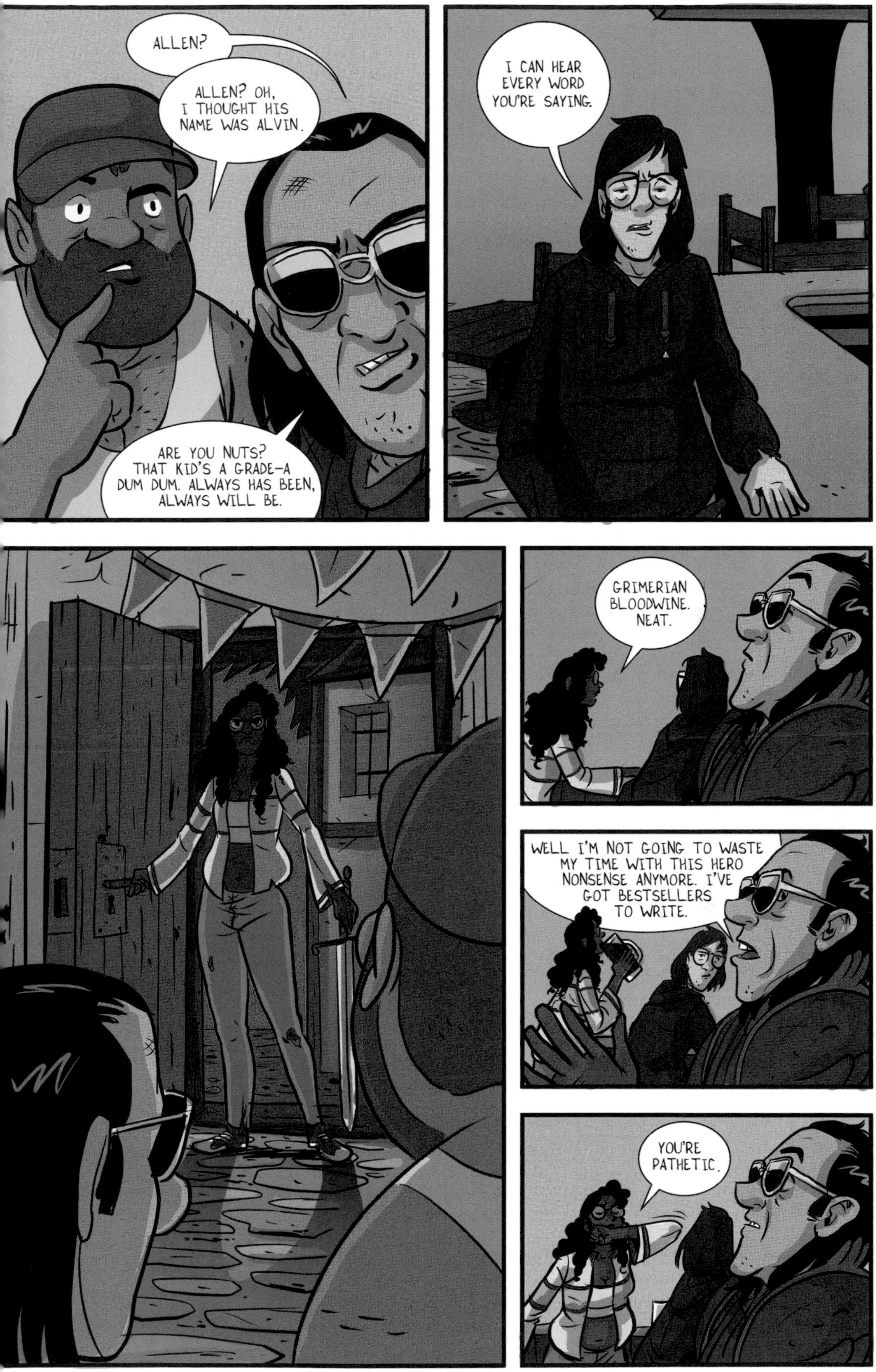
ALLEN?
ALLEN? OH, I THOUGHT HIS NAME WAS ALVIN.
ARE YOU NUTS? THAT KID'S A GRADE-A DUM DUM. ALWAYS HAS BEEN, ALWAYS WILL BE.
I CAN HEAR EVERY WORD YOU'RE SAYING.
GRIMERIAN BLOODWINE. NEAT.
WELL I'M NOT GOING TO WASTE MY TIME WITH THIS HERO NONSENSE ANYMORE. I'VE GOT BESTSELLERS TO WRITE.
YOU'RE PATHETIC.

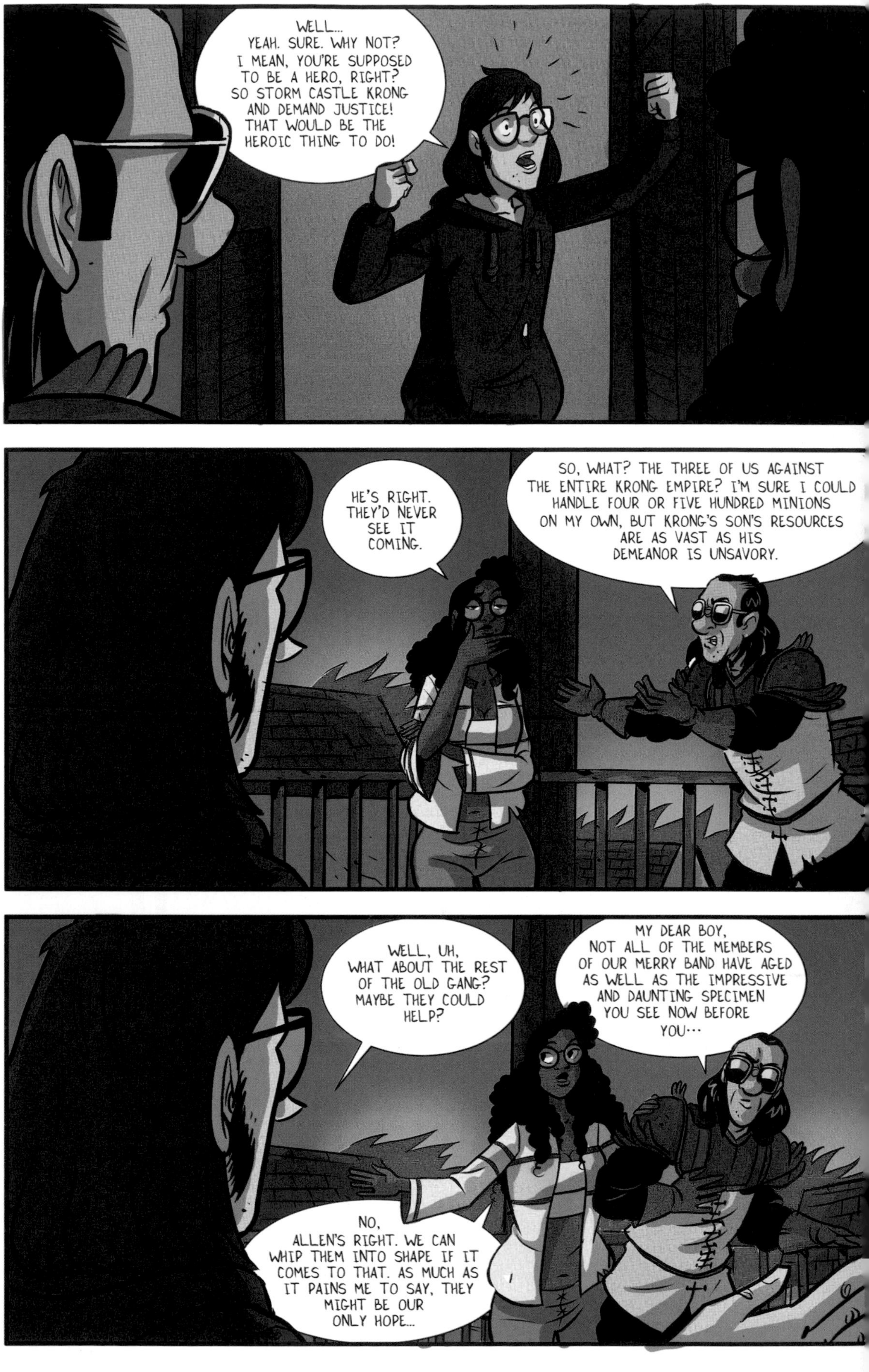
WELL... YEAH. SURE. WHY NOT? I MEAN, YOU'RE SUPPOSED TO BE A HERO, RIGHT? SO STORM CASTLE KRONG AND DEMAND JUSTICE! THAT WOULD BE THE HEROIC THING TO DO!
HE'S RIGHT. THEY'D NEVER SEE IT COMING.
SO, WHAT? THE THREE OF US AGAINST THE ENTIRE KRONG EMPIRE? I'M SURE I COULD HANDLE FOUR OR FIVE HUNDRED MINIONS ON MY OWN, BUT KRONG'S SON'S RESOURCES ARE AS VAST AS HIS DEMEANOR IS UNSAVORY.
WELL, UH, WHAT ABOUT THE REST OF THE OLD GANG? MAYBE THEY COULD HELP?
MY DEAR BOY, NOT ALL OF THE MEMBERS OF OUR MERRY BAND HAVE AGED AS WELL AS THE IMPRESSIVE AND DAUNTING SPECIMEN YOU SEE NOW BEFORE YOU...
NO, ALLEN'S RIGHT. WE CAN WHIP THEM INTO SHAPE IF IT COMES TO THAT. AS MUCH AS IT PAINS ME TO SAY, THEY MIGHT BE OUR ONLY HOPE...

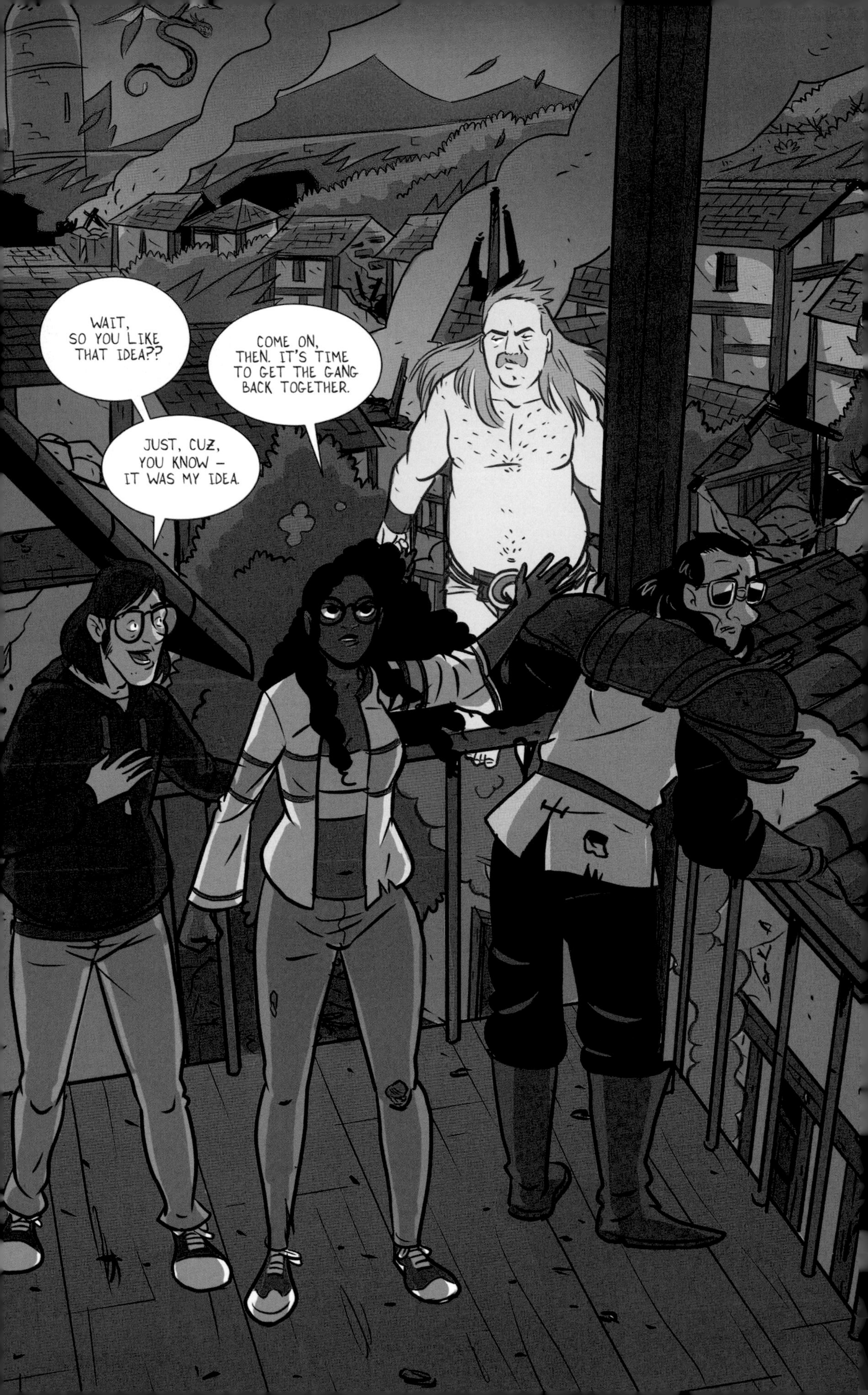
WAIT, SO YOU LIKE THAT IDEA??
JUST, CUZ, YOU KNOW – IT WAS MY IDEA.
COME ON, THEN. IT'S TIME TO GET THE GANG BACK TOGETHER.

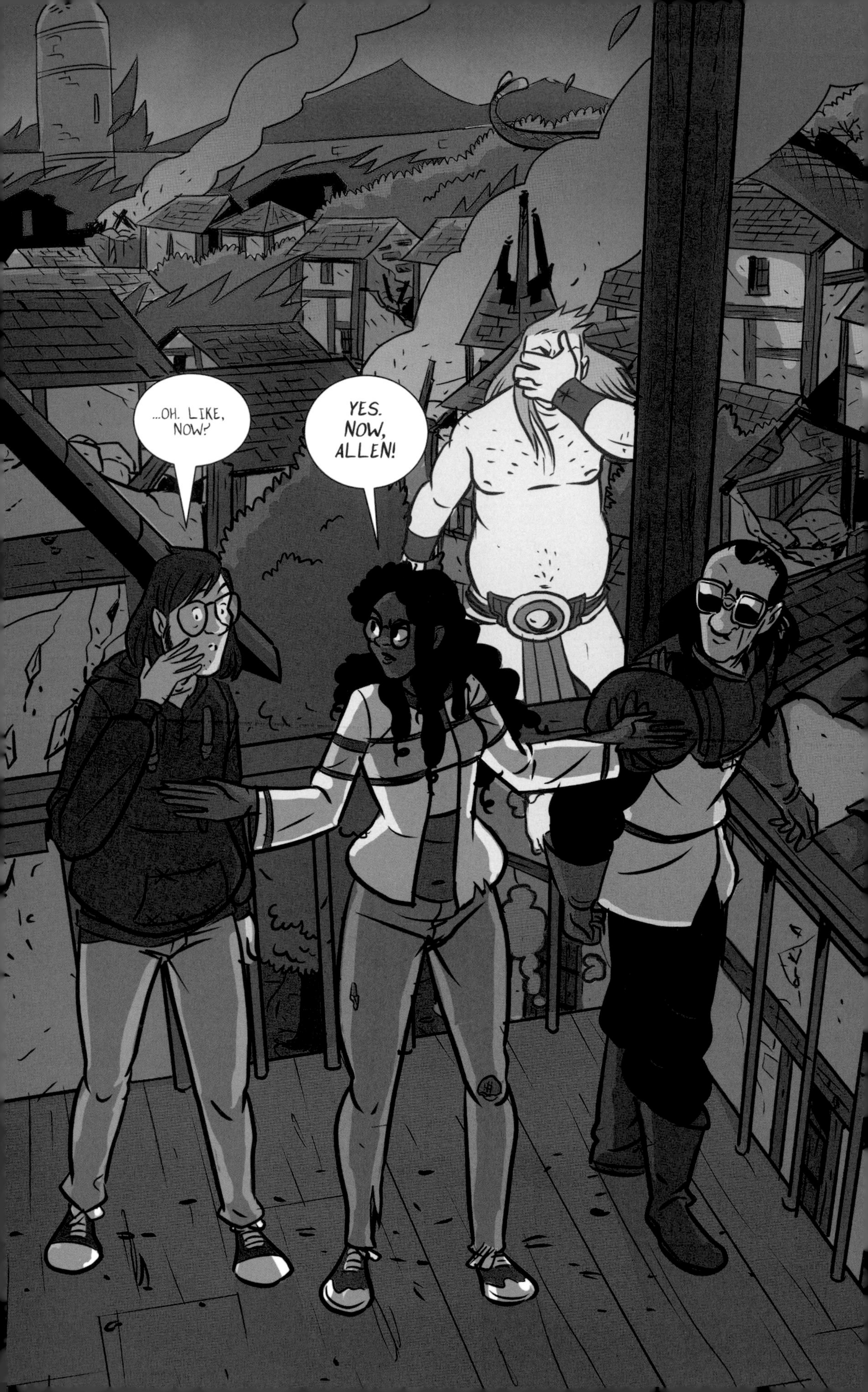
...OH. LIKE, NOW?
YES. NOW, ALLEN!

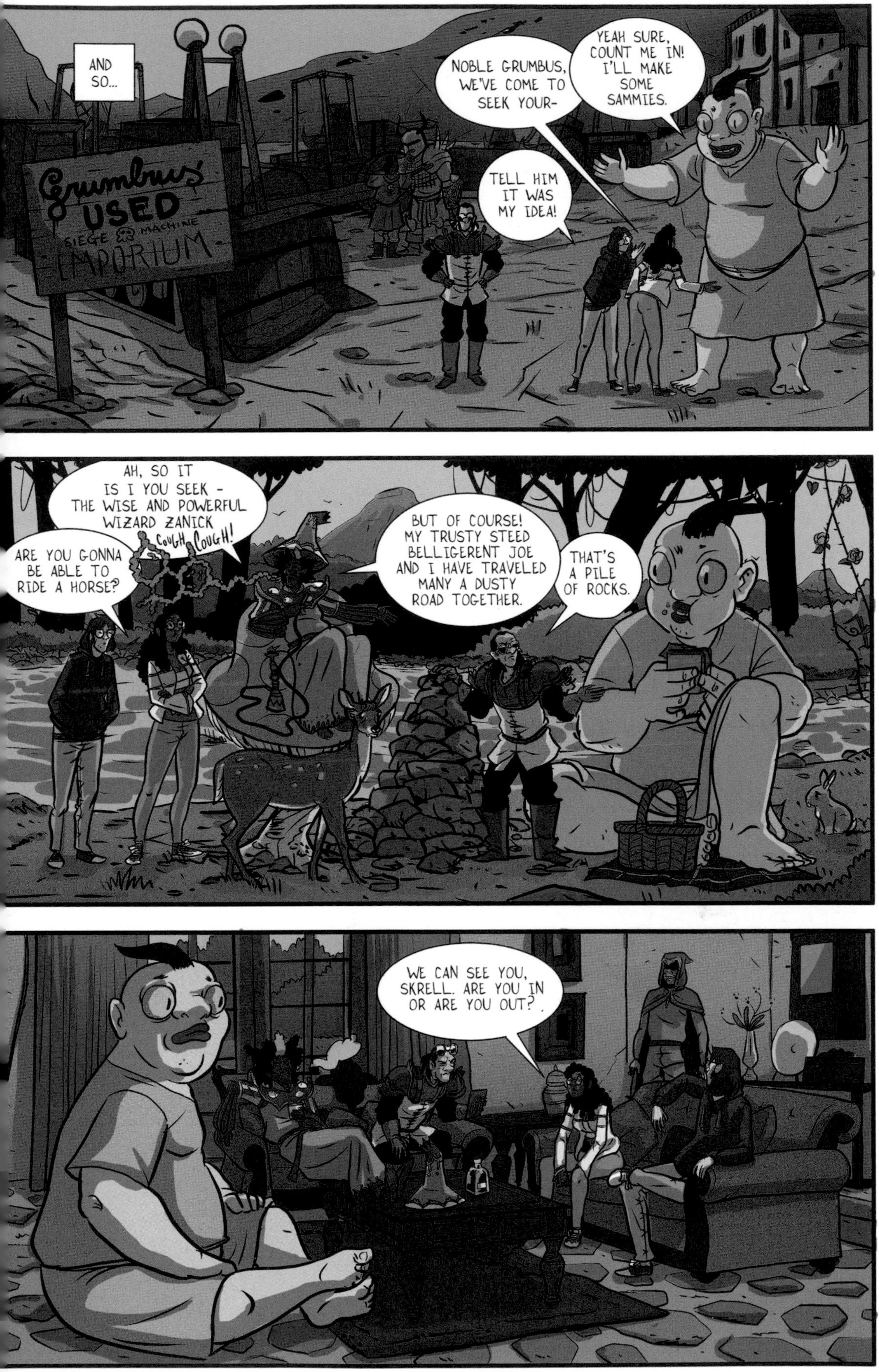
AND SO...
Grumbus' USED SIEGE MACHINE EMPORIUM
NOBLE GRUMBUS, WE'VE COME TO SEEK YOUR-
YEAH SURE, COUNT ME IN! I'LL MAKE SOME SAMMIES.
TELL HIM IT WAS MY IDEA!
AH, SO IT IS I YOU SEEK - THE WISE AND POWERFUL WIZARD ZANICK
COUGH COUGH!
ARE YOU GONNA BE ABLE TO RIDE A HORSE?
BUT OF COURSE! MY TRUSTY STEED BELLIGERENT JOE AND I HAVE TRAVELED MANY A DUSTY ROAD TOGETHER.
THAT'S A PILE OF ROCKS.
WE CAN SEE YOU, SKRELL. ARE YOU IN OR ARE YOU OUT?

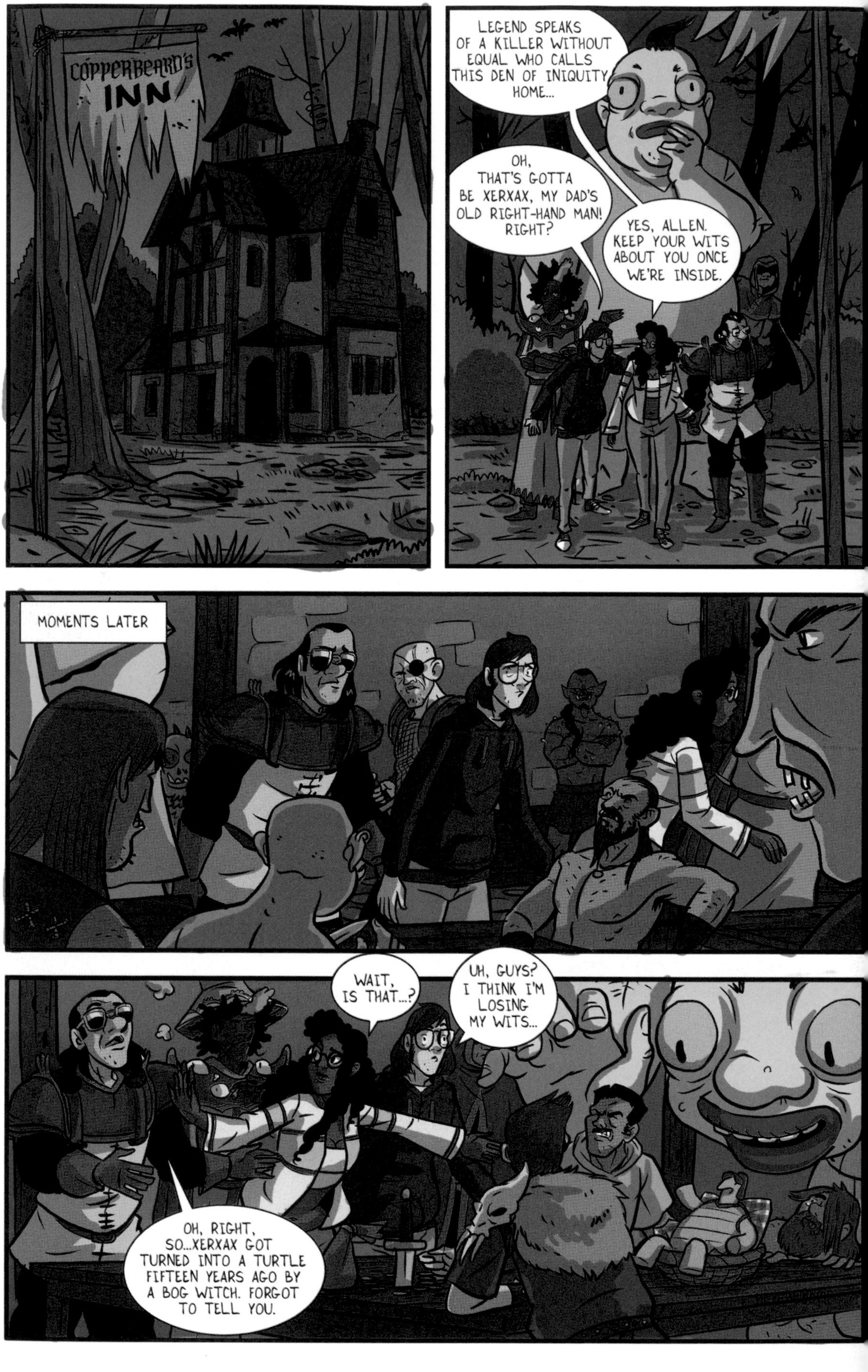
COPPERBEARD'S INN
LEGEND SPEAKS OF A KILLER WITHOUT EQUAL WHO CALLS THIS DEN OF INIQUITY HOME...
OH, THAT'S GOTTA BE XERXAX, MY DAD'S OLD RIGHT-HAND MAN! RIGHT?
YES, ALLEN. KEEP YOUR WITS ABOUT YOU ONCE WE'RE INSIDE.
MOMENTS LATER
WAIT, IS THAT...?
UH, GUYS? I THINK I'M LOSING MY WITS...
OH, RIGHT, SO...XERXAX GOT TURNED INTO A TURTLE FIFTEEN YEARS AGO BY A BOG WITCH. FORGOT TO TELL YOU.

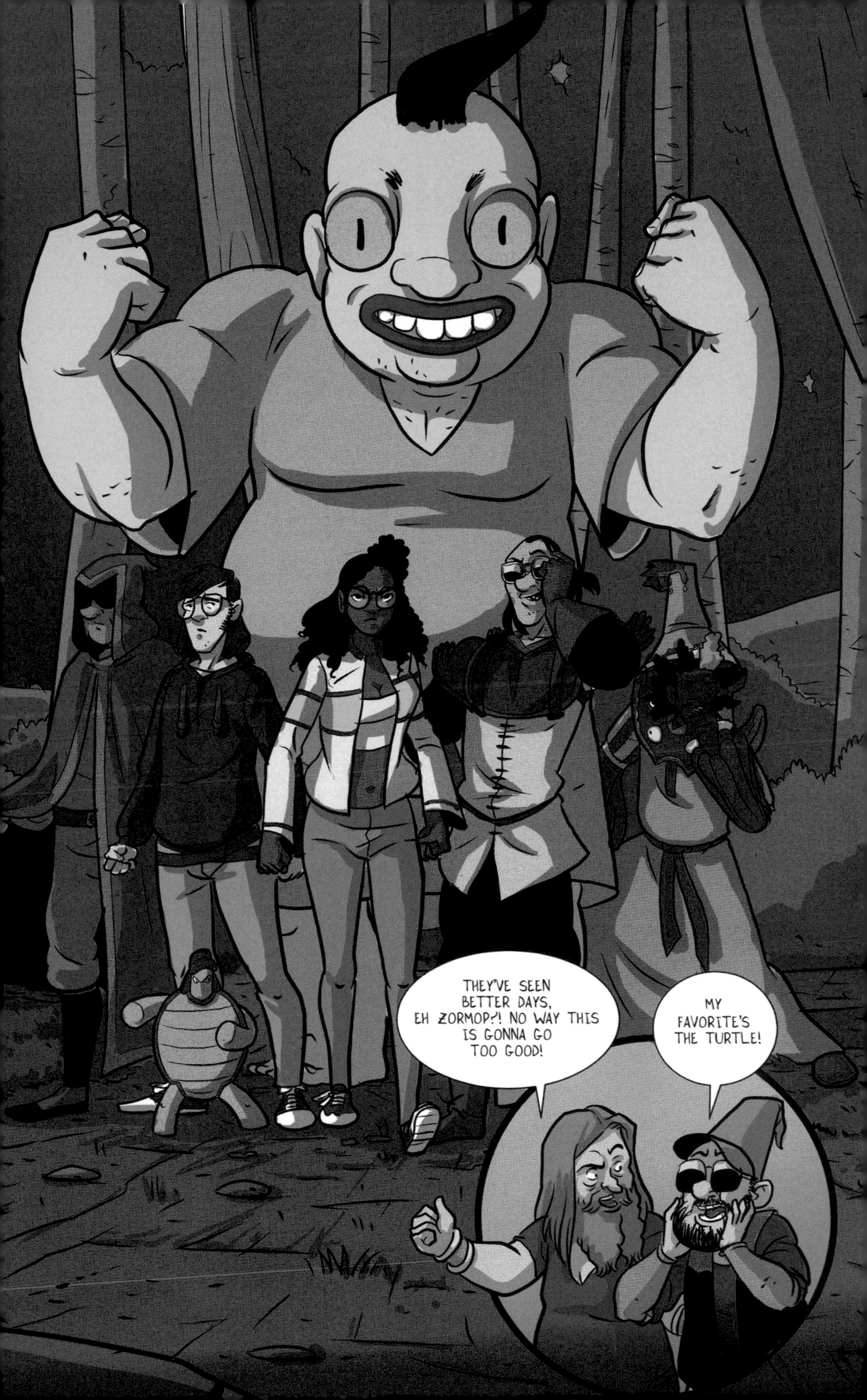
THEY'VE SEEN BETTER DAYS, EH ZORMOP?! NO WAY THIS IS GONNA GO TOO GOOD!
MY FAVORITE'S THE TURTLE!

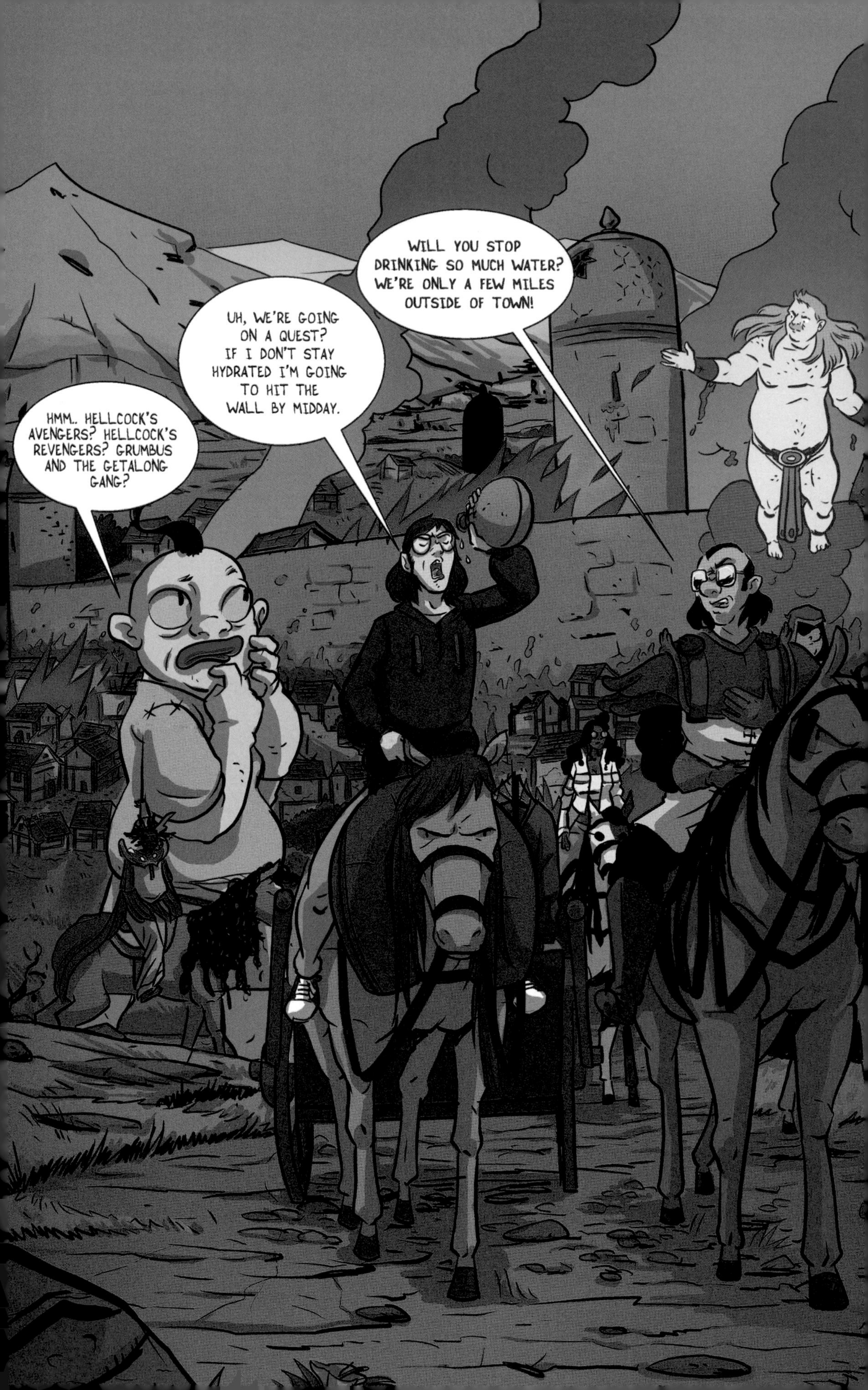
HMM.. HELLCOCK'S AVENGERS? HELLCOCK'S REVENGERS? GRUMBUS AND THE GETALONG GANG?
UH, WE'RE GOING ON A QUEST? IF I DON'T STAY HYDRATED I'M GOING TO HIT THE WALL BY MIDDAY.
WILL YOU STOP DRINKING SO MUCH WATER? WE'RE ONLY A FEW MILES OUTSIDE OF TOWN!

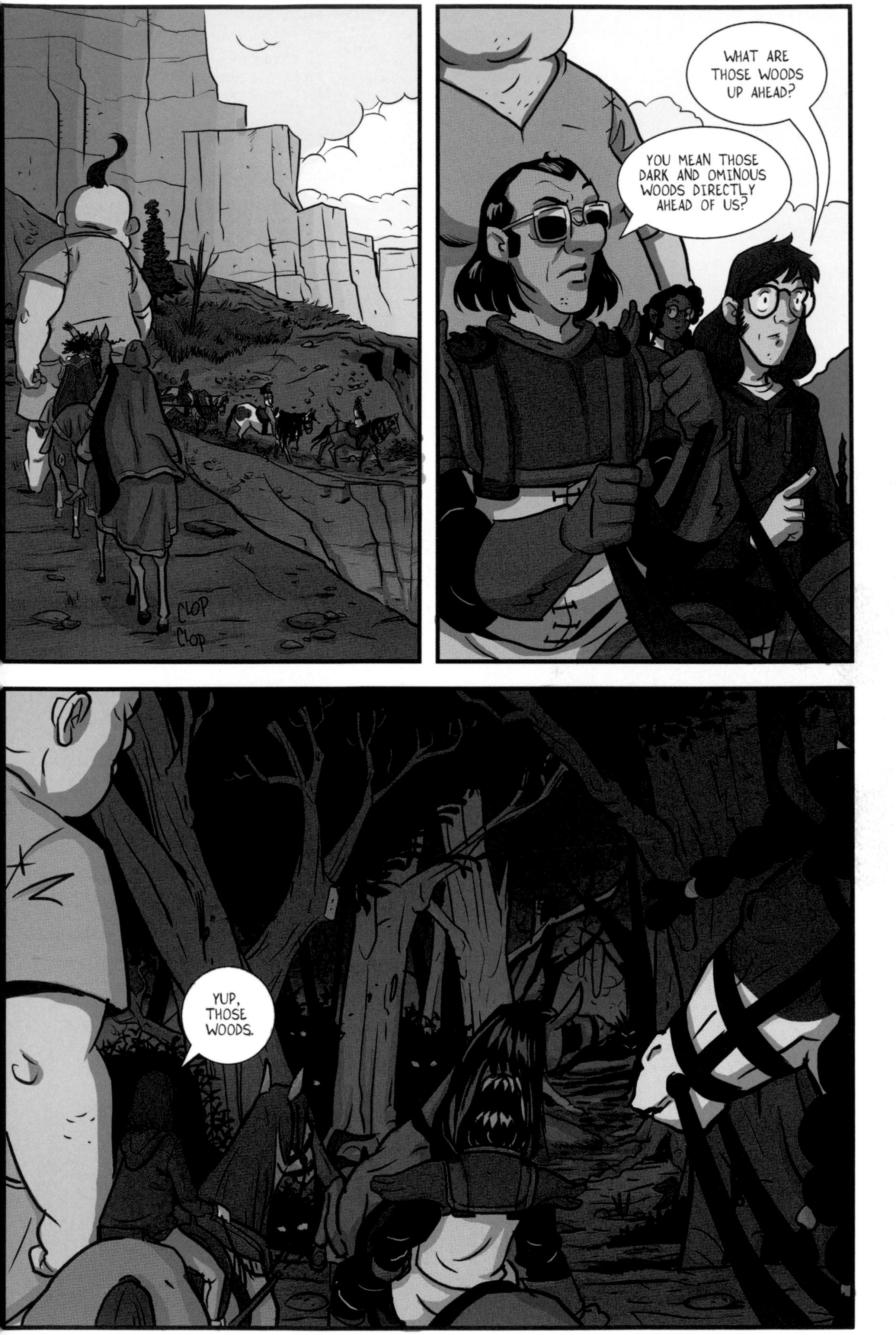
CLOP
CLOP
WHAT ARE THOSE WOODS UP AHEAD?
YOU MEAN THOSE DARK AND OMINOUS WOODS DIRECTLY AHEAD OF US?
YUP, THOSE WOODS.

MY BOY, YONDER LIE **THE PINES OF MYSTERY!**

HUH. WHAT'S IN THERE?

DARK, STRANGE, UNSPEAKABLE THINGS!

RIGHT. LIKE WHAT?

SCARY BAD THINGS!

UM, OKAYYY. GIVE ME AN EXAMPLE.

THINK OF THE MOST MONSTROUS CREATURE YOU CAN IMAGINE. NOW IMAGINE SOMETHING **TWICE** AS MONSTROUS!

SUCH AS...?

YOU SHALL SEE! OH-HO-HO! YOU SHALL SEE!!

YOU GUYS HAVE **NEVER** BEEN THERE, HAVE YOU?

WELL, NO. NOT TECHNICALLY.

CAN YOU BLAME US? LOOK AT IT! IT'S SO SPOOKY!

I'M GETTING SCARED, AND I'M A GHOST!

ALAS, WE MUST BRAVE ITS TREACHEROUS DEPTHS! IT'S THE ONLY WAY THROUGH THE MOUNTAIN PASS! UNLESS, OF COURSE, WE WERE TO TRAVERSE THE DEADLY BLACK GLACIERS OF MOUNT CRAG. NO MAN HAS EVER DONE THAT AND LIVED...

WELL LET'S GET ON WITH IT THEN...

...DRAMA QUEENS.

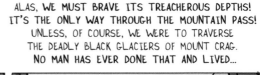

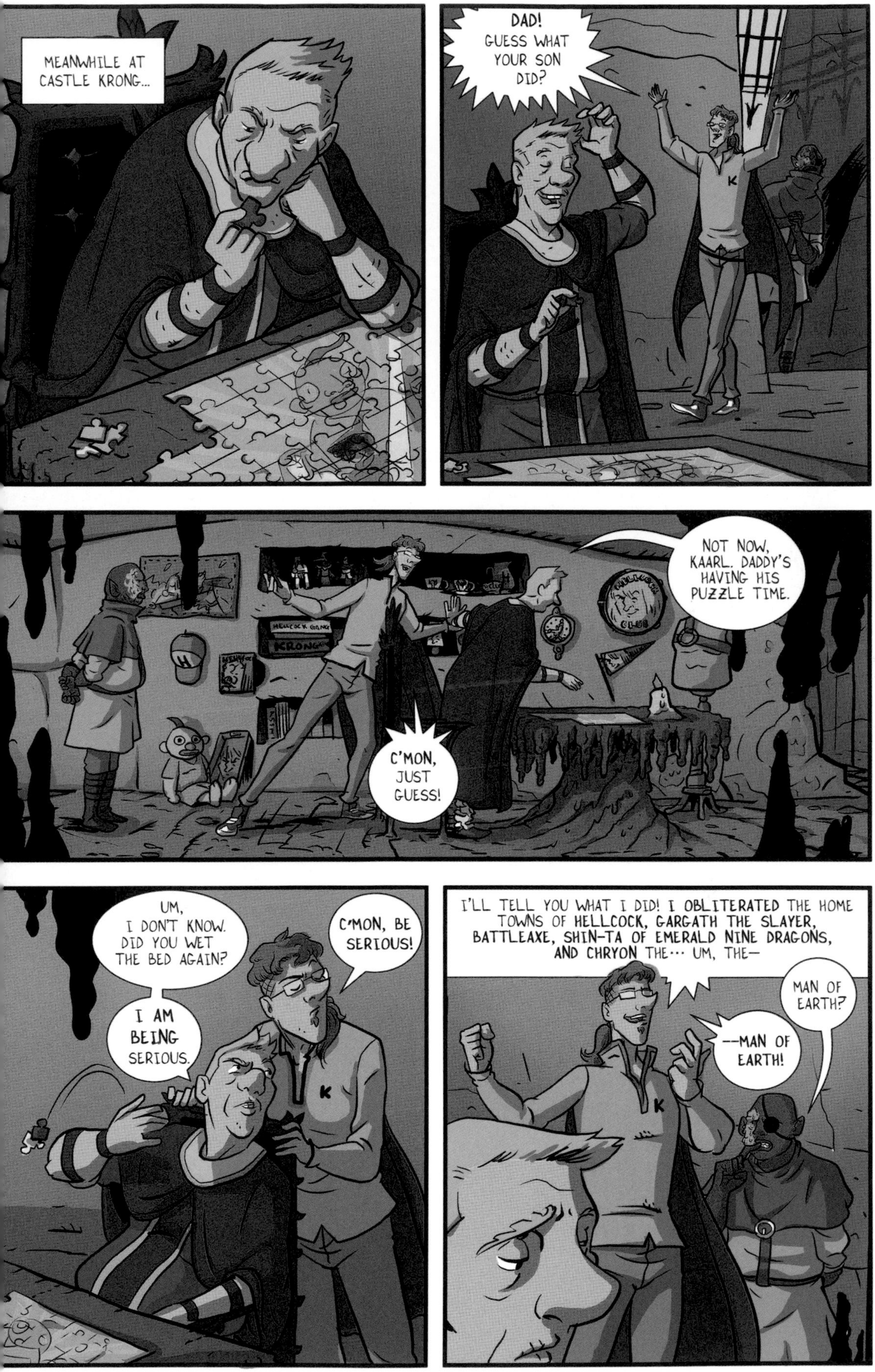
MEANWHILE AT CASTLE KRONG...
DAD! GUESS WHAT YOUR SON DID?
NOT NOW, KAARL. DADDY'S HAVING HIS PUZZLE TIME.
C'MON, JUST GUESS!
UM, I DON'T KNOW. DID YOU WET THE BED AGAIN?
C'MON, BE SERIOUS!
I AM BEING SERIOUS.
I'LL TELL YOU WHAT I DID! I OBLITERATED THE HOME TOWNS OF HELLCOCK, GARGATH THE SLAYER, BATTLEAXE, SHIN-TA OF EMERALD NINE DRAGONS, AND CHRYON THE··· UM, THE—
MAN OF EARTH?
--MAN OF EARTH!

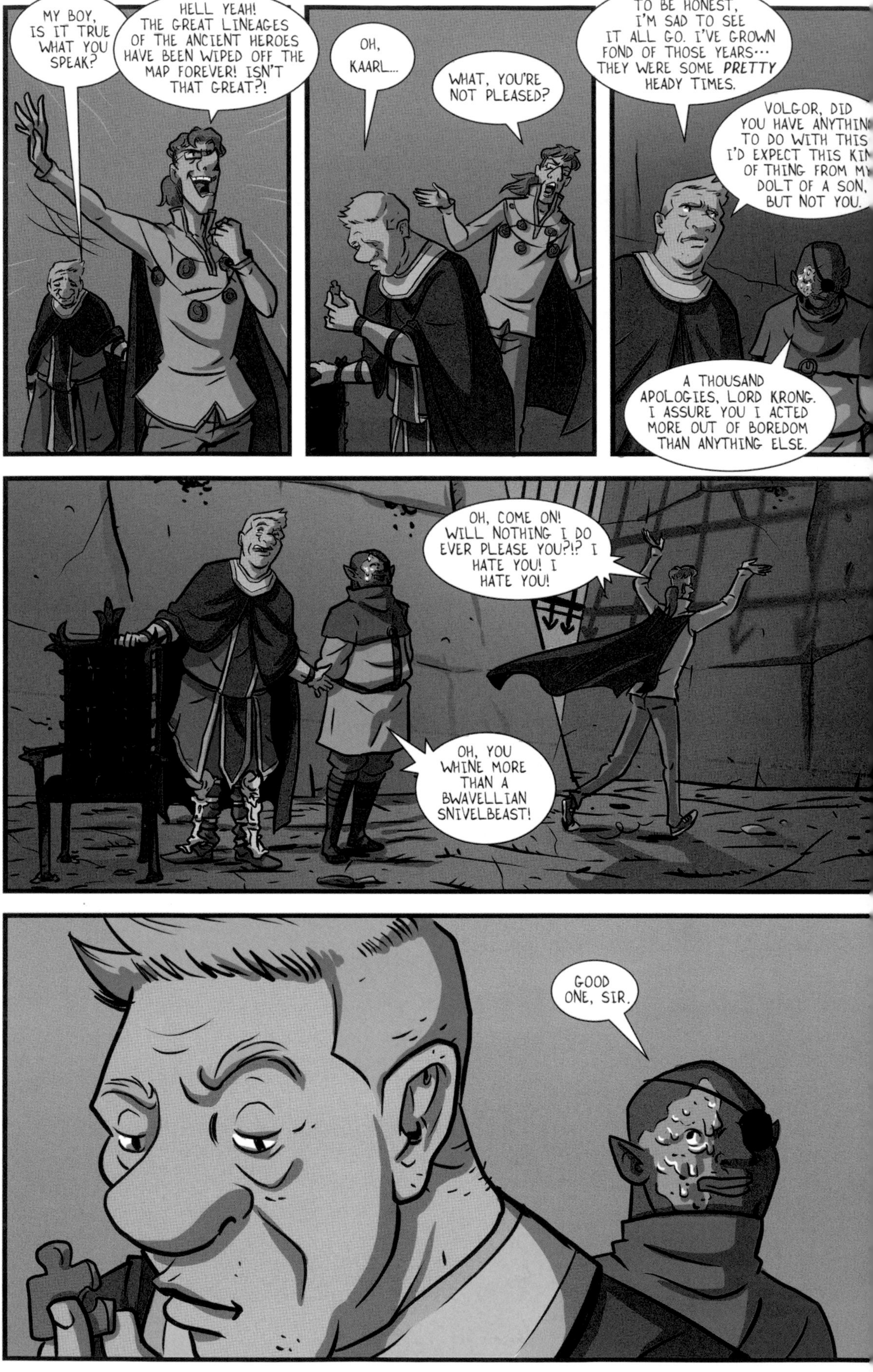
MY BOY, IS IT TRUE WHAT YOU SPEAK?
HELL YEAH! THE GREAT LINEAGES OF THE ANCIENT HEROES HAVE BEEN WIPED OFF THE MAP FOREVER! ISN'T THAT GREAT?!
OH, KAARL...
WHAT, YOU'RE NOT PLEASED?
TO BE HONEST, I'M SAD TO SEE IT ALL GO. I'VE GROWN FOND OF THOSE YEARS... THEY WERE SOME PRETTY HEADY TIMES.
VOLGOR, DID YOU HAVE ANYTHIN TO DO WITH THIS I'D EXPECT THIS KIN OF THING FROM MY DOLT OF A SON, BUT NOT YOU.
A THOUSAND APOLOGIES, LORD KRONG. I ASSURE YOU I ACTED MORE OUT OF BOREDOM THAN ANYTHING ELSE.
OH, COME ON! WILL NOTHING I DO EVER PLEASE YOU?!? I HATE YOU! I HATE YOU!
OH, YOU WHINE MORE THAN A BWAVELLIAN SNIVELBEAST!
GOOD ONE, SIR.

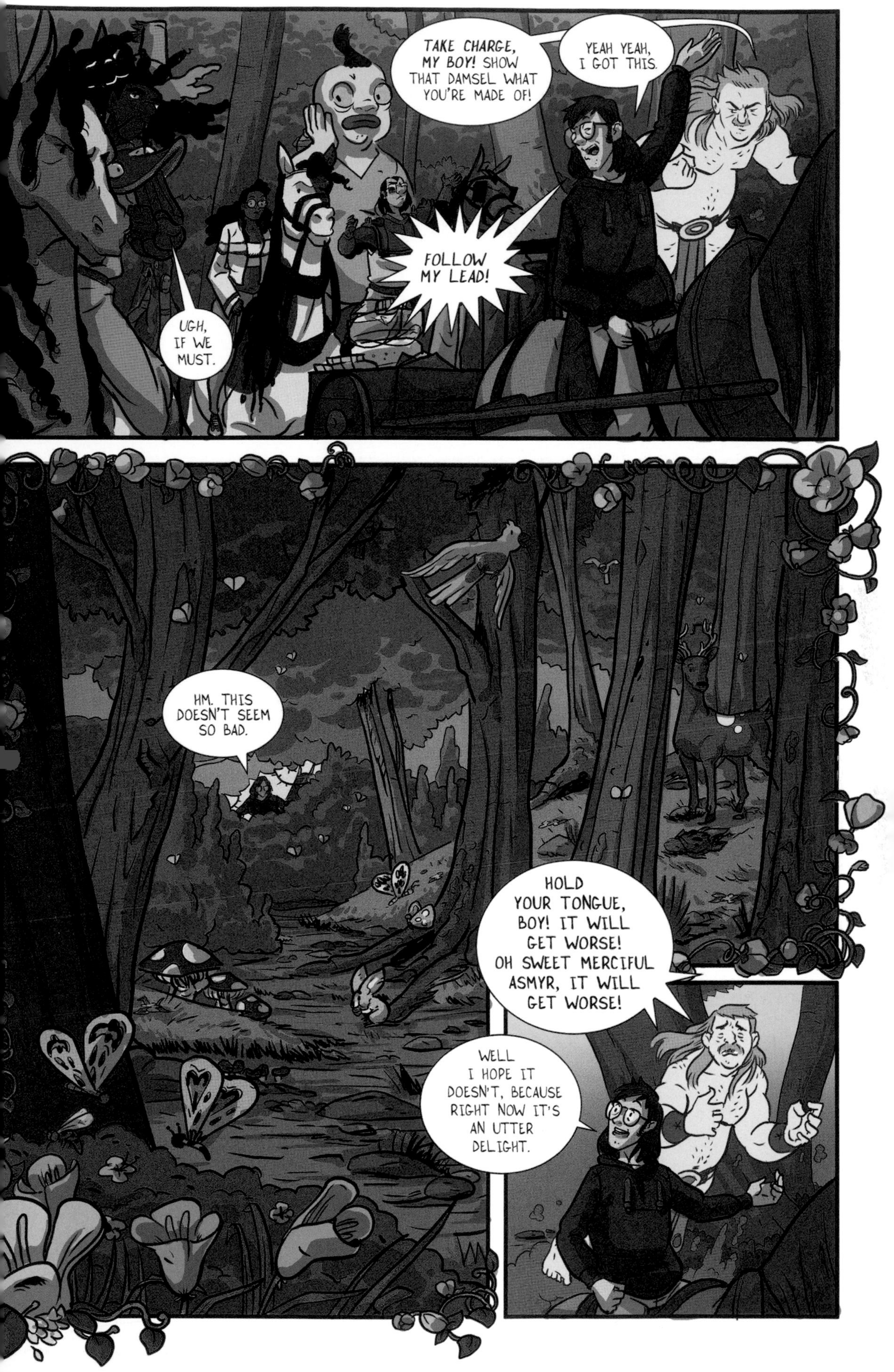
TAKE CHARGE, MY BOY! SHOW THAT DAMSEL WHAT YOU'RE MADE OF!
YEAH YEAH, I GOT THIS.
FOLLOW MY LEAD!
UGH, IF WE MUST.
HM. THIS DOESN'T SEEM SO BAD.
HOLD YOUR TONGUE, BOY! IT WILL GET WORSE! OH SWEET MERCIFUL ASMYR, IT WILL GET WORSE!
WELL I HOPE IT DOESN'T, BECAUSE RIGHT NOW IT'S AN UTTER DELIGHT.

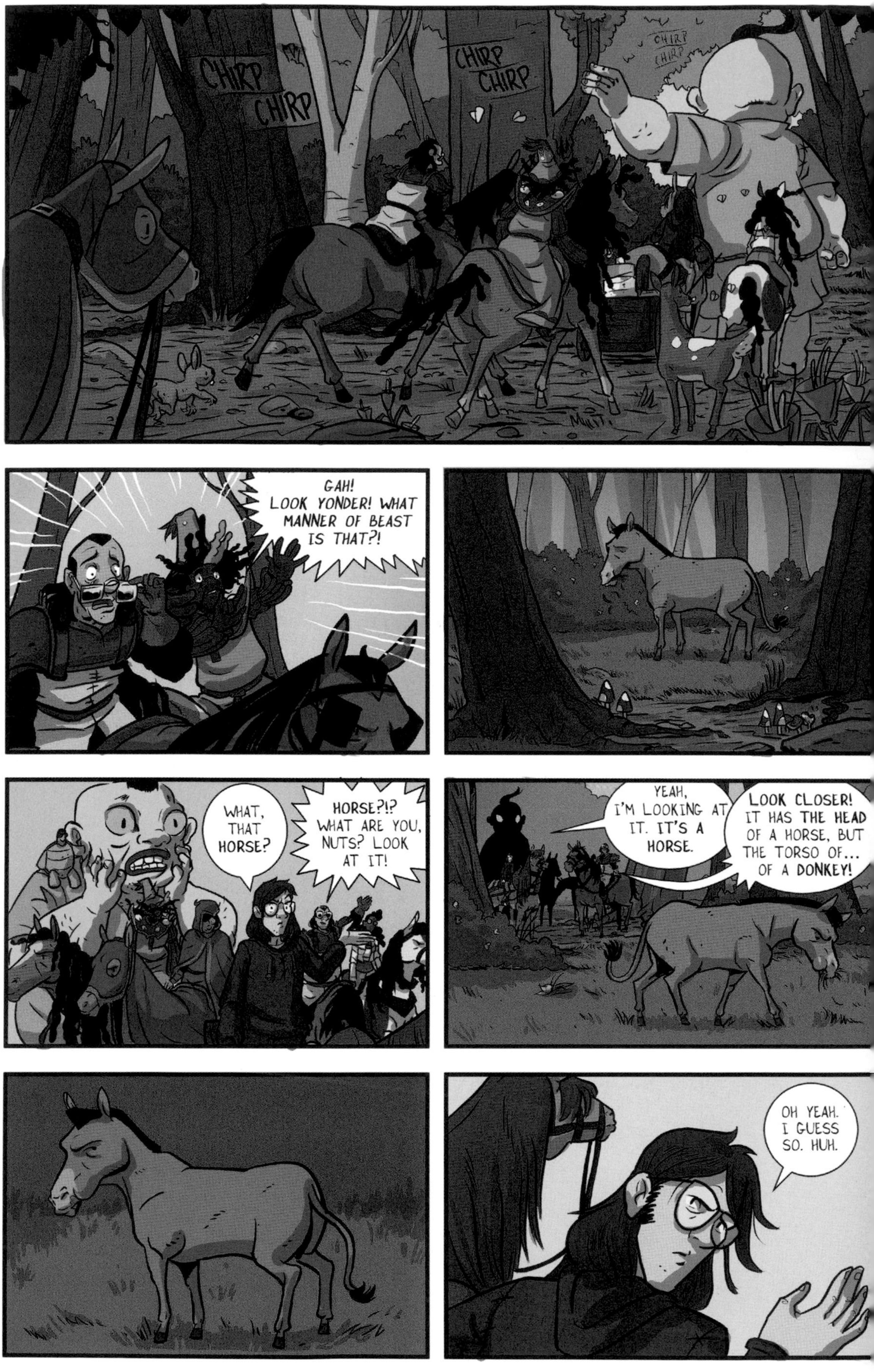
CHIRP
CHIRP
CHIRP
CHIRP
CHIRP
CHIRP
GAH! LOOK YONDER! WHAT MANNER OF BEAST IS THAT?!
WHAT, THAT HORSE?
HORSE?!? WHAT ARE YOU, NUTS? LOOK AT IT!
YEAH, I'M LOOKING AT IT. IT'S A HORSE.
LOOK CLOSER! IT HAS THE HEAD OF A HORSE, BUT THE TORSO OF... OF A DONKEY!
OH YEAH. I GUESS SO. HUH.

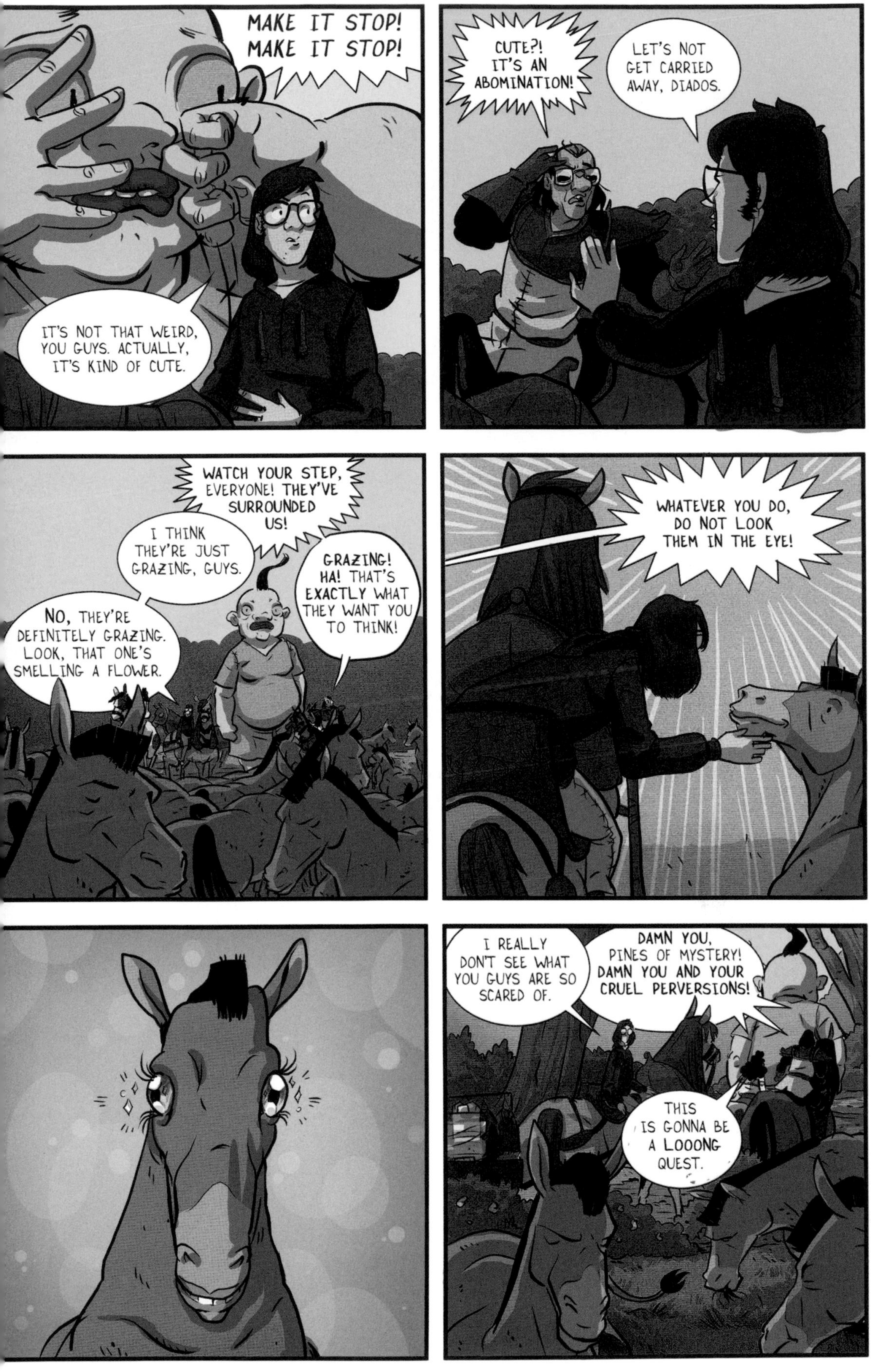
MAKE IT STOP! MAKE IT STOP!
IT'S NOT THAT WEIRD, YOU GUYS. ACTUALLY, IT'S KIND OF CUTE.
CUTE?! IT'S AN ABOMINATION!
LET'S NOT GET CARRIED AWAY, DIADOS.
WATCH YOUR STEP, EVERYONE! THEY'VE SURROUNDED US!
I THINK THEY'RE JUST GRAZING, GUYS.
GRAZING! HA! THAT'S EXACTLY WHAT THEY WANT YOU TO THINK!
NO, THEY'RE DEFINITELY GRAZING. LOOK, THAT ONE'S SMELLING A FLOWER.
WHATEVER YOU DO, DO NOT LOOK THEM IN THE EYE!
I REALLY DON'T SEE WHAT YOU GUYS ARE SO SCARED OF.
DAMN YOU, PINES OF MYSTERY! DAMN YOU AND YOUR CRUEL PERVERSIONS!
THIS IS GONNA BE A LOOONG QUEST.

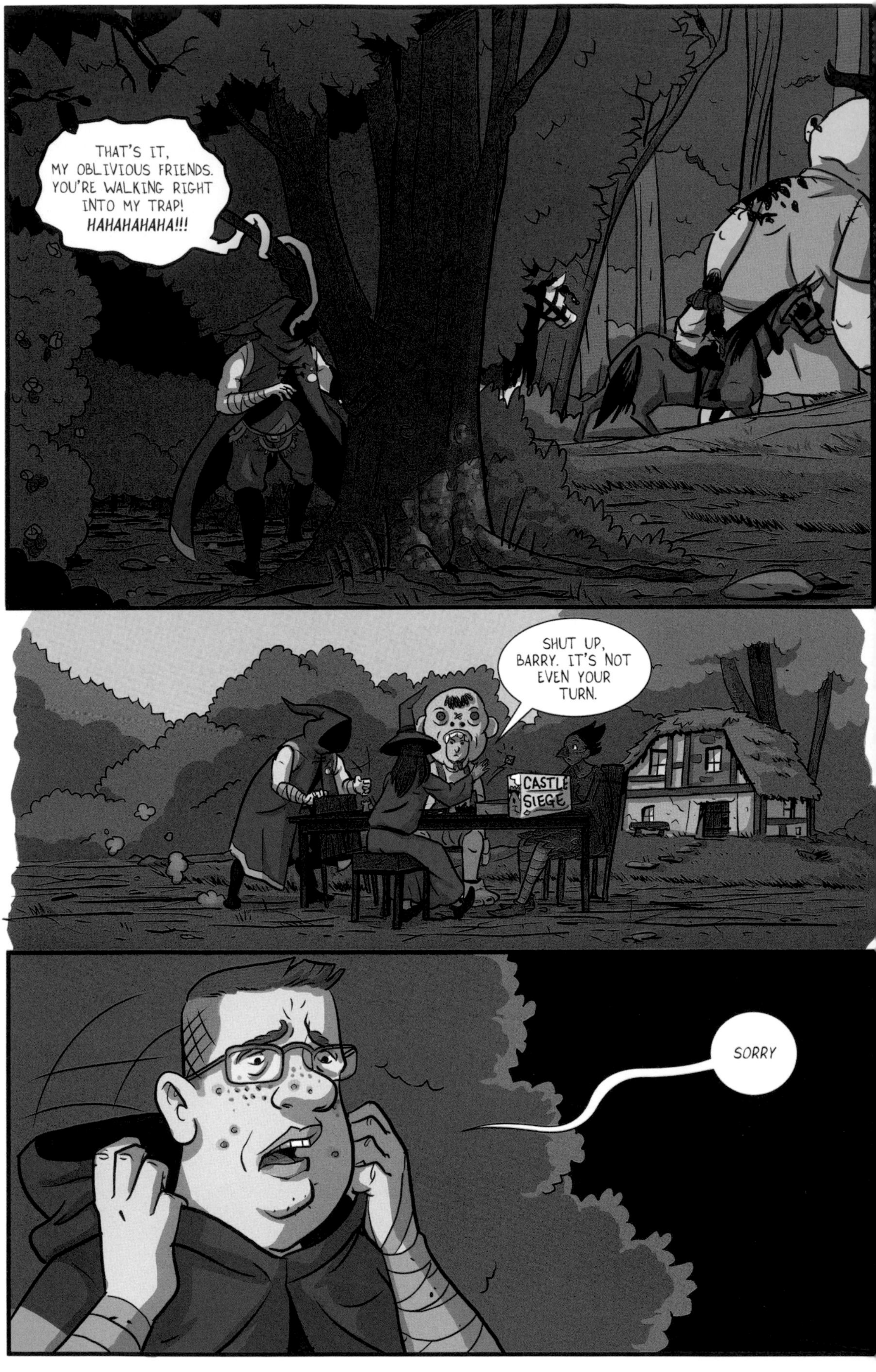
THAT'S IT, MY OBLIVIOUS FRIENDS. YOU'RE WALKING RIGHT INTO MY TRAP! **HAHAHAHAHA!!!**
SHUT UP, BARRY. IT'S NOT EVEN YOUR TURN.
CASTLE SIEGE
SORRY

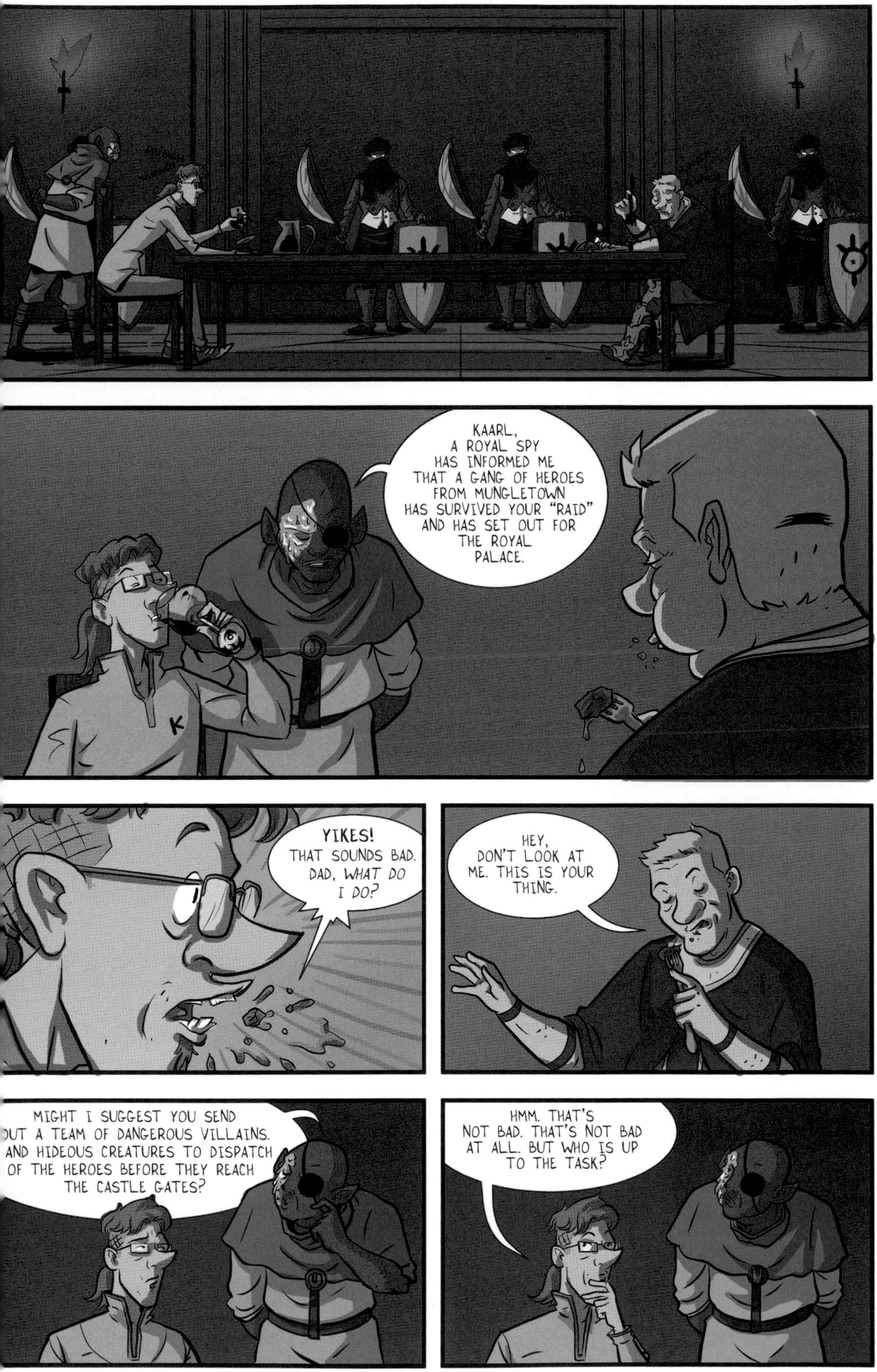
KAARL, A ROYAL SPY HAS INFORMED ME THAT A GANG OF HEROES FROM MUNGLETOWN HAS SURVIVED YOUR "RAID" AND HAS SET OUT FOR THE ROYAL PALACE.
YIKES! THAT SOUNDS BAD. DAD, WHAT DO I DO?
HEY, DON'T LOOK AT ME. THIS IS YOUR THING.
MIGHT I SUGGEST YOU SEND OUT A TEAM OF DANGEROUS VILLAINS. AND HIDEOUS CREATURES TO DISPATCH OF THE HEROES BEFORE THEY REACH THE CASTLE GATES?
HMM. THAT'S NOT BAD. THAT'S NOT BAD AT ALL. BUT WHO IS UP TO THE TASK?

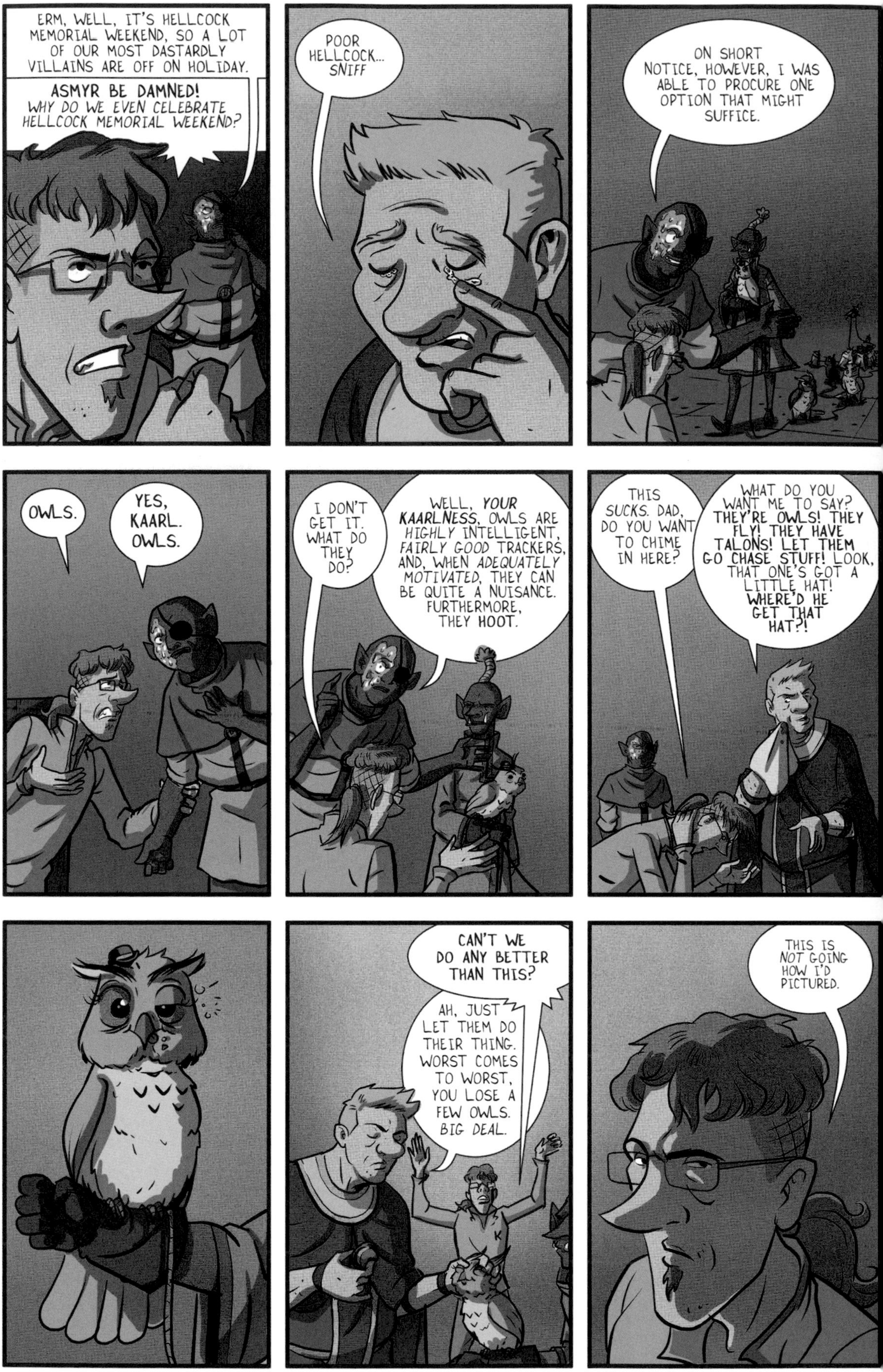
ERM, WELL, IT'S HELLCOCK MEMORIAL WEEKEND, SO A LOT OF OUR MOST DASTARDLY VILLAINS ARE OFF ON HOLIDAY.
ASMYR BE DAMNED! WHY DO WE EVEN CELEBRATE HELLCOCK MEMORIAL WEEKEND?
POOR HELLCOCK... SNIFF
ON SHORT NOTICE, HOWEVER, I WAS ABLE TO PROCURE ONE OPTION THAT MIGHT SUFFICE.
OWLS.
YES, KAARL. OWLS.
I DON'T GET IT. WHAT DO THEY DO?
WELL, YOUR KAARLNESS, OWLS ARE HIGHLY INTELLIGENT, FAIRLY GOOD TRACKERS, AND, WHEN ADEQUATELY MOTIVATED, THEY CAN BE QUITE A NUISANCE. FURTHERMORE, THEY HOOT.
THIS SUCKS. DAD, DO YOU WANT TO CHIME IN HERE?
WHAT DO YOU WANT ME TO SAY? THEY'RE OWLS! THEY FLY! THEY HAVE TALONS! LET THEM GO CHASE STUFF! LOOK, THAT ONE'S GOT A LITTLE HAT! WHERE'D HE GET THAT HAT?!
CAN'T WE DO ANY BETTER THAN THIS?
AH, JUST LET THEM DO THEIR THING. WORST COMES TO WORST, YOU LOSE A FEW OWLS. BIG DEAL.
THIS IS NOT GOING HOW I'D PICTURED.

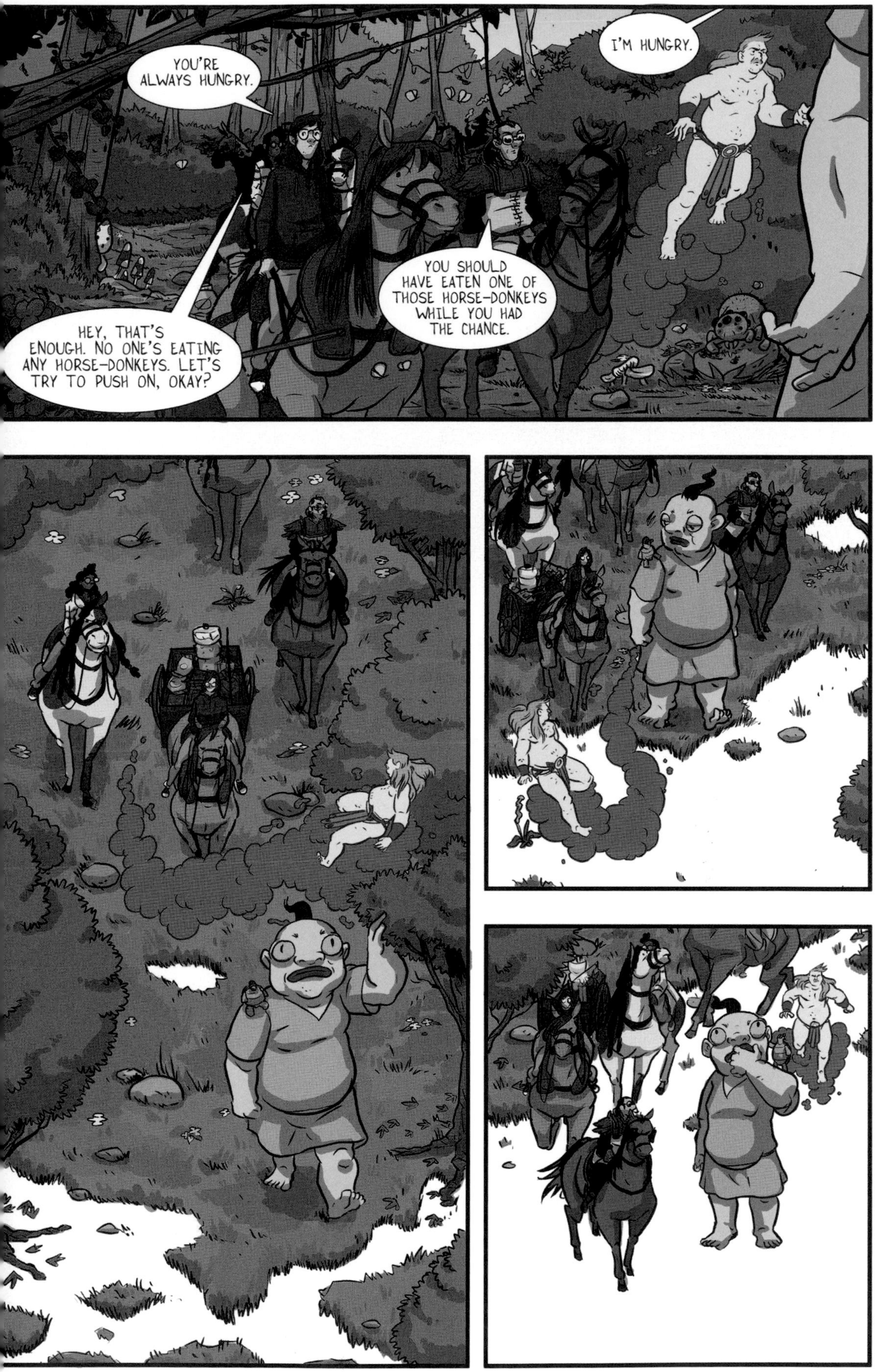
I'M HUNGRY.
YOU'RE ALWAYS HUNGRY.
YOU SHOULD HAVE EATEN ONE OF THOSE HORSE-DONKEYS WHILE YOU HAD THE CHANCE.
HEY, THAT'S ENOUGH. NO ONE'S EATING ANY HORSE-DONKEYS. LET'S TRY TO PUSH ON, OKAY?

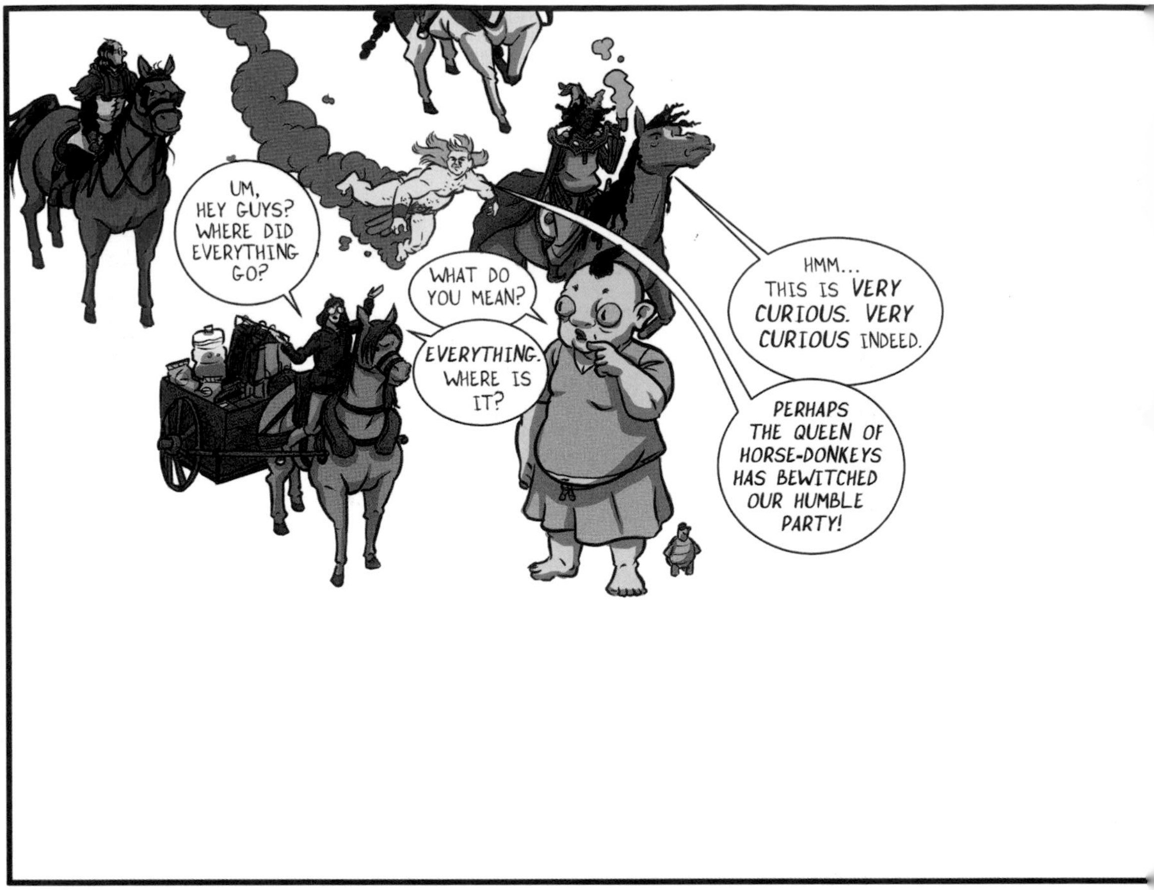
UM, HEY GUYS? WHERE DID EVERYTHING GO?
WHAT DO YOU MEAN?
EVERYTHING. WHERE IS IT?
HMM... THIS IS VERY CURIOUS. VERY CURIOUS INDEED.
PERHAPS THE QUEEN OF HORSE-DONKEYS HAS BEWITCHED OUR HUMBLE PARTY!

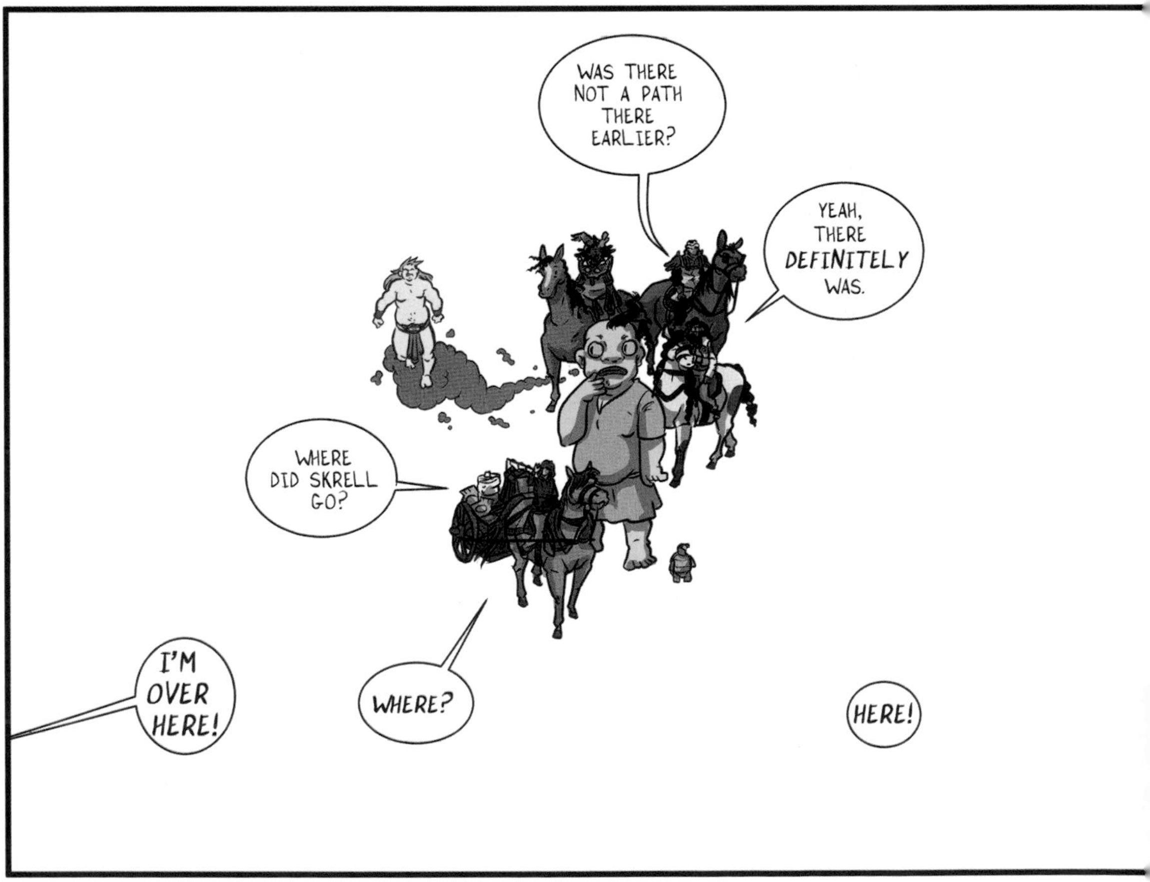
WAS THERE NOT A PATH THERE EARLIER?
YEAH, THERE DEFINITELY WAS.
WHERE DID SKRELL GO?
I'M OVER HERE!
WHERE?
HERE!

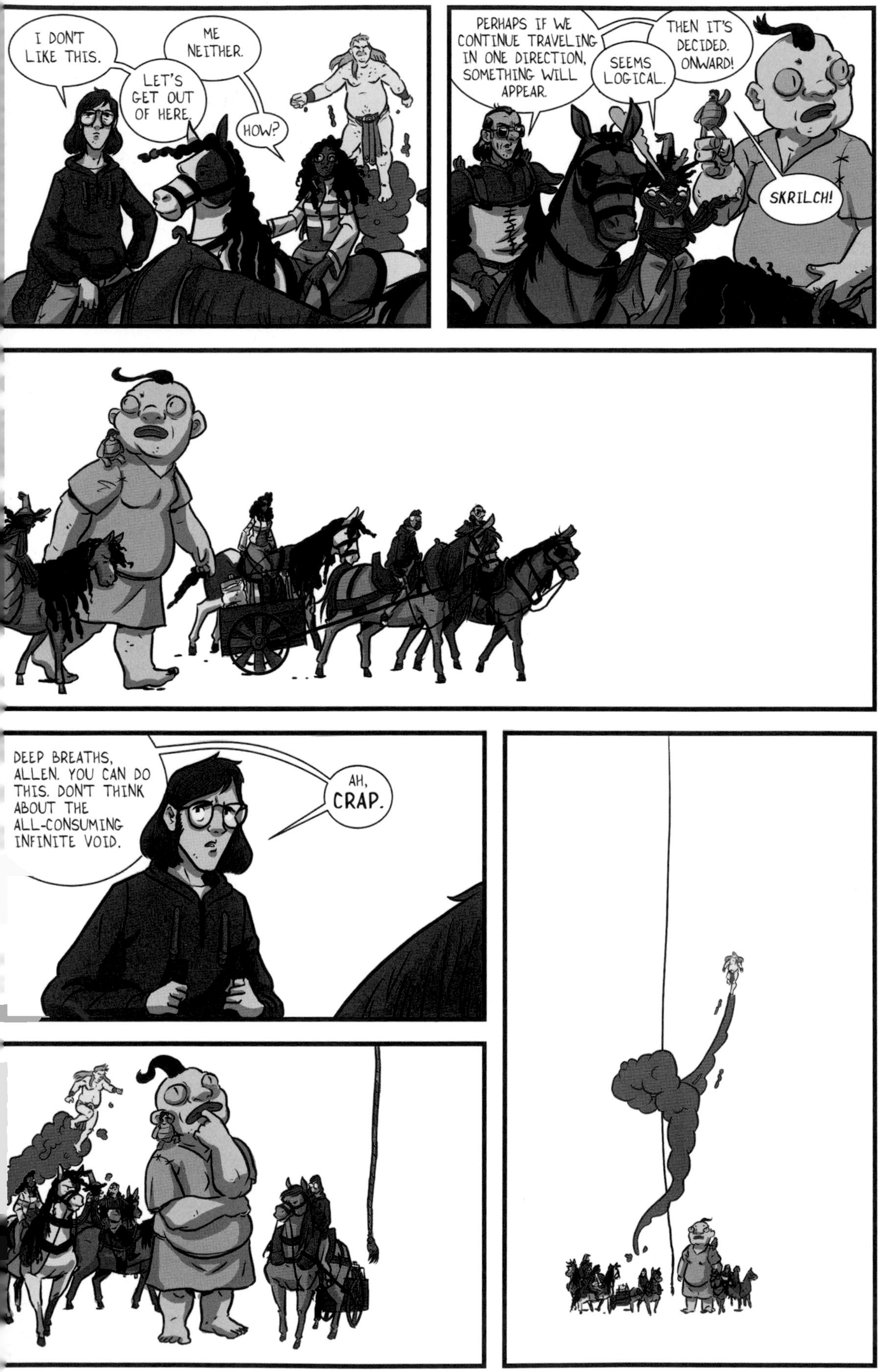
I DON'T LIKE THIS.
ME NEITHER.
LET'S GET OUT OF HERE.
HOW?
PERHAPS IF WE CONTINUE TRAVELING IN ONE DIRECTION, SOMETHING WILL APPEAR.
SEEMS LOGICAL.
THEN IT'S DECIDED. ONWARD!
SKRILCH!
DEEP BREATHS, ALLEN. YOU CAN DO THIS. DON'T THINK ABOUT THE ALL-CONSUMING INFINITE VOID.
AH, CRAP.

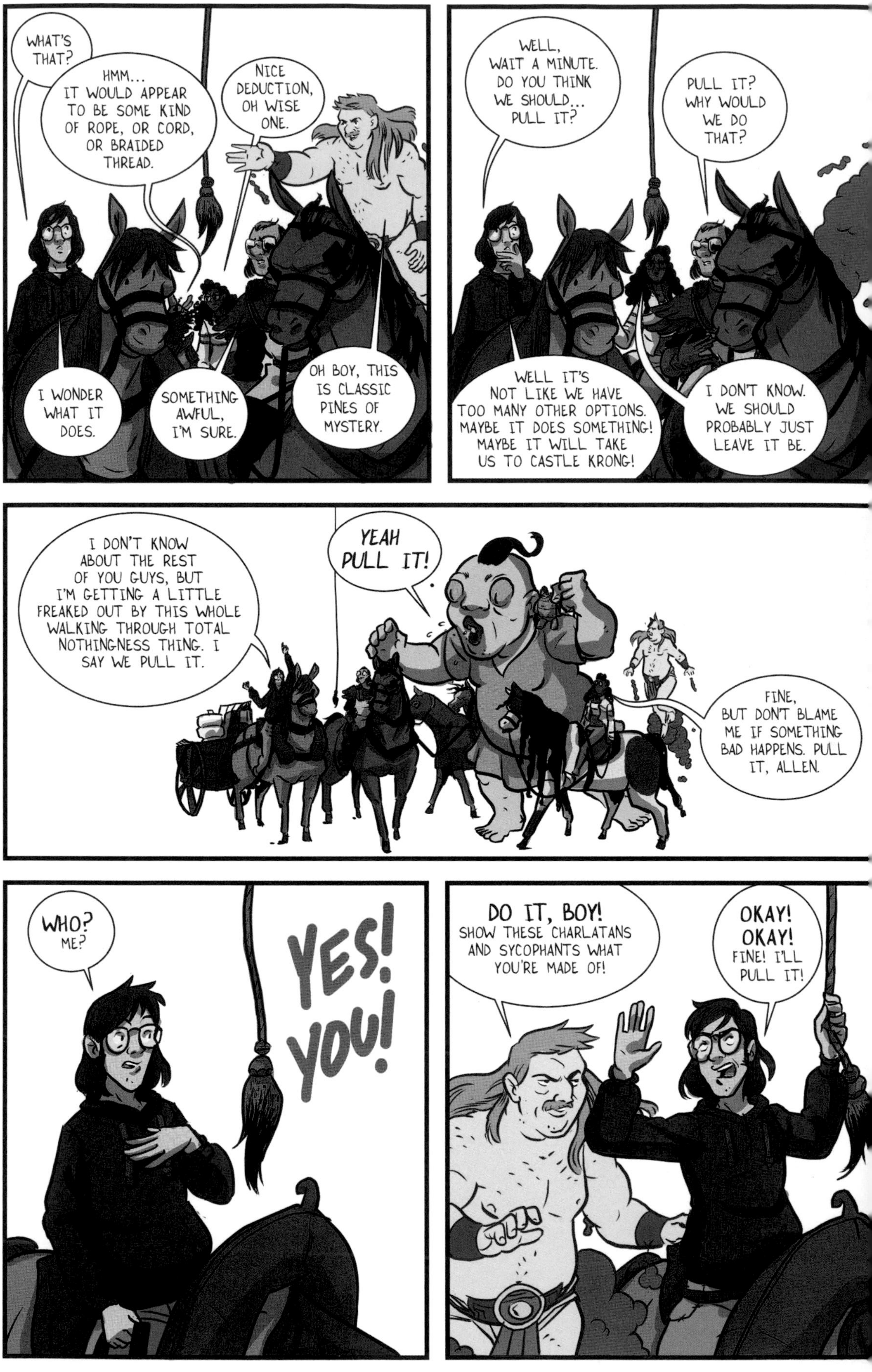
WHAT'S THAT?
HMM... IT WOULD APPEAR TO BE SOME KIND OF ROPE, OR CORD, OR BRAIDED THREAD.
NICE DEDUCTION, OH WISE ONE.
I WONDER WHAT IT DOES.
SOMETHING AWFUL, I'M SURE.
OH BOY, THIS IS CLASSIC PINES OF MYSTERY.
WELL, WAIT A MINUTE. DO YOU THINK WE SHOULD... PULL IT?
PULL IT? WHY WOULD WE DO THAT?
WELL IT'S NOT LIKE WE HAVE TOO MANY OTHER OPTIONS. MAYBE IT DOES SOMETHING! MAYBE IT WILL TAKE US TO CASTLE KRONG!
I DON'T KNOW. WE SHOULD PROBABLY JUST LEAVE IT BE.
I DON'T KNOW ABOUT THE REST OF YOU GUYS, BUT I'M GETTING A LITTLE FREAKED OUT BY THIS WHOLE WALKING THROUGH TOTAL NOTHINGNESS THING. I SAY WE PULL IT.
YEAH PULL IT!
FINE, BUT DON'T BLAME ME IF SOMETHING BAD HAPPENS. PULL IT, ALLEN.
WHO? ME?
YES! YOU!
DO IT, BOY! SHOW THESE CHARLATANS AND SYCOPHANTS WHAT YOU'RE MADE OF!
OKAY! OKAY! FINE! I'LL PULL IT!

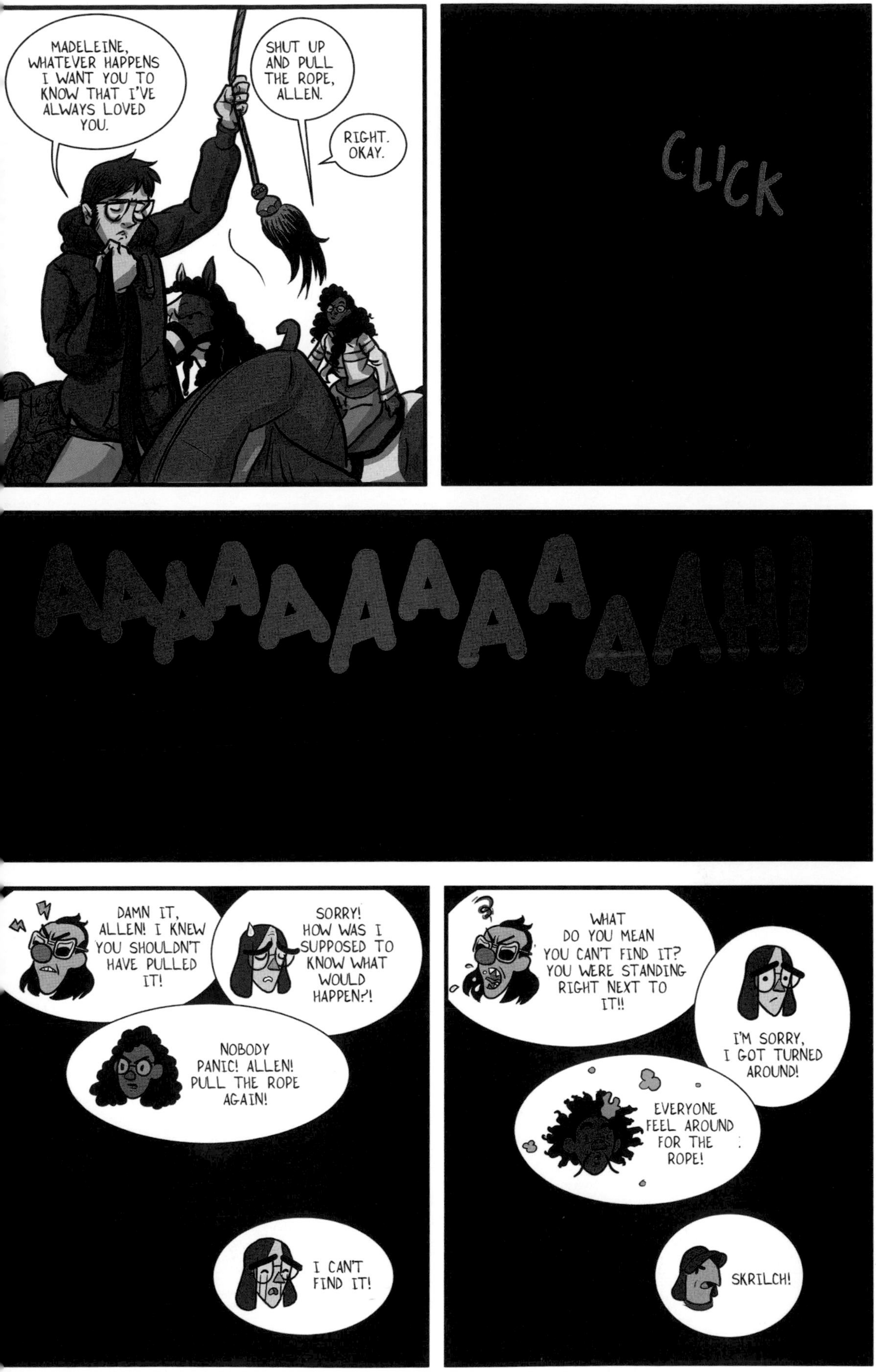
MADELEINE, WHATEVER HAPPENS I WANT YOU TO KNOW THAT I'VE ALWAYS LOVED YOU.
SHUT UP AND PULL THE ROPE, ALLEN.
RIGHT. OKAY.
CLICK
AAAAAAAAAAAH!
DAMN IT, ALLEN! I KNEW YOU SHOULDN'T HAVE PULLED IT!
SORRY! HOW WAS I SUPPOSED TO KNOW WHAT WOULD HAPPEN?!
NOBODY PANIC! ALLEN! PULL THE ROPE AGAIN!
I CAN'T FIND IT!
WHAT DO YOU MEAN YOU CAN'T FIND IT? YOU WERE STANDING RIGHT NEXT TO IT!!
I'M SORRY, I GOT TURNED AROUND!
EVERYONE FEEL AROUND FOR THE ROPE!
SKRILCH!

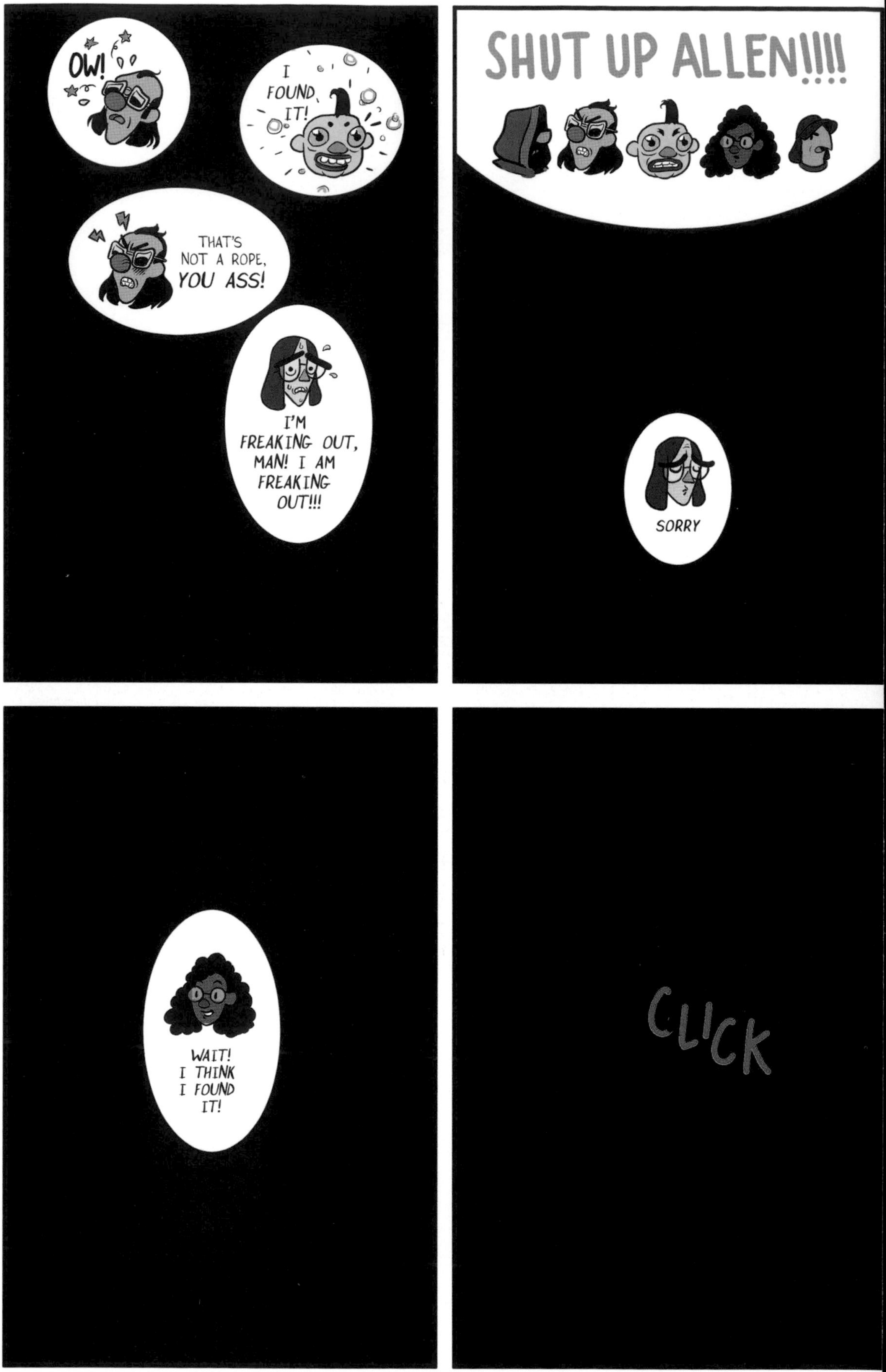
OW!
I FOUND IT!
THAT'S NOT A ROPE, YOU ASS!
I'M FREAKING OUT, MAN! I AM FREAKING OUT!!!
SHUT UP ALLEN!!!!!
SORRY
WAIT! I THINK I FOUND IT!
CLICK

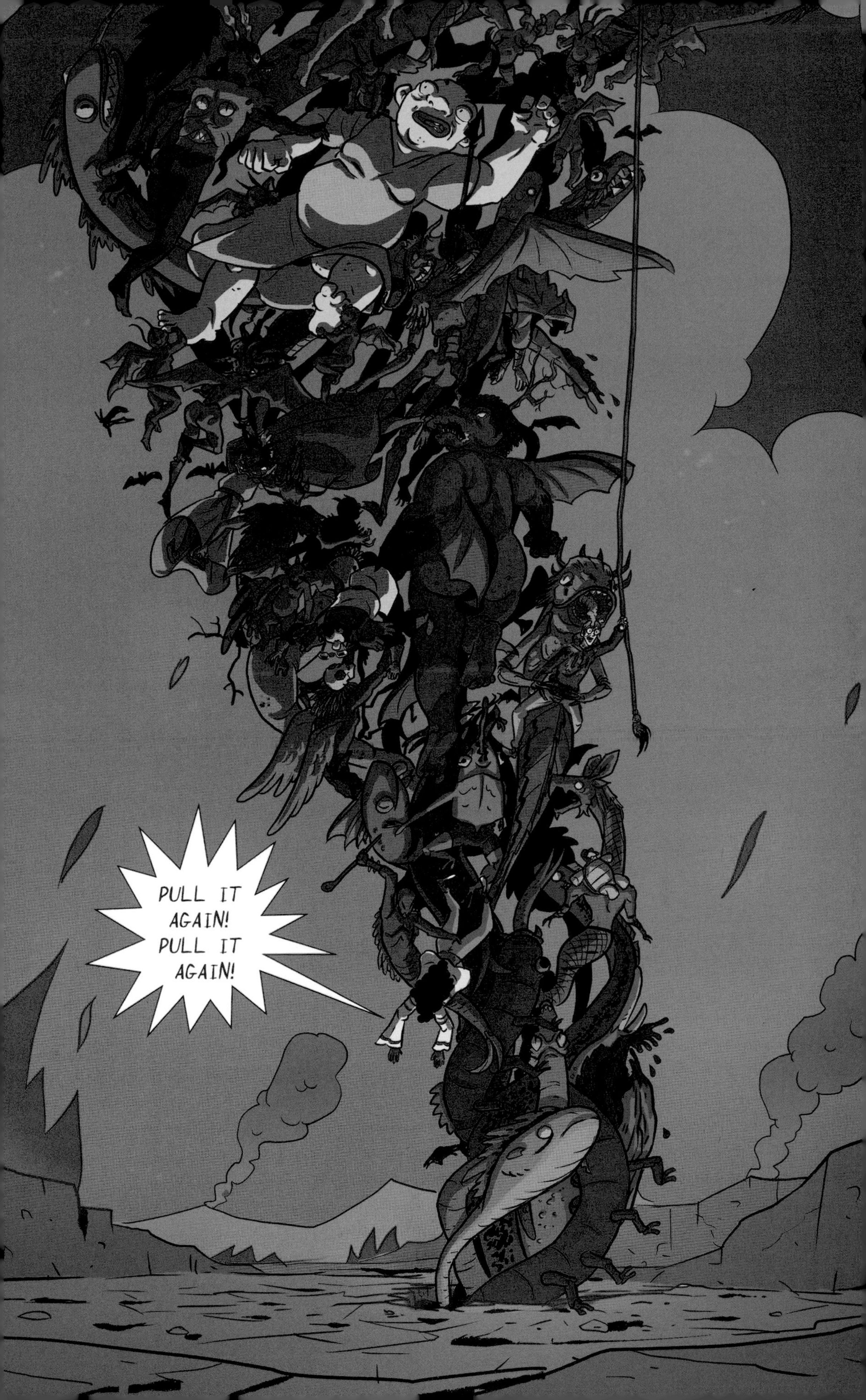
PULL IT AGAIN! PULL IT AGAIN!

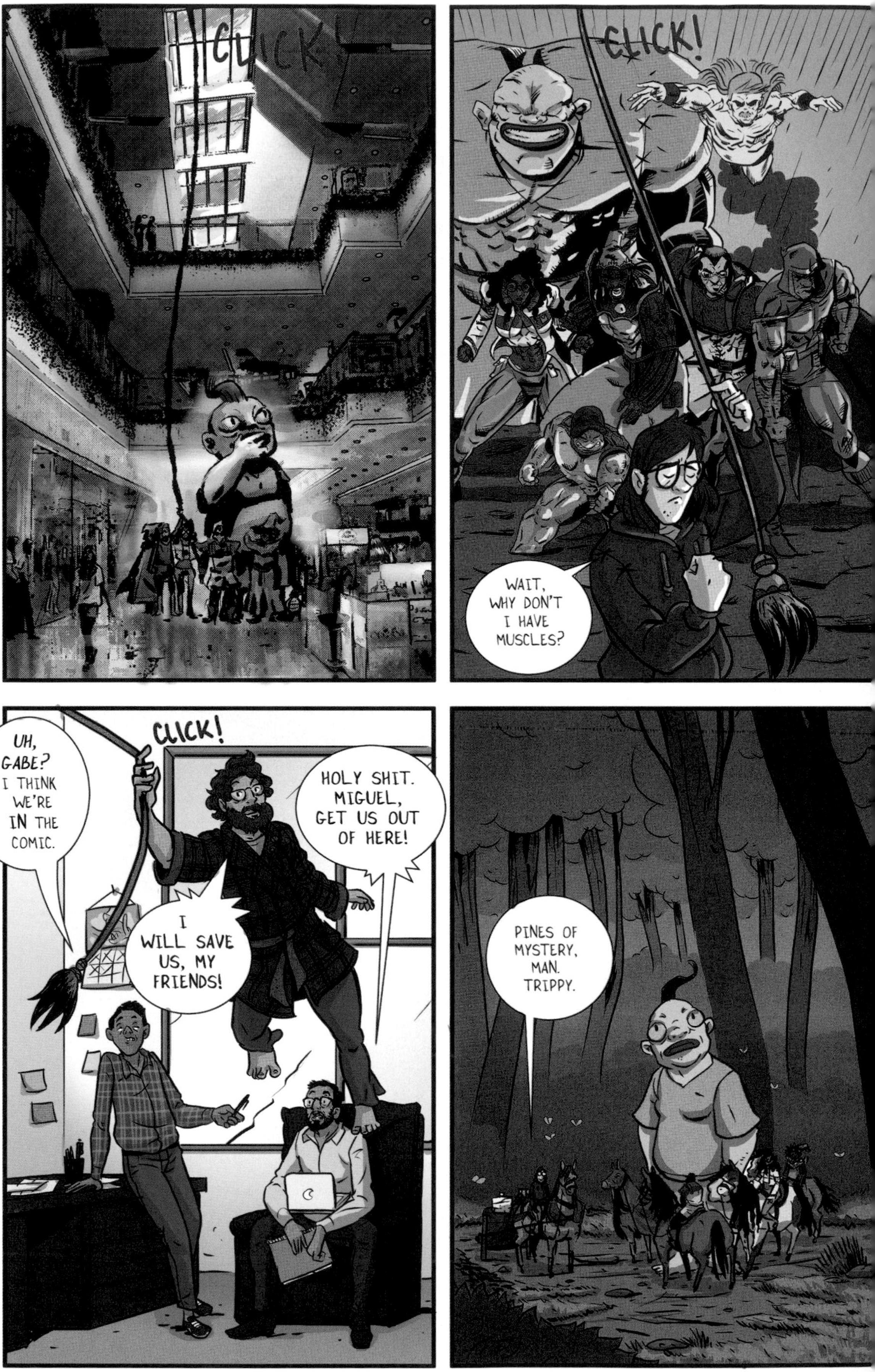
CLICK!
CLICK!
WAIT, WHY DON'T I HAVE MUSCLES?
UH, GABE? I THINK WE'RE IN THE COMIC.
CLICK!
HOLY SHIT. MIGUEL, GET US OUT OF HERE!
I WILL SAVE US, MY FRIENDS!
PINES OF MYSTERY, MAN. TRIPPY.

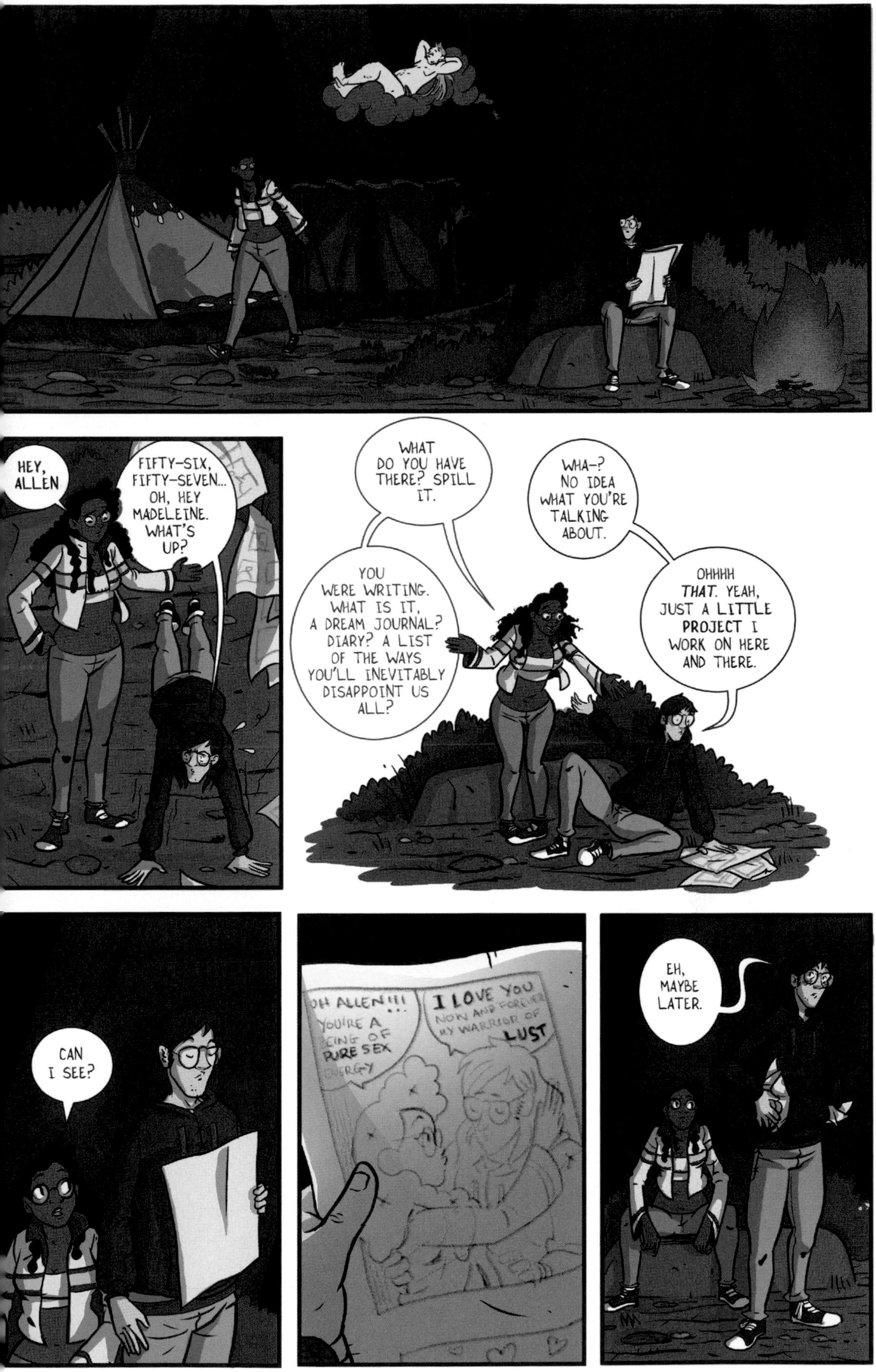
HEY, ALLEN
FIFTY-SIX, FIFTY-SEVEN... OH, HEY MADELEINE. WHAT'S UP?
WHAT DO YOU HAVE THERE? SPILL IT.
YOU WERE WRITING. WHAT IS IT, A DREAM JOURNAL? DIARY? A LIST OF THE WAYS YOU'LL INEVITABLY DISAPPOINT US ALL?
WHA-? NO IDEA WHAT YOU'RE TALKING ABOUT.
OHHHH THAT. YEAH, JUST A LITTLE PROJECT I WORK ON HERE AND THERE.
CAN I SEE?
OH ALLEN!!!
YOU'RE A
PURE SEX
I LOVE YOU
NOW AND FOREVER MY WARRIOR OF LUST
EH, MAYBE LATER.

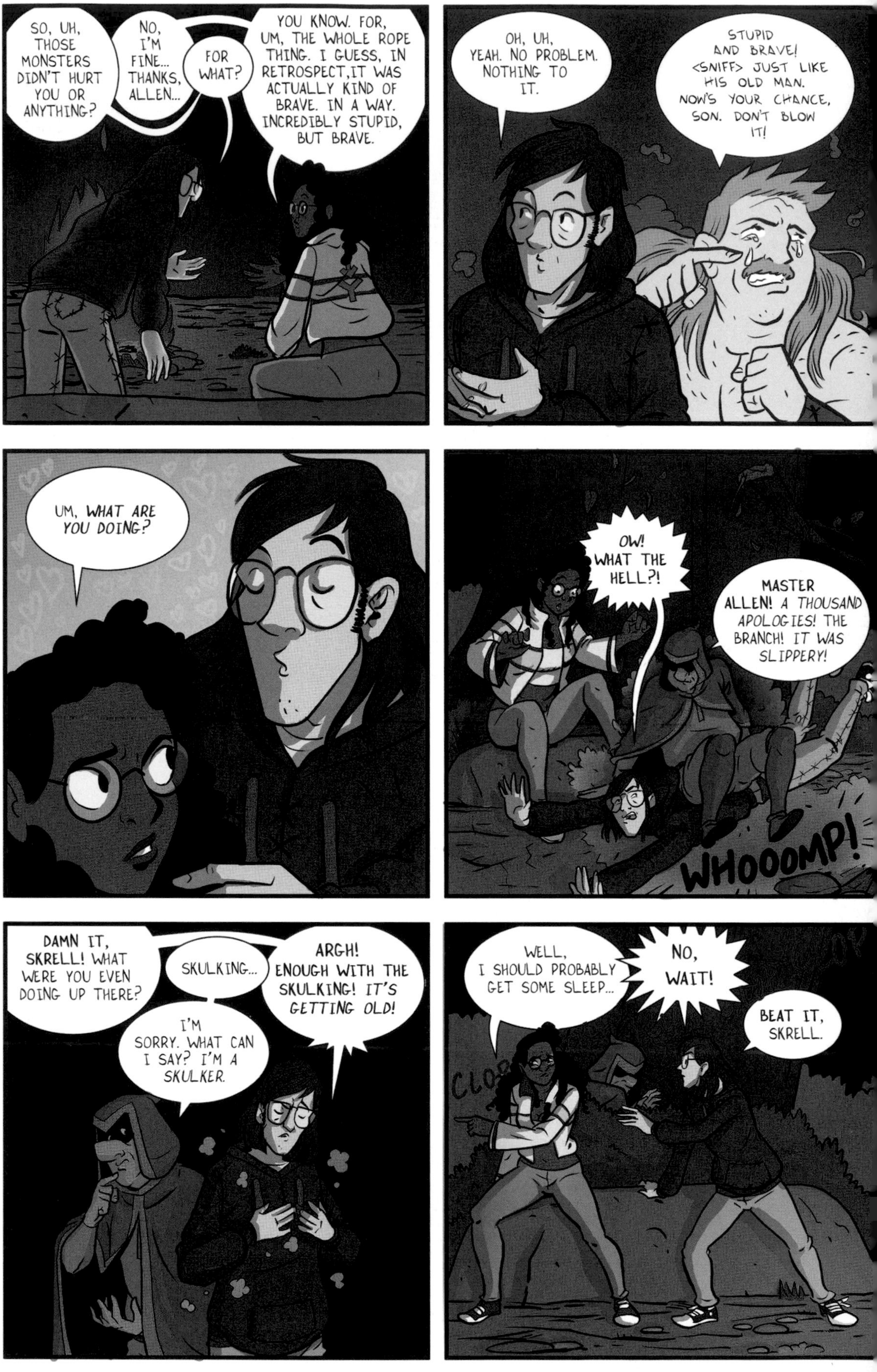

SO, UH, THOSE MONSTERS DIDN'T HURT YOU OR ANYTHING?
NO, I'M FINE... THANKS, ALLEN...
FOR WHAT?
YOU KNOW. FOR, UM, THE WHOLE ROPE THING. I GUESS, IN RETROSPECT, IT WAS ACTUALLY KIND OF BRAVE. IN A WAY. INCREDIBLY STUPID, BUT BRAVE.
OH, UH, YEAH. NO PROBLEM. NOTHING TO IT.
STUPID AND BRAVE! <SNIFF> JUST LIKE HIS OLD MAN. NOW'S YOUR CHANCE, SON. DON'T BLOW IT!
UM, WHAT ARE YOU DOING?
OW! WHAT THE HELL?!
MASTER ALLEN! A THOUSAND APOLOGIES! THE BRANCH! IT WAS SLIPPERY!
WHOOOMP!
DAMN IT, SKRELL! WHAT WERE YOU EVEN DOING UP THERE?
SKULKING...
ARGH! ENOUGH WITH THE SKULKING! IT'S GETTING OLD!
I'M SORRY. WHAT CAN I SAY? I'M A SKULKER.
WELL, I SHOULD PROBABLY GET SOME SLEEP...
NO, WAIT!
BEAT IT, SKRELL.

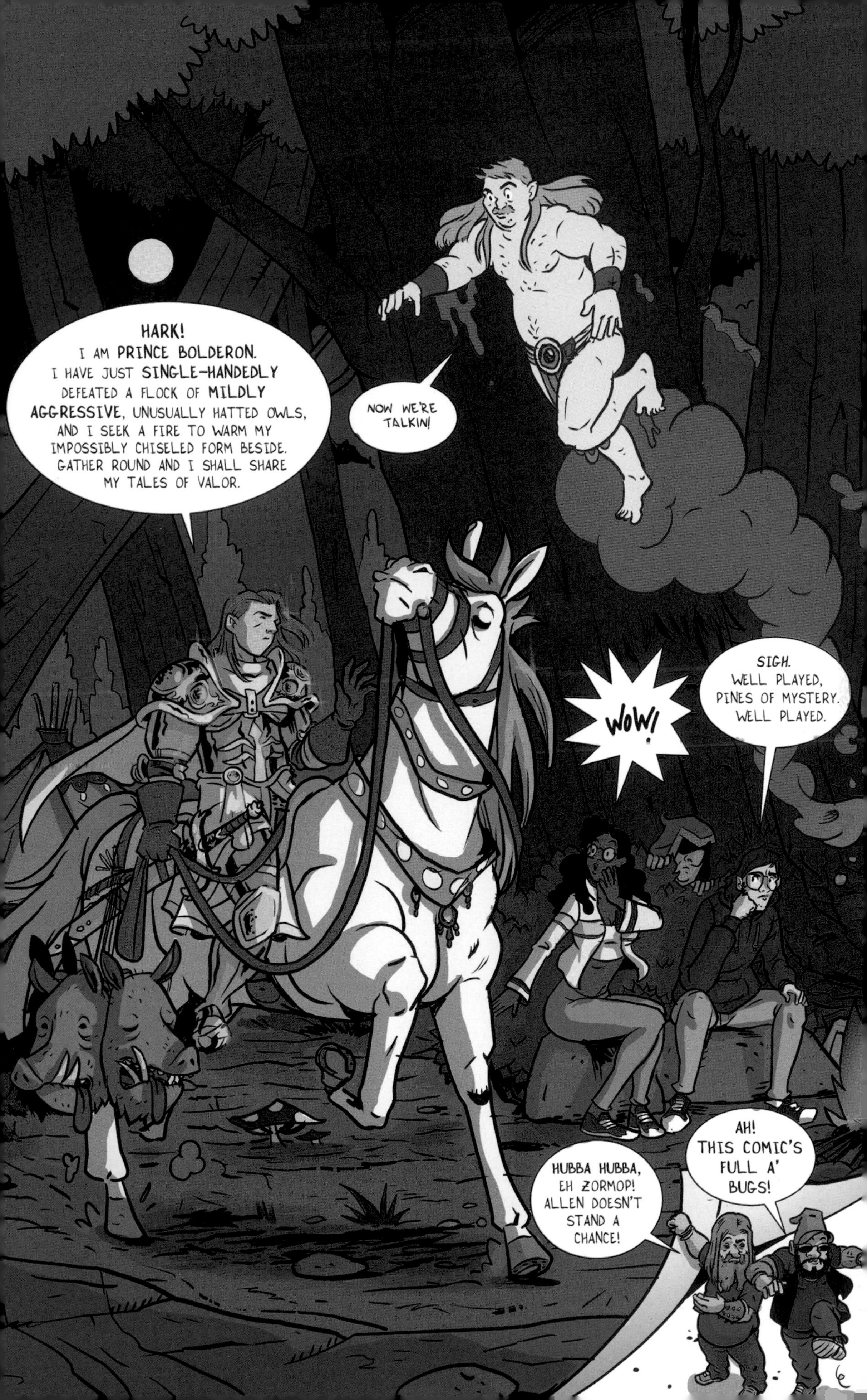
HARK!
I AM PRINCE BOLDERON.
I HAVE JUST SINGLE-HANDEDLY DEFEATED A FLOCK OF MILDLY AGGRESSIVE, UNUSUALLY HATTED OWLS, AND I SEEK A FIRE TO WARM MY IMPOSSIBLY CHISELED FORM BESIDE. GATHER ROUND AND I SHALL SHARE MY TALES OF VALOR.
NOW WE'RE TALKIN!
WOW!
SIGH. WELL PLAYED, PINES OF MYSTERY. WELL PLAYED.
HUBBA HUBBA, EH ZORMOP! ALLEN DOESN'T STAND A CHANCE!
AH! THIS COMIC'S FULL A' BUGS!

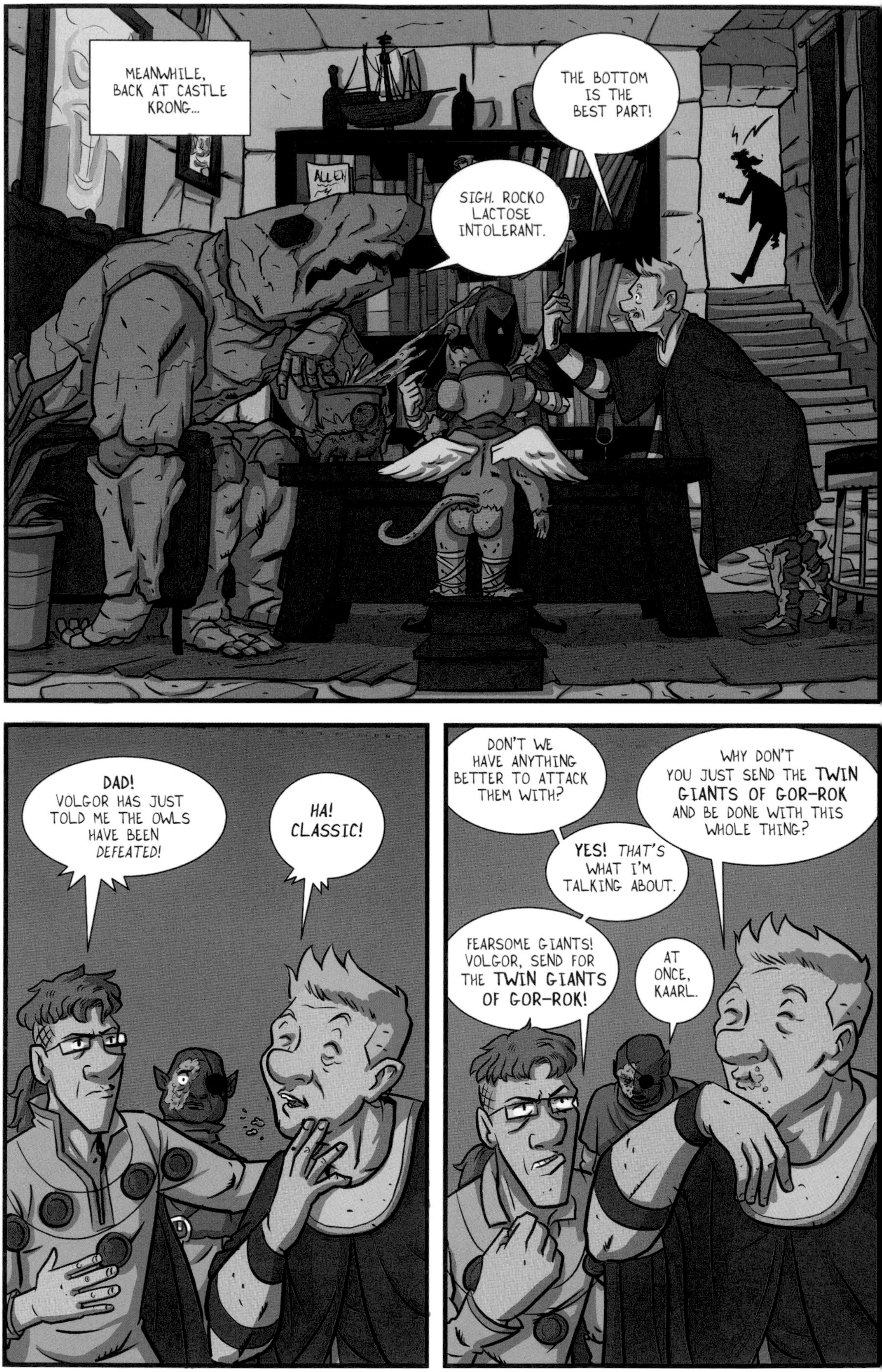
MEANWHILE, BACK AT CASTLE KRONG...
THE BOTTOM IS THE BEST PART!
SIGH. ROCKO LACTOSE INTOLERANT.
ALLEN
DAD! VOLGOR HAS JUST TOLD ME THE OWLS HAVE BEEN DEFEATED!
HA! CLASSIC!
DON'T WE HAVE ANYTHING BETTER TO ATTACK THEM WITH?
WHY DON'T YOU JUST SEND THE TWIN GIANTS OF GOR-ROK AND BE DONE WITH THIS WHOLE THING?
YES! THAT'S WHAT I'M TALKING ABOUT.
FEARSOME GIANTS! VOLGOR, SEND FOR THE TWIN GIANTS OF GOR-ROK!
AT ONCE, KAARL.

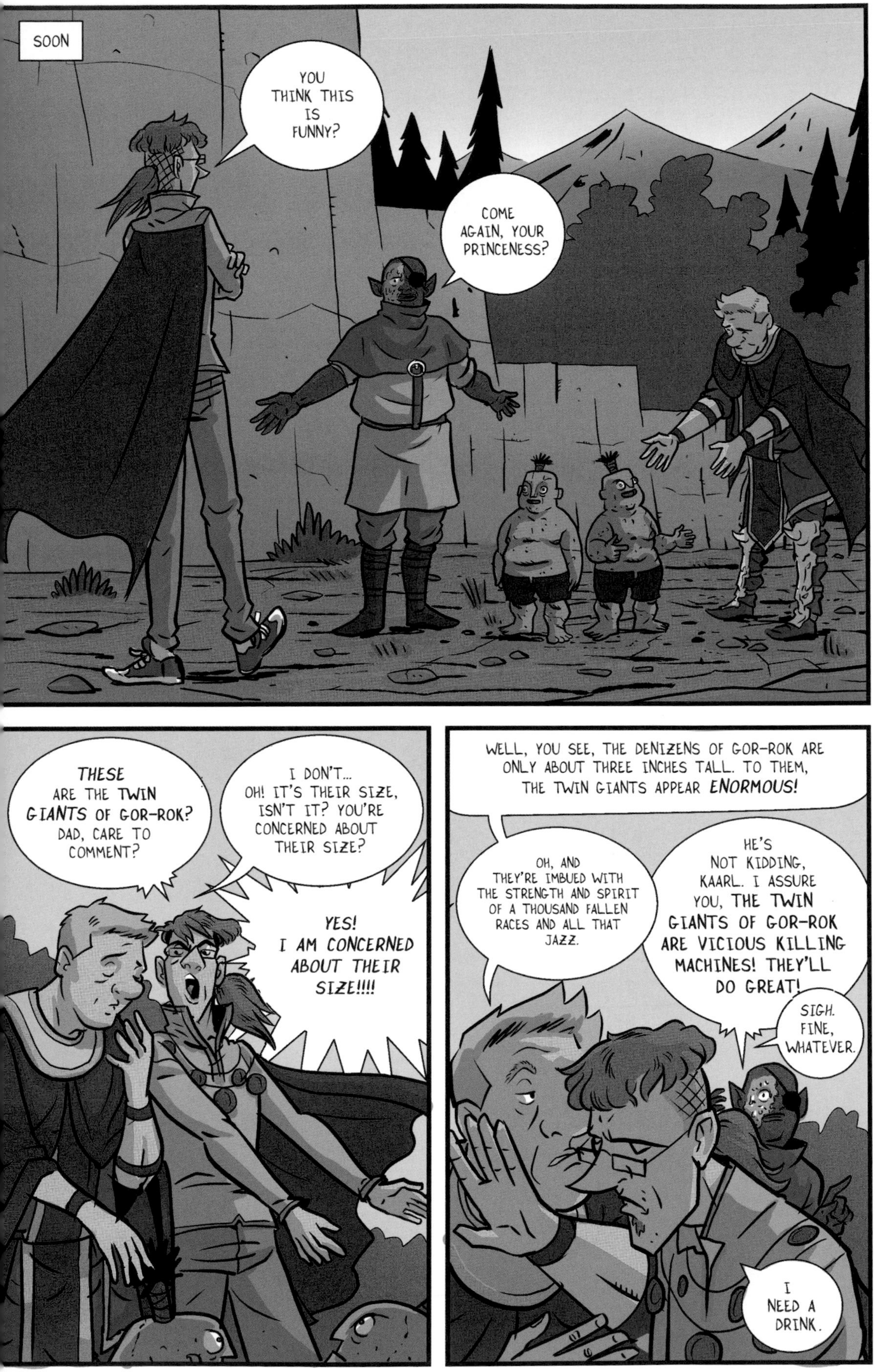
SOON
YOU THINK THIS IS FUNNY?
COME AGAIN, YOUR PRINCENESS?
THESE ARE THE TWIN GIANTS OF GOR-ROK? DAD, CARE TO COMMENT?
I DON'T... OH! IT'S THEIR SIZE, ISN'T IT? YOU'RE CONCERNED ABOUT THEIR SIZE?
YES! I AM CONCERNED ABOUT THEIR SIZE!!!!
WELL, YOU SEE, THE DENIZENS OF GOR-ROK ARE ONLY ABOUT THREE INCHES TALL. TO THEM, THE TWIN GIANTS APPEAR ENORMOUS!
OH, AND THEY'RE IMBUED WITH THE STRENGTH AND SPIRIT OF A THOUSAND FALLEN RACES AND ALL THAT JAZZ.
HE'S NOT KIDDING, KAARL. I ASSURE YOU, THE TWIN GIANTS OF GOR-ROK ARE VICIOUS KILLING MACHINES! THEY'LL DO GREAT!
SIGH. FINE, WHATEVER.
I NEED A DRINK.

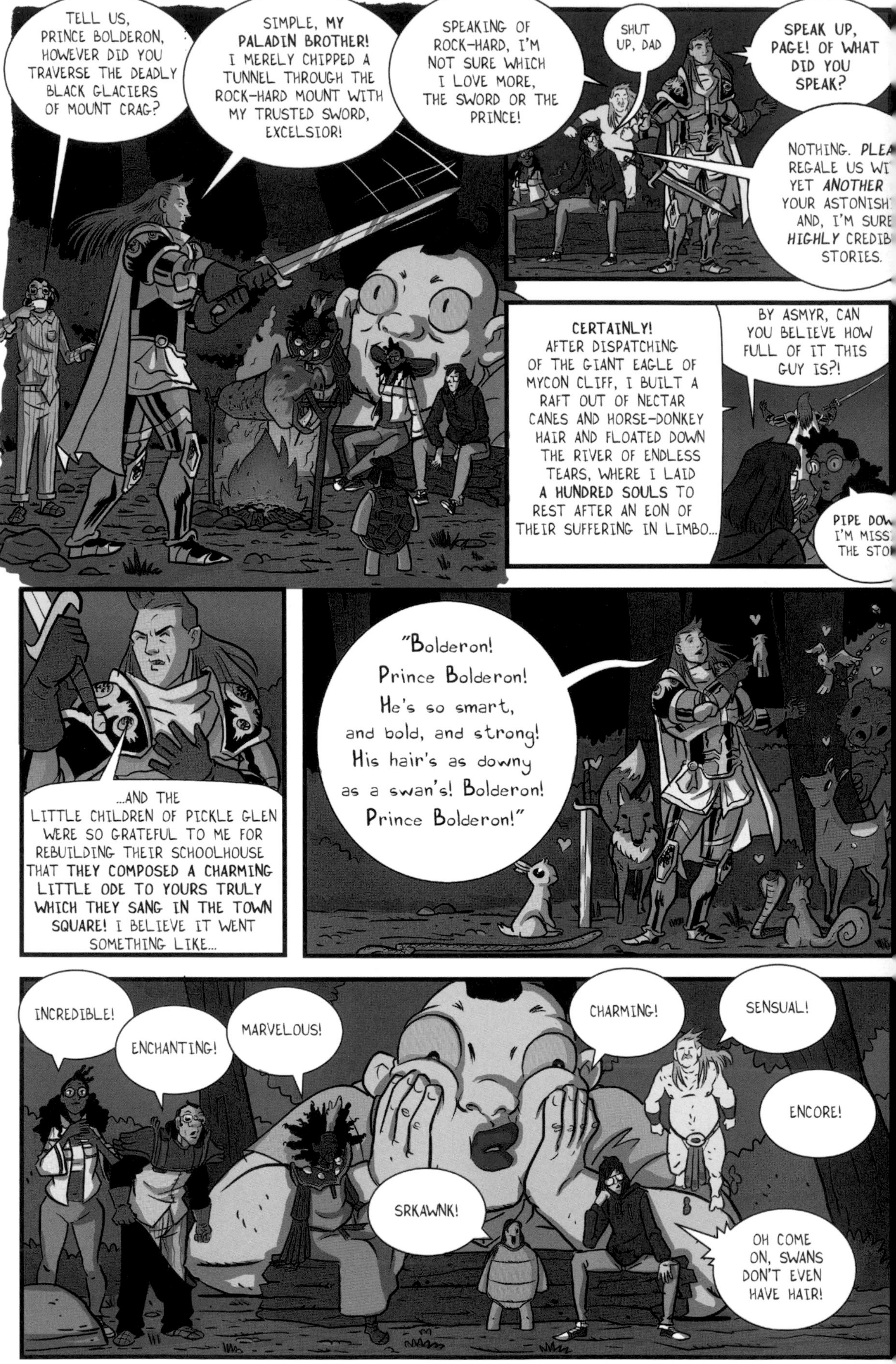
TELL US, PRINCE BOLDERON, HOWEVER DID YOU TRAVERSE THE DEADLY BLACK GLACIERS OF MOUNT CRAG?
SIMPLE, MY **PALADIN BROTHER!** I MERELY CHIPPED A TUNNEL THROUGH THE ROCK-HARD MOUNT WITH MY TRUSTED SWORD, EXCELSIOR!
SPEAKING OF ROCK-HARD, I'M NOT SURE WHICH I LOVE MORE, THE SWORD OR THE PRINCE!
SHUT UP, DAD
SPEAK UP, PAGE! OF WHAT DID YOU SPEAK?
NOTHING. **PLEA**
REGALE US WI
YET ***ANOTHER***
YOUR ASTONISH
AND, I'M SURE
HIGHLY CREDIB
STORIES.
CERTAINLY! AFTER DISPATCHING OF THE GIANT EAGLE OF MYCON CLIFF, I BUILT A RAFT OUT OF NECTAR CANES AND HORSE-DONKEY HAIR AND FLOATED DOWN THE RIVER OF ENDLESS TEARS, WHERE I LAID **A HUNDRED SOULS** TO REST AFTER AN EON OF THEIR SUFFERING IN LIMBO...
BY ASMYR, CAN YOU BELIEVE HOW FULL OF IT THIS GUY IS?!
PIPE DOW
I'M MISS
THE STO
...AND THE LITTLE CHILDREN OF PICKLE GLEN WERE SO GRATEFUL TO ME FOR REBUILDING THEIR SCHOOLHOUSE THAT **THEY COMPOSED A CHARMING LITTLE ODE TO YOURS TRULY WHICH THEY SANG IN THE TOWN SQUARE!** I BELIEVE IT WENT SOMETHING LIKE...
"Bolderon! Prince Bolderon! He's so smart, and bold, and strong! His hair's as downy as a swan's! Bolderon! Prince Bolderon!"
INCREDIBLE!
ENCHANTING!
MARVELOUS!
CHARMING!
SENSUAL!
ENCORE!
SRKAWNK!
OH COME ON, SWANS DON'T EVEN HAVE HAIR!

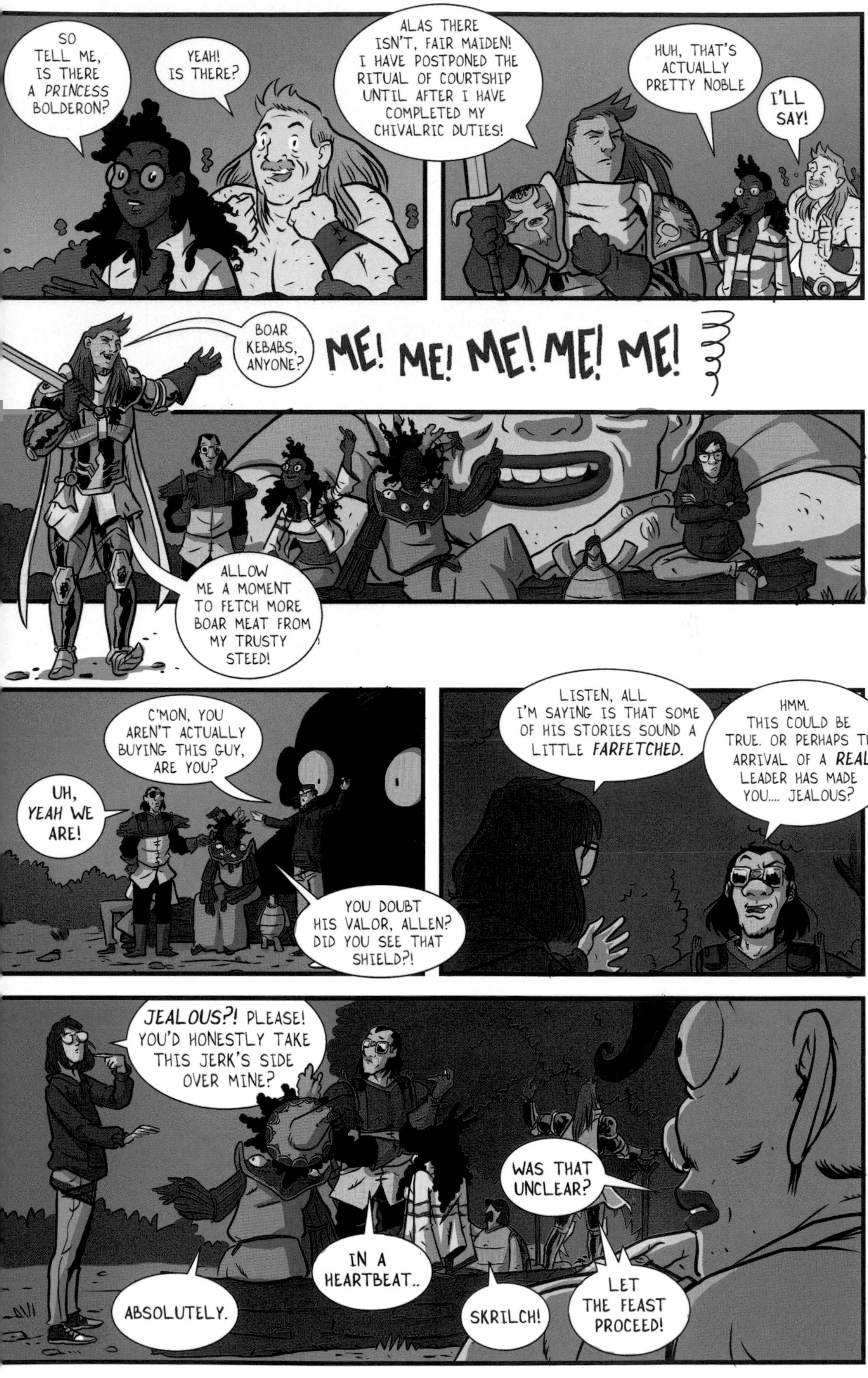
SO TELL ME, IS THERE A PRINCESS BOLDERON?
YEAH! IS THERE?
ALAS THERE ISN'T, FAIR MAIDEN! I HAVE POSTPONED THE RITUAL OF COURTSHIP UNTIL AFTER I HAVE COMPLETED MY CHIVALRIC DUTIES!
HUH, THAT'S ACTUALLY PRETTY NOBLE
I'LL SAY!
BOAR KEBABS, ANYONE?
ME! ME! ME! ME! ME!
ALLOW ME A MOMENT TO FETCH MORE BOAR MEAT FROM MY TRUSTY STEED!
C'MON, YOU AREN'T ACTUALLY BUYING THIS GUY, ARE YOU?
UH, YEAH WE ARE!
YOU DOUBT HIS VALOR, ALLEN? DID YOU SEE THAT SHIELD?!
LISTEN, ALL I'M SAYING IS THAT SOME OF HIS STORIES SOUND A LITTLE FARFETCHED.
HMM. THIS COULD BE TRUE. OR PERHAPS THE ARRIVAL OF A REAL LEADER HAS MADE YOU.... JEALOUS?
JEALOUS?! PLEASE! YOU'D HONESTLY TAKE THIS JERK'S SIDE OVER MINE?
ABSOLUTELY.
IN A HEARTBEAT..
WAS THAT UNCLEAR?
SKRILCH!
LET THE FEAST PROCEED!

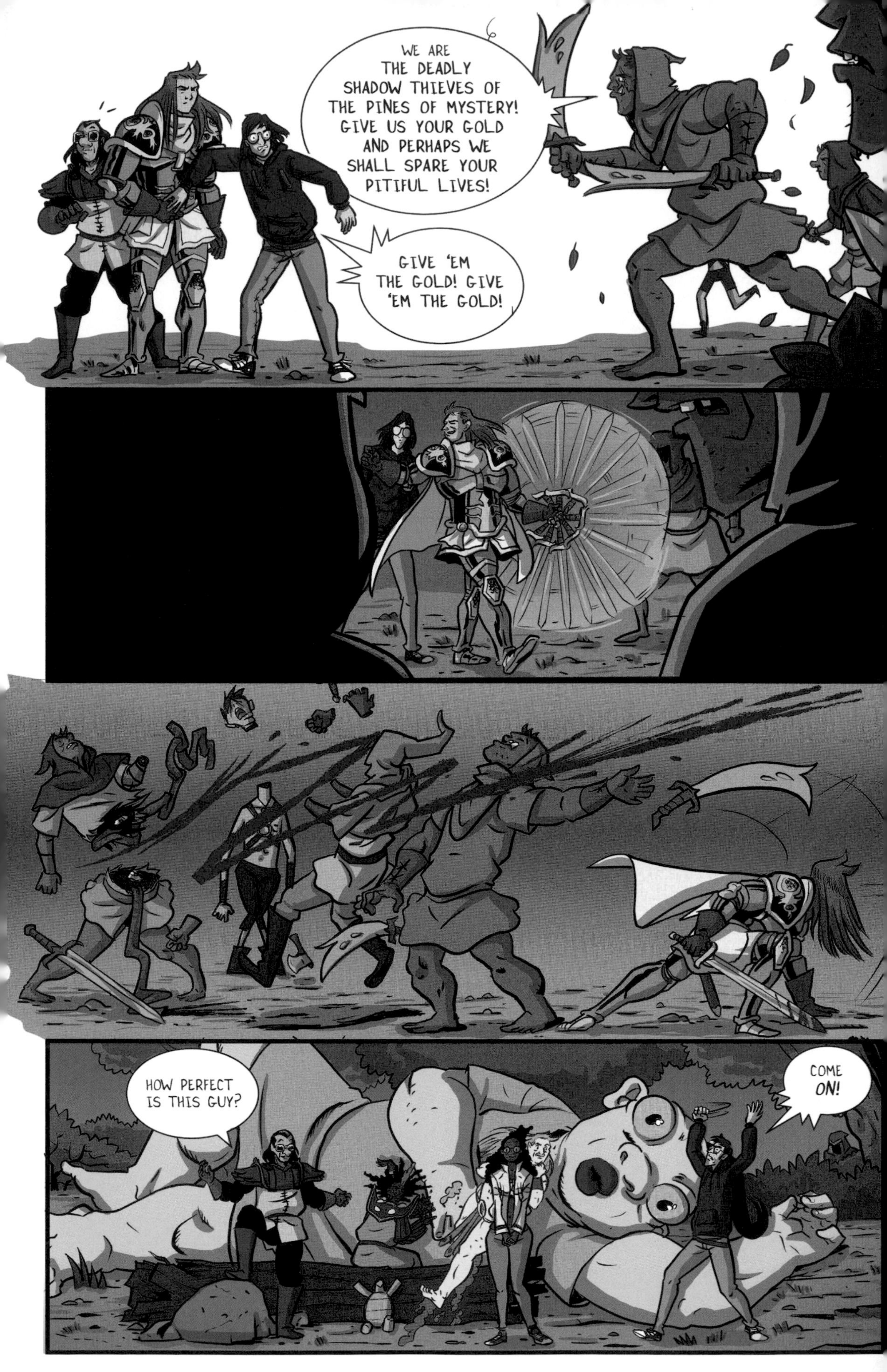
WE ARE THE DEADLY SHADOW THIEVES OF THE PINES OF MYSTERY! GIVE US YOUR GOLD AND PERHAPS WE SHALL SPARE YOUR PITIFUL LIVES!
GIVE 'EM THE GOLD! GIVE 'EM THE GOLD!
HOW PERFECT IS THIS GUY?
COME ON!

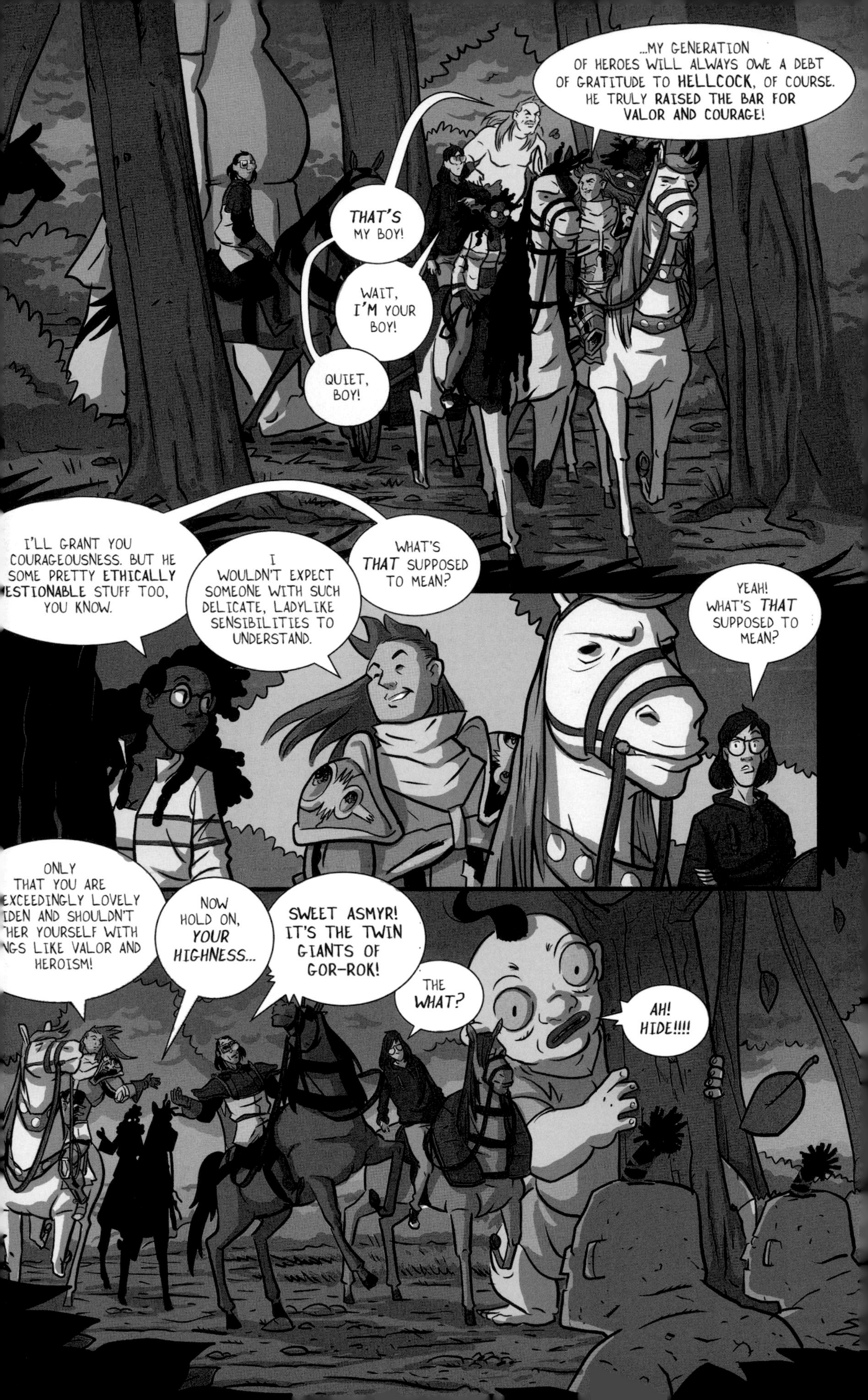
...MY GENERATION OF HEROES WILL ALWAYS OWE A DEBT OF GRATITUDE TO HELLCOCK, OF COURSE. HE TRULY RAISED THE BAR FOR VALOR AND COURAGE!
THAT'S MY BOY!
WAIT, I'M YOUR BOY!
QUIET, BOY!
I'LL GRANT YOU COURAGEOUSNESS. BUT HE SOME PRETTY ETHICALLY ESTIONABLE STUFF TOO, YOU KNOW.
I WOULDN'T EXPECT SOMEONE WITH SUCH DELICATE, LADYLIKE SENSIBILITIES TO UNDERSTAND.
WHAT'S THAT SUPPOSED TO MEAN?
YEAH! WHAT'S THAT SUPPOSED TO MEAN?
ONLY THAT YOU ARE EXCEEDINGLY LOVELY IDEN AND SHOULDN'T THER YOURSELF WITH NGS LIKE VALOR AND HEROISM!
NOW HOLD ON, YOUR HIGHNESS...
SWEET ASMYR! IT'S THE TWIN GIANTS OF GOR-ROK!
THE WHAT?
AH! HIDE!!!!

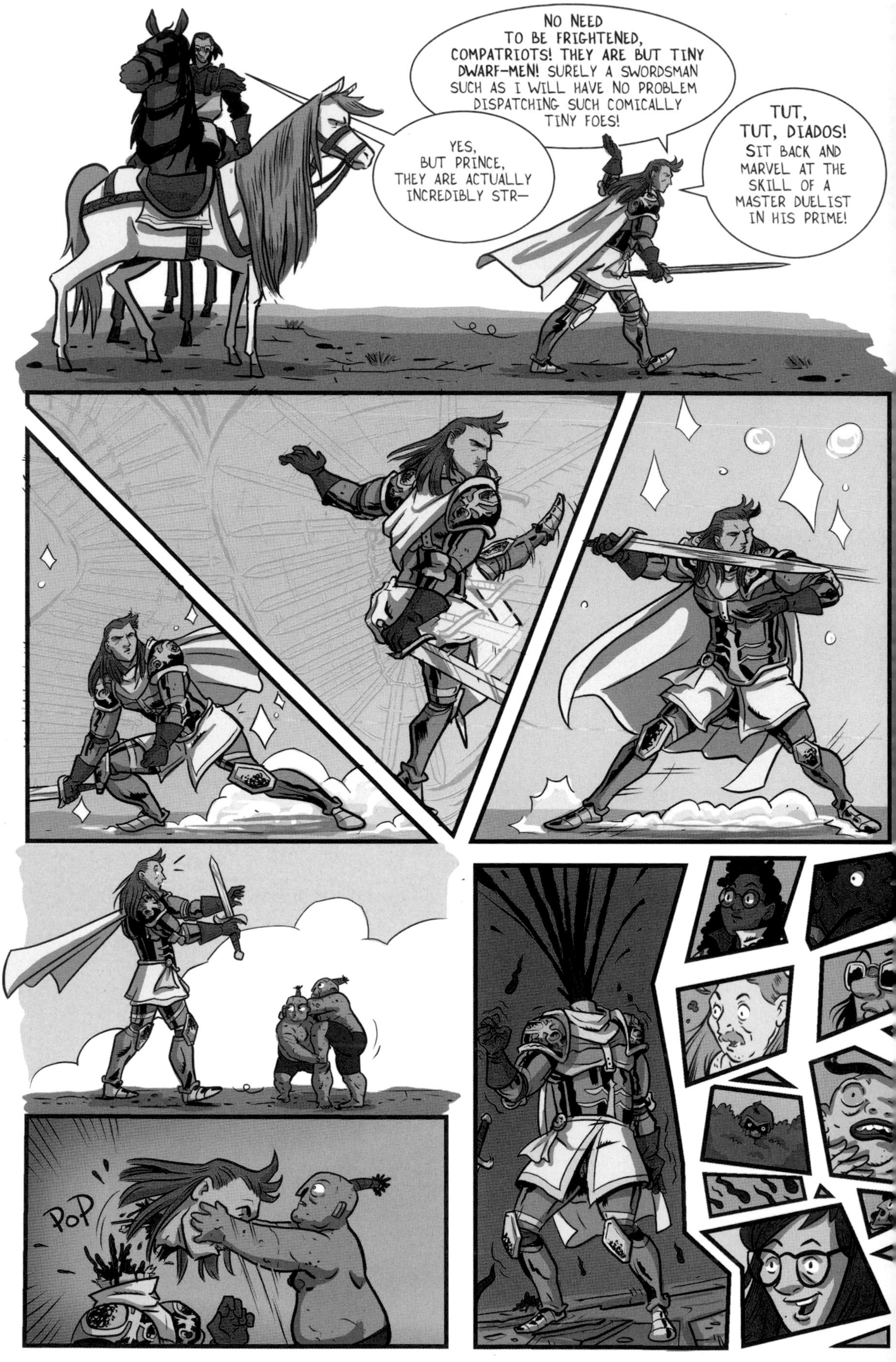
NO NEED TO BE FRIGHTENED, COMPATRIOTS! THEY ARE BUT TINY DWARF-MEN! SURELY A SWORDSMAN SUCH AS I WILL HAVE NO PROBLEM DISPATCHING SUCH COMICALLY TINY FOES!
YES, BUT PRINCE, THEY ARE ACTUALLY INCREDIBLY STR—
TUT, TUT, DIADOS! SIT BACK AND MARVEL AT THE SKILL OF A MASTER DUELIST IN HIS PRIME!
POP

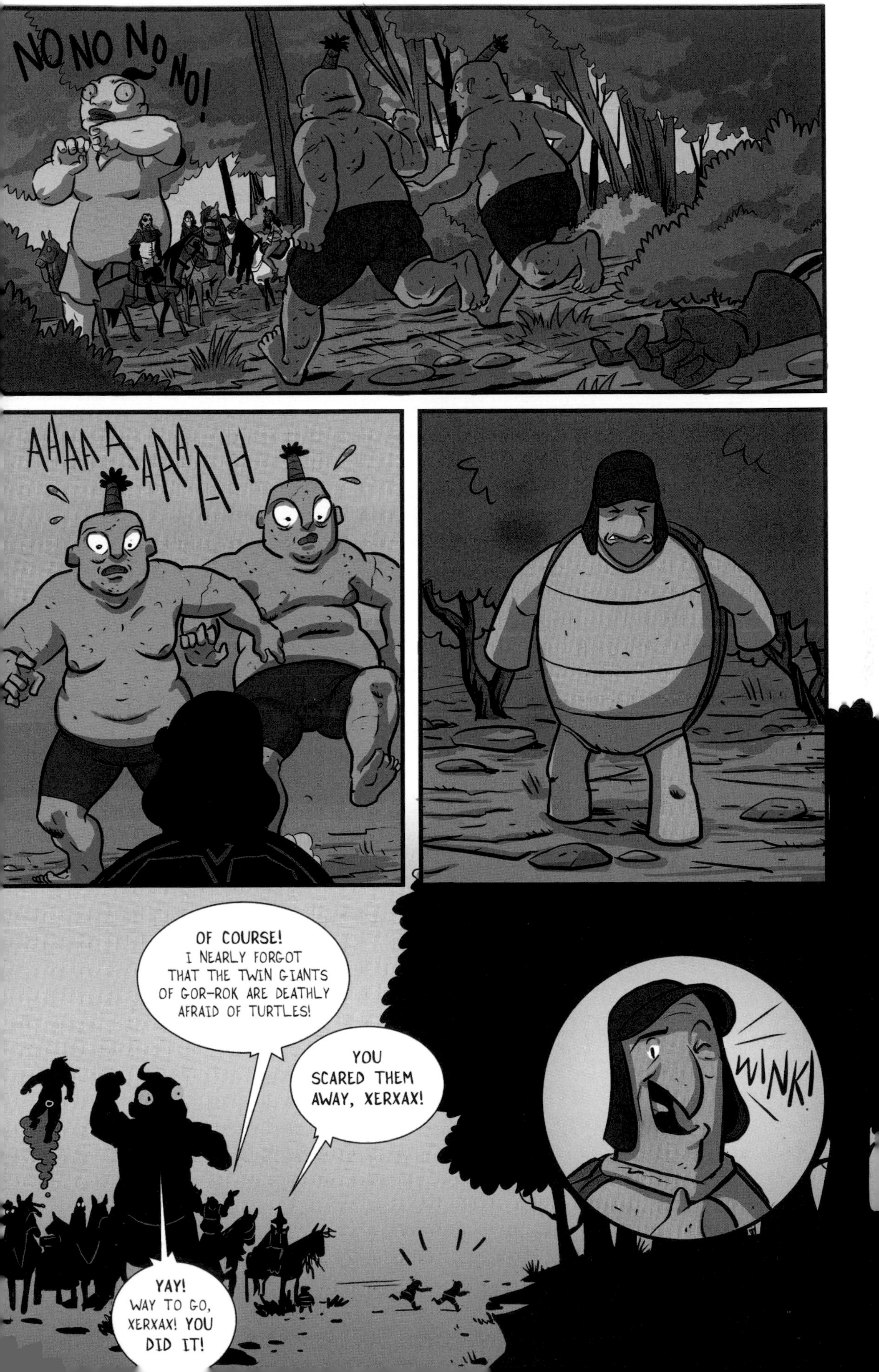
NO NO NO NO NO!
AHAAAAAAAH
OF COURSE! I NEARLY FORGOT THAT THE TWIN GIANTS OF GOR-ROK ARE DEATHLY AFRAID OF TURTLES!
YOU SCARED THEM AWAY, XERXAX!
YAY! WAY TO GO, XERXAX! YOU DID IT!
WINK!

LATER...

AH! ANOTHER **BEAUTIFUL** DAY FOR QUESTING, EH? LET'S GET A MOVE ON!

FIRST WE MUST PERFORM THE FUNERAL RITES FOR POOR, POOR PRINCE BOLDERON.

SNIFFLE...

ALLEN, WOULD YOU CARE TO SAY A FEW WORDS?

WHO, ME?

YES, YOU. YOU ARE THE LEADER OF THIS EXPEDITION... TECHNICALLY...

YEAH, BUT YOU SEE, I DIDN'T KNOW THE GUY VERY WELL.

JUST SAY WHATEVER IS IN YOUR HEART, ALLEN.

UH, **RIGHT**. SURE. OKAY.

SOON...

AHEM. GOOD MORNING. UH, WE ARE GATHERED HERE TODAY TO MOURN THE MEMORY OF A VERY... WELL-HAIRCUTTED... PERSON. PRINCE BOLDERON WAS A MAN WHO LOVED MANY THINGS. HE LOVED **KEBABS, WEAPONS,** AND...CAMPFIRES?

WHY, ASYMR, WHY?!

BUT MOST OF ALL, HE LOVED TO TALK **ENDLESSLY** ABOUT ALL OF THE ADVENTURES HE **CLAIMED** TO HAVE BEEN ON. OH, HOW HE LOVED TO **TALK** AND TALK AND TALK. AND TALK.

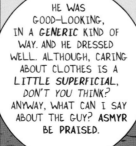

HE WAS GOOD-LOOKING, IN A **GENERIC** KIND OF WAY. AND HE DRESSED WELL. ALTHOUGH, CARING ABOUT CLOTHES IS A **LITTLE SUPERFICIAL**, DON'T YOU THINK? ANYWAY, WHAT CAN I SAY ABOUT THE GUY? **ASYMR** BE PRAISED.

WE WILL NOW FIRE THE CEREMONIAL FLAME ARROW!

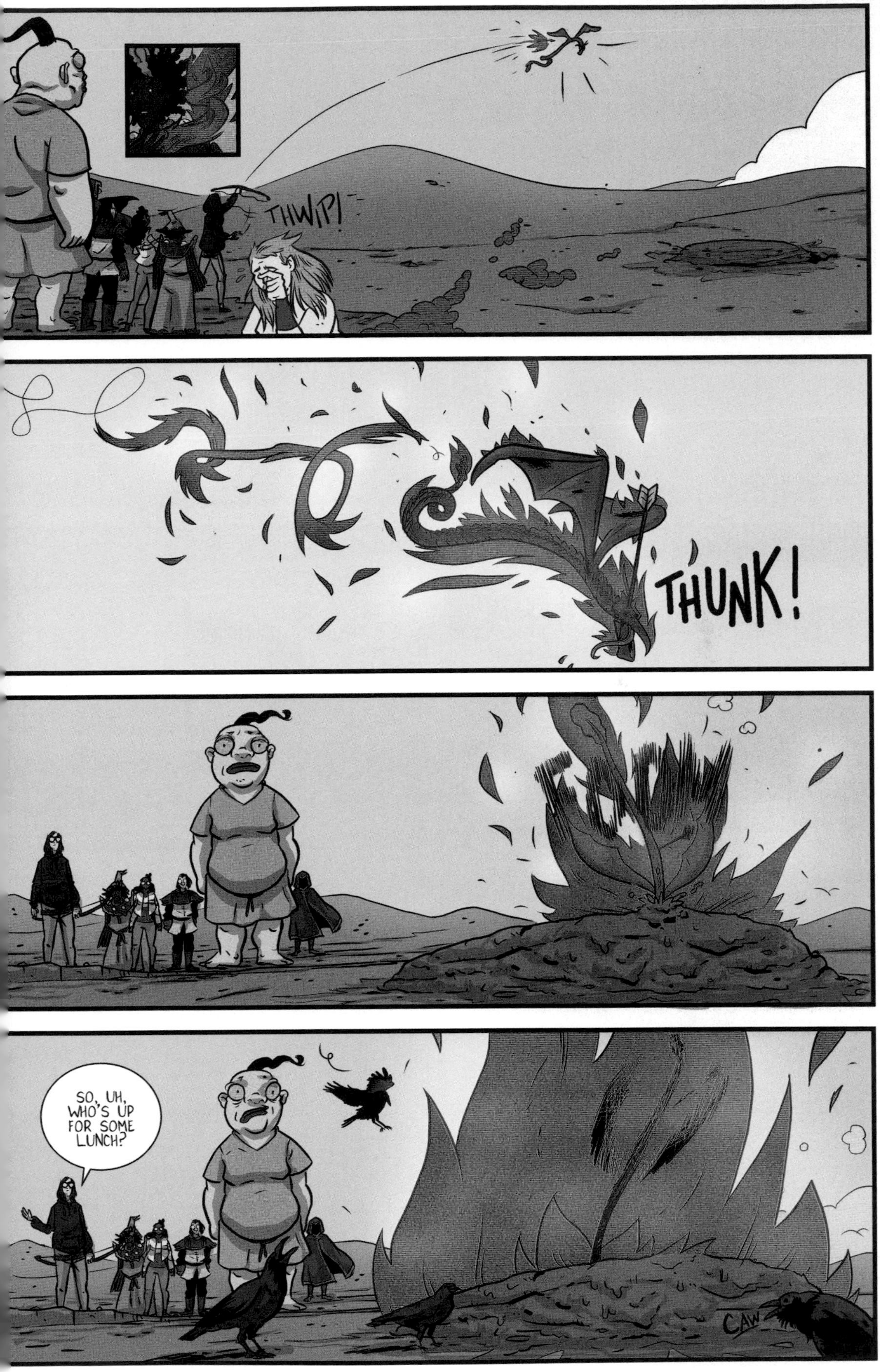
THWIP!
THUNK!
SO, UH, WHO'S UP FOR SOME LUNCH?
CAW

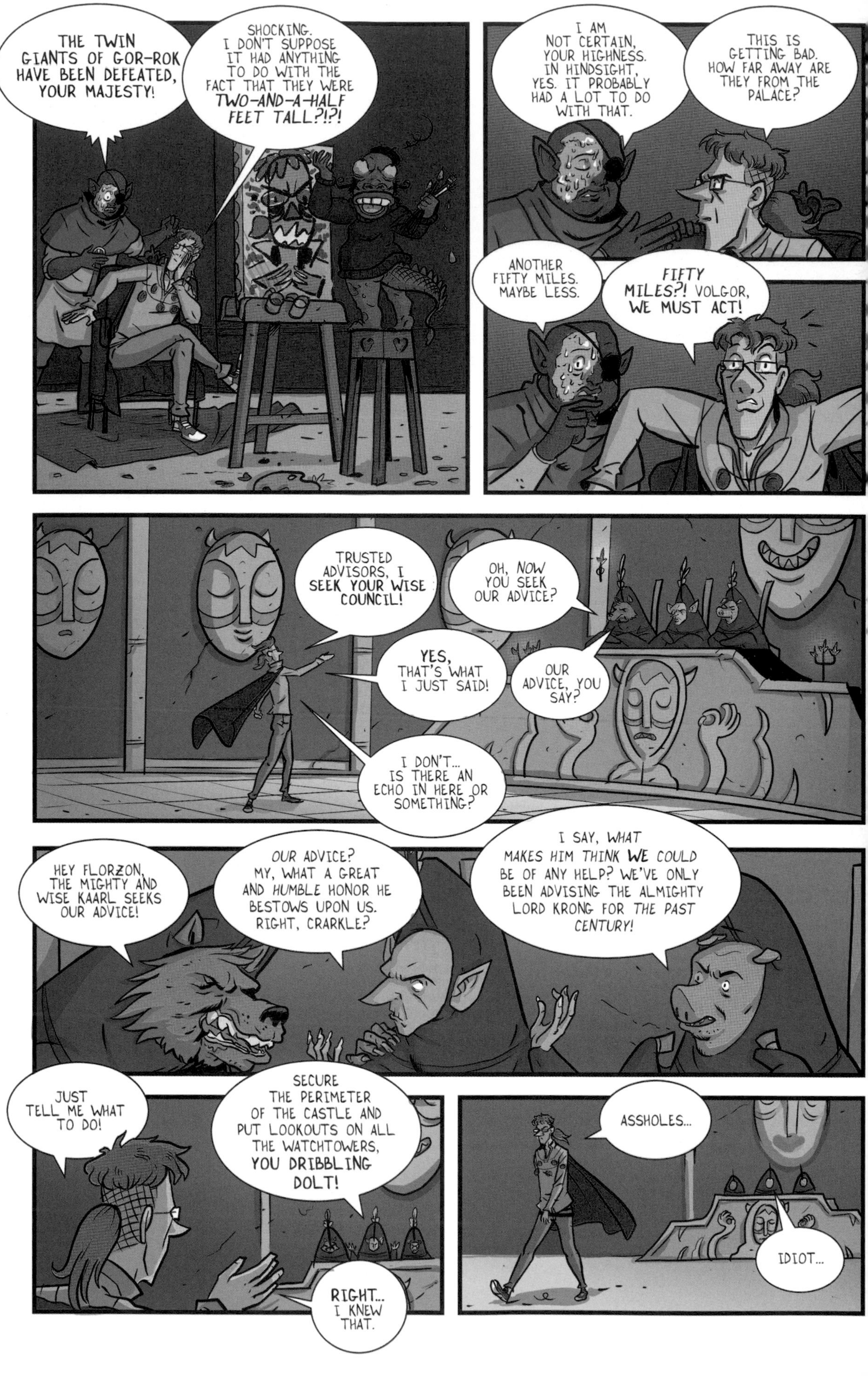
THE TWIN GIANTS OF GOR-ROK HAVE BEEN DEFEATED, YOUR MAJESTY!
SHOCKING. I DON'T SUPPOSE IT HAD ANYTHING TO DO WITH THE FACT THAT THEY WERE TWO-AND-A-HALF FEET TALL?!?!
I AM NOT CERTAIN, YOUR HIGHNESS. IN HINDSIGHT, YES. IT PROBABLY HAD A LOT TO DO WITH THAT.
THIS IS GETTING BAD. HOW FAR AWAY ARE THEY FROM THE PALACE?
ANOTHER FIFTY MILES. MAYBE LESS.
FIFTY MILES?! VOLGOR, WE MUST ACT!
TRUSTED ADVISORS, I SEEK YOUR WISE COUNCIL!
OH, NOW YOU SEEK OUR ADVICE?
YES, THAT'S WHAT I JUST SAID!
OUR ADVICE, YOU SAY?
I DON'T... IS THERE AN ECHO IN HERE OR SOMETHING?
HEY FLORZON, THE MIGHTY AND WISE KAARL SEEKS OUR ADVICE!
OUR ADVICE? MY, WHAT A GREAT AND HUMBLE HONOR HE BESTOWS UPON US. RIGHT, CRARKLE?
I SAY, WHAT MAKES HIM THINK WE COULD BE OF ANY HELP? WE'VE ONLY BEEN ADVISING THE ALMIGHTY LORD KRONG FOR THE PAST CENTURY!
JUST TELL ME WHAT TO DO!
SECURE THE PERIMETER OF THE CASTLE AND PUT LOOKOUTS ON ALL THE WATCHTOWERS, YOU DRIBBLING DOLT!
RIGHT... I KNEW THAT.
ASSHOLES...
IDIOT...

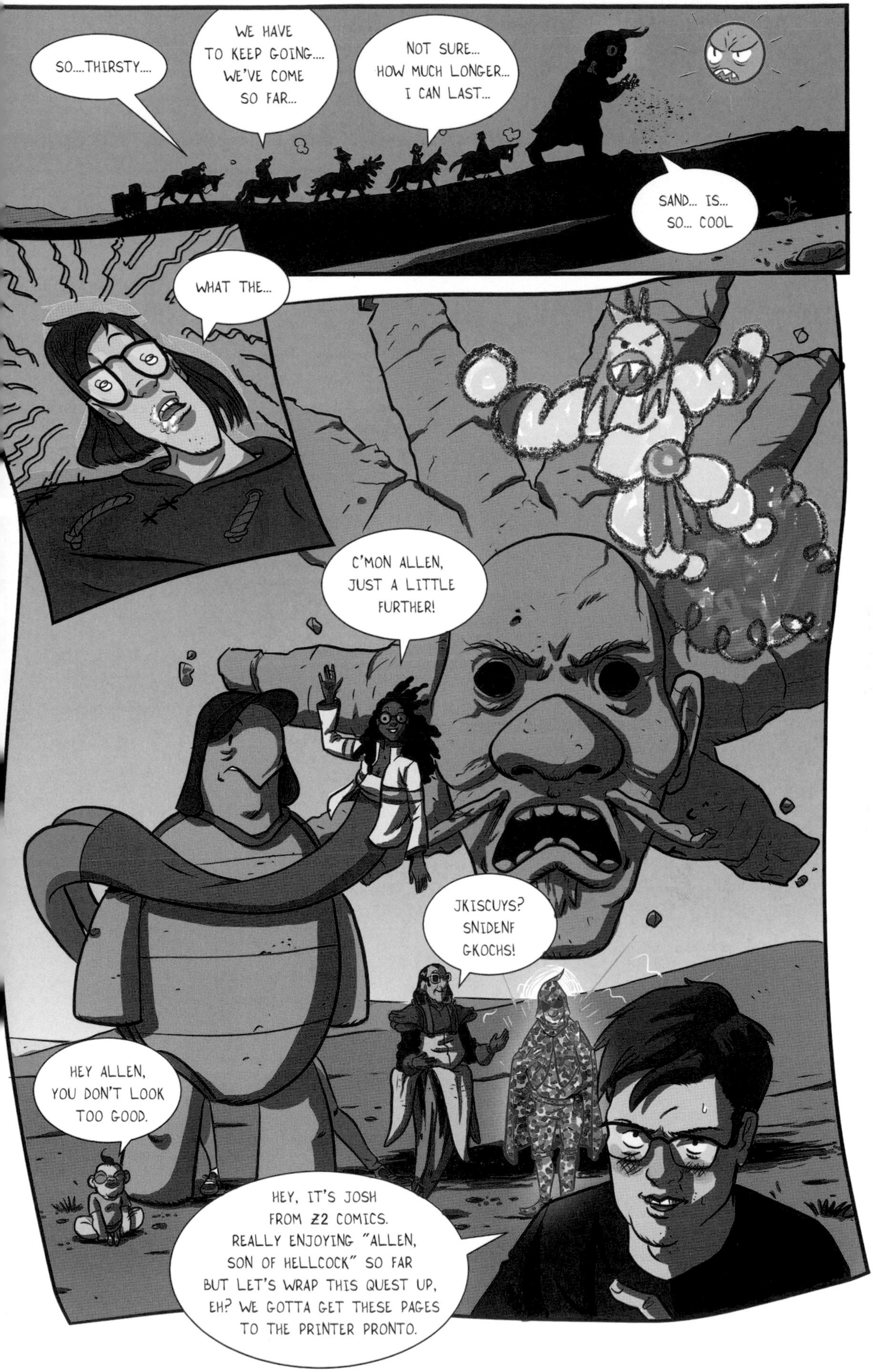
SO....THIRSTY....
WE HAVE TO KEEP GOING.... WE'VE COME SO FAR...
NOT SURE... HOW MUCH LONGER... I CAN LAST...
SAND... IS... SO... COOL
WHAT THE...
C'MON ALLEN, JUST A LITTLE FURTHER!
JKISCUYS? SNIDENF GKOCHS!
HEY ALLEN, YOU DON'T LOOK TOO GOOD.
HEY, IT'S JOSH FROM Z2 COMICS. REALLY ENJOYING "ALLEN, SON OF HELLCOCK" SO FAR BUT LET'S WRAP THIS QUEST UP, EH? WE GOTTA GET THESE PAGES TO THE PRINTER PRONTO.

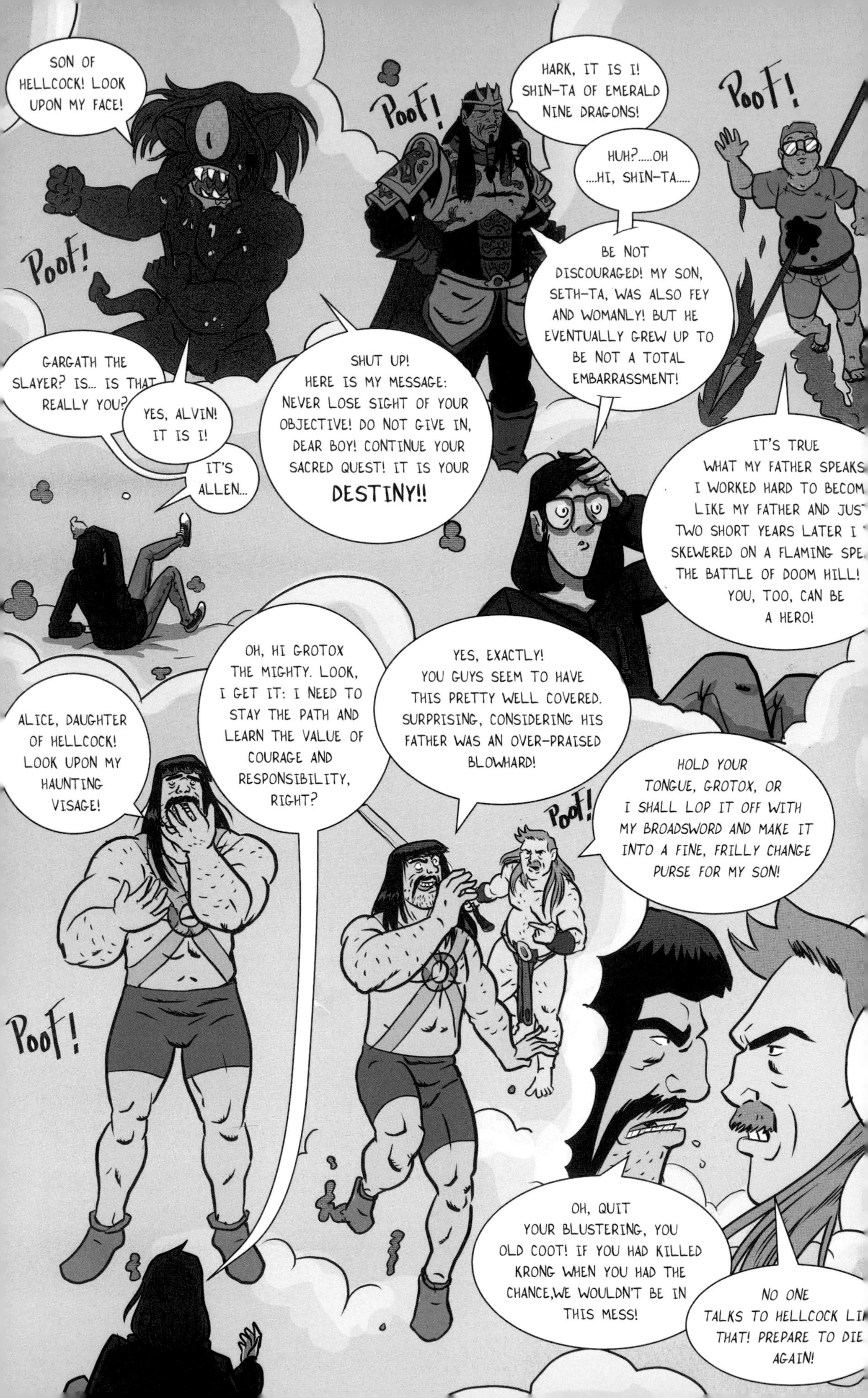
SON OF HELLCOCK! LOOK UPON MY FACE!
POOF!
POOF!
HARK, IT IS I! SHIN-TA OF EMERALD NINE DRAGONS!
HUH?.....OH ....HI, SHIN-TA.....
BE NOT DISCOURAGED! MY SON, SETH-TA, WAS ALSO FEY AND WOMANLY! BUT HE EVENTUALLY GREW UP TO BE NOT A TOTAL EMBARRASSMENT!
POOF!
GARGATH THE SLAYER? IS... IS THAT REALLY YOU?
YES, ALVIN! IT IS I!
IT'S ALLEN...
SHUT UP! HERE IS MY MESSAGE: NEVER LOSE SIGHT OF YOUR OBJECTIVE! DO NOT GIVE IN, DEAR BOY! CONTINUE YOUR SACRED QUEST! IT IS YOUR DESTINY!!
IT'S TRUE WHAT MY FATHER SPEAKS I WORKED HARD TO BECOM LIKE MY FATHER AND JUS TWO SHORT YEARS LATER I SKEWERED ON A FLAMING SPE THE BATTLE OF DOOM HILL! YOU, TOO, CAN BE A HERO!
ALICE, DAUGHTER OF HELLCOCK! LOOK UPON MY HAUNTING VISAGE!
POOF!
OH, HI GROTOX THE MIGHTY. LOOK, I GET IT: I NEED TO STAY THE PATH AND LEARN THE VALUE OF COURAGE AND RESPONSIBILITY, RIGHT?
YES, EXACTLY! YOU GUYS SEEM TO HAVE THIS PRETTY WELL COVERED. SURPRISING, CONSIDERING HIS FATHER WAS AN OVER-PRAISED BLOWHARD!
POOF!
HOLD YOUR TONGUE, GROTOX, OR I SHALL LOP IT OFF WITH MY BROADSWORD AND MAKE IT INTO A FINE, FRILLY CHANGE PURSE FOR MY SON!
OH, QUIT YOUR BLUSTERING, YOU OLD COOT! IF YOU HAD KILLED KRONG WHEN YOU HAD THE CHANCE,WE WOULDN'T BE IN THIS MESS!
NO ONE TALKS TO HELLCOCK LI THAT! PREPARE TO DIE AGAIN!

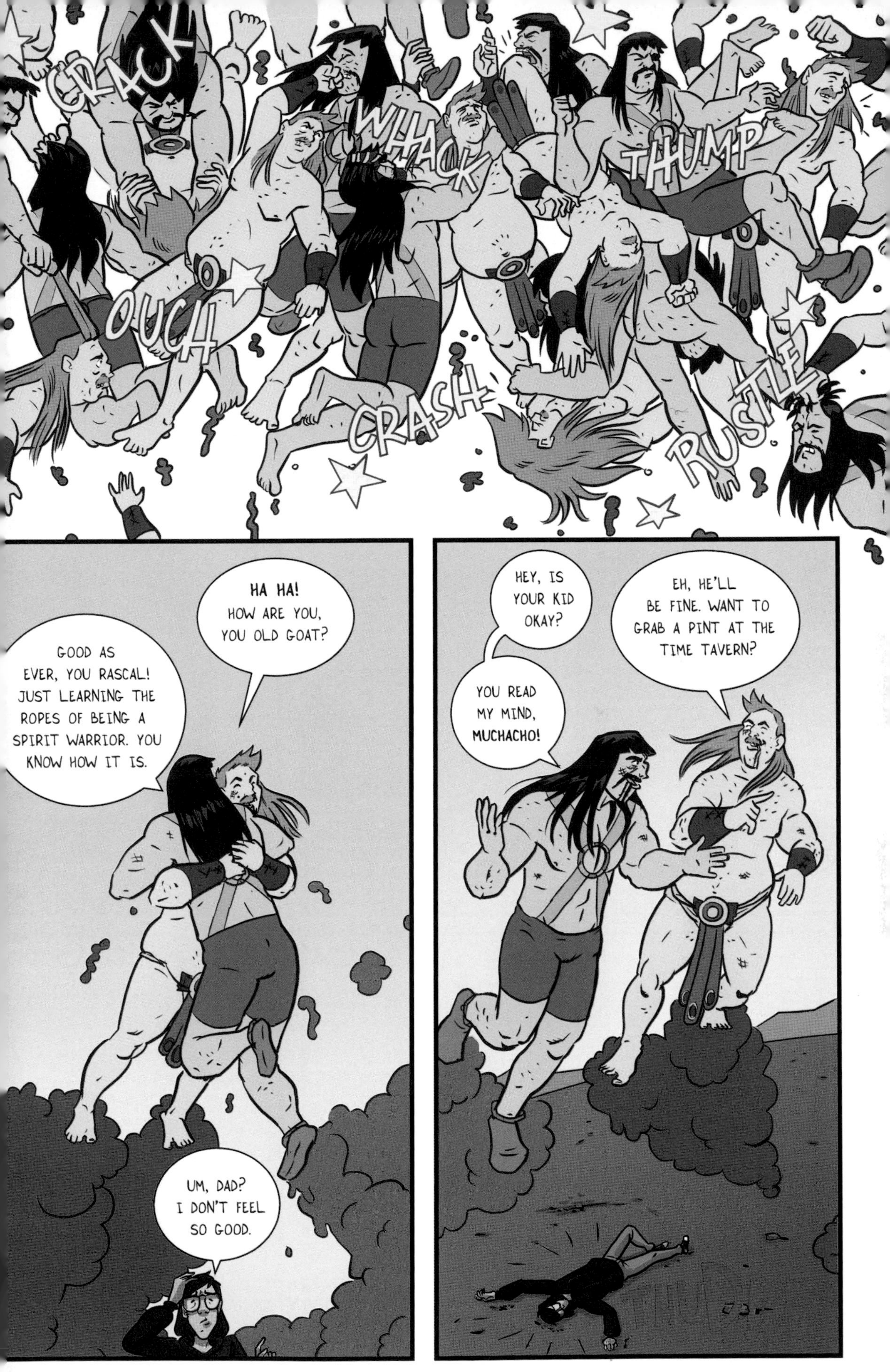
CRACK
WHACK
THUMP
OUCH
CRASH
RUSTLE
HA HA! HOW ARE YOU, YOU OLD GOAT?
GOOD AS EVER, YOU RASCAL! JUST LEARNING THE ROPES OF BEING A SPIRIT WARRIOR. YOU KNOW HOW IT IS.
UM, DAD? I DON'T FEEL SO GOOD.
HEY, IS YOUR KID OKAY?
EH, HE'LL BE FINE. WANT TO GRAB A PINT AT THE TIME TAVERN?
YOU READ MY MIND, MUCHACHO!

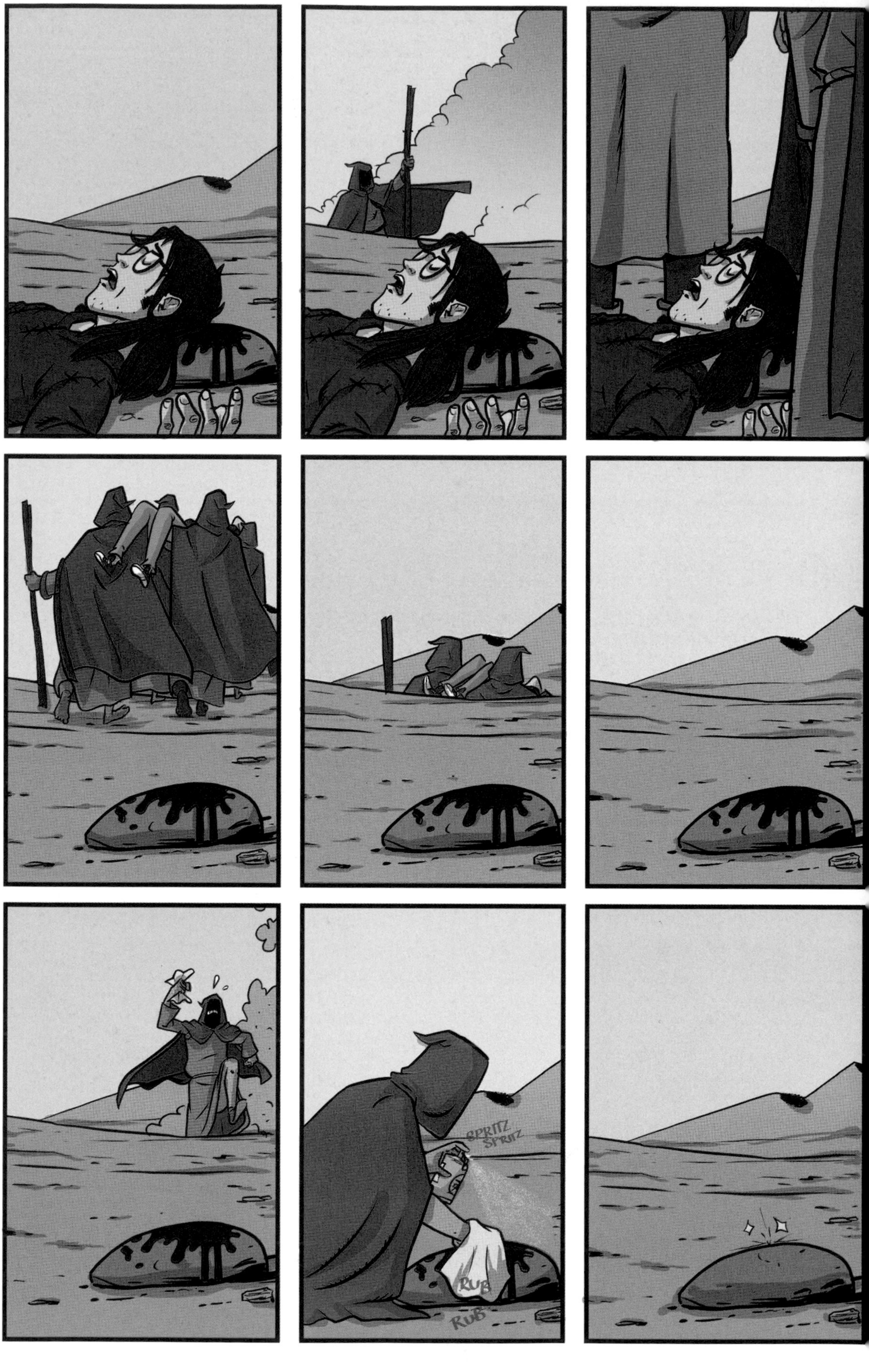
SPRITZ
SPRITZ
RUB
RUB

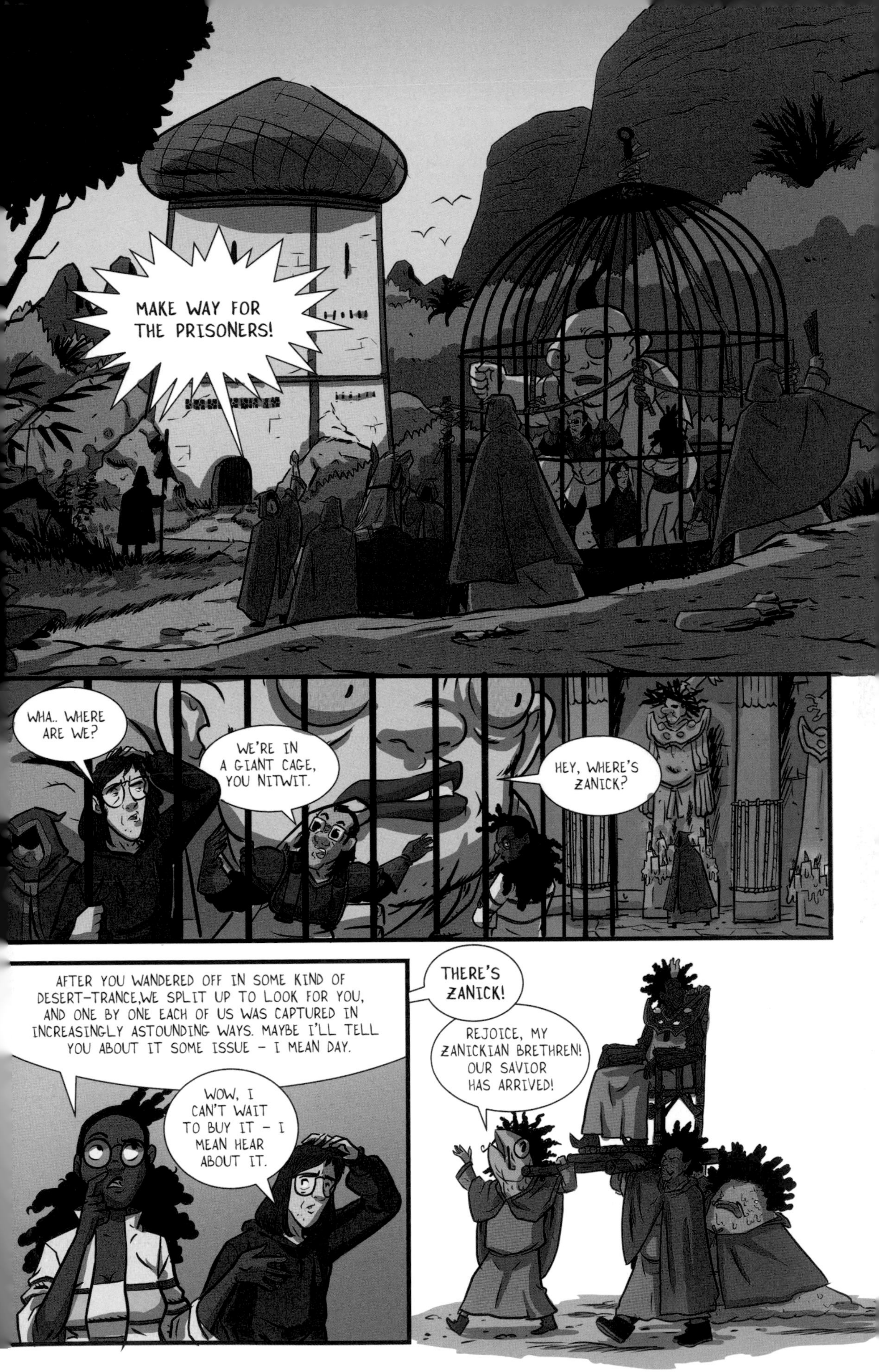
MAKE WAY FOR THE PRISONERS!
WHA.. WHERE ARE WE?
WE'RE IN A GIANT CAGE, YOU NITWIT.
HEY, WHERE'S ZANICK?
AFTER YOU WANDERED OFF IN SOME KIND OF DESERT-TRANCE,WE SPLIT UP TO LOOK FOR YOU, AND ONE BY ONE EACH OF US WAS CAPTURED IN INCREASINGLY ASTOUNDING WAYS. MAYBE I'LL TELL YOU ABOUT IT SOME ISSUE - I MEAN DAY.
WOW, I CAN'T WAIT TO BUY IT - I MEAN HEAR ABOUT IT.
THERE'S ZANICK!
REJOICE, MY ZANICKIAN BRETHREN! OUR SAVIOR HAS ARRIVED!

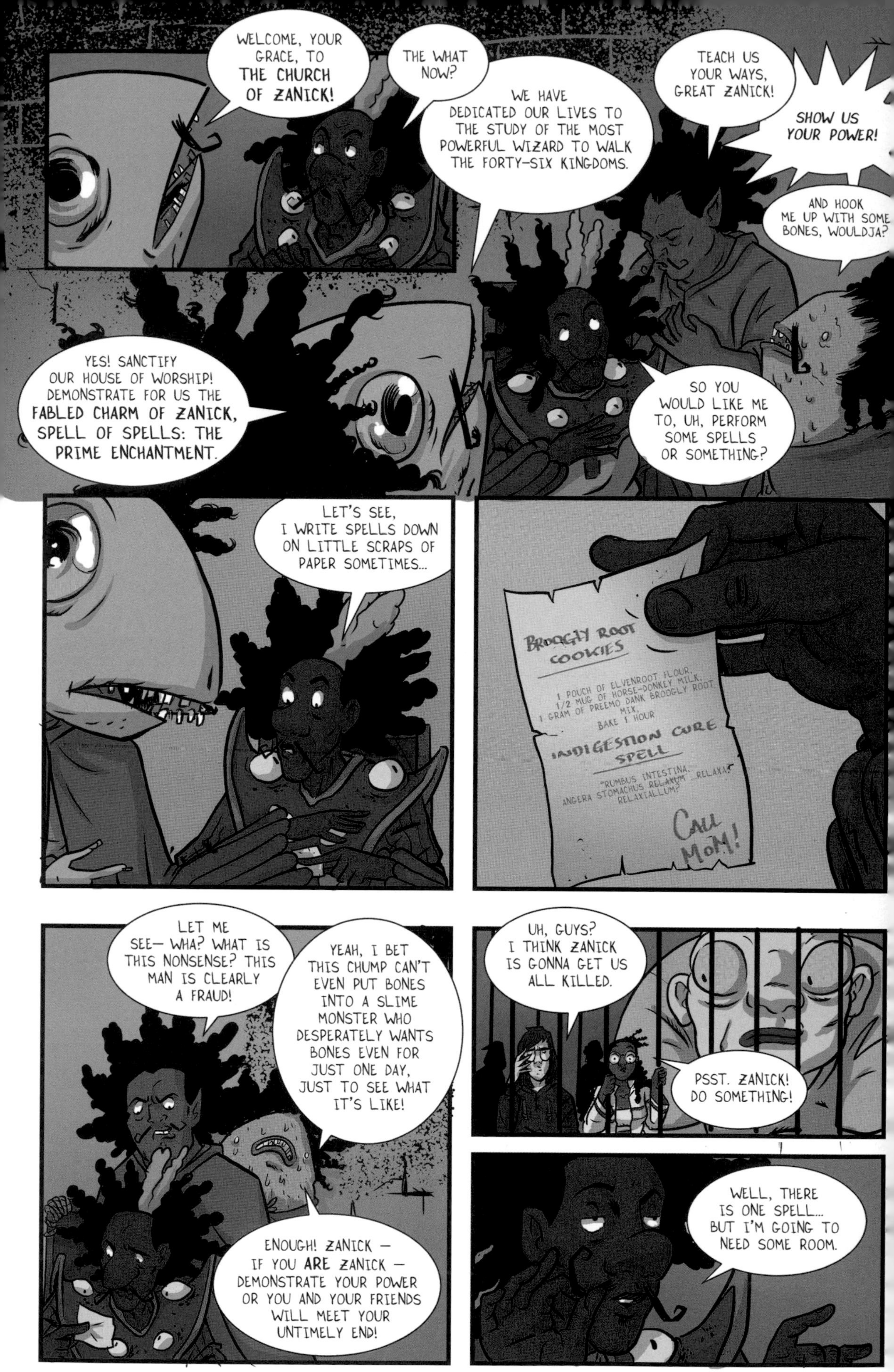
WELCOME, YOUR GRACE, TO THE CHURCH OF ZANICK!
THE WHAT NOW?
WE HAVE DEDICATED OUR LIVES TO THE STUDY OF THE MOST POWERFUL WIZARD TO WALK THE FORTY-SIX KINGDOMS.
TEACH US YOUR WAYS, GREAT ZANICK!
SHOW US YOUR POWER!
AND HOOK ME UP WITH SOME BONES, WOULDJA?
YES! SANCTIFY OUR HOUSE OF WORSHIP! DEMONSTRATE FOR US THE FABLED CHARM OF ZANICK, SPELL OF SPELLS: THE PRIME ENCHANTMENT.
SO YOU WOULD LIKE ME TO, UH, PERFORM SOME SPELLS OR SOMETHING?
LET'S SEE, I WRITE SPELLS DOWN ON LITTLE SCRAPS OF PAPER SOMETIMES...
BROOGLY ROOT COOKIES
1 POUCH OF ELVENROOT FLOUR,
1/2 MUG OF HORSE-DONKEY MILK,
1 GRAM OF PREEMO DANK BROOGLY ROOT MIX,
BAKE 1 HOUR
INDIGESTION CURE SPELL
"RUMBUS INTESTINA, ANGERA STOMACHUS ~~RELAXUM~~ ...RELAXAS? RELAXIALLUM?
CALL MOM!
LET ME SEE— WHA? WHAT IS THIS NONSENSE? THIS MAN IS CLEARLY A FRAUD!
YEAH, I BET THIS CHUMP CAN'T EVEN PUT BONES INTO A SLIME MONSTER WHO DESPERATELY WANTS BONES EVEN FOR JUST ONE DAY, JUST TO SEE WHAT IT'S LIKE!
ENOUGH! ZANICK — IF YOU ARE ZANICK — DEMONSTRATE YOUR POWER OR YOU AND YOUR FRIENDS WILL MEET YOUR UNTIMELY END!
UH, GUYS? I THINK ZANICK IS GONNA GET US ALL KILLED.
PSST. ZANICK! DO SOMETHING!
WELL, THERE IS ONE SPELL... BUT I'M GOING TO NEED SOME ROOM.

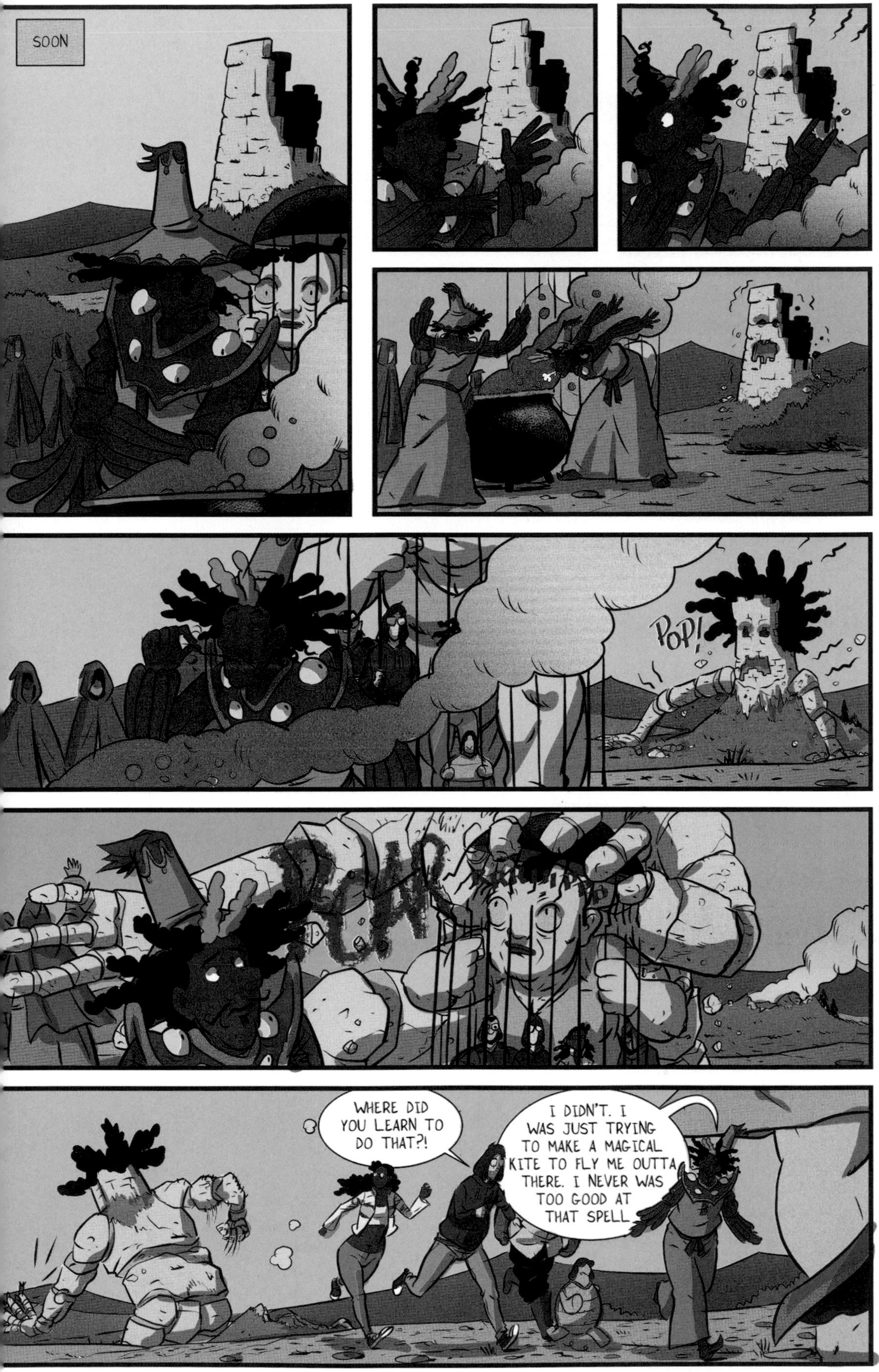
SOON
POP!
WHERE DID YOU LEARN TO DO THAT?!
I DIDN'T. I WAS JUST TRYING TO MAKE A MAGICAL KITE TO FLY ME OUTTA THERE. I NEVER WAS TOO GOOD AT THAT SPELL.

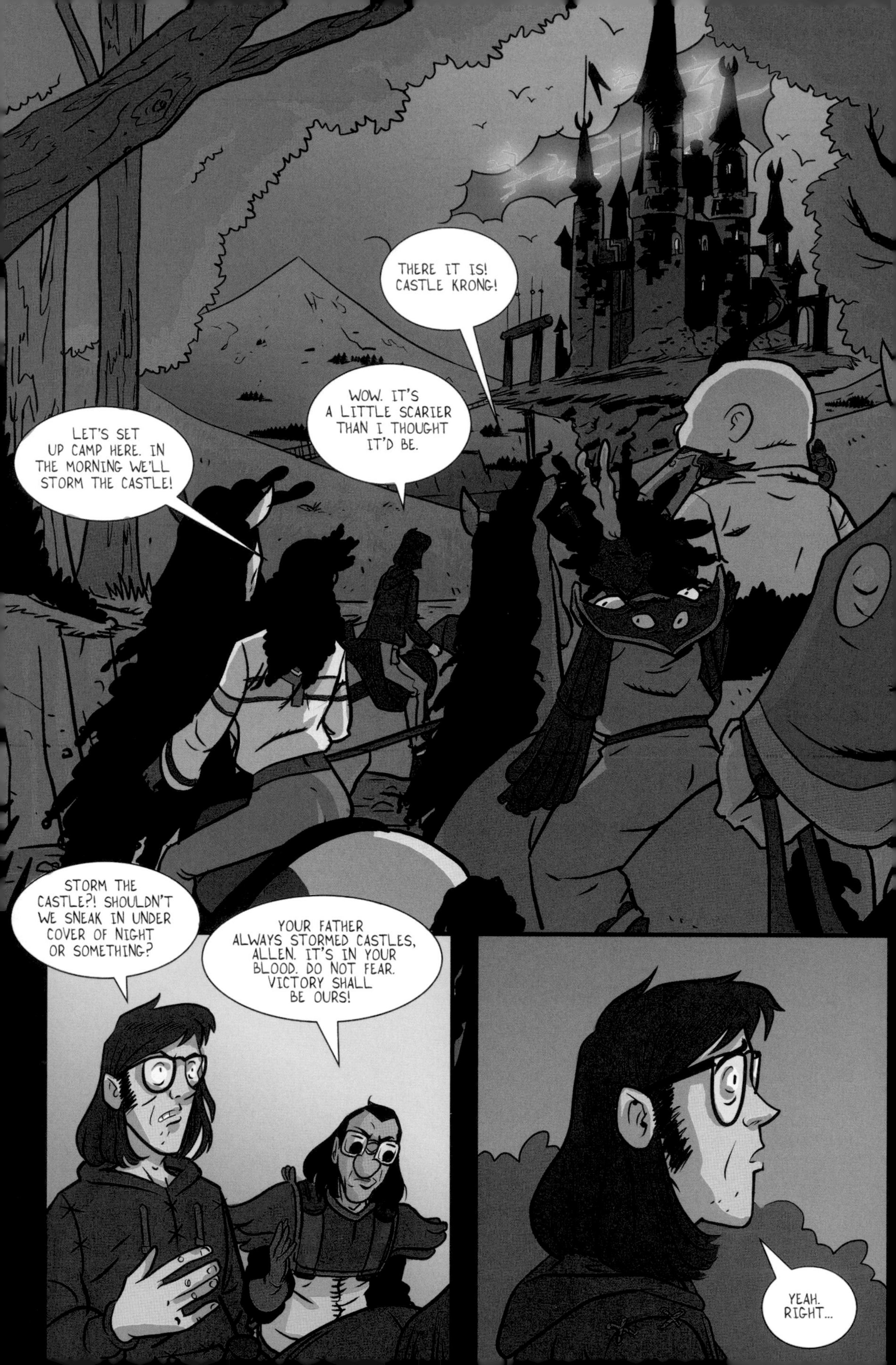
THERE IT IS! CASTLE KRONG!
WOW. IT'S A LITTLE SCARIER THAN I THOUGHT IT'D BE.
LET'S SET UP CAMP HERE. IN THE MORNING WE'LL STORM THE CASTLE!
STORM THE CASTLE?! SHOULDN'T WE SNEAK IN UNDER COVER OF NIGHT OR SOMETHING?
YOUR FATHER ALWAYS STORMED CASTLES, ALLEN. IT'S IN YOUR BLOOD. DO NOT FEAR. VICTORY SHALL BE OURS!
YEAH. RIGHT...

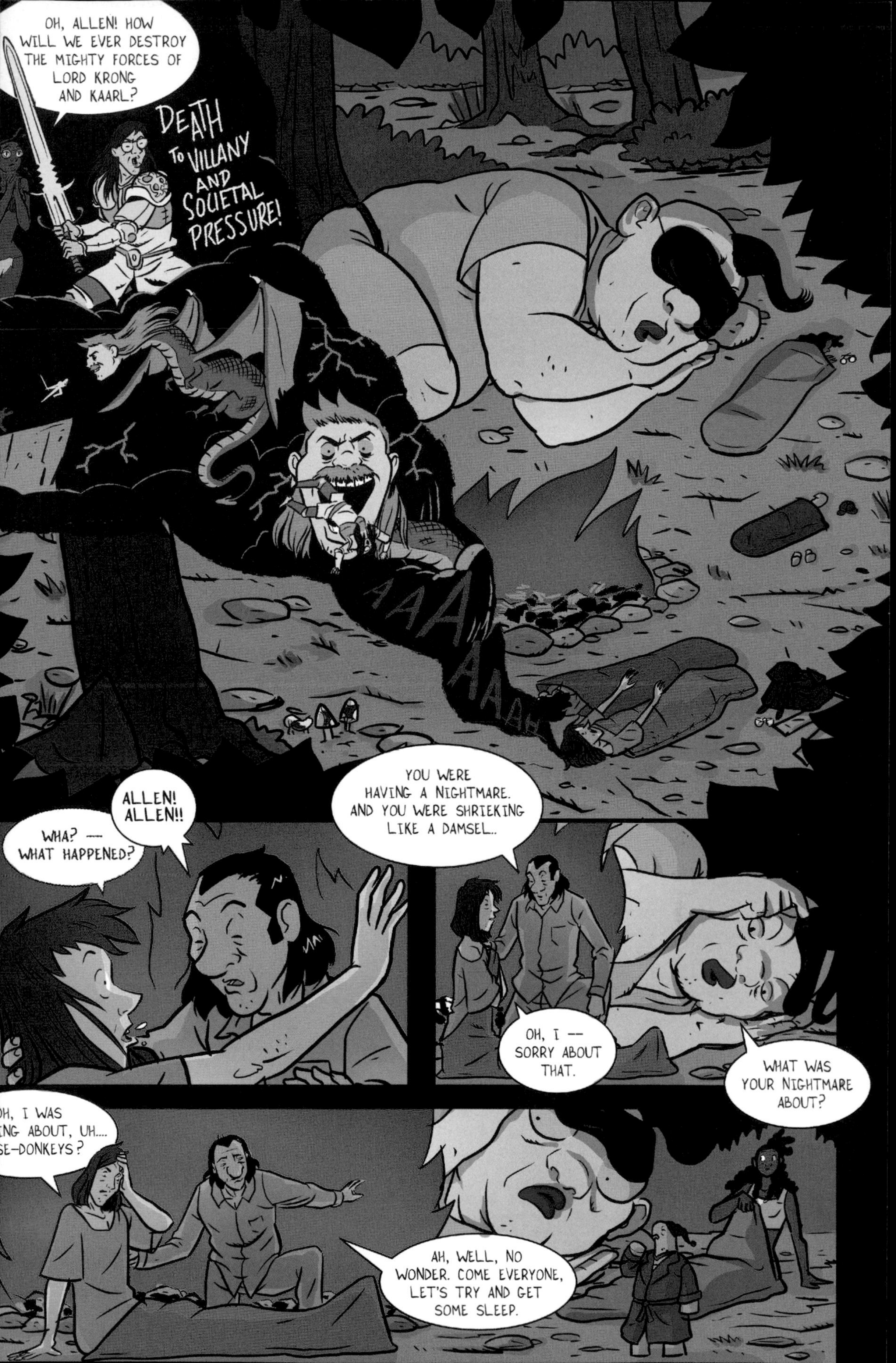
OH, ALLEN! HOW WILL WE EVER DESTROY THE MIGHTY FORCES OF LORD KRONG AND KAARL?
DEATH TO VILLANY AND SOCIETAL PRESSURE!
AAAAAAH
ALLEN! ALLEN!!
WHA? — WHAT HAPPENED?
YOU WERE HAVING A NIGHTMARE. AND YOU WERE SHRIEKING LIKE A DAMSEL..
OH, I — SORRY ABOUT THAT.
WHAT WAS YOUR NIGHTMARE ABOUT?
H, I WAS ING ABOUT, UH.... SE-DONKEYS?
AH, WELL, NO WONDER. COME EVERYONE, LET'S TRY AND GET SOME SLEEP.

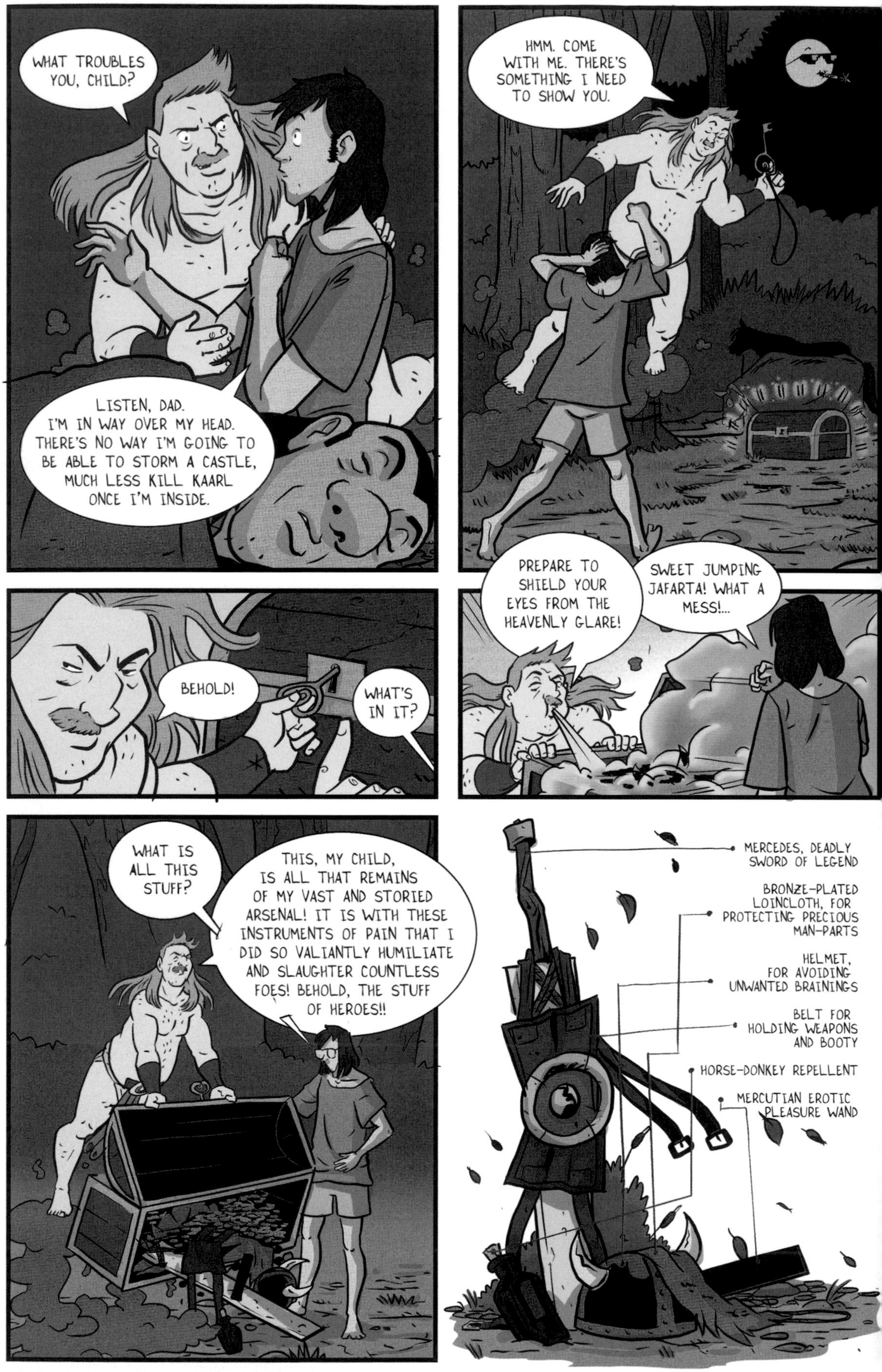
WHAT TROUBLES YOU, CHILD?
LISTEN, DAD. I'M IN WAY OVER MY HEAD. THERE'S NO WAY I'M GOING TO BE ABLE TO STORM A CASTLE, MUCH LESS KILL KAARL ONCE I'M INSIDE.
HMM. COME WITH ME. THERE'S SOMETHING I NEED TO SHOW YOU.
BEHOLD!
WHAT'S IN IT?
PREPARE TO SHIELD YOUR EYES FROM THE HEAVENLY GLARE!
SWEET JUMPING JAFARTA! WHAT A MESS!...
WHAT IS ALL THIS STUFF?
THIS, MY CHILD, IS ALL THAT REMAINS OF MY VAST AND STORIED ARSENAL! IT IS WITH THESE INSTRUMENTS OF PAIN THAT I DID SO VALIANTLY HUMILIATE AND SLAUGHTER COUNTLESS FOES! BEHOLD, THE STUFF OF HEROES!!
MERCEDES, DEADLY SWORD OF LEGEND
BRONZE-PLATED LOINCLOTH, FOR PROTECTING PRECIOUS MAN-PARTS
HELMET, FOR AVOIDING UNWANTED BRAININGS
BELT FOR HOLDING WEAPONS AND BOOTY
HORSE-DONKEY REPELLENT
MERCUTIAN EROTIC PLEASURE WAND

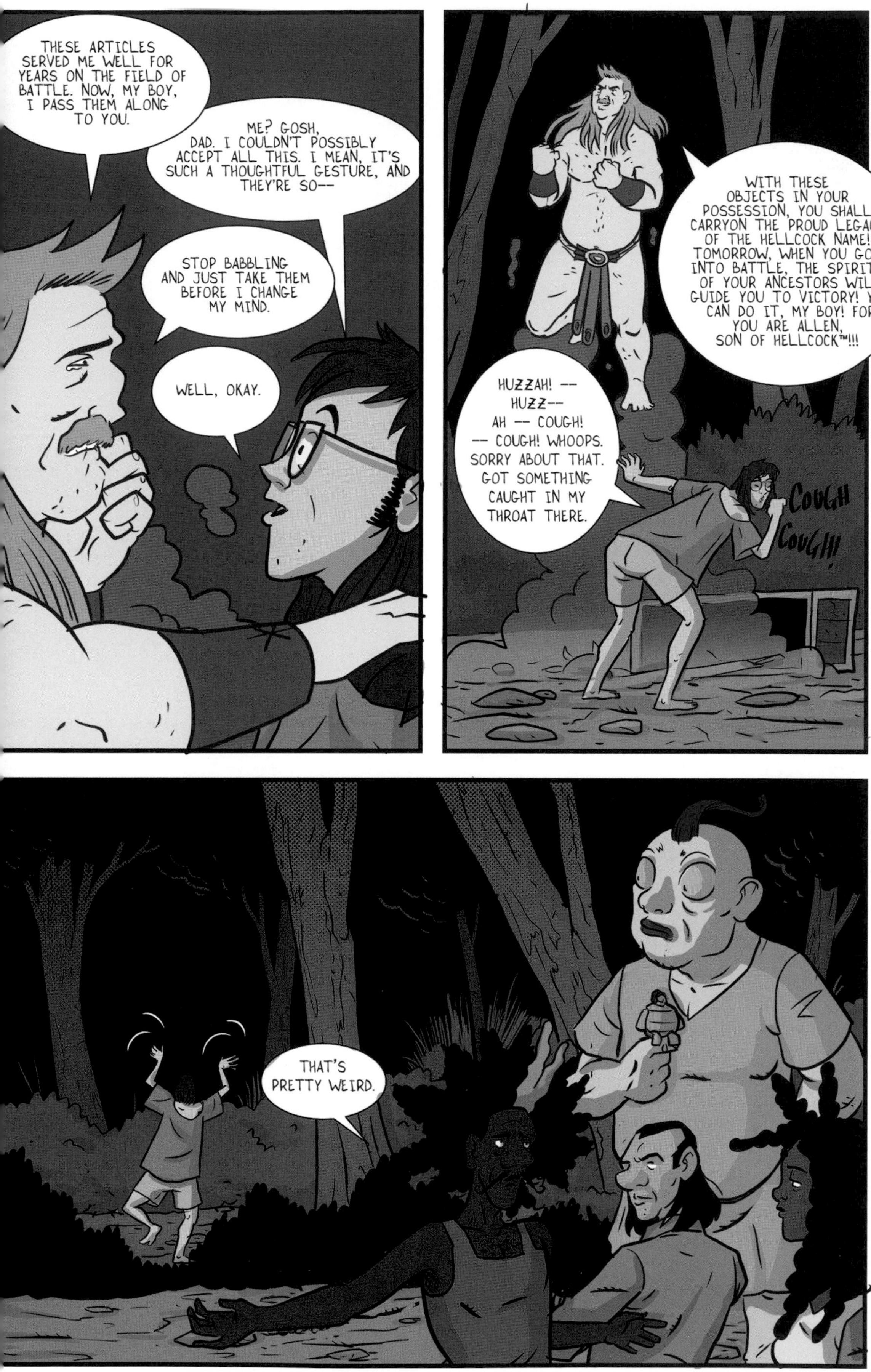
THESE ARTICLES SERVED ME WELL FOR YEARS ON THE FIELD OF BATTLE. NOW, MY BOY, I PASS THEM ALONG TO YOU.
ME? GOSH, DAD. I COULDN'T POSSIBLY ACCEPT ALL THIS. I MEAN, IT'S SUCH A THOUGHTFUL GESTURE, AND THEY'RE SO--
STOP BABBLING AND JUST TAKE THEM BEFORE I CHANGE MY MIND.
WELL, OKAY.
WITH THESE OBJECTS IN YOUR POSSESSION, YOU SHALL CARRYON THE PROUD LEGACY OF THE HELLCOCK NAME! TOMORROW, WHEN YOU GO INTO BATTLE, THE SPIRITS OF YOUR ANCESTORS WILL GUIDE YOU TO VICTORY! YOU CAN DO IT, MY BOY! FOR YOU ARE ALLEN, SON OF HELLCOCK™!!!
HUZZAH! -- HUZZ-- AH -- COUGH! -- COUGH! WHOOPS. SORRY ABOUT THAT. GOT SOMETHING CAUGHT IN MY THROAT THERE.
COUGH
COUGH!
THAT'S PRETTY WEIRD.

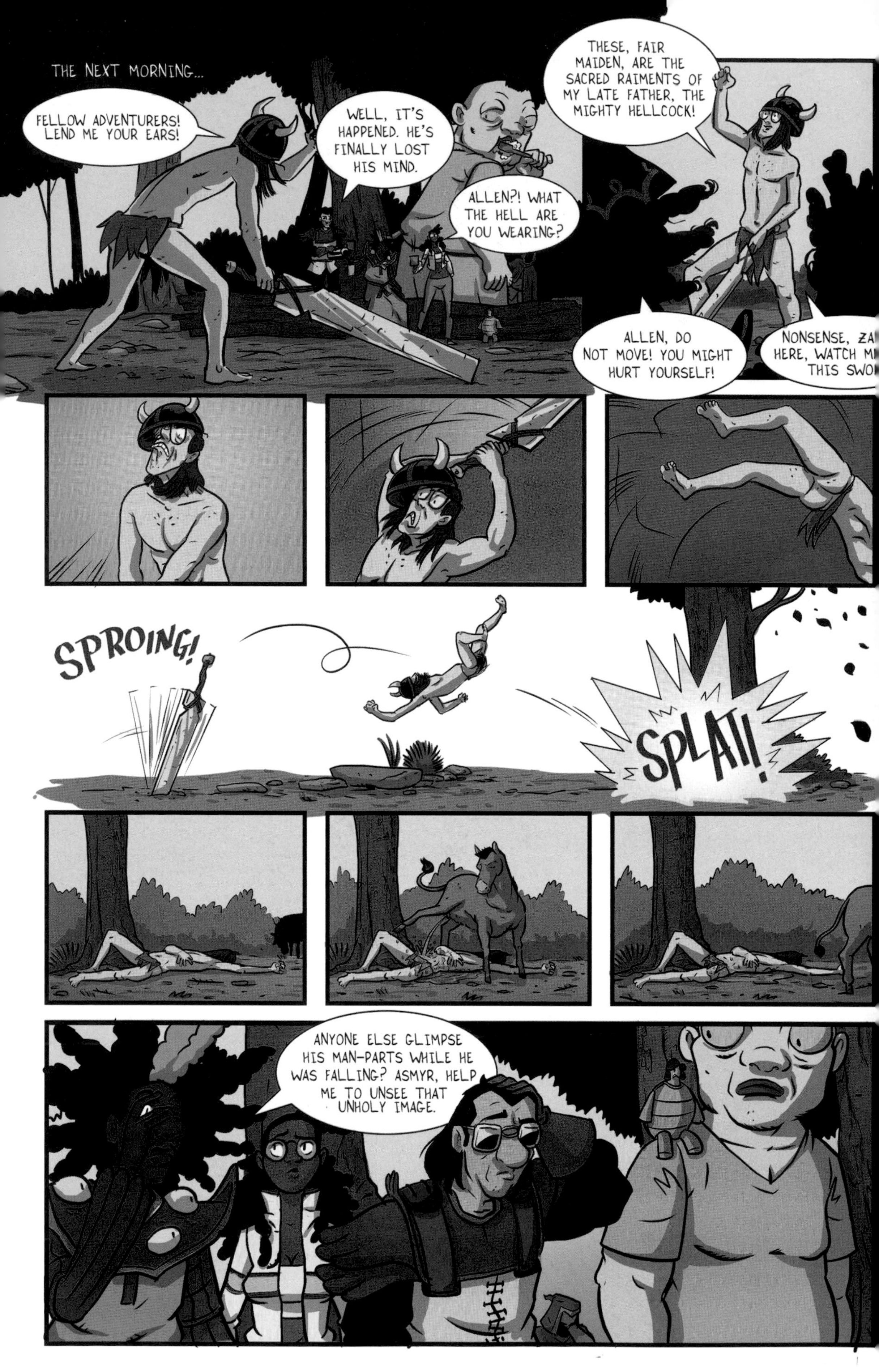
THE NEXT MORNING...
FELLOW ADVENTURERS! LEND ME YOUR EARS!
WELL, IT'S HAPPENED. HE'S FINALLY LOST HIS MIND.
ALLEN?! WHAT THE HELL ARE YOU WEARING?
THESE, FAIR MAIDEN, ARE THE SACRED RAIMENTS OF MY LATE FATHER, THE MIGHTY HELLCOCK!
ALLEN, DO NOT MOVE! YOU MIGHT HURT YOURSELF!
NONSENSE, ZA
HERE, WATCH M
THIS SWO
SPROING!
SPLAT!!
ANYONE ELSE GLIMPSE HIS MAN-PARTS WHILE HE WAS FALLING? ASMYR, HELP ME TO UNSEE THAT UNHOLY IMAGE.

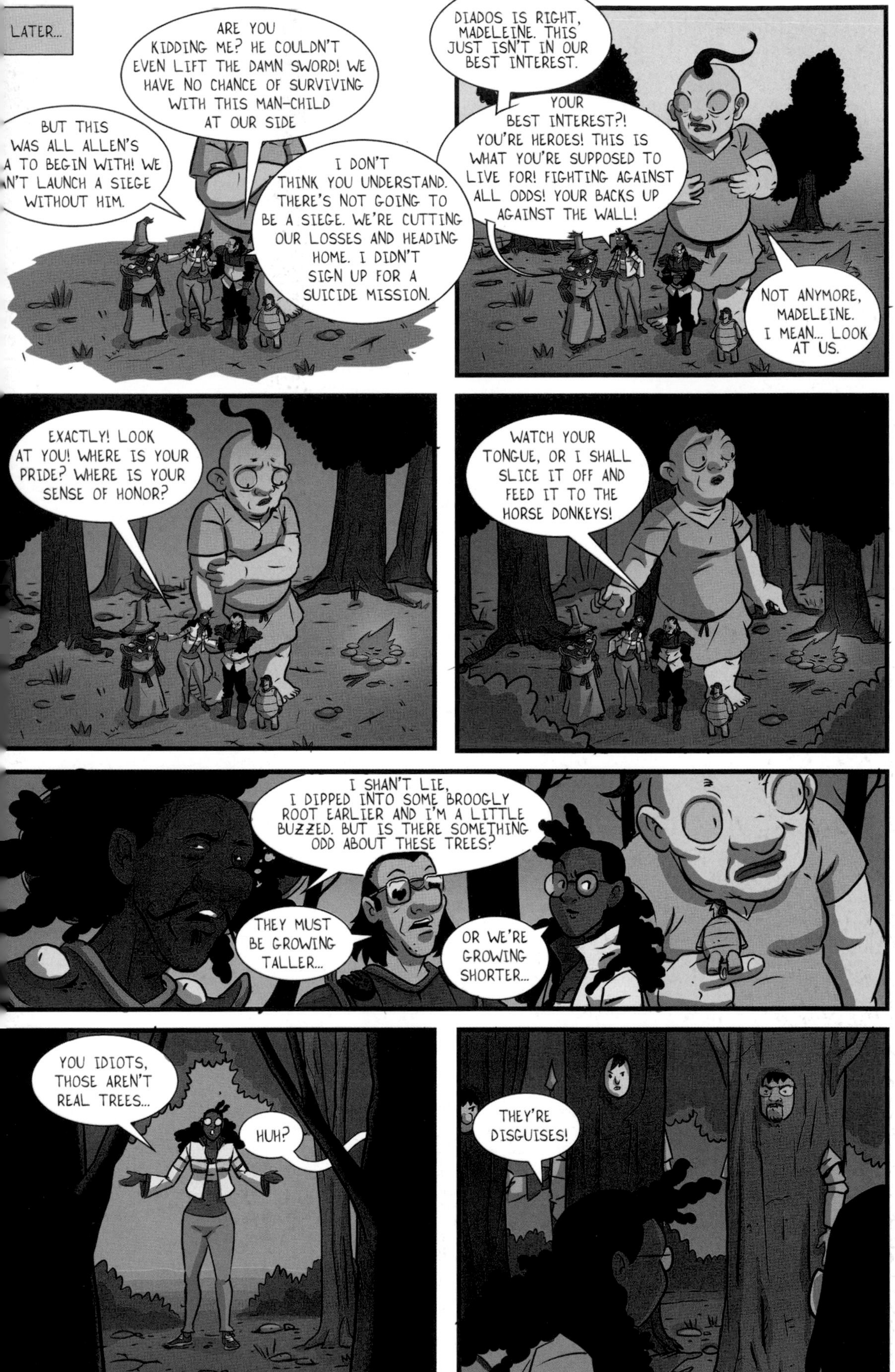
LATER...
ARE YOU KIDDING ME? HE COULDN'T EVEN LIFT THE DAMN SWORD! WE HAVE NO CHANCE OF SURVIVING WITH THIS MAN-CHILD AT OUR SIDE
BUT THIS WAS ALL ALLEN'S
A TO BEGIN WITH! WE
N'T LAUNCH A SIEGE WITHOUT HIM.
I DON'T THINK YOU UNDERSTAND. THERE'S NOT GOING TO BE A SIEGE. WE'RE CUTTING OUR LOSSES AND HEADING HOME. I DIDN'T SIGN UP FOR A SUICIDE MISSION.
DIADOS IS RIGHT, MADELEINE. THIS JUST ISN'T IN OUR BEST INTEREST.
YOUR BEST INTEREST?! YOU'RE HEROES! THIS IS WHAT YOU'RE SUPPOSED TO LIVE FOR! FIGHTING AGAINST ALL ODDS! YOUR BACKS UP AGAINST THE WALL!
NOT ANYMORE, MADELEINE. I MEAN... LOOK AT US.
EXACTLY! LOOK AT YOU! WHERE IS YOUR PRIDE? WHERE IS YOUR SENSE OF HONOR?
WATCH YOUR TONGUE, OR I SHALL SLICE IT OFF AND FEED IT TO THE HORSE DONKEYS!
I SHAN'T LIE, I DIPPED INTO SOME BROOGLY ROOT EARLIER AND I'M A LITTLE BUZZED. BUT IS THERE SOMETHING ODD ABOUT THESE TREES?
THEY MUST BE GROWING TALLER...
OR WE'RE GROWING SHORTER...
YOU IDIOTS, THOSE AREN'T REAL TREES...
HUH?
THEY'RE DISGUISES!

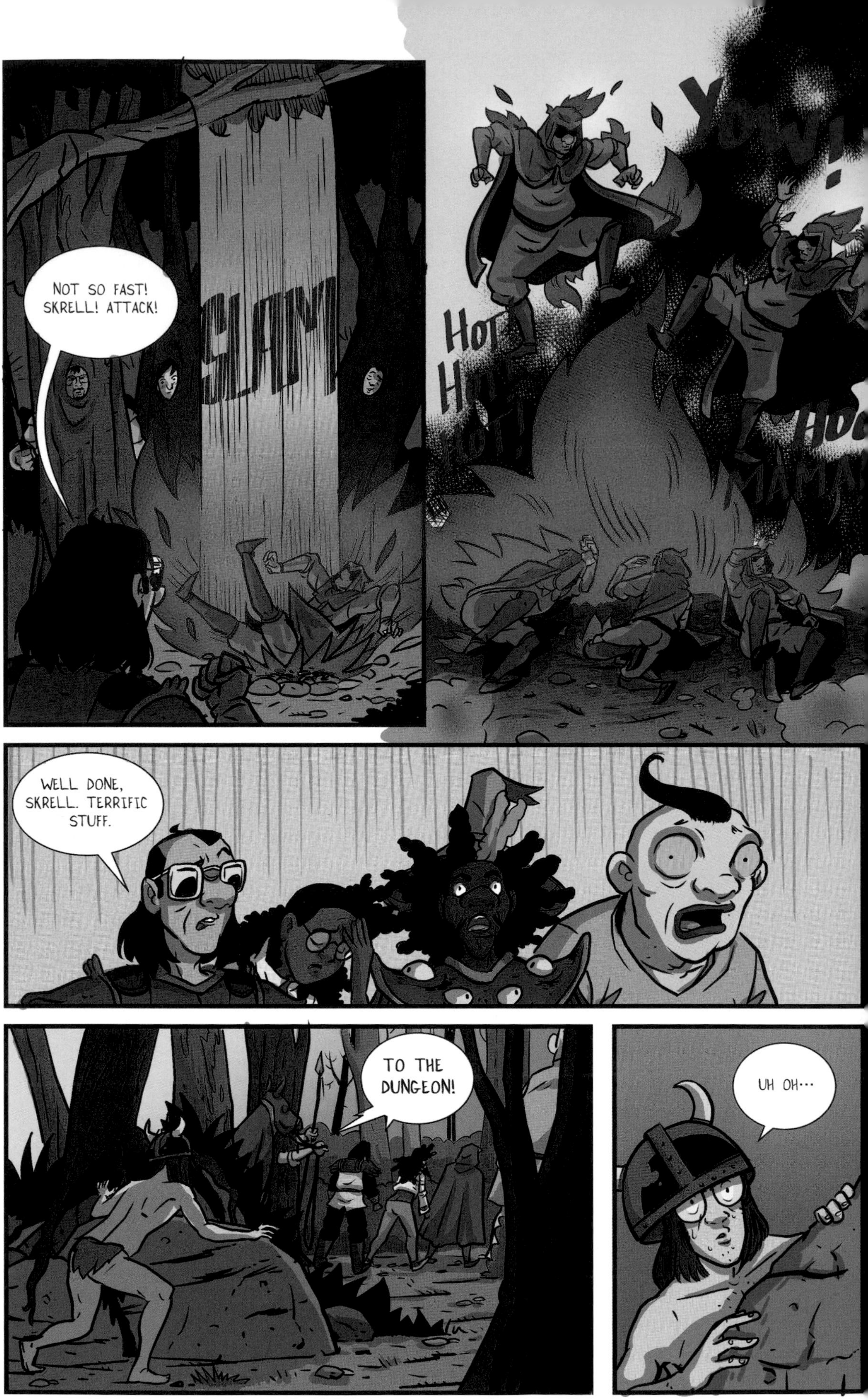
NOT SO FAST! SKRELL! ATTACK!
SLAM!
YOW!
WELL DONE, SKRELL. TERRIFIC STUFF.
TO THE DUNGEON!
UH OH…

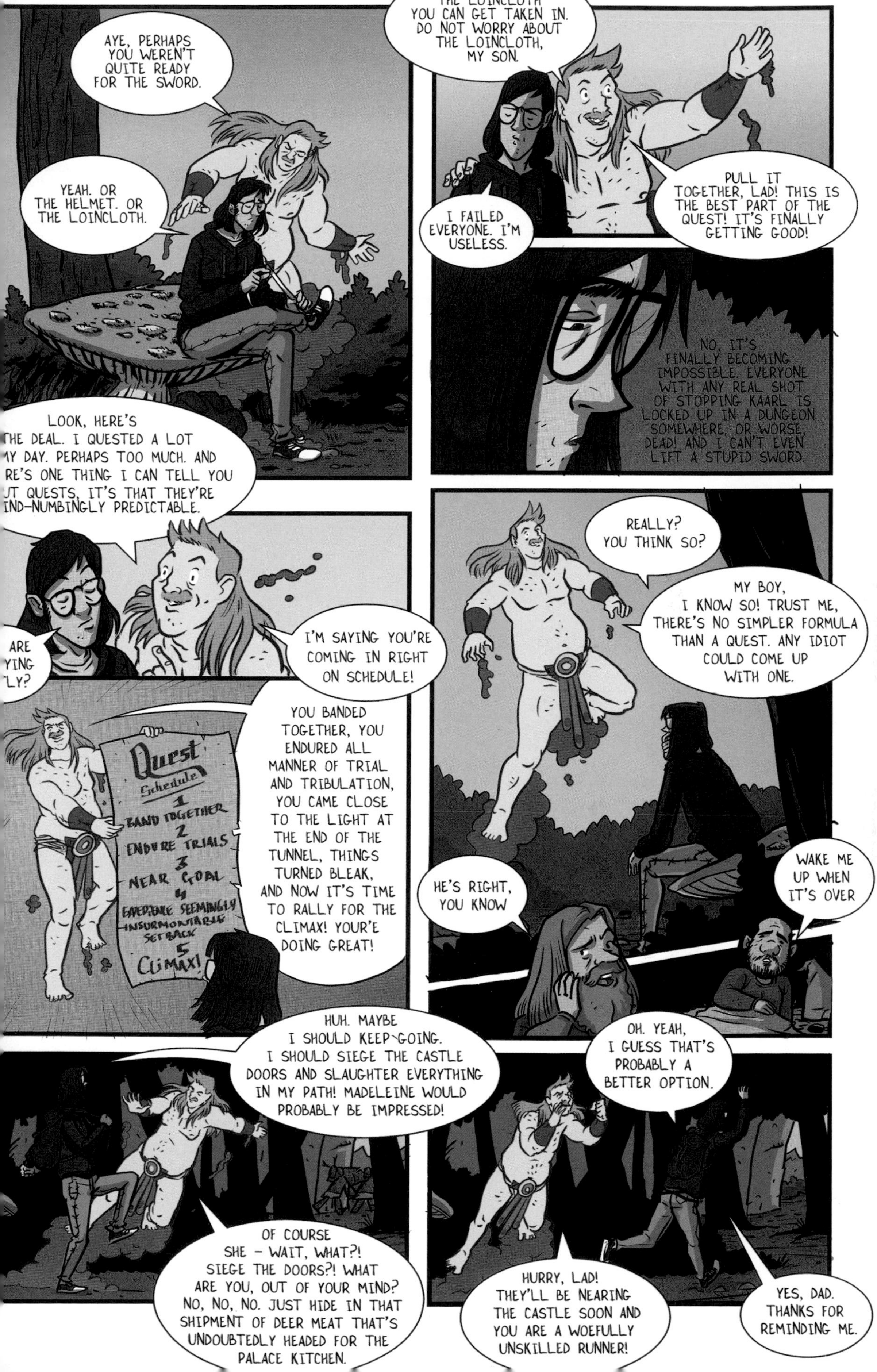
AYE, PERHAPS YOU WEREN'T QUITE READY FOR THE SWORD.
YEAH. OR THE HELMET. OR THE LOINCLOTH.
THE LOINCLOTH YOU CAN GET TAKEN IN. DO NOT WORRY ABOUT THE LOINCLOTH, MY SON.
I FAILED EVERYONE. I'M USELESS.
PULL IT TOGETHER, LAD! THIS IS THE BEST PART OF THE QUEST! IT'S FINALLY GETTING GOOD!
NO, IT'S FINALLY BECOMING IMPOSSIBLE. EVERYONE WITH ANY REAL SHOT OF STOPPING KAARL IS LOCKED UP IN A DUNGEON SOMEWHERE. OR WORSE, DEAD! AND I CAN'T EVEN LIFT A STUPID SWORD.
LOOK, HERE'S THE DEAL. I QUESTED A LOT MY DAY. PERHAPS TOO MUCH. AND RE'S ONE THING I CAN TELL YOU UT QUESTS, IT'S THAT THEY'RE IND-NUMBINGLY PREDICTABLE.
ARE YING LY?
I'M SAYING YOU'RE COMING IN RIGHT ON SCHEDULE!
REALLY? YOU THINK SO?
MY BOY, I KNOW SO! TRUST ME, THERE'S NO SIMPLER FORMULA THAN A QUEST. ANY IDIOT COULD COME UP WITH ONE.
Quest Schedule
1 BAND TOGETHER
2 ENDURE TRIALS
3 NEAR GOAL
4 EXPERIENCE SEEMINGLY INSURMONTABLE SETBACK
5 CLIMAX!
YOU BANDED TOGETHER, YOU ENDURED ALL MANNER OF TRIAL AND TRIBULATION, YOU CAME CLOSE TO THE LIGHT AT THE END OF THE TUNNEL, THINGS TURNED BLEAK, AND NOW IT'S TIME TO RALLY FOR THE CLIMAX! YOUR'E DOING GREAT!
HE'S RIGHT, YOU KNOW
WAKE ME UP WHEN IT'S OVER
HUH. MAYBE I SHOULD KEEP GOING. I SHOULD SIEGE THE CASTLE DOORS AND SLAUGHTER EVERYTHING IN MY PATH! MADELEINE WOULD PROBABLY BE IMPRESSED!
OF COURSE SHE – WAIT, WHAT?! SIEGE THE DOORS?! WHAT ARE YOU, OUT OF YOUR MIND? NO, NO, NO. JUST HIDE IN THAT SHIPMENT OF DEER MEAT THAT'S UNDOUBTEDLY HEADED FOR THE PALACE KITCHEN.
OH. YEAH, I GUESS THAT'S PROBABLY A BETTER OPTION.
HURRY, LAD! THEY'LL BE NEARING THE CASTLE SOON AND YOU ARE A WOEFULLY UNSKILLED RUNNER!
YES, DAD. THANKS FOR REMINDING ME.

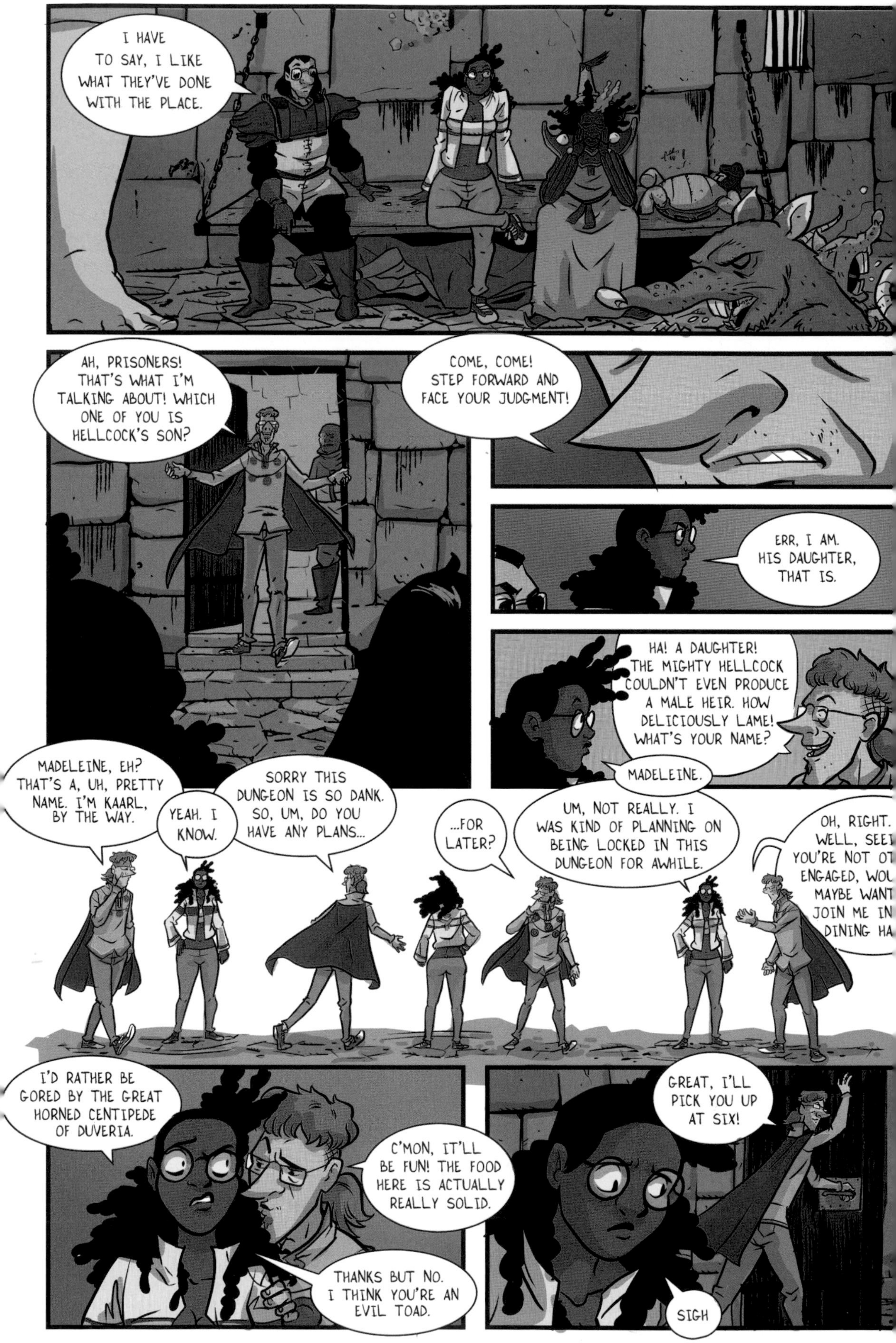
I HAVE TO SAY, I LIKE WHAT THEY'VE DONE WITH THE PLACE.
AH, PRISONERS! THAT'S WHAT I'M TALKING ABOUT! WHICH ONE OF YOU IS HELLCOCK'S SON?
COME, COME! STEP FORWARD AND FACE YOUR JUDGMENT!
ERR, I AM. HIS DAUGHTER, THAT IS.
HA! A DAUGHTER! THE MIGHTY HELLCOCK COULDN'T EVEN PRODUCE A MALE HEIR. HOW DELICIOUSLY LAME! WHAT'S YOUR NAME?
MADELEINE.
MADELEINE, EH? THAT'S A, UH, PRETTY NAME. I'M KAARL, BY THE WAY.
YEAH. I KNOW.
SORRY THIS DUNGEON IS SO DANK. SO, UM, DO YOU HAVE ANY PLANS...
...FOR LATER?
UM, NOT REALLY. I WAS KIND OF PLANNING ON BEING LOCKED IN THIS DUNGEON FOR AWHILE.
OH, RIGHT. WELL, SEE YOU'RE NOT OT ENGAGED, WOU MAYBE WANT JOIN ME IN DINING HA
I'D RATHER BE GORED BY THE GREAT HORNED CENTIPEDE OF DUVERIA.
C'MON, IT'LL BE FUN! THE FOOD HERE IS ACTUALLY REALLY SOLID.
THANKS BUT NO. I THINK YOU'RE AN EVIL TOAD.
GREAT, I'LL PICK YOU UP AT SIX!
SIGH

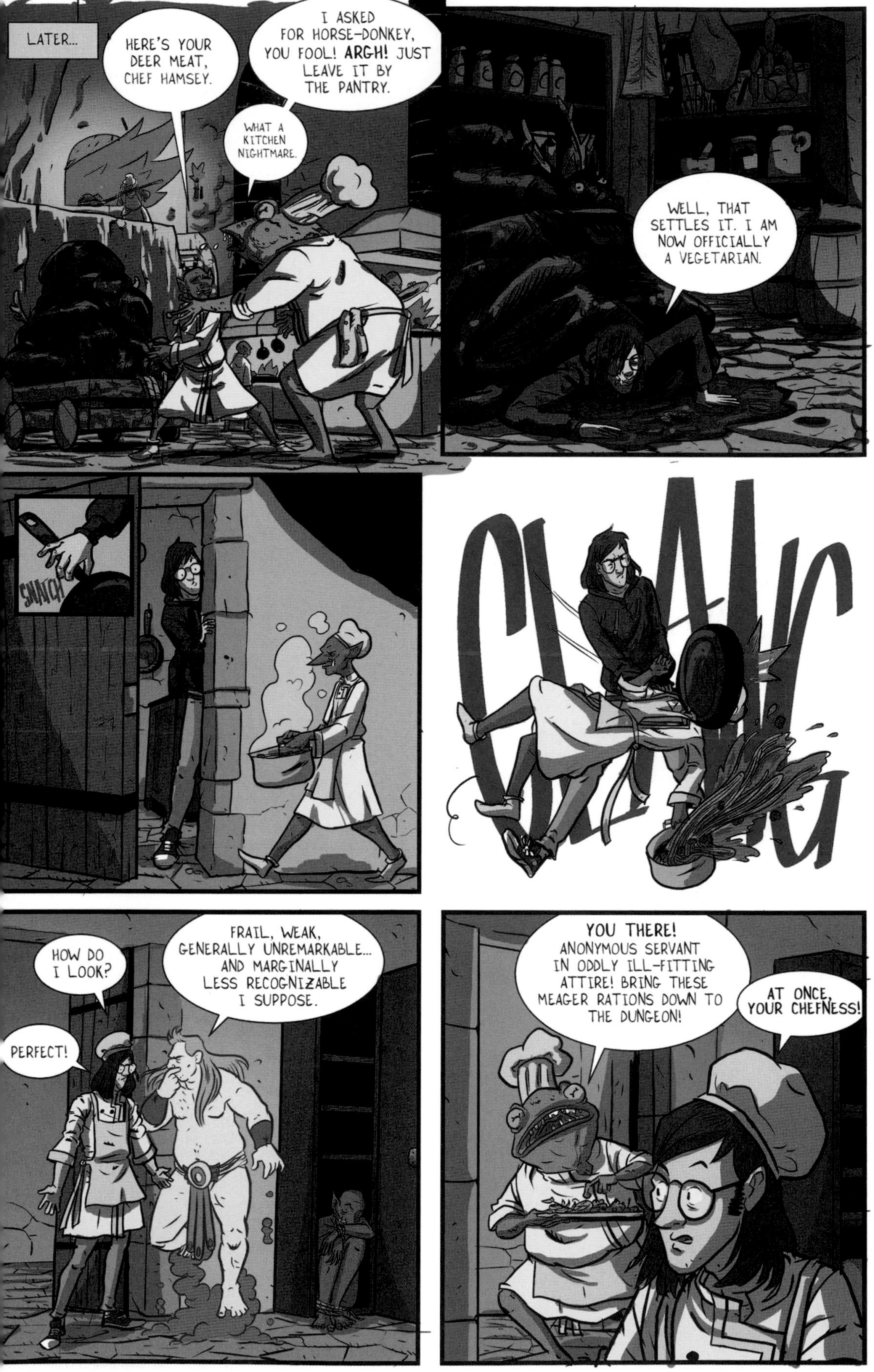
LATER...
HERE'S YOUR DEER MEAT, CHEF HAMSEY.
I ASKED FOR HORSE-DONKEY, YOU FOOL! **ARGH!** JUST LEAVE IT BY THE PANTRY.
WHAT A KITCHEN NIGHTMARE.
WELL, THAT SETTLES IT. I AM NOW OFFICIALLY A VEGETARIAN.
SNATCH
HOW DO I LOOK?
FRAIL, WEAK, GENERALLY UNREMARKABLE... AND MARGINALLY LESS RECOGNIZABLE I SUPPOSE.
PERFECT!
YOU THERE! ANONYMOUS SERVANT IN ODDLY ILL-FITTING ATTIRE! BRING THESE MEAGER RATIONS DOWN TO THE DUNGEON!
AT ONCE, YOUR CHEFNESS!

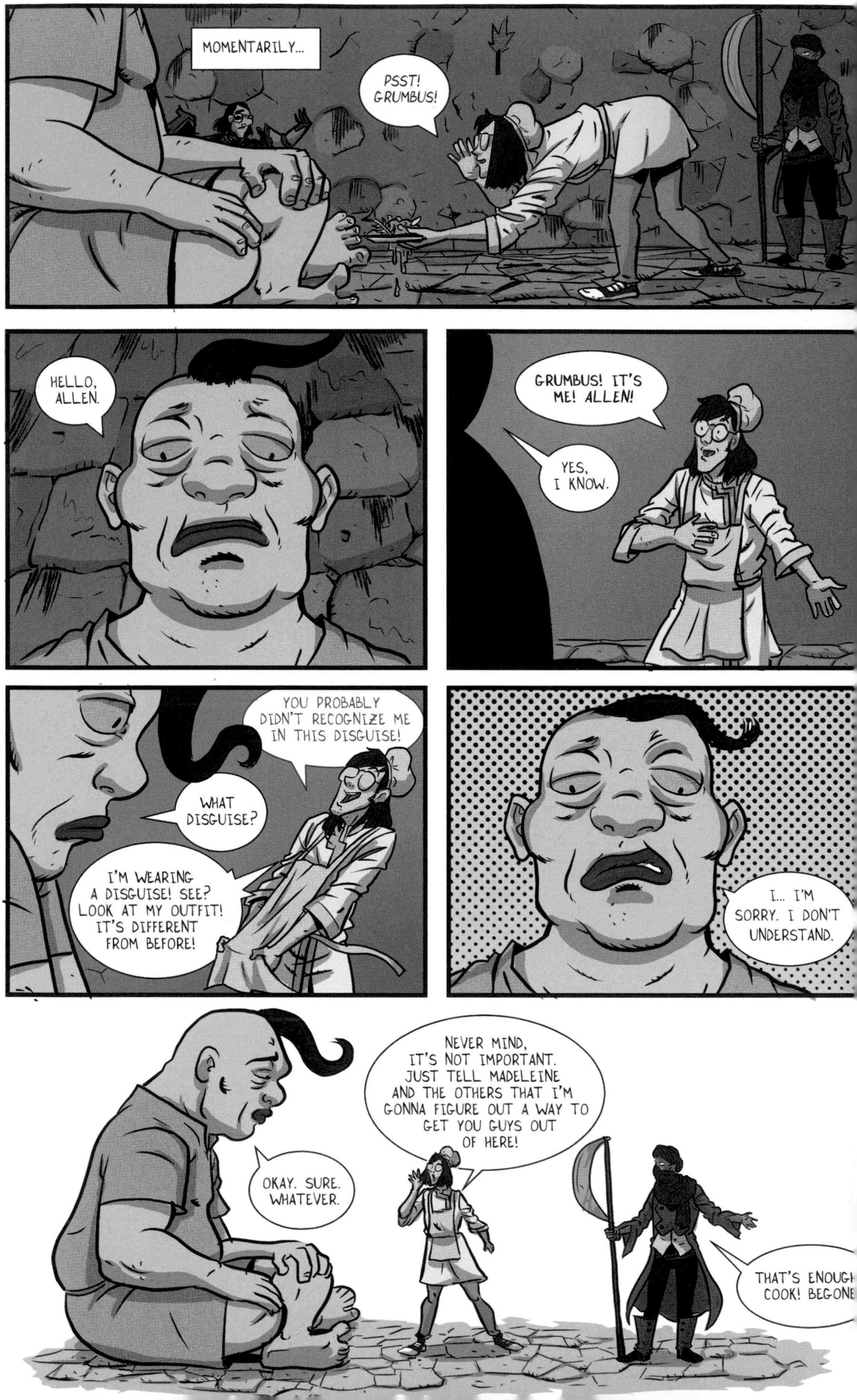
MOMENTARILY...
PSST! GRUMBUS!
HELLO, ALLEN.
GRUMBUS! IT'S ME! ALLEN!
YES, I KNOW.
YOU PROBABLY DIDN'T RECOGNIZE ME IN THIS DISGUISE!
WHAT DISGUISE?
I'M WEARING A DISGUISE! SEE? LOOK AT MY OUTFIT! IT'S DIFFERENT FROM BEFORE!
I... I'M SORRY. I DON'T UNDERSTAND.
NEVER MIND, IT'S NOT IMPORTANT. JUST TELL MADELEINE AND THE OTHERS THAT I'M GONNA FIGURE OUT A WAY TO GET YOU GUYS OUT OF HERE!
OKAY. SURE. WHATEVER.
THAT'S ENOUG COOK! BEGONE

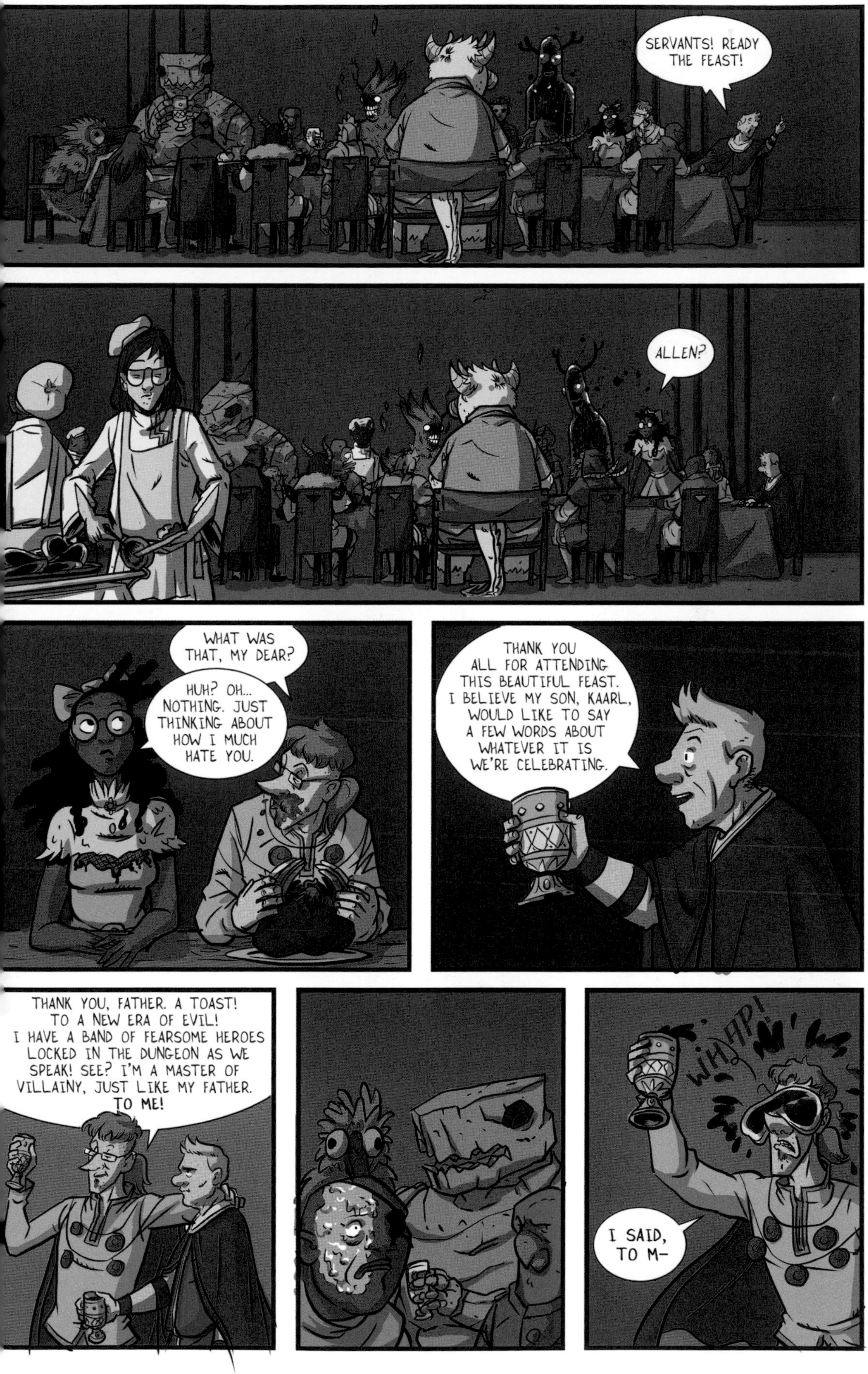
SERVANTS! READY THE FEAST!
ALLEN?
WHAT WAS THAT, MY DEAR?
HUH? OH... NOTHING. JUST THINKING ABOUT HOW I MUCH HATE YOU.
THANK YOU ALL FOR ATTENDING THIS BEAUTIFUL FEAST. I BELIEVE MY SON, KAARL, WOULD LIKE TO SAY A FEW WORDS ABOUT WHATEVER IT IS WE'RE CELEBRATING.
THANK YOU, FATHER. A TOAST! TO A NEW ERA OF EVIL! I HAVE A BAND OF FEARSOME HEROES LOCKED IN THE DUNGEON AS WE SPEAK! SEE? I'M A MASTER OF VILLAINY, JUST LIKE MY FATHER. TO ME!
WHAP!
I SAID, TO M-

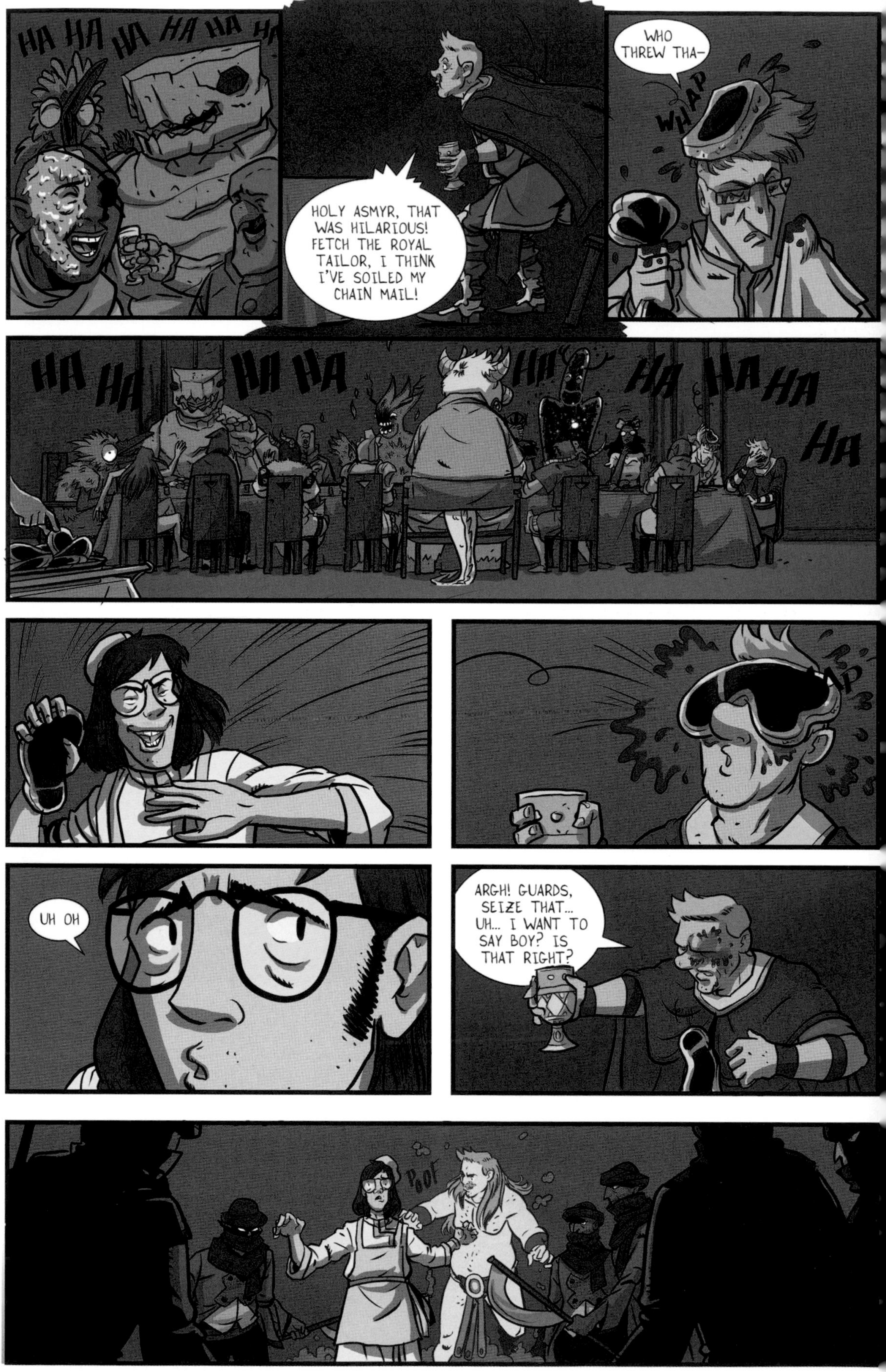
HA HA HA HA HA
HOLY ASMYR, THAT WAS HILARIOUS! FETCH THE ROYAL TAILOR, I THINK I'VE SOILED MY CHAIN MAIL!
WHO THREW THA-
WHAP
HA HA HA HA
HA HA HA HA HA HA
UH OH
ARGH! GUARDS, SEIZE THAT... UH... I WANT TO SAY BOY? IS THAT RIGHT?
POOF

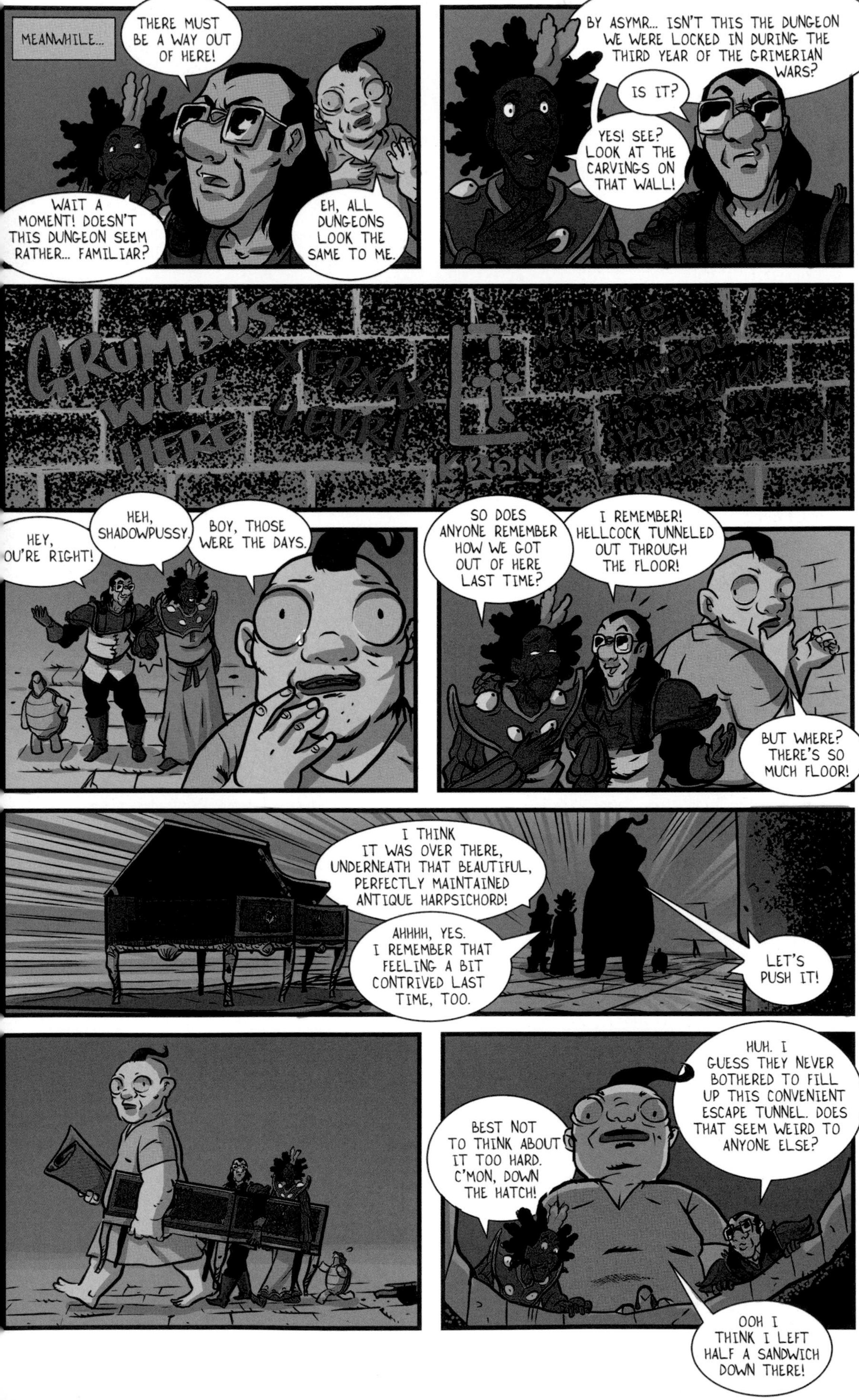
MEANWHILE...
THERE MUST BE A WAY OUT OF HERE!
WAIT A MOMENT! DOESN'T THIS DUNGEON SEEM RATHER... FAMILIAR?
EH, ALL DUNGEONS LOOK THE SAME TO ME.
BY ASYMR... ISN'T THIS THE DUNGEON WE WERE LOCKED IN DURING THE THIRD YEAR OF THE GRIMERIAN WARS?
IS IT?
YES! SEE? LOOK AT THE CARVINGS ON THAT WALL!
GRUMBUS WUZ HERE
XERXAS 4EVR!
KRONG
HEY, OU'RE RIGHT!
HEH, SHADOWPUSSY.
BOY, THOSE WERE THE DAYS.
SO DOES ANYONE REMEMBER HOW WE GOT OUT OF HERE LAST TIME?
I REMEMBER! HELLCOCK TUNNELED OUT THROUGH THE FLOOR!
BUT WHERE? THERE'S SO MUCH FLOOR!
I THINK IT WAS OVER THERE, UNDERNEATH THAT BEAUTIFUL, PERFECTLY MAINTAINED ANTIQUE HARPSICHORD!
AHHHH, YES. I REMEMBER THAT FEELING A BIT CONTRIVED LAST TIME, TOO.
LET'S PUSH IT!
HUH. I GUESS THEY NEVER BOTHERED TO FILL UP THIS CONVENIENT ESCAPE TUNNEL. DOES THAT SEEM WEIRD TO ANYONE ELSE?
BEST NOT TO THINK ABOUT IT TOO HARD. C'MON, DOWN THE HATCH!
OOH I THINK I LEFT HALF A SANDWICH DOWN THERE!

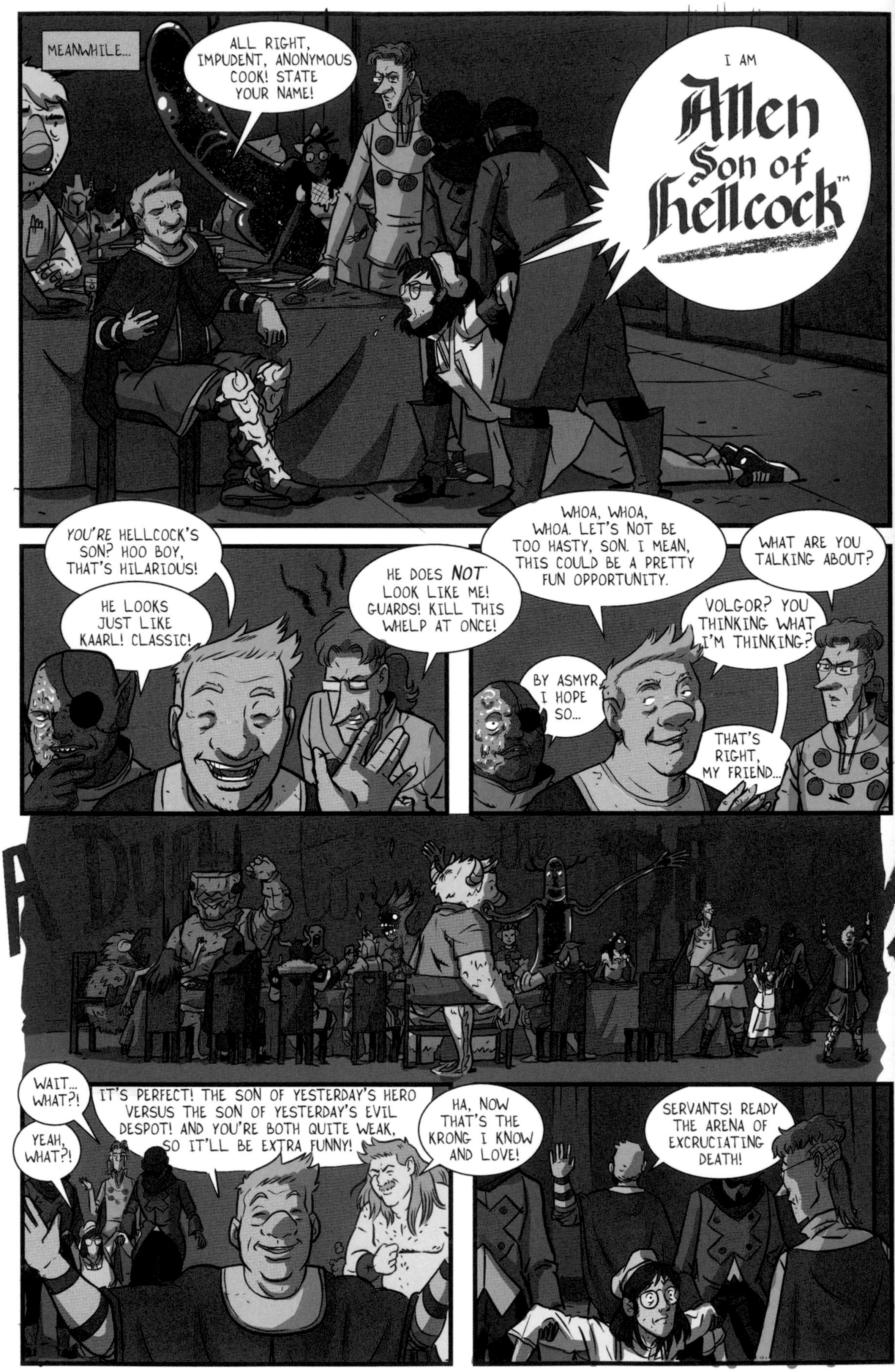
MEANWHILE...
ALL RIGHT, IMPUDENT, ANONYMOUS COOK! STATE YOUR NAME!
I AM Allen Son of Hellcock™
YOU'RE HELLCOCK'S SON? HOO BOY, THAT'S HILARIOUS!
HE LOOKS JUST LIKE KAARL! CLASSIC!
HE DOES NOT LOOK LIKE ME! GUARDS! KILL THIS WHELP AT ONCE!
WHOA, WHOA, WHOA. LET'S NOT BE TOO HASTY, SON. I MEAN, THIS COULD BE A PRETTY FUN OPPORTUNITY.
WHAT ARE YOU TALKING ABOUT?
VOLGOR? YOU THINKING WHAT I'M THINKING?
BY ASMYR, I HOPE SO...
THAT'S RIGHT, MY FRIEND...
WAIT... WHAT?!
YEAH, WHAT?!
IT'S PERFECT! THE SON OF YESTERDAY'S HERO VERSUS THE SON OF YESTERDAY'S EVIL DESPOT! AND YOU'RE BOTH QUITE WEAK, SO IT'LL BE EXTRA FUNNY!
HA, NOW THAT'S THE KRONG I KNOW AND LOVE!
SERVANTS! READY THE ARENA OF EXCRUCIATING DEATH!

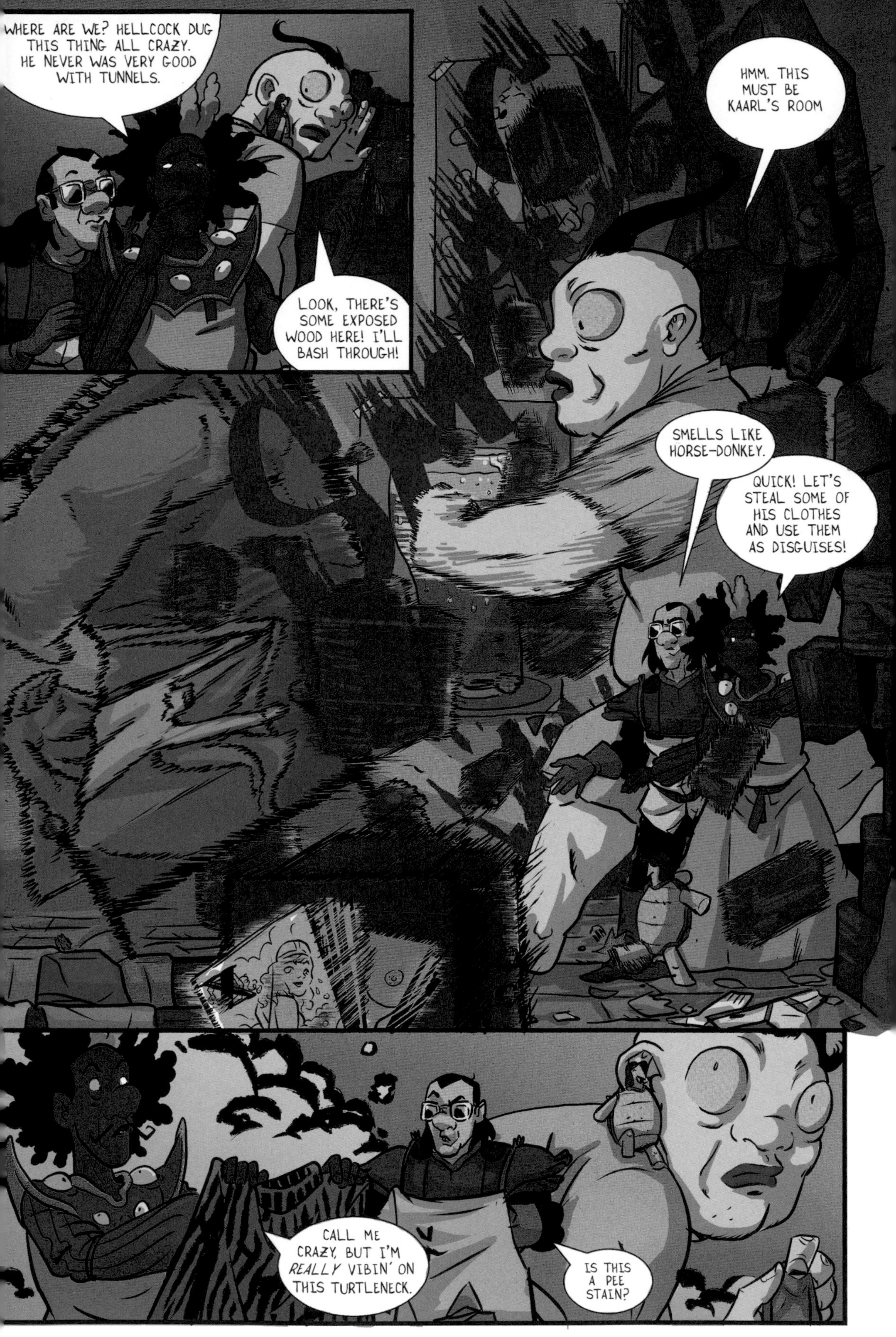
WHERE ARE WE? HELLCOCK DUG THIS THING ALL CRAZY. HE NEVER WAS VERY GOOD WITH TUNNELS.
LOOK, THERE'S SOME EXPOSED WOOD HERE! I'LL BASH THROUGH!
HMM. THIS MUST BE KAARL'S ROOM
SMELLS LIKE HORSE-DONKEY.
QUICK! LET'S STEAL SOME OF HIS CLOTHES AND USE THEM AS DISGUISES!
CALL ME CRAZY, BUT I'M REALLY VIBIN' ON THIS TURTLENECK.
IS THIS A PEE STAIN?

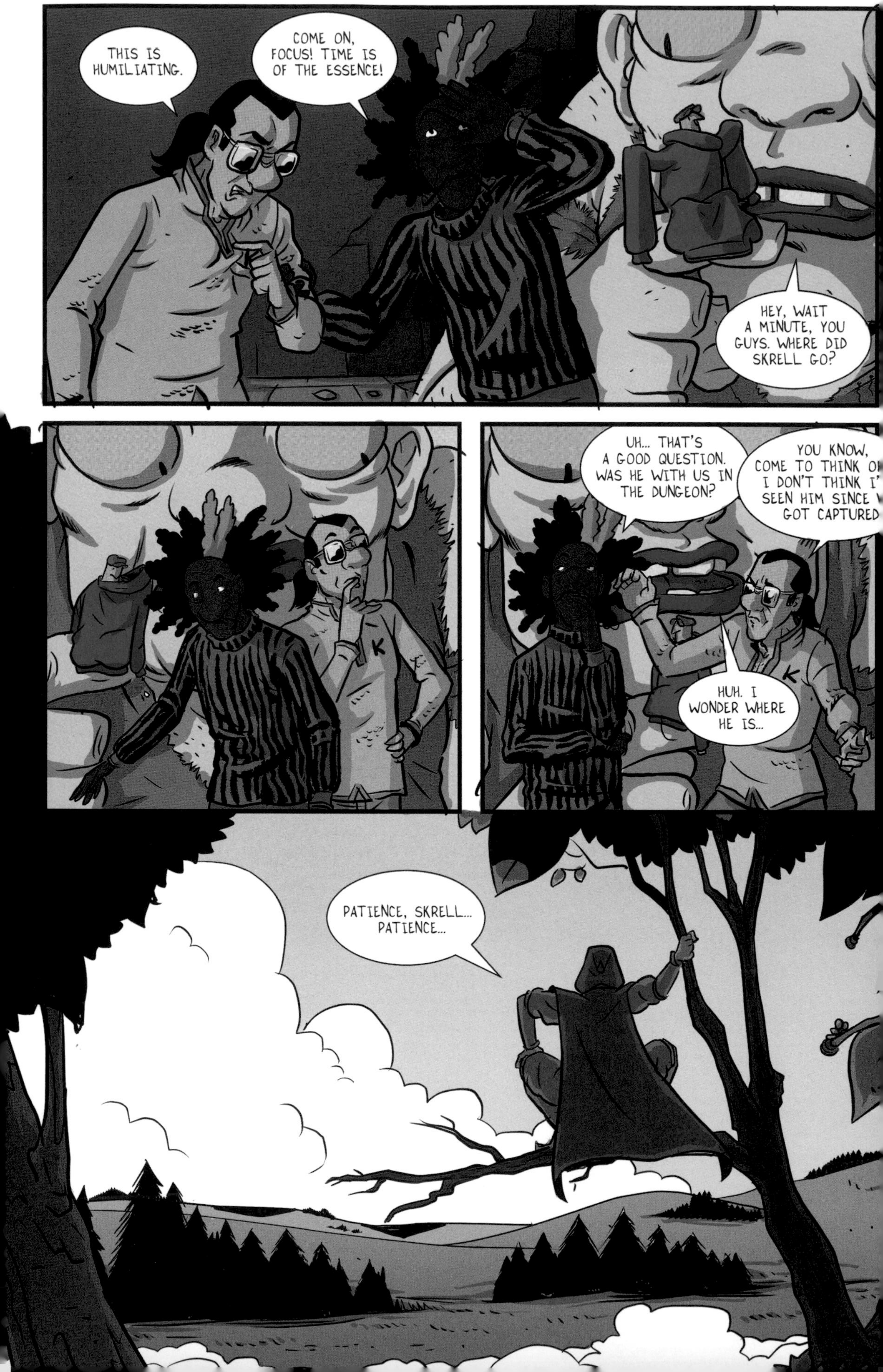
THIS IS HUMILIATING.
COME ON, FOCUS! TIME IS OF THE ESSENCE!
HEY, WAIT A MINUTE, YOU GUYS. WHERE DID SKRELL GO?
UH... THAT'S A GOOD QUESTION. WAS HE WITH US IN THE DUNGEON?
YOU KNOW, COME TO THINK O I DON'T THINK I' SEEN HIM SINCE GOT CAPTURED
HUH. I WONDER WHERE HE IS...
PATIENCE, SKRELL... PATIENCE...

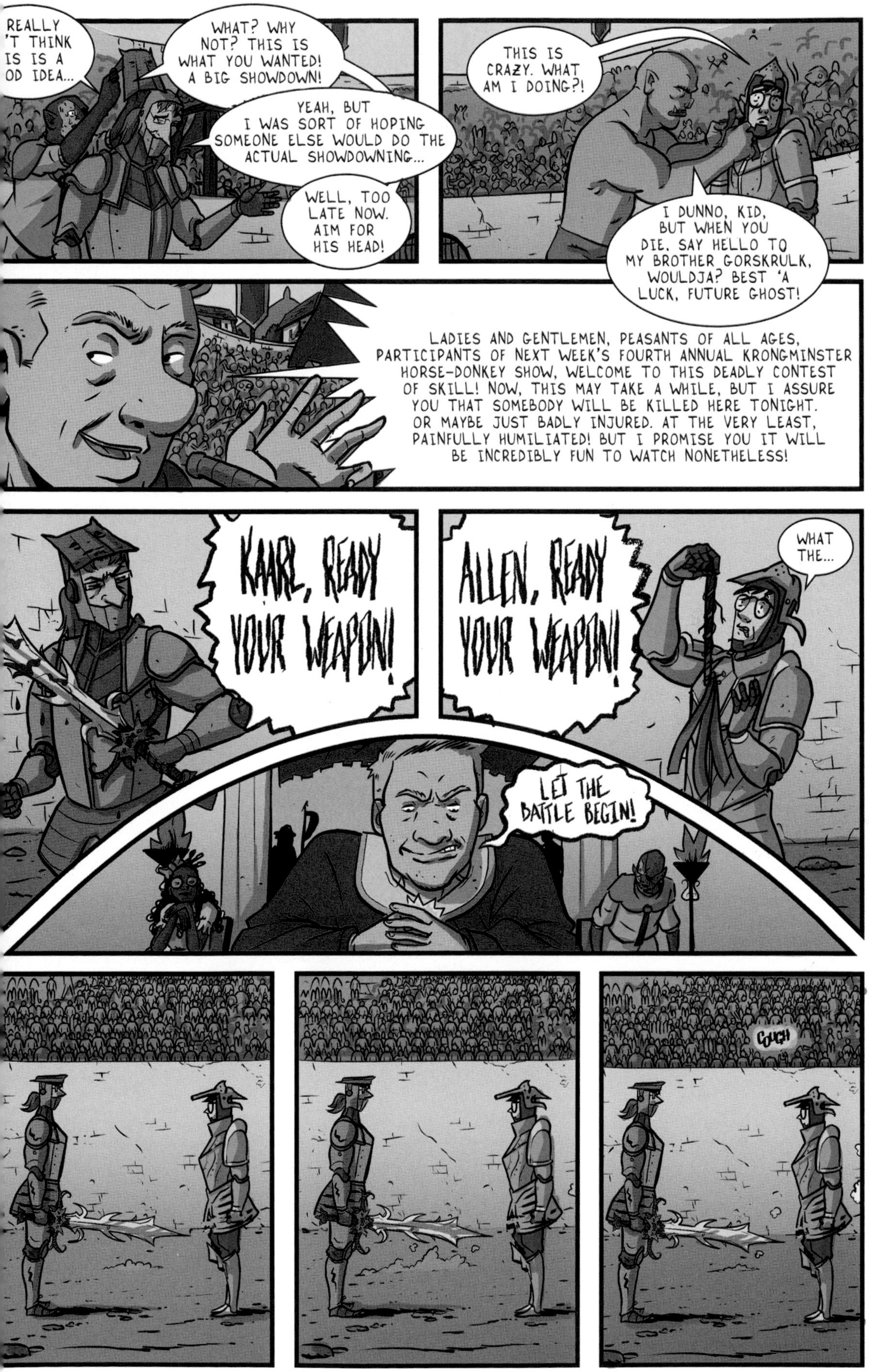
REALLY 'T THINK IS IS A OD IDEA...
WHAT? WHY NOT? THIS IS WHAT YOU WANTED! A BIG SHOWDOWN!
YEAH, BUT I WAS SORT OF HOPING SOMEONE ELSE WOULD DO THE ACTUAL SHOWDOWNING...
WELL, TOO LATE NOW. AIM FOR HIS HEAD!
THIS IS CRAZY. WHAT AM I DOING?!
I DUNNO, KID, BUT WHEN YOU DIE, SAY HELLO TO MY BROTHER GORSKRULK, WOULDJA? BEST 'A LUCK, FUTURE GHOST!
LADIES AND GENTLEMEN, PEASANTS OF ALL AGES, PARTICIPANTS OF NEXT WEEK'S FOURTH ANNUAL KRONGMINSTER HORSE-DONKEY SHOW, WELCOME TO THIS DEADLY CONTEST OF SKILL! NOW, THIS MAY TAKE A WHILE, BUT I ASSURE YOU THAT SOMEBODY WILL BE KILLED HERE TONIGHT. OR MAYBE JUST BADLY INJURED. AT THE VERY LEAST, PAINFULLY HUMILIATED! BUT I PROMISE YOU IT WILL BE INCREDIBLY FUN TO WATCH NONETHELESS!
KAARL, READY YOUR WEAPON!
ALLEN, READY YOUR WEAPON!
WHAT THE...
LET THE BATTLE BEGIN!
COUGH

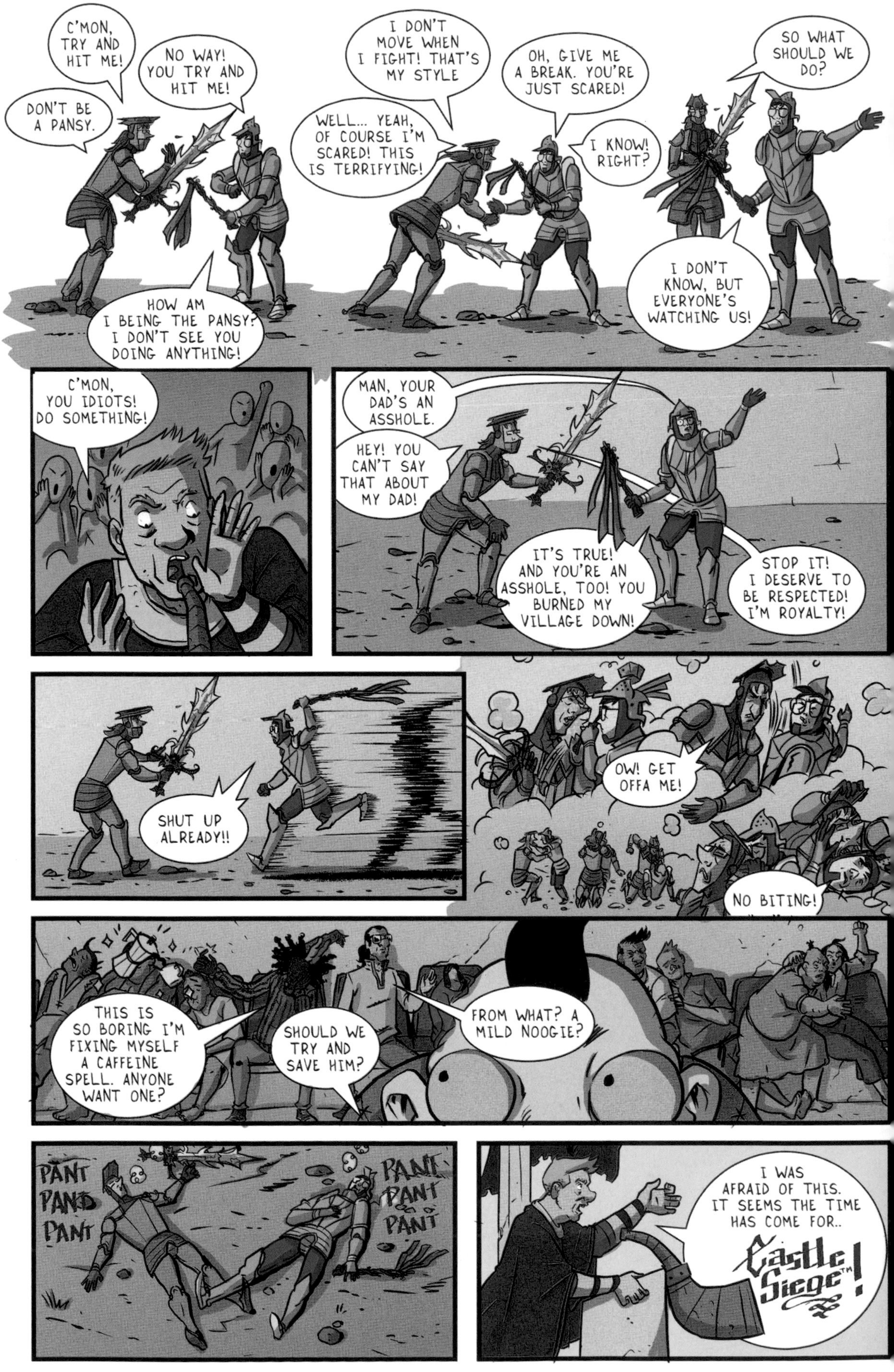

DON'T BE A PANSY.
C'MON, TRY AND HIT ME!
NO WAY! YOU TRY AND HIT ME!
HOW AM I BEING THE PANSY? I DON'T SEE YOU DOING ANYTHING!
I DON'T MOVE WHEN I FIGHT! THAT'S MY STYLE
OH, GIVE ME A BREAK. YOU'RE JUST SCARED!
WELL... YEAH, OF COURSE I'M SCARED! THIS IS TERRIFYING!
I KNOW! RIGHT?
SO WHAT SHOULD WE DO?
I DON'T KNOW, BUT EVERYONE'S WATCHING US!
C'MON, YOU IDIOTS! DO SOMETHING!
MAN, YOUR DAD'S AN ASSHOLE.
HEY! YOU CAN'T SAY THAT ABOUT MY DAD!
IT'S TRUE! AND YOU'RE AN ASSHOLE, TOO! YOU BURNED MY VILLAGE DOWN!
STOP IT! I DESERVE TO BE RESPECTED! I'M ROYALTY!
SHUT UP ALREADY!!
OW! GET OFFA ME!
NO BITING!
THIS IS SO BORING I'M FIXING MYSELF A CAFFEINE SPELL. ANYONE WANT ONE?
SHOULD WE TRY AND SAVE HIM?
FROM WHAT? A MILD NOOGIE?
PANT PANT PANT
PANT PANT PANT
I WAS AFRAID OF THIS. IT SEEMS THE TIME HAS COME FOR..
Castle Siege™!

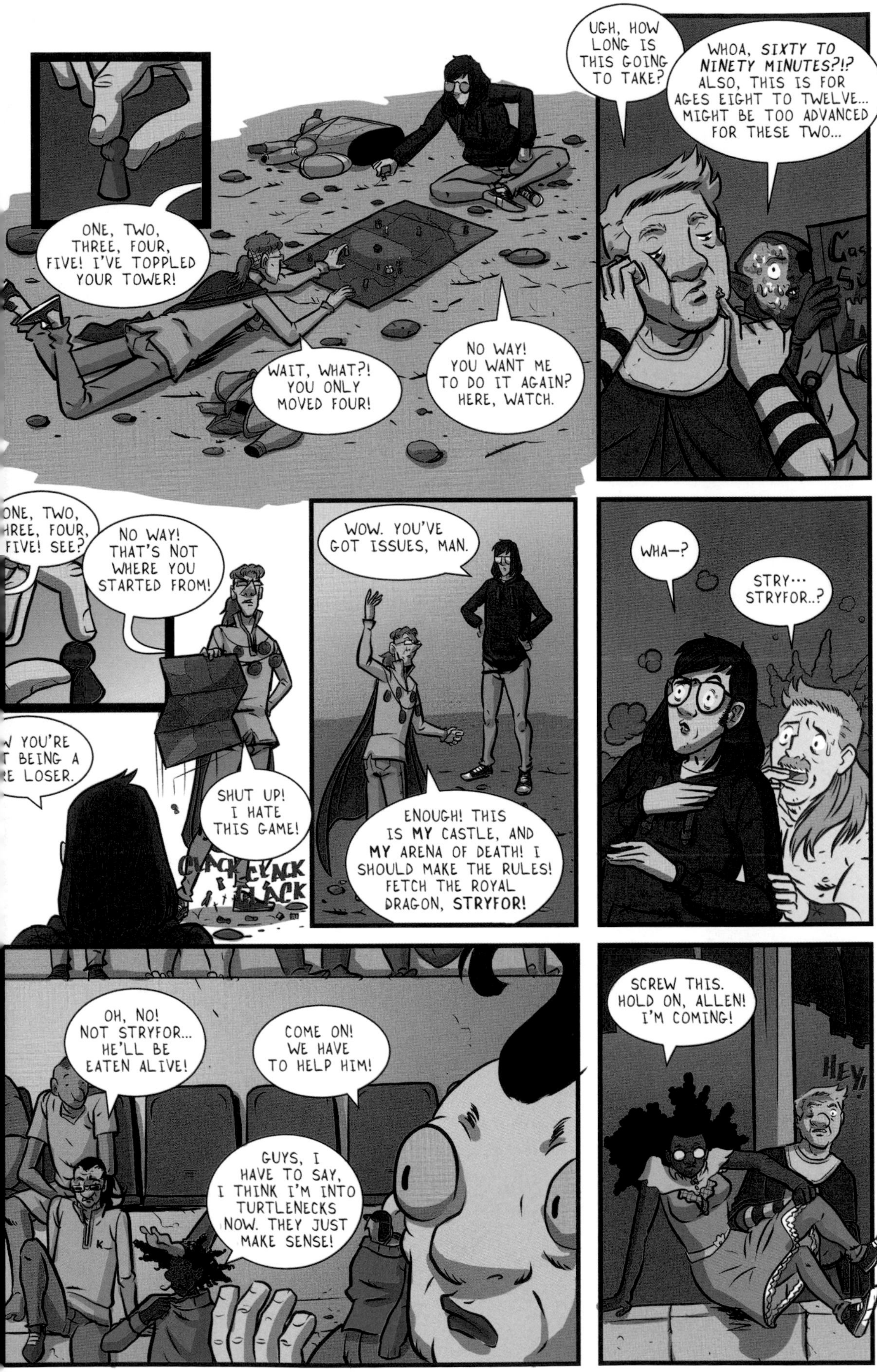
ONE, TWO, THREE, FOUR, FIVE! I'VE TOPPLED YOUR TOWER!
WAIT, WHAT?! YOU ONLY MOVED FOUR!
NO WAY! YOU WANT ME TO DO IT AGAIN? HERE, WATCH.
UGH, HOW LONG IS THIS GOING TO TAKE?
WHOA, SIXTY TO NINETY MINUTES?!? ALSO, THIS IS FOR AGES EIGHT TO TWELVE... MIGHT BE TOO ADVANCED FOR THESE TWO...
ONE, TWO, HREE, FOUR, FIVE! SEE?
NO WAY! THAT'S NOT WHERE YOU STARTED FROM!
W YOU'RE T BEING A E LOSER.
SHUT UP! I HATE THIS GAME!
WOW. YOU'VE GOT ISSUES, MAN.
ENOUGH! THIS IS MY CASTLE, AND MY ARENA OF DEATH! I SHOULD MAKE THE RULES! FETCH THE ROYAL DRAGON, STRYFOR!
WHA—?
STRY... STRYFOR..?
OH, NO! NOT STRYFOR... HE'LL BE EATEN ALIVE!
COME ON! WE HAVE TO HELP HIM!
GUYS, I HAVE TO SAY, I THINK I'M INTO TURTLENECKS NOW. THEY JUST MAKE SENSE!
SCREW THIS. HOLD ON, ALLEN! I'M COMING!
HEY!

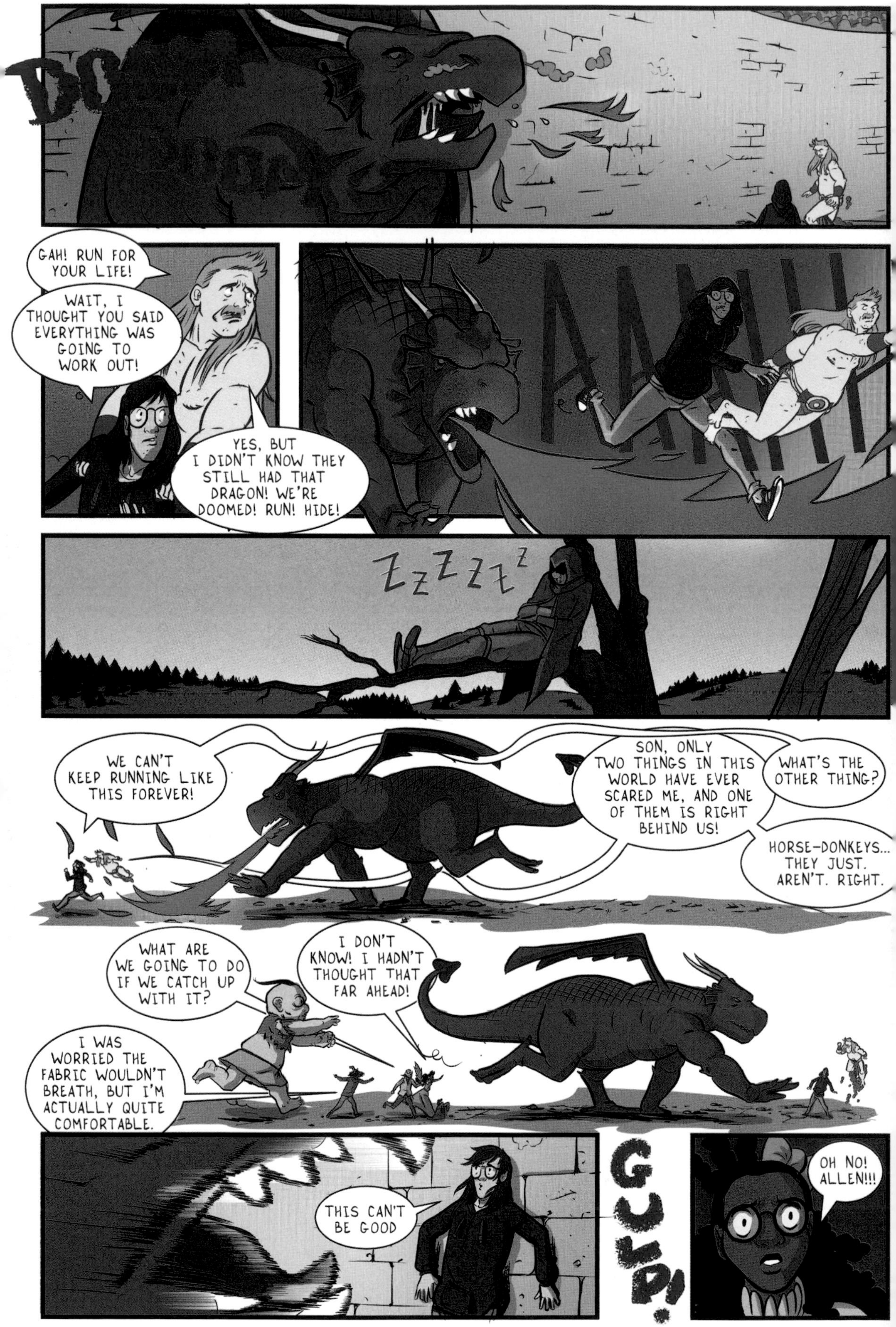
GAH! RUN FOR YOUR LIFE!
WAIT, I THOUGHT YOU SAID EVERYTHING WAS GOING TO WORK OUT!
YES, BUT I DIDN'T KNOW THEY STILL HAD THAT DRAGON! WE'RE DOOMED! RUN! HIDE!
ZZZZZZ
WE CAN'T KEEP RUNNING LIKE THIS FOREVER!
SON, ONLY TWO THINGS IN THIS WORLD HAVE EVER SCARED ME, AND ONE OF THEM IS RIGHT BEHIND US!
WHAT'S THE OTHER THING?
HORSE-DONKEYS... THEY JUST. AREN'T. RIGHT.
WHAT ARE WE GOING TO DO IF WE CATCH UP WITH IT?
I DON'T KNOW! I HADN'T THOUGHT THAT FAR AHEAD!
I WAS WORRIED THE FABRIC WOULDN'T BREATH, BUT I'M ACTUALLY QUITE COMFORTABLE.
THIS CAN'T BE GOOD
GULP!
OH NO! ALLEN!!!

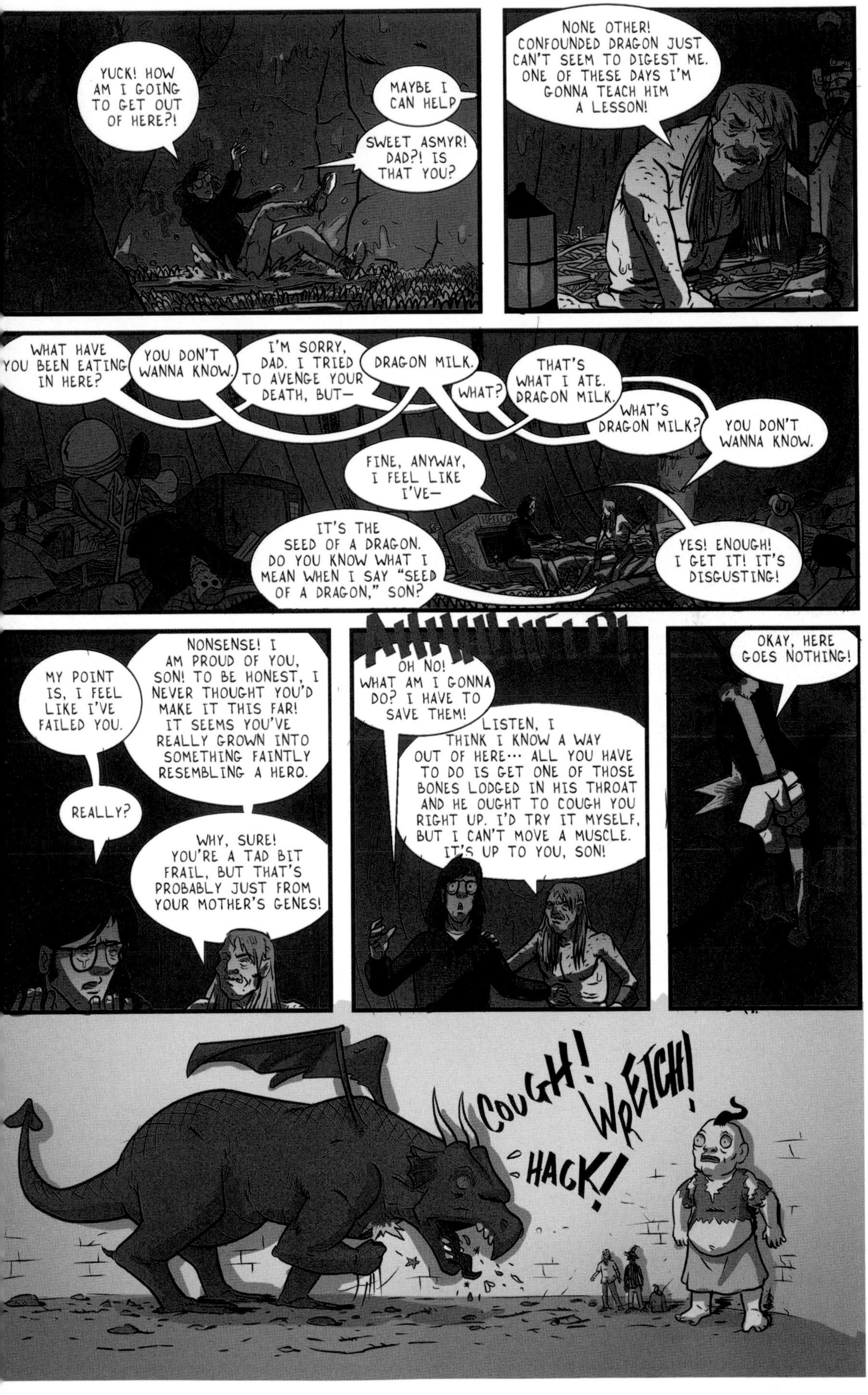
YUCK! HOW AM I GOING TO GET OUT OF HERE?!
MAYBE I CAN HELP
SWEET ASMYR! DAD?! IS THAT YOU?
NONE OTHER! CONFOUNDED DRAGON JUST CAN'T SEEM TO DIGEST ME. ONE OF THESE DAYS I'M GONNA TEACH HIM A LESSON!
WHAT HAVE YOU BEEN EATING IN HERE?
YOU DON'T WANNA KNOW.
I'M SORRY, DAD. I TRIED TO AVENGE YOUR DEATH, BUT—
DRAGON MILK.
WHAT?
THAT'S WHAT I ATE. DRAGON MILK.
WHAT'S DRAGON MILK?
YOU DON'T WANNA KNOW.
FINE, ANYWAY, I FEEL LIKE I'VE—
IT'S THE SEED OF A DRAGON. DO YOU KNOW WHAT I MEAN WHEN I SAY "SEED OF A DRAGON," SON?
YES! ENOUGH! I GET IT! IT'S DISGUSTING!
MY POINT IS, I FEEL LIKE I'VE FAILED YOU.
NONSENSE! I AM PROUD OF YOU, SON! TO BE HONEST, I NEVER THOUGHT YOU'D MAKE IT THIS FAR! IT SEEMS YOU'VE REALLY GROWN INTO SOMETHING FAINTLY RESEMBLING A HERO.
REALLY?
WHY, SURE! YOU'RE A TAD BIT FRAIL, BUT THAT'S PROBABLY JUST FROM YOUR MOTHER'S GENES!
OH NO! WHAT AM I GONNA DO? I HAVE TO SAVE THEM!
LISTEN, I THINK I KNOW A WAY OUT OF HERE… ALL YOU HAVE TO DO IS GET ONE OF THOSE BONES LODGED IN HIS THROAT AND HE OUGHT TO COUGH YOU RIGHT UP. I'D TRY IT MYSELF, BUT I CAN'T MOVE A MUSCLE. IT'S UP TO YOU, SON!
OKAY, HERE GOES NOTHING!
COUGH!
WRETCH!
HACK!

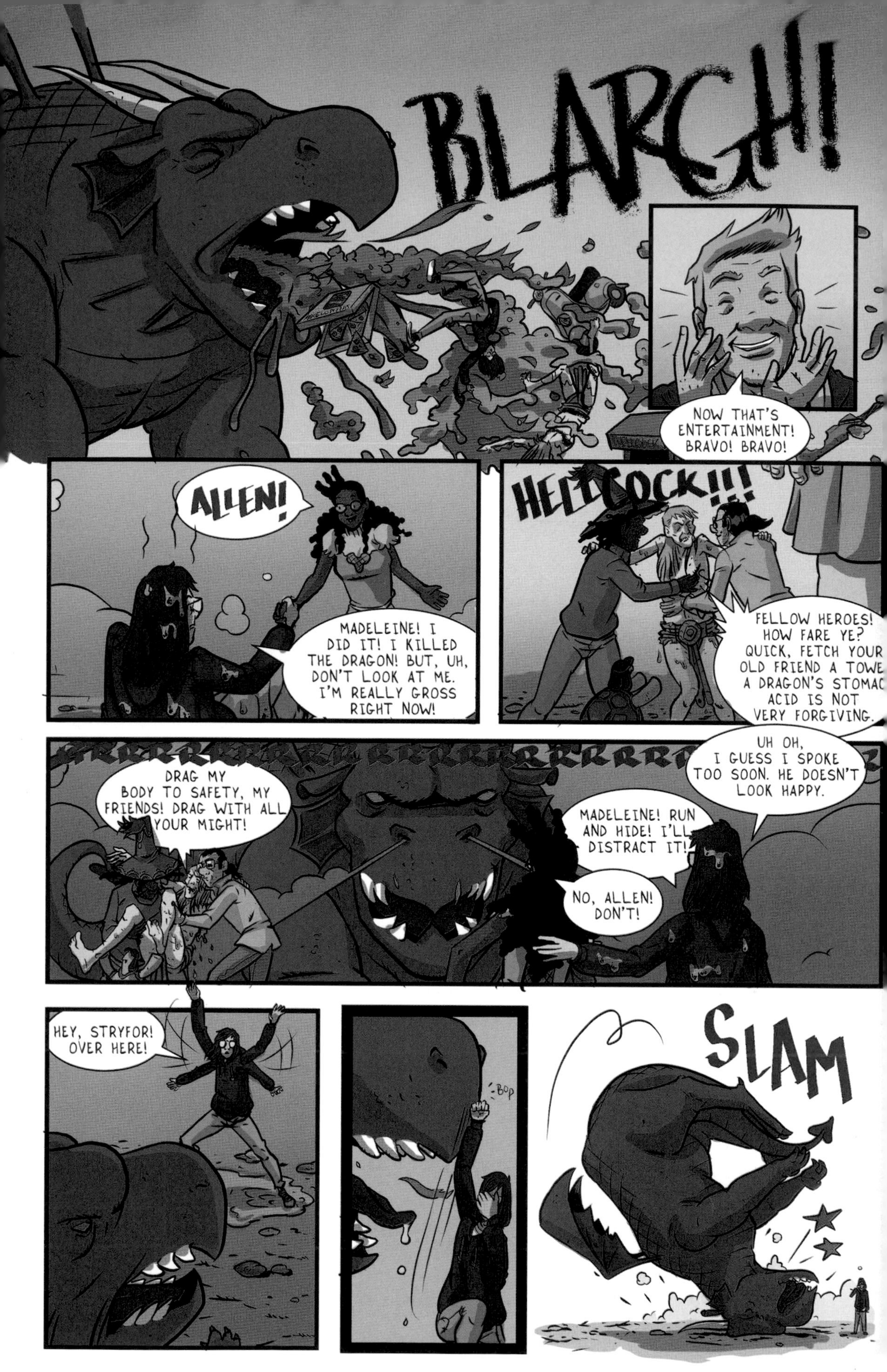
BLARGH!
NOW THAT'S ENTERTAINMENT! BRAVO! BRAVO!
ALLEN!
MADELEINE! I DID IT! I KILLED THE DRAGON! BUT, UH, DON'T LOOK AT ME. I'M REALLY GROSS RIGHT NOW!
HELLCOCK!!!
FELLOW HEROES! HOW FARE YE? QUICK, FETCH YOUR OLD FRIEND A TOWE A DRAGON'S STOMAC ACID IS NOT VERY FORGIVING.
UH OH, I GUESS I SPOKE TOO SOON. HE DOESN'T LOOK HAPPY.
DRAG MY BODY TO SAFETY, MY FRIENDS! DRAG WITH ALL YOUR MIGHT!
MADELEINE! RUN AND HIDE! I'LL DISTRACT IT!
NO, ALLEN! DON'T!
HEY, STRYFOR! OVER HERE!
BOP
SLAM

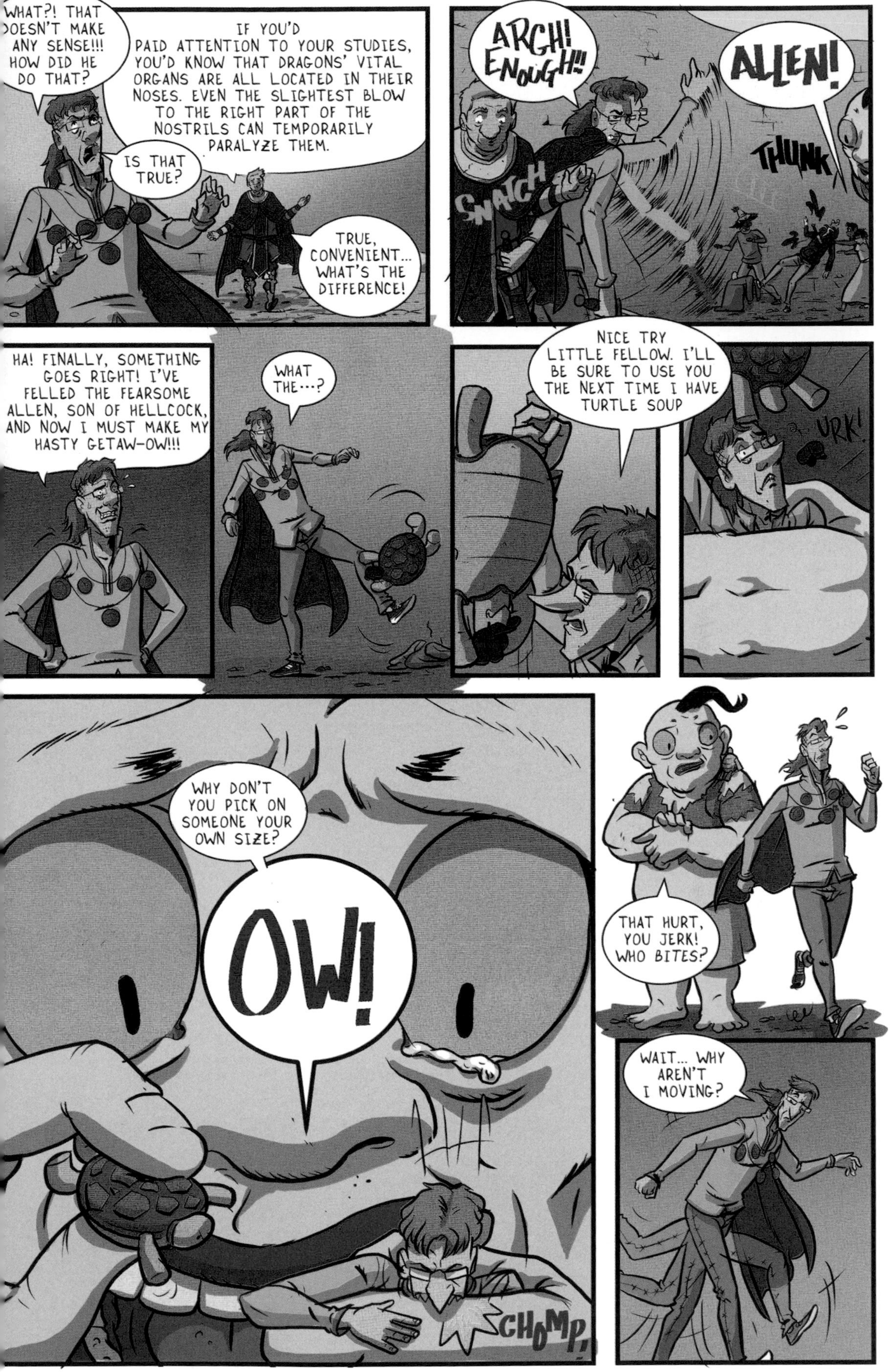
WHAT?! THAT DOESN'T MAKE ANY SENSE!!! HOW DID HE DO THAT?
IF YOU'D PAID ATTENTION TO YOUR STUDIES, YOU'D KNOW THAT DRAGONS' VITAL ORGANS ARE ALL LOCATED IN THEIR NOSES. EVEN THE SLIGHTEST BLOW TO THE RIGHT PART OF THE NOSTRILS CAN TEMPORARILY PARALYZE THEM.
IS THAT TRUE?
TRUE, CONVENIENT... WHAT'S THE DIFFERENCE!
ARCH! ENOUGH!!
SNATCH
ALLEN!
THUNK
HA! FINALLY, SOMETHING GOES RIGHT! I'VE FELLED THE FEARSOME ALLEN, SON OF HELLCOCK, AND NOW I MUST MAKE MY HASTY GETAW-OW!!!
WHAT THE...?
NICE TRY LITTLE FELLOW. I'LL BE SURE TO USE YOU THE NEXT TIME I HAVE TURTLE SOUP
URK!
WHY DON'T YOU PICK ON SOMEONE YOUR OWN SIZE?
OW!
CHOMP
THAT HURT, YOU JERK! WHO BITES?
WAIT... WHY AREN'T I MOVING?

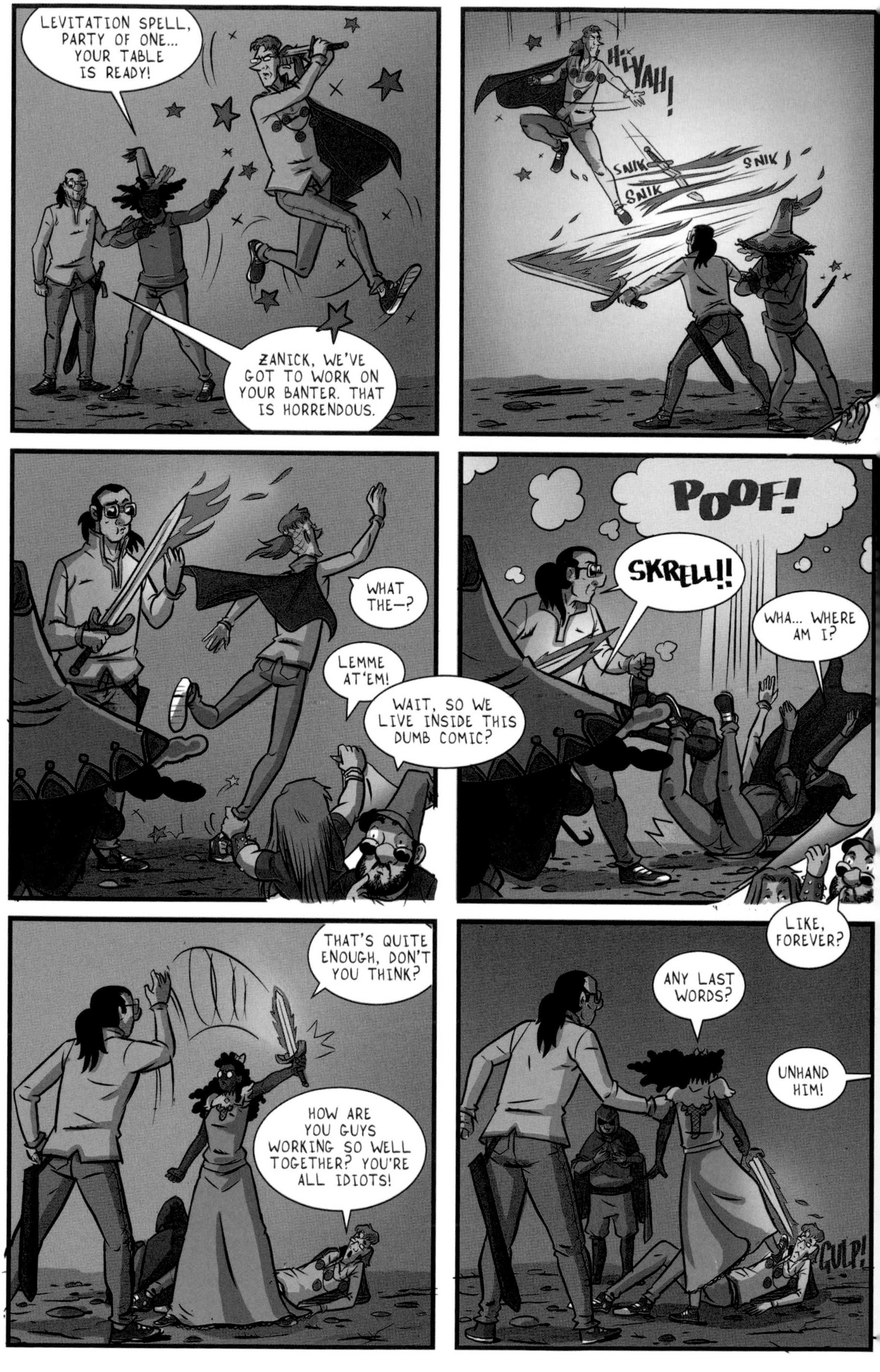
LEVITATION SPELL, PARTY OF ONE... YOUR TABLE IS READY!
ZANICK, WE'VE GOT TO WORK ON YOUR BANTER. THAT IS HORRENDOUS.
HI-YAH!
SNIK
SNIK
SNIK
WHAT THE—?
LEMME AT'EM!
WAIT, SO WE LIVE INSIDE THIS DUMB COMIC?
POOF!
SKRELL!!
WHA... WHERE AM I?
LIKE, FOREVER?
THAT'S QUITE ENOUGH, DON'T YOU THINK?
HOW ARE YOU GUYS WORKING SO WELL TOGETHER? YOU'RE ALL IDIOTS!
ANY LAST WORDS?
UNHAND HIM!
GULP!

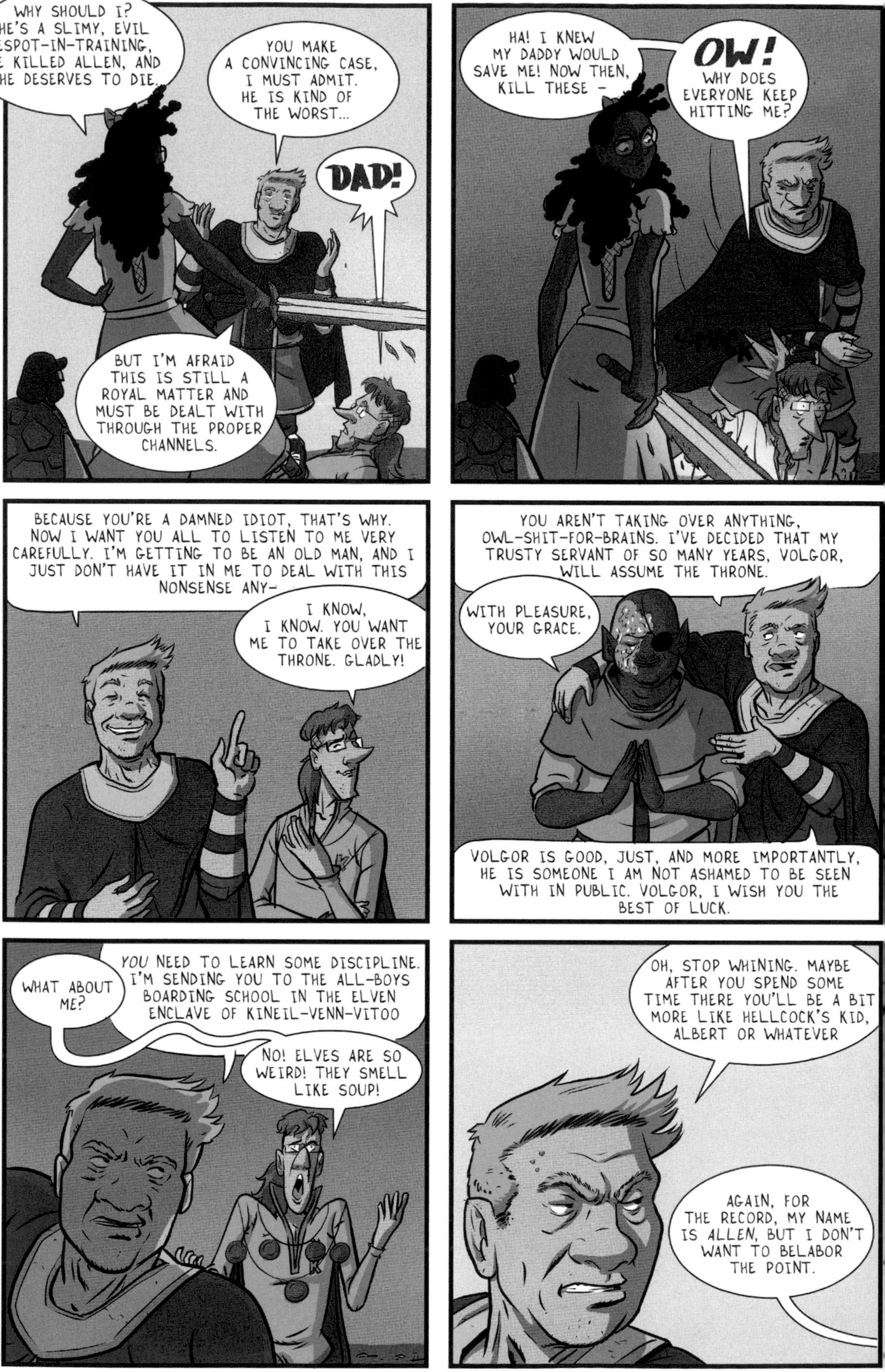
WHY SHOULD I? HE'S A SLIMY, EVIL DESPOT-IN-TRAINING, HE KILLED ALLEN, AND HE DESERVES TO DIE.
YOU MAKE A CONVINCING CASE, I MUST ADMIT. HE IS KIND OF THE WORST...
DAD!
BUT I'M AFRAID THIS IS STILL A ROYAL MATTER AND MUST BE DEALT WITH THROUGH THE PROPER CHANNELS.
HA! I KNEW MY DADDY WOULD SAVE ME! NOW THEN, KILL THESE -
OW! WHY DOES EVERYONE KEEP HITTING ME?
BECAUSE YOU'RE A DAMNED IDIOT, THAT'S WHY. NOW I WANT YOU ALL TO LISTEN TO ME VERY CAREFULLY. I'M GETTING TO BE AN OLD MAN, AND I JUST DON'T HAVE IT IN ME TO DEAL WITH THIS NONSENSE ANY-
I KNOW, I KNOW. YOU WANT ME TO TAKE OVER THE THRONE. GLADLY!
YOU AREN'T TAKING OVER ANYTHING, OWL-SHIT-FOR-BRAINS. I'VE DECIDED THAT MY TRUSTY SERVANT OF SO MANY YEARS, VOLGOR, WILL ASSUME THE THRONE.
WITH PLEASURE, YOUR GRACE.
VOLGOR IS GOOD, JUST, AND MORE IMPORTANTLY, HE IS SOMEONE I AM NOT ASHAMED TO BE SEEN WITH IN PUBLIC. VOLGOR, I WISH YOU THE BEST OF LUCK.
WHAT ABOUT ME?
YOU NEED TO LEARN SOME DISCIPLINE. I'M SENDING YOU TO THE ALL-BOYS BOARDING SCHOOL IN THE ELVEN ENCLAVE OF KINEIL-VENN-VITOO
NO! ELVES ARE SO WEIRD! THEY SMELL LIKE SOUP!
OH, STOP WHINING. MAYBE AFTER YOU SPEND SOME TIME THERE YOU'LL BE A BIT MORE LIKE HELLCOCK'S KID, ALBERT OR WHATEVER
AGAIN, FOR THE RECORD, MY NAME IS ALLEN, BUT I DON'T WANT TO BELABOR THE POINT.

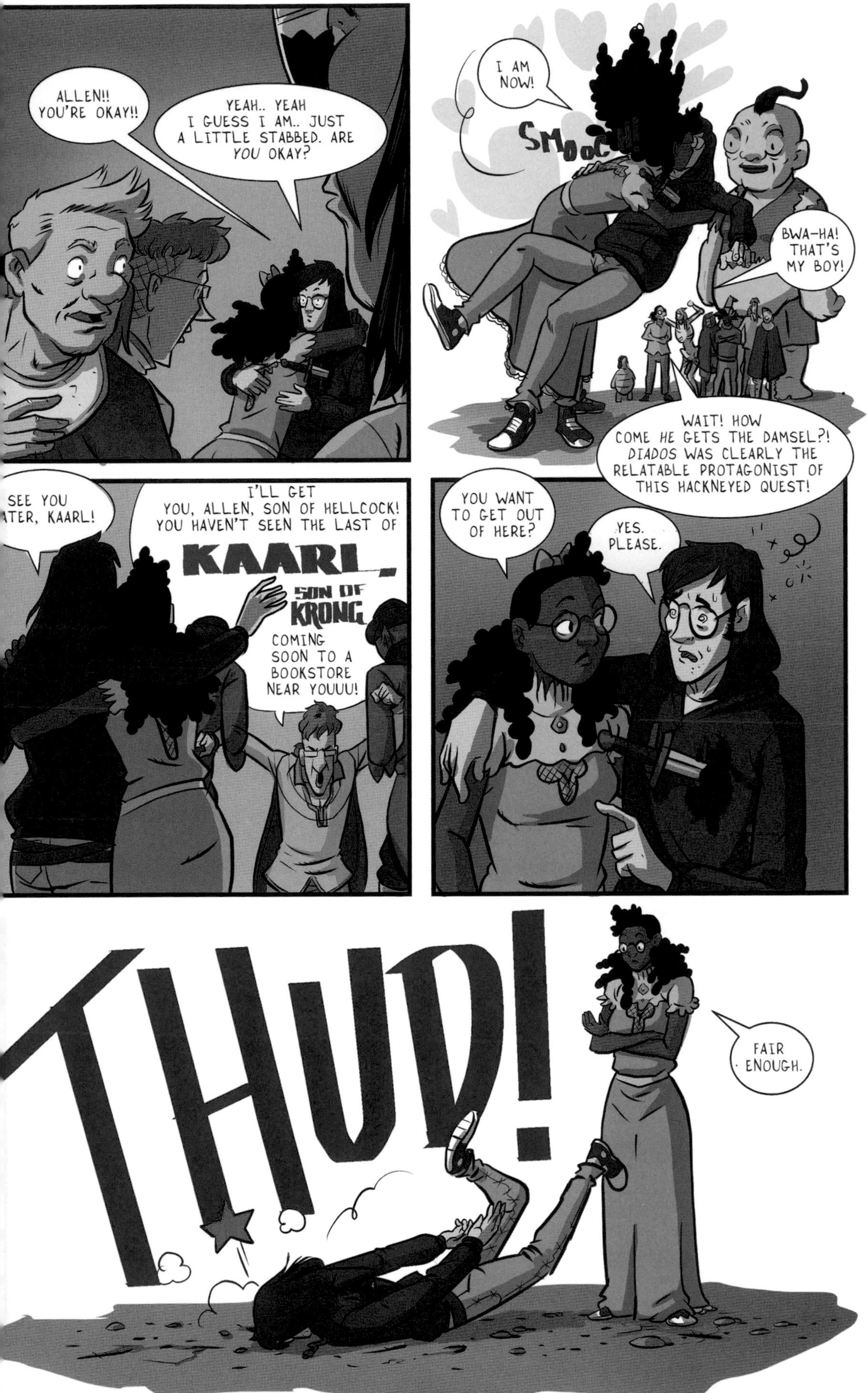
ALLEN!! YOU'RE OKAY!!
YEAH.. YEAH I GUESS I AM.. JUST A LITTLE STABBED. ARE YOU OKAY?
I AM NOW!
SMOOCH!
BWA-HA! THAT'S MY BOY!
WAIT! HOW COME HE GETS THE DAMSEL?! DIADOS WAS CLEARLY THE RELATABLE PROTAGONIST OF THIS HACKNEYED QUEST!
SEE YOU LATER, KAARL!
I'LL GET YOU, ALLEN, SON OF HELLCOCK! YOU HAVEN'T SEEN THE LAST OF
KAARL, SON OF KRONG
COMING SOON TO A BOOKSTORE NEAR YOUUU!
YOU WANT TO GET OUT OF HERE?
YES. PLEASE.
THUD!
FAIR ENOUGH.

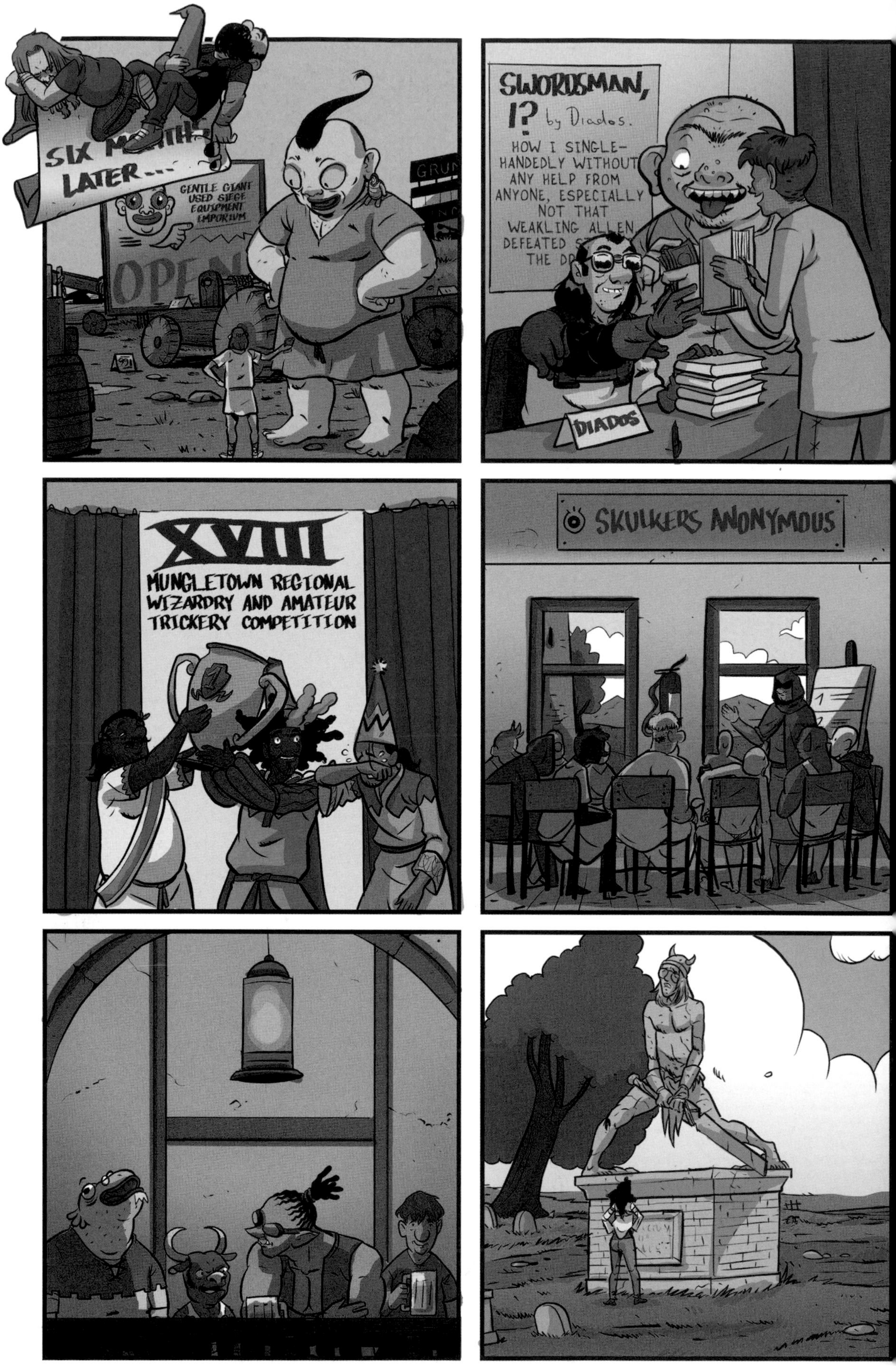

SIX
LATER...
GENTLE GIANT USED SIEGE EQUIPMENT EMPORIUM
OPE
GRUN
SWORDSMAN, I? by Diados.
HOW I SINGLE-HANDEDLY WITHOUT ANY HELP FROM ANYONE, ESPECIALLY NOT THAT WEAKLING ALLEN DEFEATED S THE DR
DIADOS
XVIII
MUNGLETOWN REGIONAL WIZARDRY AND AMATEUR TRICKERY COMPETITION
SKULKERS ANONYMOUS

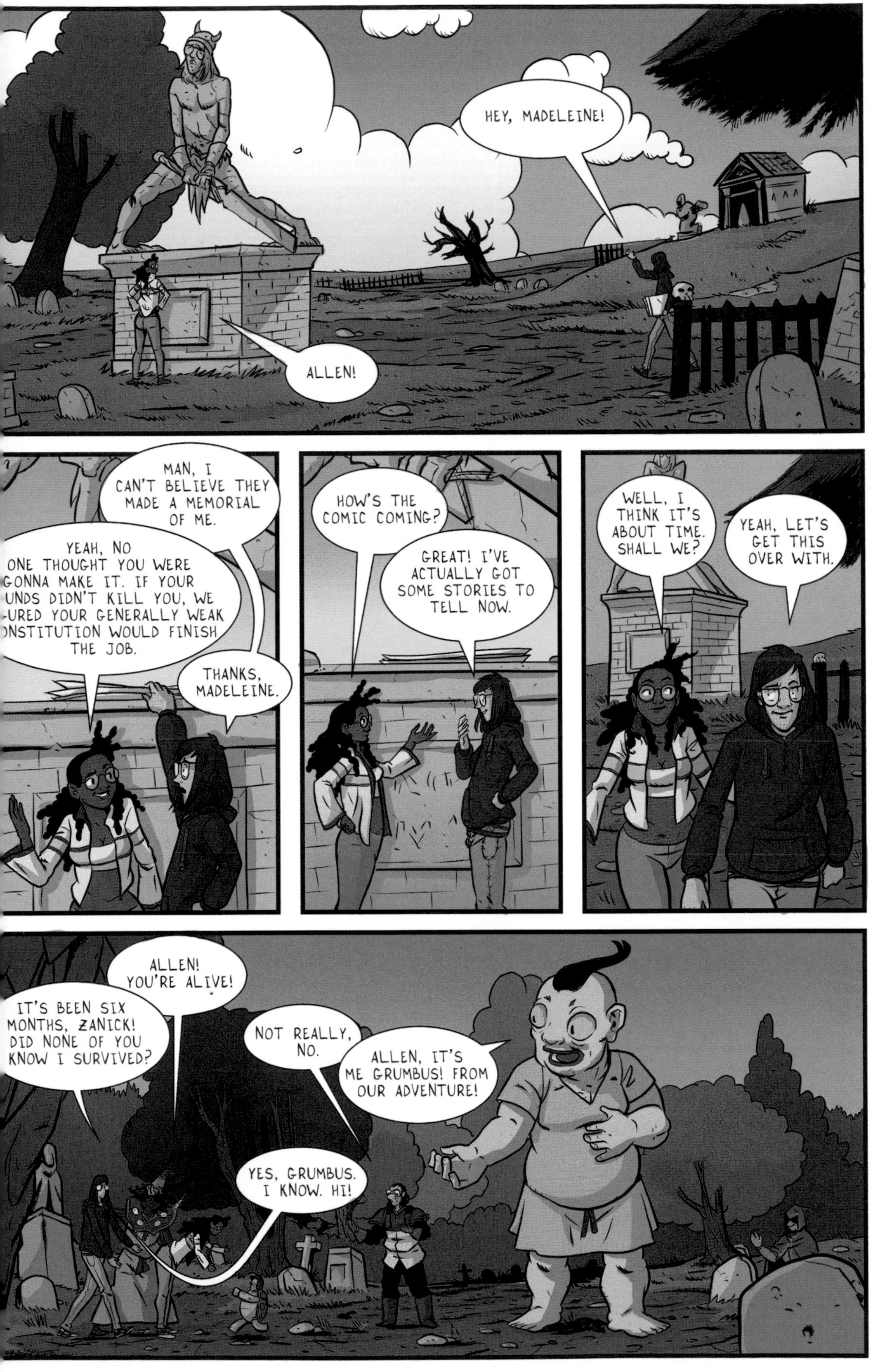
HEY, MADELEINE!
ALLEN!
MAN, I CAN'T BELIEVE THEY MADE A MEMORIAL OF ME.
YEAH, NO ONE THOUGHT YOU WERE GONNA MAKE IT. IF YOUR UNDS DIDN'T KILL YOU, WE URED YOUR GENERALLY WEAK NSTITUTION WOULD FINISH THE JOB.
THANKS, MADELEINE.
HOW'S THE COMIC COMING?
GREAT! I'VE ACTUALLY GOT SOME STORIES TO TELL NOW.
WELL, I THINK IT'S ABOUT TIME. SHALL WE?
YEAH, LET'S GET THIS OVER WITH.
ALLEN! YOU'RE ALIVE!
IT'S BEEN SIX MONTHS, ZANICK! DID NONE OF YOU KNOW I SURVIVED?
NOT REALLY, NO.
ALLEN, IT'S ME GRUMBUS! FROM OUR ADVENTURE!
YES, GRUMBUS. I KNOW. HI!

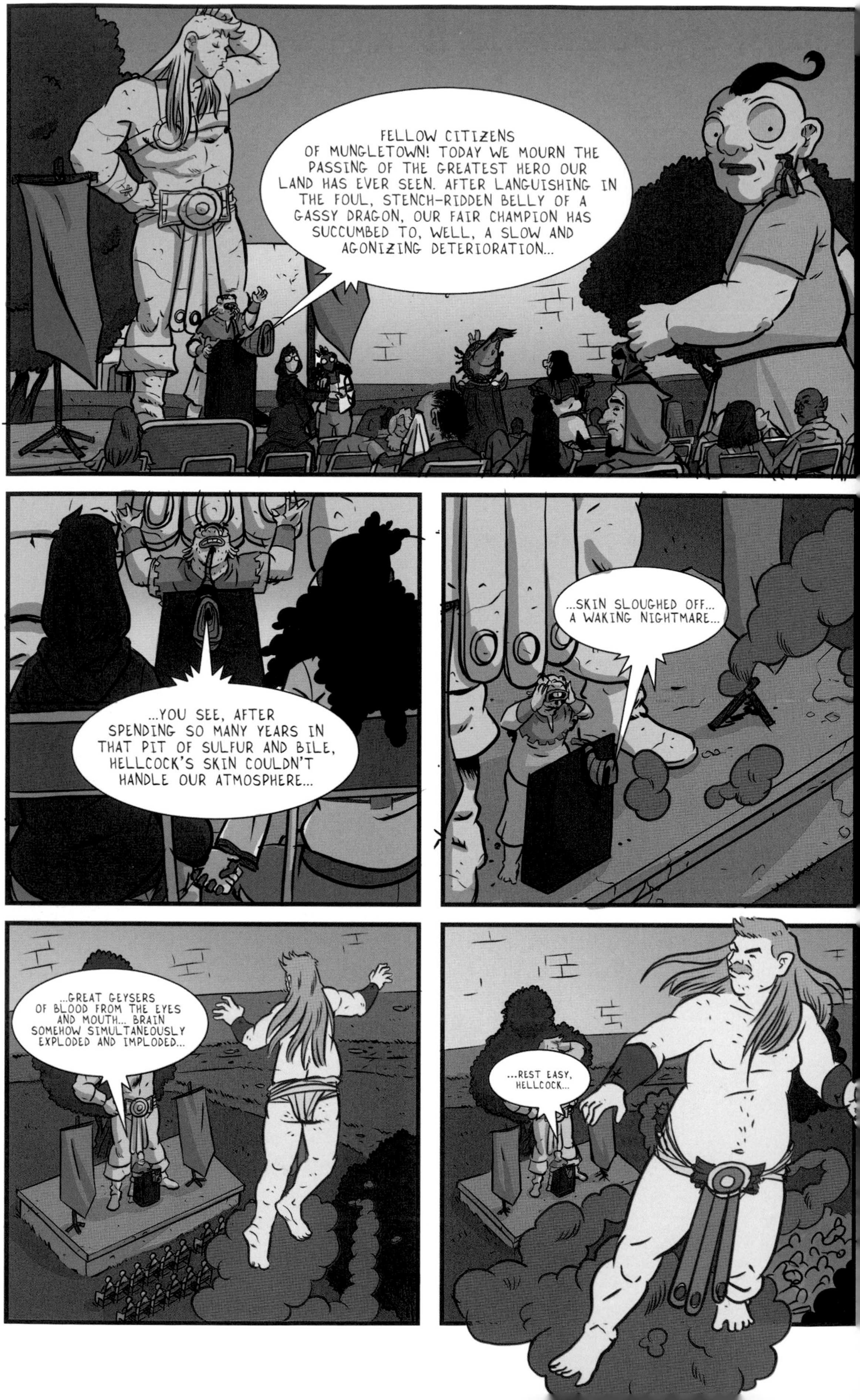
FELLOW CITIZENS OF MUNGLETOWN! TODAY WE MOURN THE PASSING OF THE GREATEST HERO OUR LAND HAS EVER SEEN. AFTER LANGUISHING IN THE FOUL, STENCH-RIDDEN BELLY OF A GASSY DRAGON, OUR FAIR CHAMPION HAS SUCCUMBED TO, WELL, A SLOW AND AGONIZING DETERIORATION...
...YOU SEE, AFTER SPENDING SO MANY YEARS IN THAT PIT OF SULFUR AND BILE, HELLCOCK'S SKIN COULDN'T HANDLE OUR ATMOSPHERE...
...SKIN SLOUGHED OFF... A WAKING NIGHTMARE...
...GREAT GEYSERS OF BLOOD FROM THE EYES AND MOUTH... BRAIN SOMEHOW SIMULTANEOUSLY EXPLODED AND IMPLODED...
...REST EASY, HELLCOCK...

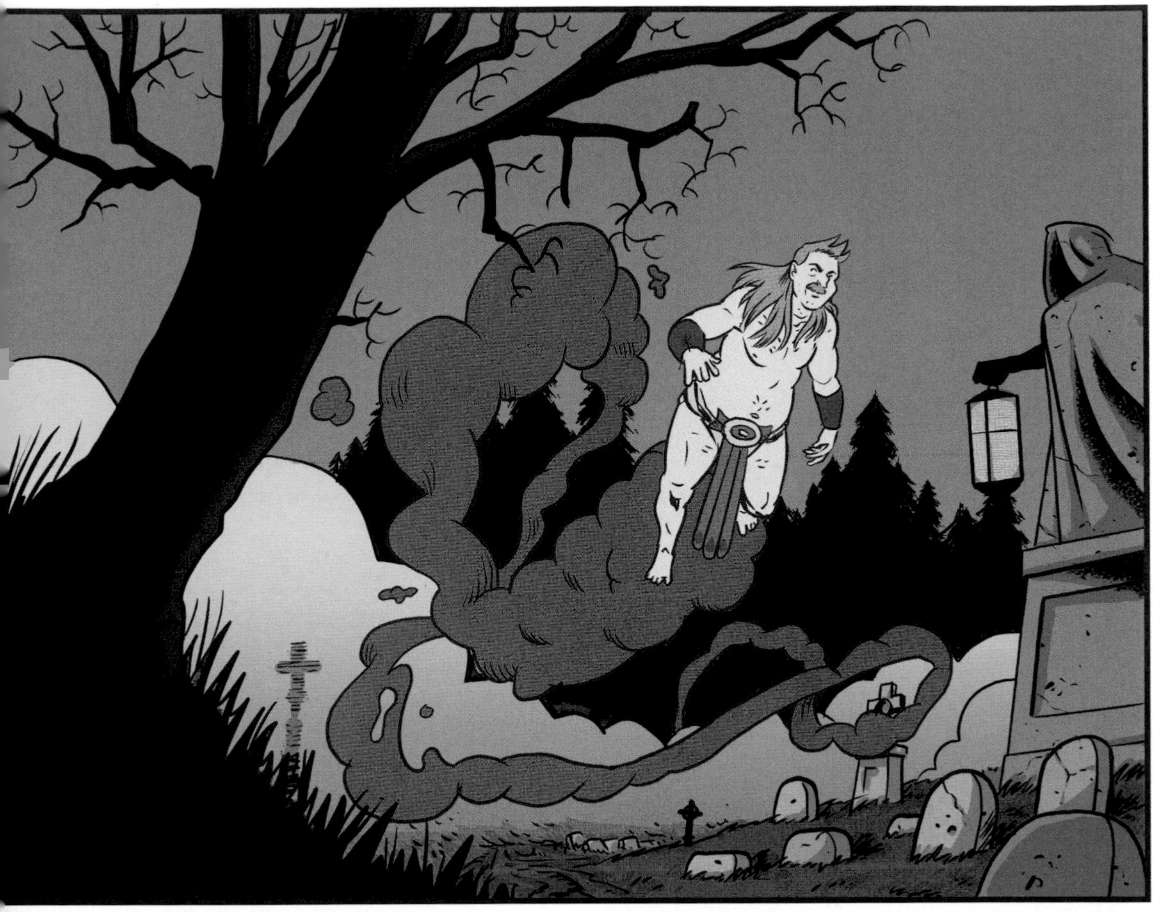

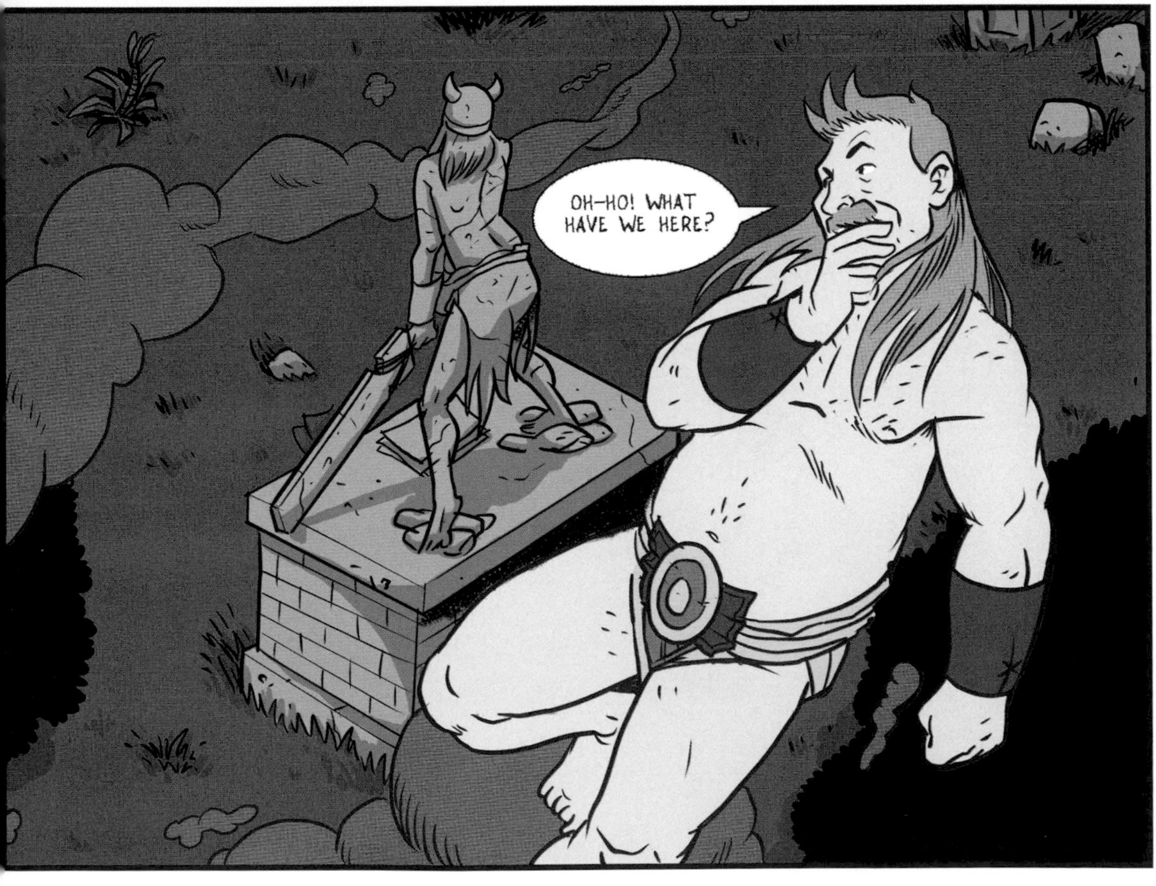
OH-HO! WHAT HAVE WE HERE?

A PICTURE BOOK! AND BY THE LOOKS OF IT, NOT HALF BAD!

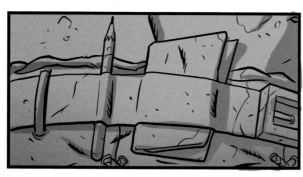

ACTUALLY IT'S ALLEN...

OH, WAIT... THIS PART NEEDS CONSIDERABLE WORK.

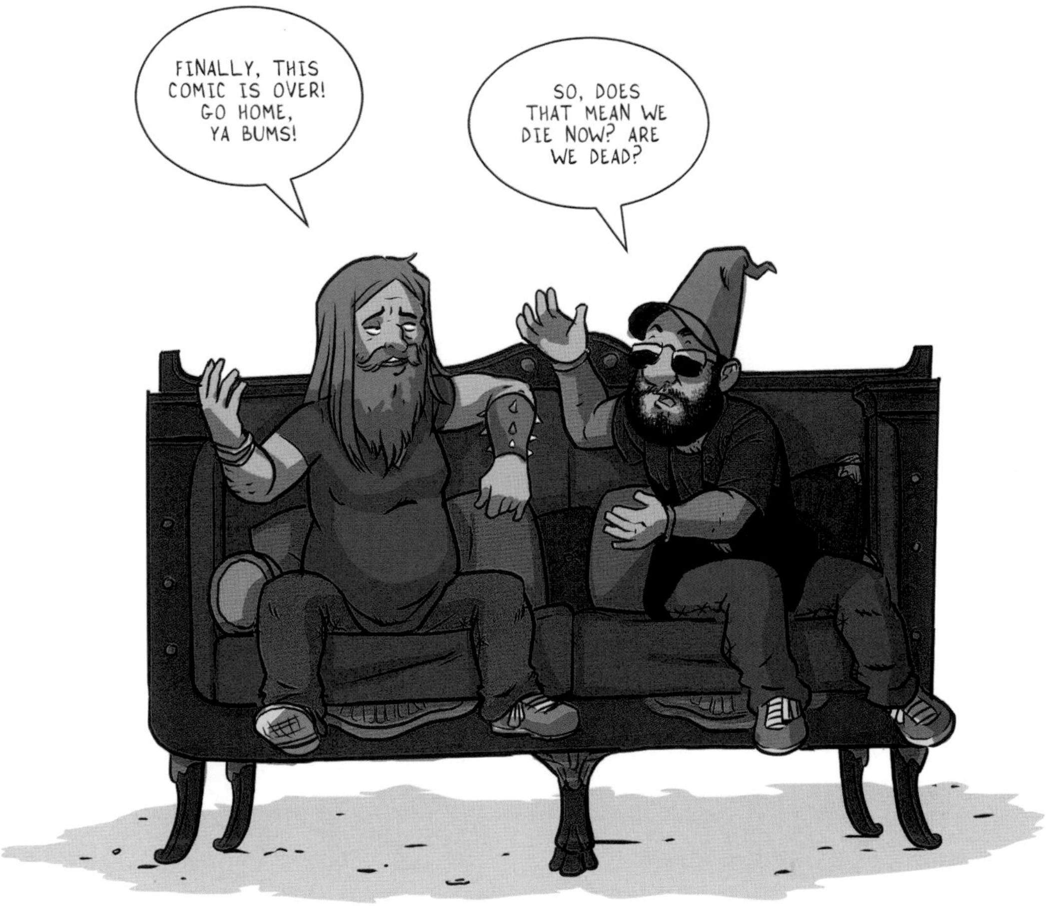
FINALLY, THIS COMIC IS OVER! GO HOME, YA BUMS!
SO, DOES THAT MEAN WE DIE NOW? ARE WE DEAD?

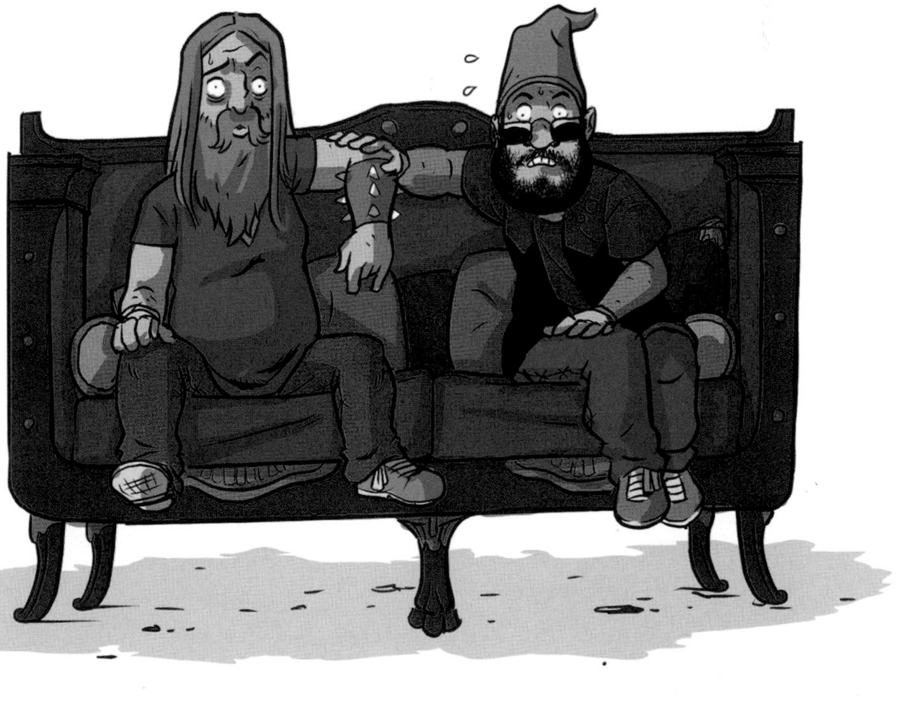

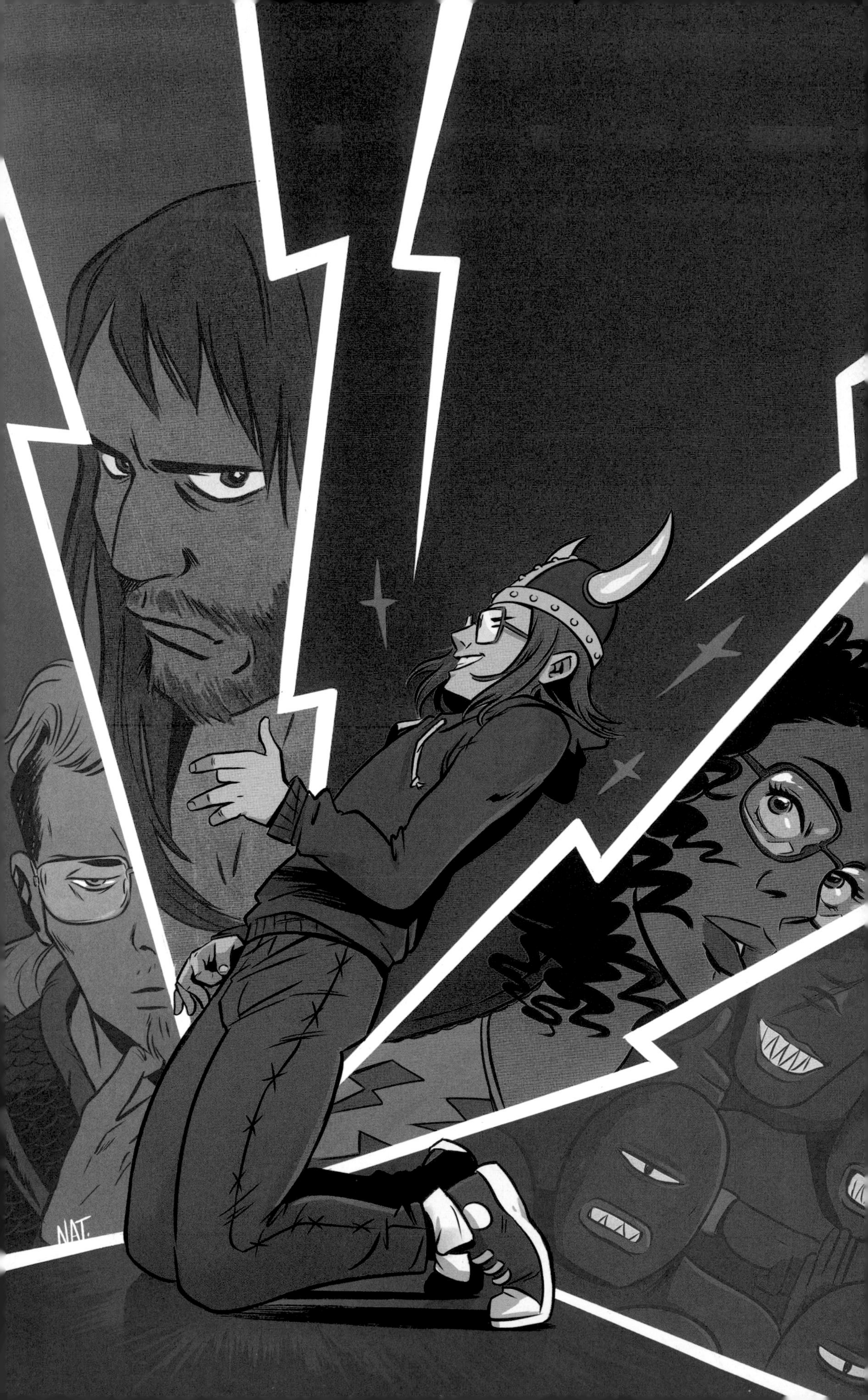
NAT.

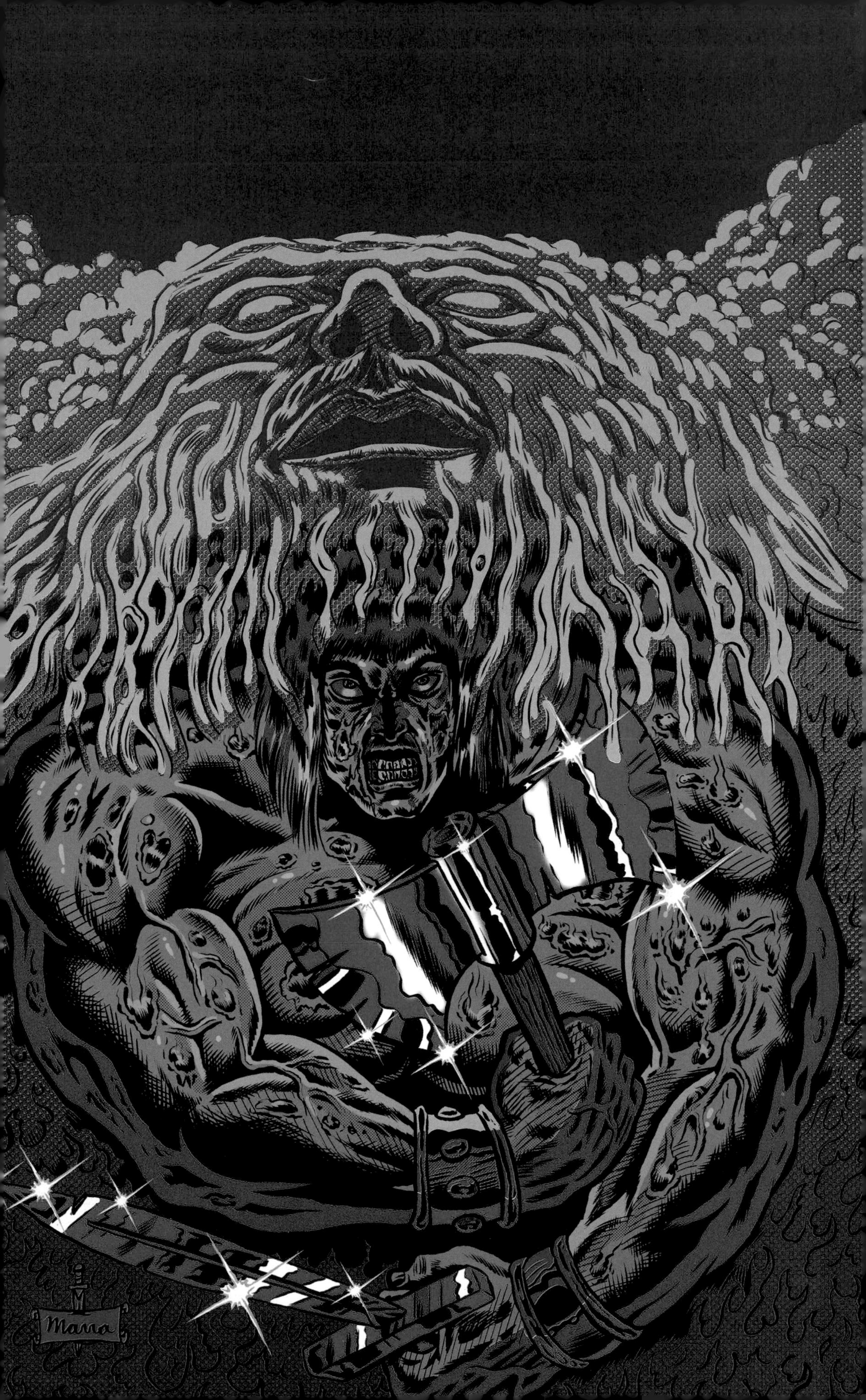
Mana

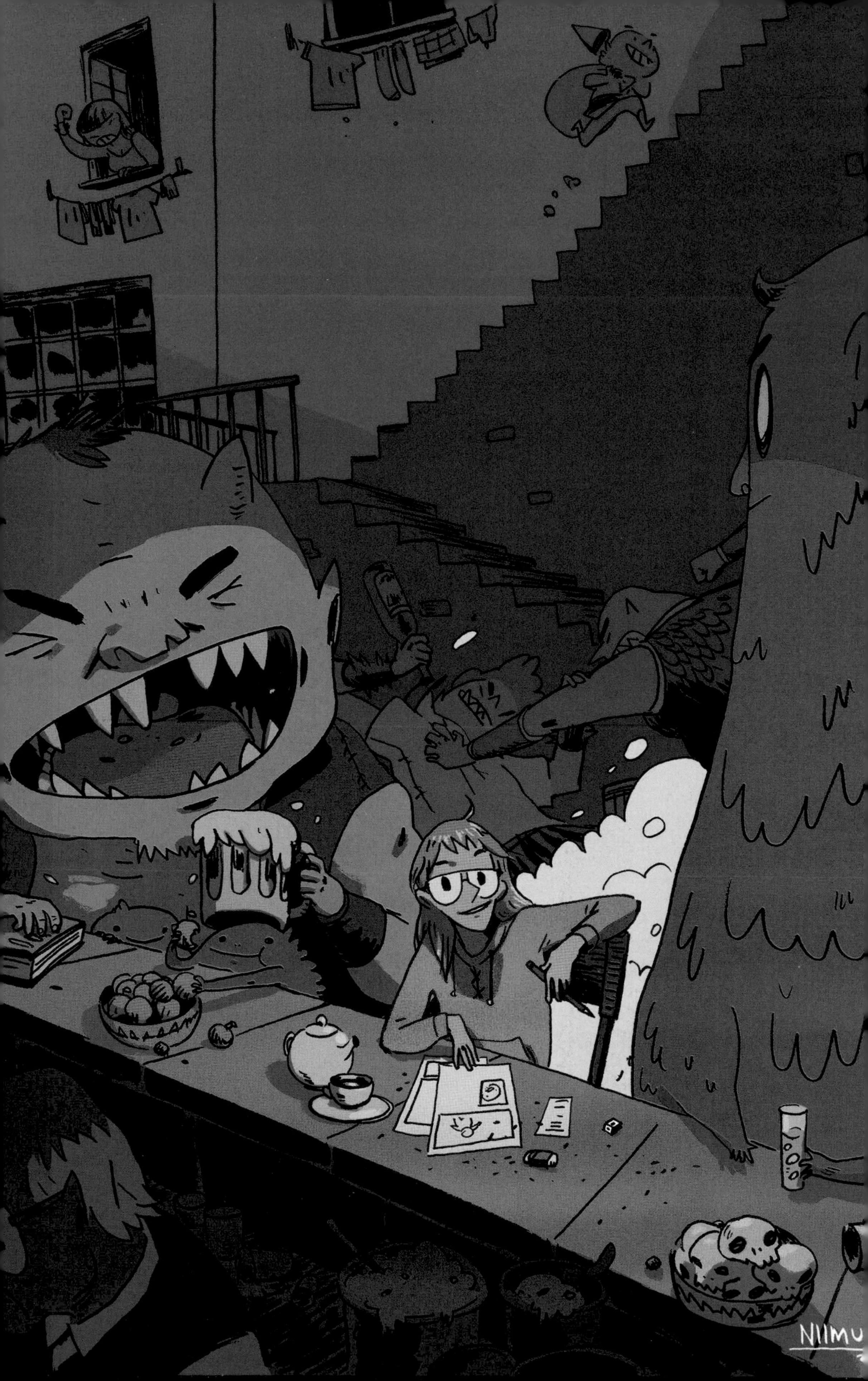
NIIMU